THE WINDING ROAD HOME

SALLY JOHN

HARVEST HOUSE PUBLISHERS

EUGENE, OREGON

Unless otherwise indicated, all Scripture quotations are taken from The New English Bible, © Oxford University Press and Cambridge University Press 1961, 1970. All rights reserved.

Cover by Garborg Design Works, Minneapolis, Minnesota

Published in association with the literary agency of Alive Communications, Inc., 7680 Goddard Street, Suite 200, Colorado Springs, CO 80920.

This is a work of fiction. Names, characters, places, and incidents are products of the author's imagination or are used fictitiously. Any resemblance to actual persons, living or dead, or to events or locales, is entirely coincidental.

THE WINDING ROAD HOME
Copyright © 2003 by Sally John
Published by Harvest House Publishers
Eugene, Oregon 97402
www.harvesthousepublishers.com

ISBN-13: 978-0-7369-2094-0
ISBN-10: 0-7369-2094-3

Library of Congress Cataloging-in-Publication Data
John, Sally D., 1951-
    The winding road home / Sally John.
        p. cm.—(The other way home series ; bk. 4)
    ISBN-13: 978-0-7369-1170-2
    ISBN-10: 0-7369-1170-7
    1. Women—Middle West—Fiction. 2. Female friendship—Fiction. 3. Middle West—Fiction.
I. Title.
    PS3560.O323W56 2003
    813'.54—dc21   2003001832

Printed in the United States of America

08 09 10 11 12 13 14 15 / LB-CF / 11 10 9 8 7 6 5 4 3 2 1

Acknowledgments

As always, the writing has been a collaborative effort. My thanks go to those who have been a part of *The Winding Road Home:*

Kristi Ruud for pottery lessons and her real-life model of *Adele's* home studio.

Mindy Carls for her example of spirit I've instilled in *Kate* and *Rusty,* who by no means resemble the *Orion Gazette's* managing editor in any other way.

Tracy John for her unflagging, enthusiastic help as my "other editor."

Elizabeth John for her technical assistance and constant support.

Christopher John for caring.

Michael Skelton for drawing the map.

Trudy Watson for her Volkswagen expertise and gracious research.

Sally Weckel for jumping in with both feet as "press agent."

Kim Moore of Harvest House for generally being everything one could ask for in an editor.

And Tim...for taking care of everything else along the way.

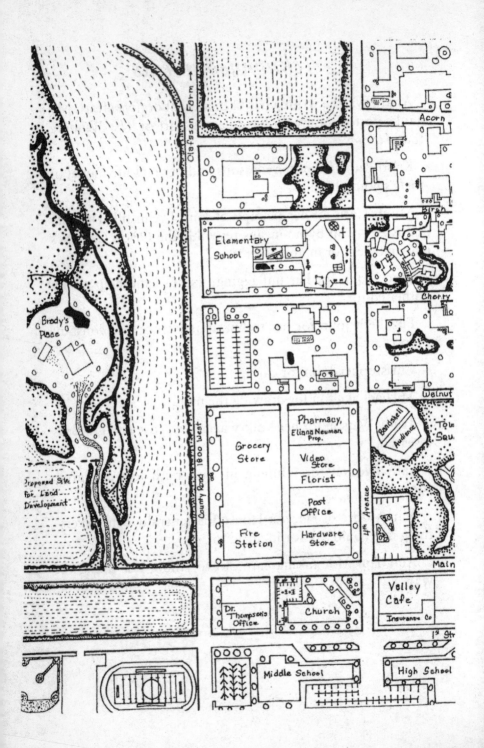

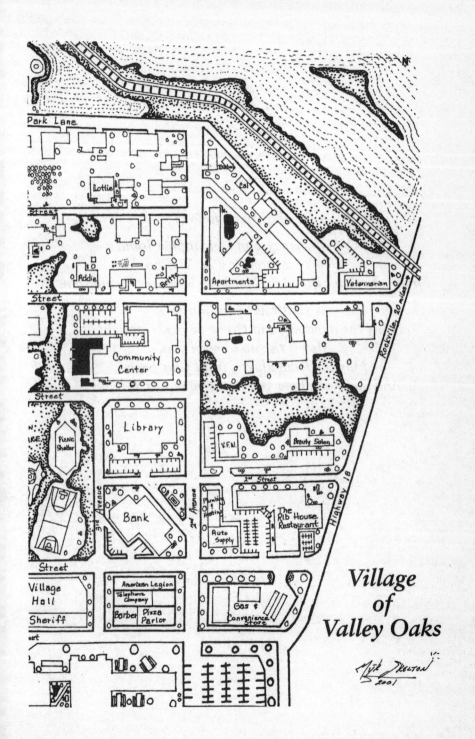

Village
of
Valley Oaks

~

For those who follow:

Elizabeth, Tracy, and Christopher John;
Cassie Carlson; Joshua Watson;
Emilee, Nathan, Brendan, Matthew, Kyle, and Justin John

As you travel your journey,
May the winding road Home be made straight,
May it rise up to meet you,
May the wind always be at your back,
And may God hold you in the palm of His hand.

~

Prologue

Wait quietly for the LORD,
Be patient till he comes...
—Psalm 37:7

"Ladies and gentlemen!" The jaunty emcee spoke in a deep radio announcer's voice. He stood on the stage between two preteen girls, a microphone in his hand. "Let's congratulate this year's winner of the countywide spelling bee, who now advances to the state competition, and from there, we hope, on to nationals!"

The sparse crowd in the school auditorium applauded politely. As family members of the participants, they were naturally inclined to exhibit more enthusiasm for their own child. By the time the winner was announced, only one group of relatives held any genuine interest in the program.

The girl who knew how to spell "metamorphosis" smiled politely in return. As the host lauded the runner-up, the county's best 12-year-old speller waited as if she were quite at home taking first place.

The girl who had not known 30 seconds ago how to spell "metamorphosis" took a trembling breath, smiling sweetly through tears. There was a slight increase in the level of applause. Blonde and blue-eyed, she had won over the audience with her display of anxiety at each word aimed her way and unabashed joy with each correct spelling.

The host congratulated the winner now, shaking her hand. Shorter than average, she lifted her chin, looked him straight in the eye, and thanked him, clearly mature beyond her 12 years. Her straight, reddish hair was pulled back into a ponytail. She had played the game well. Intensely. Focused. Never hesitant.

"Tell us," the emcee said, "what would you like to do when you grow up?"

"I'd like to be a White House correspondent. A Helen Thomas for the twenty-first century."

Laughter rippled through the audience.

Though it easily could have been construed as being aimed at her, the girl didn't seem to mind. She gazed at the cluster of people in the front row still cheering for her. Why would she need the crowd's approval? She had a loving family and a plan for her life.

A young woman sat huddled in a pew, a large bulging knapsack beside her. Groups of people were scattered throughout the sanctuary. The wind rattled the stained-glass windows.

Another woman, somewhat older in appearance, walked along the pew before hers and sat down, facing her. "The snowstorm isn't letting up. We should leave now. Your bus won't be going anywhere tonight."

"You're sure?"

She nodded. "The highways are closed down. Please, I've food and plenty of space for you."

"I'll just stay here." There was a stony edge to her tone. Hard, resolute.

"It's too uncomfortable and drafty. I think enough towns-folk have shown up to take all the stranded travelers home for the night."

The young woman blinked. Her curly hair hung about her shoulders, matted. "Why would you take me home?"

The other woman smiled. "Someone took me home once. It's my turn."

"You don't know the first thing about me."

"I know you need a place to sleep."

"I'm pregnant. Nineteen. Single. No means of support. People react to me as if I were a leper."

The older woman bowed her head for a moment, her forehead against the back of the pew. When she raised it, tears glistened in her eyes. "Sweetheart, I was there. My daughter is eleven now. She's always wanted a baby sister. Or brother." Holding out her hand to the other, she stood. "Let's go home."

One

Seventeen years later

No dictionary contained the precise word to describe the scene unfolding before Kate Kilpatrick.

Oh, there were plenty of words all right. Peculiar. Sweet. Bizarre. Touching. Unreal. Heartwarming. Hokey. Sensational.

But not one of them fit, not exactly.

Worse yet, there was no way on earth she knew how to incorporate the indescribable, personal scene into a *news* article. Her notepad and pen dangled at her side in a mitten-covered hand. The camera, its strap slung over her shoulder, rested against her hip, adding dead weight to the already heavy jacket. Like steam in a kettle curling toward its whistling hole, pressure mounted in her chest. With a loud puff that jiggled her lips and fanned her bangs, she released it. *Welcome to the big time, Kilpatrick*, she thought ruefully.

Kate stood inside the Valley Oaks High School in an area which just that morning she learned was referred to as the commons. The term was new to her. Though the place was large and airy, the dominant odor was distinctly school, as if its walls were made of books and paper and pencils and cafeteria food and gym shoes. Evidently all doorways led to the commons. On her way in she had glimpsed a ring of entrances: hallways, gym, glassed-in office, back parking lot.

The location also appeared to be the gathering place for unusual events.

Unusual. Poignant. Quaint. Singular events.

An expert in the fine art of elbow-prodding, Kate had pressed her way through a sea of bodies and now stood at its center. The sea was comprised predominantly of adolescents. Quiet adolescents, standing on tiptoes, their faces expectant with O-shaped mouths and raised brows. That in itself would be curious enough, but that wasn't the main event. The students' attention was riveted on two adults in the center, surrounded by the crowd. Those two were the main event.

She knew the man was Joel Kingsley, principal of the high school, because he had been the one who called the office. He said that at precisely 8:37 A.M. he would be centrally located in the commons and that he fully expected a newsworthy event to unfold there at that time. It wasn't only his voice, trim body, and nearly buzzed black hair that hinted at military. A soldierly aura emanated from him even as he smiled during an intense, hushed exchange of what must have been personal words. The aura remained now as he planted a knee into the linoleum.

He held the hand of a woman Kate recognized as Britte Olafsson, girls basketball coach. She looked as if she'd just stepped off the plane from Scandinavia, from her height to her blonde hair to the slightly shell-shocked appearance about her eyes that anyone would exhibit after a ten-hour flight. Kate suspected her dazed expression wasn't due to jet lag. The man had just proclaimed in a voice for all to hear, "Miss O, I'd like your permission to court you."

The red-faced coach glanced about, maybe in search of a hole to climb into. At last she cried out, "All right! Yes, you have my permission!"

The crowd of quiet adolescents burst apart at the seams, whooping and hollering. If Kate closed her eyes, she would believe herself inside a gym at a sporting event. But she wasn't. She wished she were because *that* she would know how to describe. But *this*... This was a public display of pure *romance*. Tender, but incomprehensible on an early Monday morning in a rural high school two days before Valentine's Day.

The man stood now, clutching the woman's hands between his against his chest.

Kate felt a nudge against her arm and turned. A guy, more mature-looking than the students, pointed at her camera. The cheering drowned out his voice. She read his lips asking, "Take a picture?"

She could not realign her face into anything other than a blank stare. What did he think? They were witnessing *news*?

He held his hand out, palm up, toward her shoulder. In a glance she took in his expensive, ecru cable-stitched sweater, likely hand-knit in Ireland. He had the build of a husky fisherman, but his olive skin tone, dark eyes, and wavy black hair grazing the top of the sweater's neckline declared his ancestors didn't fish off the coast of Ireland. More plausibly it would have been in the Mediterranean.

Kate shrugged the camera strap off into his waiting hand and thought, *Go for it, buddy.*

She turned back to the main attraction, where an intense but inaudible conversation flowed between the couple. Kate predicted the scene had to end in a kiss because two people could not look at each other in that way without giving physical expression to their love. Even if they *were* being watched by roughly 400 pairs of eyes.

Tanner Carlucci removed the camera's lens cap and grinned to himself. Britte, the fire-breathing varsity coach and no-nonsense math teacher, was blushing. Joel, the ex-Marine and by-the-book high school principal, had knelt on bended knee. It was a priceless moment, and the woman with the camera had stood stock-still and missed it! Well, he'd snap a shot of the kiss that no doubt was coming to seal whatever it was they were discussing now about courtship.

He aimed the camera, noting with approval that it was a manual focus. The woman had nice taste.

She was a stranger to the school. Though Tanner was only a substitute teacher and freshmen girls basketball coach, he would have noticed her before now. She was by far the quirkiest character he had ever seen in real life.

First off was her red hair. Not flaming, not orangey, not purplish nor dark. Just a nice shade of shiny copper penny red that resembled a mop head caught up in a clip, its ends sticking out every which way. She was small, but she had easily hustled her way through a rampart of hearty teenage boys and whispering girls. She wore rectangular, tortoise-shell glasses; a bulky, deep green jacket three sizes too large; a long skirt; clunky boots; and one mitten.

He had no idea what she was doing there, but she carried a camera that he felt could be put to better use than to decorate her shoulder. He clicked a shot now of the principal and coach, their heads close together, hands clasped, their expressions absorbed in each other. He clicked another shot, catching their emerging smiles.

Joel called for attention, though his eyes never left Britte's face. The noise abated some, and in that commanding voice of his he said, "What you are about to witness is inappropriate behavior for students in the halls."

Tanner had the camera ready. The kiss was gentle, brief. He captured it only once.

The kids erupted again, but Tanner knew that with Joel Kingsley in charge things were under control. He turned to the redhead. There was a pained expression on her face as if she couldn't process what she was witnessing. He understood the feeling. She must be new to Valley Oaks.

He looked again at Joel, who was now raising his arms and directing everyone back to class, his broad grin not in the least diminishing his effectiveness. Tanner couldn't help but chuckle at Britte. Always-in-control Miss O looked dazed and confused. He took one last snapshot and turned.

The redhead was gone. Tanner peered between the blabbering students as they slowly departed from the center of the commons. He saw her through the glass doors of the entryway. She was already climbing into an old model, light blue Volkswagen parked at the curb.

He shrugged. She would remember her camera eventually.

Kate parked her Bug on Second Avenue outside the tiny *Valley Oaks Weekly Times* office. Despite the fact that the Pizza Parlor next door was closed on Mondays, the aroma of garlic hovered. It always hovered, defying the physics of old brick walls, concrete sidewalks, and arctic breezes. It was the best advertising going. Why did the owners bother to take out an ad in the weekly? She'd been in town 17 days and eaten there a total of 13 times. And that wasn't counting coffee breaks. Her stomach rumbled.

A cowbell clanked above her head as she opened the *Times'* front door. She lingered in the doorway a moment longer than necessary, allowing a cloud of cigarette smoke to escape. The office consisted of one room that was just large enough for a counter, two desks, and a worktable. A faint glimmer of winter sunlight filtered through dirty venetian blinds covering the lone window.

At the far back corner desk, the managing editor pecked away at an electric typewriter, a cigarette dangling from the corner of her mouth. Kate knew the woman was finishing up an in-depth study of the sewer system for tomorrow's deadline and hadn't even heard the cowbell. Still, they needed to talk. "Rusty?"

No response.

Kate hung her coat on one of the wooden pegs attached to the front wall. She walked around the counter to her desk, rolled her creaky wooden chair over near the other desk, and plopped into it. "Rusty?"

"Yeah, kid?" It was the older woman's way. Sixty-two with short, straight, iron gray hair, she resembled a news reporter from the original black-and-white *Superman* television series. Clark Kent's boss, not Lois Lane. She had the personality down flat. She only needed a 1950s-style man's hat, gray suit coat, and narrow tie.

"Rusty, you have got to be kidding."

The woman's chuckle was a gravelly rumble that more often than not deteriorated into a cough. It did so now as she swiveled away from the typewriter to face Kate, removing the unfiltered cigarette from her mouth. She nearly managed to get it to the ashtray before the ash fell onto the floor.

Kate sighed inwardly. She prayed daily for the woman's health as well as her own.

Rusty found her voice, as low and gravelly as the chuckle. "What's that Marine up to now?"

Marine. That validated her hunch about the principal. "He just—in front of the entire school population—asked Britte Olafsson for permission to *court* her."

Rusty roared like a lion with bronchitis.

"It's not news."

"Welcome to Valley Oaks, kid."

"It's not news!"

Still chuckling, Rusty took a drag on her cigarette. "Then make it news, kid. It's what's happening in town this week. It's a big deal. Joel Kingsley has turned that high school on its ear with a slew of policy changes. And he's got the hutzpah to enforce them. A lot of folks don't like it. This could be one more nail in his coffin. Was Bruce Waverly there?"

Kate blinked.

"School superintendent. Dapper little guy."

"I don't know."

"Track him down. Find out what he thinks. Of course, you'll want to ask Kingsley what he's up to. Get some parents' opinions. Interview a couple of students, two or three school board members." She dug through a pile of papers on her desk. "Here's a list of them. Be sure you talk to Norton Pinsky. He always goes against the grain. We want to get all sides quoted."

Kate took the paper from her and stood. "Okay."

"What was Olafsson's answer?"

"She said yes."

Rusty smiled. "Good for her. We need to get this in Thursday's edition. It's timely, related to Valentine's Day."

"We can do a follow-up article next week." Kate rolled her chair out of the way and shuffled toward the door. "What they did on their first date. What they wore. Did they go Dutch treat? Did they double with another couple?"

"Katy-girl."

She unhooked her coat from its peg and turned.

"Lesson number one. You gotta pay your dues. Nobody makes it to DC without 'em." Rusty swiveled back to her typewriter. "Did you get a photo?"

Photo! *Oh, fiddlesticks!* The camera! "Uh, I think so. At least, the camera clicked. See you later."

Outdoors on the sidewalk Kate stood a moment and inhaled the garlic-scented frigid air. *I'm sorry, Lord. Was that a lie? It felt like one.* She'd better hustle over to the school and find the Sweater. Hopefully the guy knew how to take a decent picture.

Two

Kate entered the high school's main office, a humming beehive of activity. Several students and teachers milled about, talking and laughing. According to her school experience, the scene wasn't believable. Either the morning's public display of romance had set an abnormally merry tone or else her glasses had taken on a rosy tint, skewing her vision.

The room was divided in half by a counter. Behind that stood a short, 40-something woman. From her crisp white blouse tucked into a gray skirt to her kind, brisk manner of directing traffic, Kate knew she was in charge.

Kate stepped to the counter. "Hi. I'm Kate Kilpatrick from the *Times*."

Smiling, the woman reached over and firmly shook Kate's outstretched hand. "Well, hello. I heard we had a new reporter. Nice to meet you. I'm Lynnie Powell, secretary. Hey!" She directed her commanding voice over Kate's shoulder, "Quiet down!" The hubbub lessened a degree. "How may I help you?"

"I was here earlier, in the commons—"

"He didn't!"

"Beg your pardon?"

"Mr. Kingsley. He called you, didn't he? I do not believe it." She chuckled and raised her hands in a helpless gesture, as if the man were an endearing, precocious child.

"Yes, well, anyway, I loaned my camera to a guy, and I forgot to get it back from him. He was wearing this sweater—"

"Tanner. One of our subs. He's in Room 12 today." Lynnie slid a clipboard over the counter toward her. "Just put your John Henry right there. We need to keep track of who's in the building. Thank you. Room 12 is down the first hallway on your left."

"Thanks. I need to talk to Mr. Kingsley also. Do you think he'd have a few minutes this morning?"

She chuckled again. "Oh, I think it'd be a safe bet to say yes. I'll track him down. See you in a bit."

Kate crossed the commons and entered a hallway lined with brown-gray lockers. Above them hung large, framed photo collections. She paused to study one. It was a collage of roughly 60 pictures of students, all classic high school senior poses: fresh-faced girls in fuzzy sweaters smiling over their shoulders; boys in white, button-down collar shirts and ties. In the center was a sketch of a bearded Viking and the words "Valley Oaks High School, Class of 1962."

Kate quietly sighed. Such a simple thing shouldn't trigger strong reactions, but it did. It reminded her yet again that this town of 1,947 located just 20 miles southwest of where she had grown up was unfathomable. In no way, shape, or form could she relate to it. *Lord, I sure wish You'd let me in on why it is You've brought me here!*

At Room 12 she stopped in the open doorway. The Sweater lounged against the teacher's desk, half sitting on a corner of it. He was speaking to the class, not looking at the textbook in his hand.

"Psst."

He glanced her direction and immediately smiled in recognition.

Kate held out her arms in an apologetic shrug.

"Class, excuse me for a moment. Go ahead and start on the assignment." He walked around the desk and pulled her camera from a drawer.

She backed into the hall as he neared, out of earshot of the students. "I'm sorry for interrupting, but I'm in a bit of a hurry."

"No problem, Camera Lady. Here you go."

She accepted the camera from him and slung it over her shoulder. "Thank you. Do you think you got a picture? My editor seems to think the event is news."

"Oh, it is. The moment was priceless. You must be a newcomer to the newspaper."

She held out her hand. "Kate Kilpatrick, 17 days with the *Times*."

Smiling, he shook her hand. "Is that the *Los Angeles* or *New York Times?*"

"You've found me out. I'm delusional."

"Aren't we all? I'm a history professor here at the academy."

She laughed, instantly liking his open face. "Well, it's nice to meet you, whoever you are."

"My name's Tanner Carlucci."

"Carlucci. That sounds familiar—" She snapped her fingers. "I remember! We graduated the same year from Rockville High. You played guard when Tommy Kennedy played center."

"Now you're being delusional about me. I spent most of every basketball season sitting on the bench. I'm sorry, I don't remember you."

"You wouldn't. You were the jock who made news. I was the geek who wrote the news. Our paths didn't cross, but your name came up once or twice." She shrugged. "And besides, we had eight hundred and seventy-three classmates."

"High school. The ultimate delusional state." His sparkly brown-black eyes clouded. "It had nothing to do with real life. Here we are, twelve years later. I'm an athletic has-been with long hair, wondering what to do with the rest of my life. You're out there, gifts already honed, living your dream as journalist for either the *Los Angeles* or *New York Times.* You haven't said which yet."

"But you're teaching."

"Long story. Maybe we could meet for coffee, catch up on old times."

She grinned. "We didn't share any old times."

"Oh, that's right. Well..." He glanced furtively over one shoulder and then the other. As if about to share a secret, he hunched toward her and said in a low voice, "I could give you the inside scoop on the Magic Kingdom here, if you're interested."

"Magic Kingdom?"

"I know. Most people refer to it as Valley Oaks. But you'll find out if you hang around for a while," he waggled his brows, "that there is something magical about the place."

"I know there's something elusive about it. I haven't the foggiest how to relate to it."

"Then we should definitely talk." He straightened, and his voice returned to normal. "Are you living in town?"

"Yes, I'm renting a room from a woman. It's easier to reach me at the *Times* office. That's the *Valley Oaks Times.*"

"I see. *Los Angeles* or *New York* has loaned you out." He grinned. "I'd better get back in there. Nice meeting you, Kate."

"Thanks again for taking a picture."

"My pleasure. I hope it works for you." He rapped his knuckles on the doorjamb and went inside the room.

Life certainly was strange. Who would have guessed a Rockville classmate would turn up as a source? And in Valley Oaks, of all places.

⌒

Kate settled into a chair across the desk from the principal, not bothering to remove her coat. She didn't plan on being there long. "Thank you for seeing me, Mr. Kingsley."

"Please, call me Joel. And thank you for seeing *me*." A small, contented smile eased what would otherwise have been a perfectly daunting face. One look at his piercing gaze and chiseled features would hustle any adolescent down the straight and narrow. Kate felt herself sitting up a bit taller.

He continued, "Knowing Rusty, I figured she'd want details."

"You hit that nail on the head." She poised her pen above the stenographer notebook. "Why did you do it?"

"I love Britte Olafsson." No hesitation.

Kate blinked, shoving aside the fact that the interview was the most ridiculous she'd ever conducted. "Mr.—Joel, what I mean is, why did you stage this public display of an extremely personal moment?"

"I feel that as teacher and principal, Britte and I are public servants. Most of what we do is open to public scrutiny, as it should be to a certain extent, especially in front of the students. What help are we if we preach one way and live another? I want them to see how adults handle a relationship. If the community is gossiping about a romance, things get blown out of proportion." He held out his hands, palms up. "I wanted to be up front about where I stand with Miss O."

"How do you hope the community will respond?"

He thought for a moment. "Like everything I do for the school, I hope they'll accept it and give it some time until the results indicate whether or not it was the best course of action for the majority of the students."

Good heavens. The man had just tied together romance with hoping for a fair assessment of his performance as principal. What had Rusty said? Something about another nail in his coffin. Was his job in jeopardy?

"Did you get all that?" he asked.

"Um," Kate started writing again, "I think so." She skimmed over what she had written in her own version of shorthand. "But I don't understand what dating a woman has to do with keeping your job."

He chuckled. "I didn't either until recently. Welcome to Valley Oaks, Kate Kilpatrick."

Kate parked on Cherry Street in front of Adele Chandler's house and climbed out. Dusk had fallen and winter still nipped the air, keeping the six inches of snow firmly intact with no hint of a melting.

The afternoon's interviews tumbled about in her mind. She had managed to find the superintendent, two school board members, a handful of students and parents. Everyone had an opinion on the Kingsley-Olafsson development, but she still couldn't imagine coordinating the disconnected jangle into a news article. She needed a break.

Walking up the front sidewalk, she studied the white, two-story clapboard built in the 1920s. It was large, too large, according to Adele, for just herself and her 16-year-old daughter, Chelsea. Through the years she had often rented out the two rooms Kate now lived in on the first floor. Adele was a friend of a friend of Kate's mother's, a connection for which she was grateful. It saved her from commuting from Rockville or signing a lease. The rent was low, and the easy-going Chandlers were ideal roommates.

Just inside the small entryway, she slipped off her coat and heavy hiking boots. Voices came from the kitchen, and she crossed the dining room to enter it. Mother and daughter stood at the counter, chopping vegetables.

"Hi, honeys, I'm home!"

"Kate!" Chelsea cried, spinning around to face her. "Was that the wildest thing you've ever witnessed in your entire life or what?"

"I assume you're referring to the scene in the commons?"

"Yeah! I saw you come in."

"I didn't notice you, but then last night your hair was white blonde."

"That was my winter look." She patted her mass of long, bright red natural curls, "Now it's Valentine's Day and time for red."

"Lucky me, I'm all set." Kate exchanged a smile with Adele. Though the slightly older woman wore her natural, dark blonde waves in a shorter, bouncy style, the Chandlers resembled each other. They both had large, gray-blue eyes, medium builds, and a distinct artistic fluidity about their dress and personalities. Even their lilting voices were similar.

Adele dried her hands on a towel. "So what do you think, Kate?"

"I think it was charming and bizarre, but my opinion doesn't count when it comes to reporting. Tell me what you two think. On the record."

"Oh, Kate," Adele laughed, "I hope you're not going to quote me often. Even after seventeen years I'm still a major oddball to three-fourths of Valley Oaks. I'm not seen as a typical community member."

"Why is that?"

"I'm a single mom with a pottery studio in my basement and I dress funny."

"What's funny about colorful, flowing skirts?" She glanced down at her own African-print skirt and crocheted gold sweater over a forest green shirt. "At least you don't wear combat boots and your brother's winter jacket."

Laughing, Chelsea added, "And only one mitten."

"I wear two mittens." She watched the almost imperceptible raise of their brows. "Don't I?"

Adele grinned. "We've only seen one."

Kate sat at the table and pulled her notepad from her oversized shoulder bag. "Anyway, you're not an oddball in this matter. You're a parent. What do you think?"

"I like Joel Kingsley's honesty. He's devoted to the school and to the students. Based on his track record, I trust his judgment. If he wants to take the opportunity to present a life lesson using his own personal experience, it's all right by me. All the better that the kids see him walk his talk."

Kate wrote Adele's words. They more or less echoed what Bruce Waverly, two teachers, and one board member had told her that afternoon. Of course, those had been from politically correct people adept at speaking without the emotion coating Adele's rendition.

She turned to Chelsea. "And what do you think?"

"I want a man like Mr. Kingsley for my mom!"

Her mother groaned.

"I would have preferred *him*, but I guess he's unavailable now. They're about the same age you know. Mom's thirty-six. When he first came, I told her he was *different* and we should have him over for dinner, that she would like his no-nonsense attitude. But she dragged her feet and now Miss O has snapped him right off the market—"

Adele grabbed her daughter around the shoulders with one hand and stuck a carrot into her open mouth with the other. "Chelsea Chandler! How did you ever become so full of jabberwocky?"

The girl bit off the tip of the carrot and giggled around her chewing, "I had a good teacher who doubles as my mother!"

"No way!"

"Mom, you should hear yourself. Like in the pharmacy the other day."

As the teasing continued, Kate heard muted strands of Beethoven's Fifth emanating from her bag. She dug out the new cell phone and walked into the dining room, away from their noisy banter. "Hello."

"Kate? It's Tanner."

"Hi!"

"I called your office and Rusty gave me this number. Do you have dinner plans? I'm still in town, and the Rib House is calling my name."

In her mind's eye she saw Adele and Chelsea's mountain of chopped veggies. They always welcomed her to join them in their tasty, albeit vegetarian dinners. "I assume the Rib House serves meat?"

"All kinds. Are you a vegetarian? They have—"

"No, *I'm* not a vegetarian." Her stomach rumbled at the thought of a plateful of lipsmacking slabs of pork and beef covered in barbecue sauce. The Chandlers ate seafood and dairy products, but nothing like ribs. "The Rib House sounds great. Meet you there in ten?"

"See you."

Back in the kitchen, Kate said, "That was Tanner Carlucci, inviting me to dinner."

"Mr. Carlucci?" Chelsea exclaimed as she dramatically threw a hand against her chest. "Mr. Carlucci?" She sighed and closed her eyes. "Dinner with Mr. Carlucci?"

Kate turned to Adele, who was tossing a salad. "What?"

"His nickname—among the high school girls—is Adonis."

Kate thought of his expensive sweater and easygoing manner. Perfectly handsome as a Greek god? She hadn't really noticed. "Why?"

That sent Chelsea off on another round of squeals and swoonlike motions. "Kate! Are you blind? The guy is six feet tall with broad shoulders, gorgeous thick black hair, brown velvet eyes, and the longest eyelashes I've seen in my entire life."

Adele handed her the salad bowl. "And way too old for you to be concerned about, right?"

"Oh, Mother!"

"Right?" Her voice rose sternly. Like now, she could quickly slip back into her role as mother when she deemed the situation called for it.

"Okay, okay. Right." Chelsea set the bowl on the table, a pout forming about her mouth.

Kate cleared her throat. "You know, Adonises aren't totally what they're cracked up to be. And besides, all I'm looking for is some information and barbecued ribs!"

Three

Standing just inside the Rib House Restaurant waiting to be seated, Kate cast a surreptitious, sideways gaze at the so-called Adonis beside her. If the epitome of Adonis was tall, husky, dark, and handsome—as in a perfectly symmetrical face—then Tanner fit, hands down. His wavy black hair was stylishly long. From the side, she discerned his eyelashes were suitable for an ad touting the wonders of mascara.

"What?" He must have caught her not-so-furtive stare.

At about 5′2″, she had to tilt her head to meet his eyes. "Oh, just the reporter in me checking out a rumor. Do you know what the high school girls call you?"

He winced. "Do I want to know?"

"Sure. Knowledge is always a good thing. They call you Adonis."

The wince deepened. He was decidedly uncomfortable with the label. If not for his olive skin tone, he probably would have been blushing.

"On second thought, maybe I won't go into teaching full time."

"Look at the bright side. At least fifty percent of the student population will pay attention to you."

He rolled his eyes and touched her elbow, nudging her to follow the hostess now waiting to seat them. They crossed the main dining area, a no-frills open room of tables covered with red-checked vinyl. Every chair was occupied and the drone of conversation hummed. The woman led them to a small alcove of tables lined against a row of windows overlooking a nighttime Route 18. They sat across from each other, shrugging off their coats.

Kate said, "What do you recommend? This is my first time here."

"I like their special." He pointed to a description on her menu. "Ribs, French fries, coleslaw, and lemonade. You can get a half rack."

"I can eat a full one."

"They're huge servings."

"I hope so."

He grinned. "You can't eat a full one."

"I bet you the check I can."

"I was going to pay anyway. I invited you."

"Please don't go Sir Galahad on me. It's Dutch treat or nothing."

He held up his hands in mock surrender. "Okay, okay."

"Unless I eat a full rack."

"You're on."

A middle-aged waitress set water glasses before them, quickly took their order, and left.

"Tanner, I should buy your dinner. I owe you for the photos. They're good, clear shots."

"And poignant?"

Smiling, she rolled her eyes. "Yeah, yeah, and poignant. I'm sure Rusty will use one."

"Do I get my name in fine print beneath it?"

"Of course. But what *am* I to do with a kissing principal and teacher article? On the front page?"

"Who, what, when, where, why, and how. Just the facts, ma'am."

She glared at him over her water glass. "Now you sound like Rusty."

"Thank you. That's a compliment. Crusty Rusty is one of my favorite people."

Kate choked down a mouthful of water, laughing and coughing.

He handed her a napkin. "It's my pet name for her. She loves it."

"It's—" She coughed again. "Appropriate. Why is it you have a pet name for her?" Kate couldn't stop grinning.

"She always quotes me."

"About?"

"Ah, Kate. Your next assignment in learning the secrets of the Magic Kingdom is to read a minimum of six months' back issues of the *Times*. If you had, you'd know that I'm the freshmen girls basketball coach and sometimes varsity assistant. That's why I originally came to Valley Oaks two years ago. And then I started subbing."

"You teach and coach, but you don't know what you want to do with your life?"

"Well, those are like…" He whirled a hand in the air as if searching for a word. "Hobbies. I have a degree in business, but I don't have a teacher's certificate, though I'm working toward one. I'm a pilot too, for private charters. Of course, that's also kind of a hobby. And I enjoy photography."

"As a hobby."

He smiled. "Why settle for one hobby and call it a career? Now, what brings you to Valley Oaks? I thought Rusty pretty much handled the paper on her own, except for the publisher and part-time receptionist."

"The short version is I don't have a degree yet. I'm going for journalism from Iowa. I'll graduate as soon as I finish an internship. Nothing was available in New York or Los Angeles." She gave him a crooked smile. "Nothing in Chicago or Springfield either. My professor is an old colleague of Rusty's. So here I am. Last stop before Washington, DC."

"Why don't you have a degree yet? You were probably number one or two in our class."

She held up three fingers. "I never could beat Beth Anderson and Tracy Lyndon." She sighed dramatically. "Remember them?"

He shook his head.

"Nerds, every last one of us. Anyway, things got complicated after high school. I took a few detours along the way. You said my next assignment was to read the old *Times*. What was the first one?"

"The first one is on its way even as we speak."

The waitress set two oversized dinner plates before them, each piled high with barbecued ribs and fries.

"Eat up." He winked. "This is the most delicious inside scoop of Valley Oaks."

Tanner watched Kate with amusement as she devoured her dinner, keeping pace with him bite for bite, elbows on the table, a rib held between two hands. He was going to lose the bet.

In between bites she asked, "But seriously, Tanner, how do I write this story?"

He couldn't help but chuckle. "It's a tad hard to take you too seriously." He pointed to his own cheek, indicating where she had sauce smeared on hers.

She laughed and wiped a napkin across her face. Her laugh was infectious and suited her quirky appearance. With a forefinger, she pushed the rectangular tortoiseshell glasses up her perky little nose and asked, "Is that better?"

"Much. Okay, seriously, it's a human interest story."

"Exactly. I know how to write those, but not for page 1, above-the-fold articles."

"Kate, you've got to throw out everything you've learned in class and follow Rusty's lead. She has been around the block once or twice, you know."

"I know. Are you going to eat your coleslaw?"

"Hey, the bet was only for you to finish your own plate."

"I just didn't want it to go to waste."

"I'm a strange eater. I always save the salad for last, but if you're still hungry…" He laughed.

She joined in. "This stuff is heavenly. Have I said that already?"

"Six or seven times." He wondered where she was putting it all. Perhaps it fueled her spark plug of a personality. "Seriously, our *Times* is not a big-city paper. Unless there's a car accident or a fire or the village board discusses money, most of the news is human interest. For Valley Oaks, it works. That's all we need."

"It'd never fly in DC."

"No, it wouldn't, but this isn't DC. What's with DC anyway?"

"My next stop. I hope. I want to be the Helen Thomas of the twenty-first century. Follow the president around like his shadow. Ask him the tough questions at news conferences. Make an impact by writing, keeping the lines open between the public and the White House."

He let out a low whistle. "Sounds like a big dream. Did you know this in high school?"

She nodded, stuffing a fry into her mouth.

They may have graduated together, but she definitely walked on a different planet than he did, then and now.

She tilted her head, looking him in the face. "What was your big dream in high school?"

He blew out a puff of air. "To get through it."

"I see. Well, you sound fairly content here. As if hobby-ing in Valley Oaks is a fit."

"Maybe. But I don't live here. I have an apartment in Rockville. How about you?"

"Haven't been able to afford one of those yet. I'm living with Adele and Chelsea Chandler."

"I've had Chelsea in class. Interesting girl. What's her mother like? Chelsea looks like something from the sixties. A free-spirited hippie artist."

"They're two peas in a pod. Adele makes pottery in her spare time, but her day job is director out at the county nursing home. They're free-spirited all right, but dedicated Christians."

That was news to him. Not that he knew the Chandlers personally, but they sure didn't resemble Britte Olafsson or Anne Sutton, the basketball coaches who occasionally referred to Jesus in a decidedly noncursing manner.

Kate continued, "They're great roomies. Except they have an aversion to cooking meat." She grinned and bit into another rib.

He was missing something. What could Britte, Anne, Chelsea, and Adele have in common? He looked at the funny young woman across the table. In spite of the red hair sticking out in every direction from a plastic clip at the back, there was a fresh, healthy glow about her. An innocence in the freckled nose and in the sauce where lipstick and cheek blush should have been. She was down-to-earth. Approachable. He figured that with Kate "what you see is what you get."

Like Britte. Like Anne. Like what he'd seen of Chelsea.

Kate tilted her head again, putting herself in his line of vision. "What?"

"You're one too. A Christian." It sounded like an accusation. "What I mean is—"

"Does that negate the bet?"

"Huh?"

"Does my being a Christian mean you won't buy my dinner?" She shoved her plate toward him.

Except for the pile of bones, it was as clean as if it'd just been pulled from the dishwasher.

He laughed. "No." He couldn't remember the last time he'd laughed so much. Being with Kate was like being with the guys. Almost. He didn't know any guys this short. "As a matter of fact, I think we should do it again."

"Pizza Parlor?"

"You're on."

Tanner looked at her eyes. They were a translucent green. Not Christmas green, but combined with the red hair and colorful clothing, they added to the notion she was one heck of a surprise Santa could have left under the tree.

Kate fired up the slow beast of a computer at the newspaper office. After that delicious meal with Tanner and his lesson on what constituted news in Valley Oaks, she was ready to write the kissing principal article before heading home.

Things were looking up. She now had *four* friends in town: Rusty, Adele, Chelsea, and Tanner. Surprisingly, he was the easiest one to relate to despite their dissimilar backgrounds and approach to life. Hanging out with him was like hanging out with Beth, her best friend since high school. Almost. Beth had a husband and two little kids.

While the computer continued to grind away, its screen still dark, Kate picked up the telephone and dialed the familiar number.

"Hello," Beth Anderson Greenly answered.

"Hey. Got a minute?"

"Kate! How's it going out there in Hicksville?"

"Puh-lease. This is my home."

"For the duration."

"Uh-huh. Anyway, you'll never guess who I had dinner with tonight. Tanner Carlucci from high school."

Her friend hooted. "That jerk?"

"Come on, Beth. You didn't even know him."

"Did so. He was in my brother's group during Todd's nightmare period. They used to—"

"Don't tell me! I don't want to know what he did over twelve years ago. We had a great time. He seems like a nice guy, just like your brother is now."

"Is he still drop-dead gorgeous?"

Kate ignored the question. "And he paid."

"I guess that means, as usual, Miss Journalist didn't notice." Beth sighed loudly. "I don't know what I'm going to do with you. Well, that was kind of him to pay. I think he grew up wealthy. His dad's a doctor. Didn't he do your mom's surgery? Sidney Carlucci."

Kate thought back nearly eight years ago. "I don't know. She had so many doctors."

"I'm almost sure he did. He's a surgeon."

"He's the one we liked so much?"

"Yeah. So how did you hook up with Tanner?"

Kate relayed the details, and then she asked about the girls. Beth described her baby's latest teething bout and her two-year-old's newest favorite phrase. When at last the computer was ready, they said their goodbyes.

Kate stared at the blank screen for an inordinate amount of time. Maybe Tanner's idea was worth a try.

She went to the old newspapers piled on the floor in a corner, moved a stack of them to the table, and began skimming. Two hours later she stretched.

"As Rusty would say, 'Well, kid, it ain't DC.'" With hands on her hips and eyes closed, she twisted the kinks out of her neck and her attitude. "Thank You, Lord. It is a first step on the way there." She opened her eyes, surveyed the untidy room, and inhaled the stale smoke. "Though not the one I would have chosen!"

Four

Adele leaned over the wheelchair and gently squeezed the occupant's veined hand. "Dinner will be ready soon, Edith. Your hair looks especially nice today."

A spark of recognition flashed in the woman's watery eyes. "My granddaughter came to see me. Do you want to hear my song?"

"Maybe later, hon."

Ordinarily Adele would have lingered and listened once again to the 83-year-old's warbling rendition of "Don't Sit Under the Apple Tree," but it was 3:55. She had five minutes to spare before her appointment, and she needed every second of those five minutes to recharge.

She hurried down the hall into her office. As director of Fox Meadow Care Center, the county nursing home, she rated a space to call her own. Though cramped and windowless, it beat huddling outside in a cold minivan that took a lot longer than five minutes to warm up.

She maintained an open-door policy and so left the door ajar six inches. It was an understood signal that while she was available, if at all possible she'd rather be unavailable for just a few moments.

Turning sideways in order to fit, she stepped around the desk and slid onto her chair. Two framed five-by-seven photos caught her eye.

Maybe she should have gone to the car.

She took a couple of deep breaths. It had been an emotionally crowded day with the elderly folks. They had lost

37

Mr. Lerner at 6:08 this morning. *Why on Valentine's Day, Lord? Even if he has no family and is in a better place?* She had been called immediately and arrived by seven, shaving five minutes off the 20-minute drive. Maybe that's why she had the five minutes to spare now.

She propped her elbows on the desk and covered her face with her hands. Still, the photos loomed in her mind's eye. One was of Chelsea, 16 and a half. It was this year's school photo, her daughter's junior year, taken in the fall. She had painted orange highlights in her normally dark blonde hair. She said it was her celebration of autumn's falling leaves.

Adele could live with the hair colorings. It was the incessant, independent pulling away that gnawed at her.

The other photo was of Will...William Harrison Epstein III, wearing *casual*—a red sweater and khakis, sitting in front of her Christmas tree. Three hours from now he was taking her out for a special Valentine's dinner. She looked forward to sharing her day with him and crying on his shoulder about Mr. Lerner. Maybe even about Chelsea. *If only I can stay awake!*

"Excuse me?"

Adele jerked her hands away from her face and opened her eyes to see a stranger peeking around her door.

"Sorry. I knocked, but you must not have heard. I was told you were expecting me."

She stood, welcoming him with a smile. "Please, come in. I was just lost in thought. You must be Graham Logan."

He entered and shook her hand. "And you're Ms. Chandler."

"Adele. Nice to meet you. Have a seat."

"Thanks." He sat on the only chair, dwarfing the old ladder-back with its overly small cushion.

"I thought we could talk a bit, and then I'll give you the grand tour." She blinked, trying to refocus her tired eyes.

The guy had extraordinarily nice hair. He appeared older than she, though not by much, and yet his hair was a magnificent pewter gray color. Parted on the side. Curly in the back where it hung just below his ears.

"I don't want to take up too much of your time."

"Oh, you won't. I'm here for you. Would you like coffee or...or something?" Her mind was drawing a blank. What else did they serve in the kitchen?

He smiled. "No thank you."

"Chocolate?" She picked up a ceramic bowl of chocolate after-dinner mints and held it toward him.

He smiled again and his eyes twinkled. Piercing, steel blue eyes.

Adele reached for her coffee mug and knocked it over, spilling the contents. She grabbed a handful of tissues and began sopping it up. "Whoops."

The man stood and moved papers out of the way. "Are you all right?"

"No, not really." She held one of the framed photos toward him. "Teenager."

He raised his brows.

She glanced at the picture. It was of Will. "Oh, not that one. Here, this one."

"Ahh. I see."

"Mm-hmm." They both sat back down. "I think I have your file here somewhere." She lifted her desk blotter and peered underneath it.

"Look, we can postpone—"

"And Mr. Lerner passed away early this morning." She grabbed another tissue and dabbed her eyes. "He was such a sweetheart. I know I shouldn't get attached to the residents, but I do. I always do."

"Was he ill?"

"No, he was ninety-eight. He wanted to break the record of one hundred and seven, but I guess his heart just wasn't up for it."

"I'm sorry."

"That's kind of you to say. But it does mean we have a free bed. For your…?"

"Friend. He's been a second father to me and has no family."

"For your friend. Well." *Get a grip!* She took a deep breath and clutched her hands tightly on her lap, out of the way. "Why don't you just tell me about him."

He settled back in the chair and crossed his legs, propping ankle against knee. He wore brown corduroys, white socks, rugged brown shoes, and a bulky multi-colored sweater. No coat.

"All right," he said. "He's seventy-six and has cancer. At the most, he has only a few months to live."

"I'm so sorry."

"Thank you. We're getting…used to the idea. I'm beginning a year-long sabbatical from teaching in order to spend more time with him—"

"Sabbatical. Are you a professor?"

"Chicago area. At Northwestern. American history. Rand doesn't want to be in the city. He prefers to be out in the country, and he wants to give me the time and space to continue working. I'm researching for a book about Swedish settlers in Illinois. With this area's history, we thought it would be the ideal place."

"It is. And you'll still be close enough to easily visit the city. Do you have family there?"

"No, I'm a widower, as is Rand. No children. Siblings scattered."

Adele's heart went out to him, and she blinked back more tears. "Oh my. Do you have a place to live?"

"I just moved into an apartment in Valley Oaks. There wasn't anything in Twin Prairie." The nursing facility was located halfway between the two small towns. "I hope we can get him settled here."

"I'm sure we can, if you think he'll like it. He'll have all the medical attention he needs. It's closer than Rockville to Valley Oaks, and quieter." She stood. "Let me show you around, and then we can talk about finances."

"All right."

She squeezed past him, and he followed her out the door. It was moments like these she wanted to shut out the world and fall to her knees, asking God to change things. What a year this man was facing! And to think of the losses he'd already experienced! She stopped and faced him. "Mr.— or is it Dr. Logan?"

He gave her a half smile. "Why don't you just call me Graham?"

"Graham." Her voiced cracked. "I'm so sorry."

He stared down at her for a moment, a somber expression on his face. "I am too."

She was prettier than he imagined a Midwestern director of a nursing home in the middle of nowhere would be. And genuinely empathetic. And curiously childlike for a woman her age with such responsibility.

Graham followed Adele down a hall, trying to ignore the scent he wished was not about to become familiar. She greeted patients right and left by name, touching each one shuffling along or hunched over in a wheelchair. Jesus in a leper colony.

She glanced up at him. "I live in Valley Oaks too. I'd give you a tour there, but you won't really need one. Everything you want is within about a two-block radius. Unless you want a shopping center or a giant supermarket."

Her clothing appeared as if she'd shut her eyes and reached into the closet. But she carried it off somehow. The red sweater dress hung to her ankles, which were covered with what looked like thick white gym socks. She wore brown suede clogs. A wide belt encircled her waist; above that was a wildly colorful vest and a long necklace of beads. Her chin-length hair was curly and blonde, the shade a mature darkening of a towhead. It bounced whenever she moved her head.

They strolled through more of the building. Valentine decorations hung everywhere. She stopped at an exit door. "The gardens are lovely. Not this time of year of course." She smiled softly, her forehead pressed against the cold glass. "But he'll see the crocuses. They come up even if there's snow."

It wasn't fair. Life...was...not...fair.

They arrived back at her tiny office and sat down again. She explained finances and paperwork to him. He reached under his sweater to his shirt pocket, removed a pair of half reading glasses, and slid them on.

"Now you look like a professor," she said. "The parents of our Valley Oaks pharmacist teach at Northwestern. Do you know the Neumans? I can't remember their first names. Or what he teaches. She's a librarian. Chinese."

"Uh, yeah, I think I know who she is. It's a big place. Shall I write you a check now? He won't be needing state aid."

"That's not necessary. I'll have the accounting office prepare things. What's his name?"

"Rand. Rand Jennings."

She wrote it down. "You're welcome to move him in tomorrow, but I understand that may not be possible. And that's not a problem."

"He's anxious to get settled. We can be here a week from Friday. Will that afternoon work?"

"That'll work just fine." Her ever-present dimples deepened. "I'll be here. You can take this packet with you. It explains what you'll want to bring."

"Thank you." He stood, accepted the thick envelope, and shook her hand. She had a strong hand, as if she did more than touch the sick. "See you next week."

"Take care. Do you have a coat?"

"In the car. Goodbye." He walked out the door and started down the hall.

"Graham."

He turned to see her, hand on the doorjamb, arm stretched full length as she leaned out into the hallway.

"We'll take really good care of you and Mr. Jennings. You can trust me on that."

He nodded and continued on his way.

Fox Meadow Care Center and Adele Chandler were so much more than he had bargained for.

Adele threw the red dress on the bed and reached into her closet for another. Ten minutes and counting. She heard Chelsea and Kate's voices in her daughter's room next to hers.

"Help, you two!" she called out.

They came in.

"Oh, Mom!"

Kate asked, "What's wrong?"

Chelsea plopped on the bed and planted her elbows into the ivory chenille spread. "She doesn't know what to wear."

"Oh. Well, it's Valentine's Day. That red dress you had on seems a good choice for dinner."

Adele exchanged a look with Chelsea, who explained, "Will is *finicky*."

"Chels."

"Do you have a better word for it?"

"He's...particular. He's the administrator at the Rockville Hospital. His job is sociable and it fits him. I mean, he looks good in suits. He prefers formal as opposed to my usual mishmash."

"Mom, I don't know why you want to change for him."

"Because I like him a lot." She sat down beside her daughter. "What does it hurt if I dress now and then to please him?"

Kate pointed at the closet and asked, "Mind if I look?"

"Help yourself. And Will's kind and fun and handsome. Whoa! Speaking of handsome. This guy walked into my office today. He's moving an elderly man into the home, a close friend. I'm glad we have space for him. I guess he doesn't have long—"

"Mom, you're getting off track."

"Oh. What was I— Oh, yeah. Handsome. I felt like an ogling teenager. I got all tongue-tied and spilled my coffee."

Chelsea giggled. "I cannot believe this is my mother speaking. Your toes never curl when you talk about a guy. Not even about Will! And he's good-looking, if you like the uppity version—"

"My toes aren't curling."

"Mom, don't take it literally. So what'd he look like?"

"Kind of longish hair the color of pewter, but he wasn't old. Blue, *blue* eyes. Good build."

"This is too weird. I don't want to hear anymore!"

Adele fell back on the bed, laughing. "I have to listen to you all the time! See how ridiculous it sounds?"

Kate interrupted, holding out a dress. "Adele, how's this? It's black, dressy, simple."

"That's perfect. I forgot about that one. It's my fundraising outfit." She took it from her. "Thanks. Oh, there's the doorbell. Chels, let him in? I need two minutes. Three max."

Chelsea scooted out the door and called, "Don't forget to comb your hair!" A moment later her feet thumped down the staircase.

"So where's he taking you?" Kate sat on the bed.

"It's a surprise. Someplace special in Rockville."

"He drives all the way here from his home in Rockville, back again for dinner, here again to bring you home, and back home again. And this is the fourth time since I've been here. Sounds like love to me."

Adele paused, her hand on the back zipper. *Love?* She dropped her arms to her sides. "Kate, I haven't thought about that kind of love in eighteen years. I've been too busy. I mean, he's a great guy, and we've been dating kind of steadily for about six months. But...love! What a scary thought!"

"Well, you know the test. Are your toes curling?"

Adele laughed.

Five

Will Epstein looked very good indeed in a suit, a fact that always caught Adele by surprise. Until she had met him, men who looked good in suits did not even register on her radar screen. He was tall with boyish good looks mingled with a smooth, Wall Street executive image. As usual, heads had turned as they walked through the restaurant.

She reached now across the small candlelit table and brushed a blonde hair from his padded, pin-striped shoulder. She'd already cried, before dinner, in his car, in the parking lot.

He gave her hand a quick squeeze. "Feeling better?"

She nodded, but knew that could change in the blink of an eye. At home she'd checked the calendar and figured it was *that* week. Unfortunately, before recognizing the symptoms of emotional fireworks, she'd devoured most of the chocolate in and around her desk. She really should not have ordered the triple chocolate cake for dessert. Chocolate amplified everything, causing excessive tears and unsteady hands that knocked over coffee mugs.

"Will, I have something for you." She picked up the red gift bag at her feet and handed it to him. "Happy Valentine's Day."

He smiled the smile that crinkled his hazel eyes. "I was wondering when I'd get to open this. What is it?" He removed the tissue paper and lifted out a large, glossy black coffee mug. "You made it! It's beautiful. I like the scrolls on the handle. Hey, it's big enough for lattes. Thank you."

"You're welcome. It's your official executive mug. For the office."

"It reminds me of when we met."

"At the hospital charity thing."

"At the silent auction table."

"You bid on my set of casserole dishes."

"The ones you wanted for yourself."

She grimaced. "But I couldn't outbid you."

"You pushed me to my limit."

"They were nice."

"Still are."

She knew the dishes graced his cupboard shelves and he used them often.

He smiled softly. "You should have inscribed them 'Designed for Adele Chandler' rather than 'Designs by Addie.' Whoever she is."

Addie was a childhood name, the one she always signed on her artwork, a habit begun with coloring book pages.

"Well, Addie-Adele, I have a little something for you." He reached into his inside jacket pocket and pulled out a small box wrapped in red foil topped with a petite gold bow.

With some trepidation, she accepted the gift. *Oh, Lord, please let it be earrings! Not an engagement ring!* Kate's words replayed in her mind...*It must be love.* No, it couldn't be love. They'd never talked about love.

She opened the box and saw...a ring. A none-too-small sparkling amethyst set in gold filigree. "Oh, Will. It's so beautiful."

"It reminded me of when we met. You were wearing a wild purple outfit."

"This is too much. I can't accept—"

"Sure you can. I'm not proposing. It's simply a token of how much I care about you." His eyes were warm, full of compassion.

"Will, you pay child support, two home mortgages—"

"It was a tremendous sale. Adele, after my marriage fell apart, I didn't think I could ever let another woman into my heart. But you're there. God is real. Please accept this gift. And please don't look so scared."

She gave him a small smile. "We're both so busy, but I don't know what I'd do without our times together. You've added a whole new dimension to my life. I care very much about you. But I haven't considered a—a permanent relationship."

"The ring doesn't commit you to anything. You're free to continue dating as many guys as in the past."

She laughed. There had been exactly two other men she'd dated since Chelsea's birth, and they were ancient history. She met his gaze. Did he mean it? Since they'd met, he had been an undemanding companion who was simply sharing the present moment of life with her. He was a good friend who was treating her like a princess tonight.

Adele slipped the ring onto her right hand. "It fits! Oh, Will, you're too generous. Thank you."

"You're welcome. Here comes your chocolate."

Her good intentions to skip it slithered away. Why not indulge? It was Valentine's Day. And besides, she knew she wasn't going to sleep well tonight anyway. Princess treatment was having an unsettling effect on her.

"Adele?"

She jumped at Kate's loud voice, and the bowl she was shaping on the electric potter's wheel instantly gained a 45-degree angle.

"I'm sorry!"

"Whew." Adele turned off the humming wheel and straightened her back on the stool. "I was somewhere else."

"I know the house rule is that you're not to be disturbed down here, but it's two in the morning." She wrapped her robe around herself and sat midpoint on the stairway. As usual, she wore her glasses. Her straight red hair hung almost to her shoulders.

"Did I wake you?" Adele had placed her two wheels somewhere in the proximity of under the kitchen. Kate slept on the first floor not far from it.

"I was awake. Are you all right?"

Adele laughed and brushed her hair back with her forearm, her wet hands dripping. "No. Chocolate, PMS, Will, an amethyst ring. Oh my goodness! I've still got it on!" It was caked with wet clay. She wiped her hands on her jeans, hurried over to the sink, and carefully washed her fingers.

"Sounds like a rough night."

Adele joined her on the steps. "Will gave this to me at dinner."

Kate inspected the ring on her finger. "It's beautiful. An engagement ring?"

"Good heavens, no! But still, it's making me uncomfortable. I mean, I like him a lot, but..."

"But what?"

"He's always been kind, but this is so extravagant. Now I feel like a princess. A queen!" She sighed.

"And?"

"I like it. But I don't want to like it!" A strangled giggle escaped her throat. "I've been so independent for such a long time. This is cutting into that something awful."

"Do you love him?"

"Probably, in a way. You know, Kate, I really don't know if I've ever been in love."

"What about Chelsea's father?"

"He doesn't count. I was only nineteen and rebelling against my uptight parents. We met in Venice. We both had dropped out of college, both had enough money to bum around Europe. We traveled together. I had no morals, Kate. After a few months we went our separate ways. And then I found out I was pregnant. I came home. My dad disowned me on the spot."

"Disowned? That's an old-fashioned word."

"Not for R.J. Chandler. He refused to help in any way, shape, or form. In his eyes I had betrayed him. He burned his will in front of me."

"Adele. That's awful! What kind of man could do that?"

"An enormously successful one. His work in arbitrage consumed him. He treated me like a disposable asset. The worst of it was his lack of compassion. I don't think he loved me. But God brought me through. I kept in touch with my mother until she died about twelve years ago. He never did have a change of heart."

"How did you end up here?"

"I was on a Greyhound bus, heading from Baltimore to San Francisco. A snowstorm hit, and we were forced to stop in Valley Oaks. The community rallied around us, and people transported us over to the church. The next thing I knew, Naomi Sommers was tucking me into bed in this house."

"You're kidding. Have I met Naomi?"

"Not yet. She lived here with her daughter, Julie, who at that time was just a little girl. One thing led to another. The long and short of it is, she loved me to Jesus. Fed me, clothed me, took me to church, found me a doctor, helped me get my first job at the nursing home and then an apartment. I bought the house from her about seven years ago."

"That's quite a story."

"And off the record. Valley Oaks already knows what it needs to know of it."

Kate smiled. "You never heard from your dad? Or found Chelsea's dad?"

"Nope. I learned to forgive R.J. That took some doing. Only by my heavenly Father's power. And Naomi's mentoring. Actually, she had a similar experience as an unwed mother. The daughter of the original owner of this house, a widow, helped her when she was a pregnant teen."

"Isn't it wonderful to see how God's hand works through a string of people like that?"

"Amen. Thanks for listening, Kate. I think I've calmed down now." She stood. "I'll put away my clay and head to bed. By the way, what are you doing up?"

"Reviewing all the decisions that led me to the *Valley Oaks Times.* Telling myself that God does not make mistakes."

"Aww, Kate, I bet you knew that before you moved here."

She stood and yawned. "I thought I did, but I guess I needed another reminder. Thanks."

Six

Kate depressed the clutch, breathed a prayer that frosted the early morning air, pumped the gas pedal, and turned the key in the ignition.

"Come on, Helen," she coaxed the car as if it were a race-horse on the home stretch. After two tries it chugged awake once more. "Thank You, Lord."

The cell phone on the seat beside her played its tune.

"Hello?"

"Hey, Kate. Tanner."

"Hi." She grinned. Since their dinner last week, their paths had crossed a few times. He was a regular fixture at high school events and had sought her out at boys basketball games and a band concert. She enjoyed his company.

"How are things?"

"Not bad. It looks like Helen's going to get me to work again."

"Helen? Helen Thomas? You actually know the woman?"

"My car."

"You named your car after Helen Thomas." It was a matter-of-fact statement spoken with a trace of disbelief.

"Tell me you never named a car."

"But you're a *girl*."

"I'm going to forget you said that."

He laughed. "Here's the latest scoop for you. Girls basketball, awards banquet, tomorrow night, in the commons. Be there. It's news."

"Rusty already assigned it to me."

"Ah, she beat me. I'll pick you up at five-thirty so you can give Helen a rest. She doesn't sound so good."

Kate gunned the car. She sounded all right to her, though the heater hadn't warmed up yet.

"Which house is the Chandlers'?"

"On Cherry, across from the Community Center's parking lot, west end."

"Okay, see you there. Oh, I almost forgot. You need to bring a dish to pass."

"I thought it was a banquet, as in the food is provided?"

"Banquet is a Magic Kingdom synonym for potluck. If you don't want to cook, we'll stop at Swensen's on the way and buy something from the deli. That's what I do, if I remember. Fried chicken goes over big. Need anything from Baltimore? I'm on my way."

"Baltimore, Maryland? And you'll be back by tomorrow night?"

"I'm flying a charter, just overnight. Some guy's picking up an invalid. Give my love to Crusty Rusty."

Kate smiled. "Will do. Fly safe."

"You too." He chuckled. "My guess is that describes how you *drive*. Bye!"

"Goodbye."

She shifted into first and eased away from the curb, still smiling. The guy was better than Beth. Beth would have insisted that they cook.

⌒

"Rusty, it's archaic." Kate wasn't whining. She was just stating an opinion as calmly as she could while struggling to breathe in her boss's chimney stack of a car.

Rusty coughed, flicked her ash out the window opened just wide enough, and drove with one hand as they sped through the winter wonderland of rolling white hills. "What's archaic?"

"Driving to Twin Prairie to print the paper and then stuffing it in envelopes and then sticking those in the mail for subscribers."

"The paper doesn't go in envelopes. We just stick labels on them."

"And fold them."

"And, don't forget, then we come back, fill the vending machines, and drop some off at Lia's pharmacy and Swensen's." Rusty snorted a laugh. "Keep in mind, kid, despite the one-horse show, it's an important job we're doing. We're tuned to the pulse of the community, and it's our responsibility to publish it."

"Do you ever feel like you make a difference?"

"Sure. A lot of people tell me how much they appreciate the paper."

"I mean, do you ever change that pulse by speeding it up or slowing it down?"

"An editorial here and there."

"But do you ever uncover anything that opens people's eyes? That makes a decided change in their thought processes? This week we wrote about everything they already know or could know if they hung out long enough at the pharmacy."

"It ain't DC, kid."

Mm-hmm.

Whoops. What had happened to her middle-of-the-night surrender to God's leading? To the reminder that God was the potter, she was the clay? Probably lost between lack of sleep and the mounting desire to a pull a fire alarm. She cracked open her window. She no longer cared that it was ten degrees out there.

"Rusty, Tanner Carlucci sends his love."

The older woman roared her deep, bronchial laugh. "So you've met?"

"Actually..." Kate cleared her throat, partly from embarrassment, partly from smoke. "He took the photo of Kingsley and Olafsson."

"Ha! Good for him. I might have had to fire you if you'd missed that one."

"You can't fire an intern, can you? It's not like I'm getting paid."

"Katy-girl, you need to lighten up."

Lighten up. She knew that. Wasn't that another conclusion she'd reached at two this morning? God did not make mistakes. Like every other unplanned diversion in her life, He had directed her steps. Without a doubt, He had brought her to Valley Oaks. Now what was she going to do? Whine or lighten up?

Rusty Connelly was a gold mine of wise journalistic tidbits. After 12 hours in her company storing countless nuggets, Kate went home with a decidedly nonwhiny attitude. The village still wasn't DC, but professionally speaking, things were improving.

When she opened the front door, a sound wave of female chatter greeted her. She recalled Adele had mentioned her book club meeting was at the house tonight and that Kate was welcome to join them.

While removing her coat, she had a partial view of the living room. It looked like a packed house. She spotted Britte

Olafsson and cringed. Before she could retreat, Adele hailed her.

"Kate! Come on in. Ladies!"

The conversation died and eight pairs of eyes zeroed in on Kate.

Adele continued, "I'd like you all to meet Kate Kilpatrick."

As one, the group stood, gathered around her, and cheered.

"Good job!"

"Great job!"

"Nice writing!"

"It's perfect!"

They shook her hand, introducing themselves, patting her on the back. Their names went in one ear and out the other.

Overwhelmed, Kate finally managed to say something. "What are you all talking about?"

Adele replied, "Your article about Britte and Joel!"

Of course. Copies of the *Times* were already available in the stores and vending machines. She had placed them there herself. Evidently while she was eating pizza with Rusty, eager readers were already out buying the weekly.

"Kate." Britte beamed, no longer resembling the shell-shocked Nordic. "Thank you. We look like a couple of lovesick teenagers in the photo, but you did such a nice job of making the event sound sane rather than idiotic. I still cannot believe he called you." She shook her head.

"That makes two of us."

Kate accepted their invitation to join their book discussion. Pass up a roomful of potential sources? She didn't think twice about finding a seat.

Later that night she thought of Adele's description of the group. They referred to themselves as Club NEDD, an acronym for nurture, eat, and dabble in discussion. It was an accurate name. She had eaten and discussed. And although she knew the article was pure fluff, the women's response to it had, beyond a shadow of a doubt, *nurtured* her.

Lying in her bed, she smiled at the ceiling, warmed at the image of the loving group. Their nurturing had jiggled loose a buried thought. God had created in her the mindset and the passion to be a reporter. In all her fussing over the internship, that gift had gone dormant. To recount life's journey for others was what gave her breath, and she had been suffocating. It was time to start breathing again.

Seven

Midafternoon Friday Adele walked across the large open space of Fox Meadow's lobby. It was a hub of activity with people milling about, many of them in wheelchairs. There was a big-screen television, lots of chairs, and a table laden with baked goodies some church women had provided. Windows lined the front of the brick building, providing an unhindered view of the parking lot.

Sunshine glinted off a shiny black limousine, catching her attention. She watched as it parked on the circular drive just outside the entry. She knew immediately it was Rand Jennings. Only someone who had the ability to pay before even asking the price of admission would arrive in a limo.

Would Graham be with him?

She tried to ignore the tickle of anticipation in her stomach and hurried to grab a nearby communal wheelchair from the receptionist's office. As she pushed it toward the door, she noticed the chauffeur unloading one from the car's trunk. Naturally someone arriving in a limo would have his own. She smiled to herself and wheeled hers back.

Adele went outdoors to greet them, something she tried to do for newcomers whenever possible. Waiting on the sidewalk, she wrapped her cardigan closely and crossed her arms against the cold. Graham stood beside the open back door, bent at the waist, holding his arm toward the interior. He wore sunglasses and, again, no coat over a sweater and cords.

The man emerging from the back seat was familiar. He resembled all men over age 70 whose bodies had been ravaged by cancer and its treatments, men who spent their last days down the hall from her office. He was thin and he was bald, facts she knew despite the black winter dress coat and fur cap he wore.

He stepped now unsteadily but on his own to the chair held by the chauffeur. Graham waited near enough to grasp an arm if needed but didn't hover. His stance displayed a respect for what most men at that point desired: to remain unassisted for as long as possible.

The driver relinquished the chair to Graham, who wheeled it around and pushed it toward the door Adele now opened. As they neared, the old man looked up at her, his eyeglasses a dark tint in the bright sunlight. He raised a hand and fumbled about his shoulder, as if searching for something. Graham reached out and clutched the pale, slender fingers, continuing to push and steer with one hand.

"Hello!" She pulled the door open for them. "Welcome to Fox Meadow. Go right on inside."

Graham nodded grimly to her as he wheeled Mr. Jennings through the first set of doors.

Adele stepped around them and pushed the large blue handicapped button that automatically opened the next set. Inside she led them off to the left where there was a grouping of vacant armchairs, and she sat down in one beside the wheelchair. Graham unbuttoned the elderly man's coat and slipped it from his arms. He appeared shriveled beneath a white shirt and bright red cardigan.

She touched the old man's hand. "How do you do, Mr. Jennings."

He politely and slowly removed his hat. "You must be Adele!" His voice was low, raspy.

Taken aback that he would know her name, she replied, "Why, yes, I am."

"Graham has told me so much about you." Behind the thick bifocals now lightening a shade as they adjusted to the indoors, his eyes seemed to twinkle in the gaunt face.

"He has?" Surprise raised her voice, and then she realized he must be teasing her. She had spent a mere 45 minutes with Graham Logan. But before she could recover, he went on.

"He described you to a T and said you're the incredibly beautiful, efficient director of this place. Sold him on the spot."

"Rand!" Graham's voice jumped an octave.

"Oh, call me Pops. I always wanted to be called Pops. Never too late to start, is it?"

The man was a charmer. The nurses were going to enjoy him. "No, Mr. Jennings, it's never too late to start anything."

"Until you're dead and gone. Like I will be soon." Matter of fact, with a hint of a chuckle and no self-pity. "Where's my room?"

"Let's go right now."

She walked beside Graham, slowing her *efficient* walk to match the more sedate movement the wheelchair required. His sunglasses were atop his hair. That luscious pewter-streaked hair.

"So, Graham," she murmured, giving him a sly smile, "thanks for the compliment."

He looked decidedly uncomfortable. "You're wel— The fact is, I didn't exactly say—"

She laughed. "I know you didn't. He's charming! Shall I warn the nurses?"

Mr. Jennings turned his bald head slightly and glanced over his shoulder. "You're talking about me behind my back. Literally behind my back." His tone was amused.

"We are!" Adele took a quick double step to the front of his chair. "But it's all good stuff, Mr. Jennings. Here we go. Right in here." She led the way into a single room. "You've got a nice southeast view. Snow-covered fields and sunshine most of the day. Oh, dear. The bed's not ready. I'll grab some linens and take care of that. I imagine you're rather tired after your trip. "

"I could use a nap. You'd think the good Lord would take away the need for sleep at this stage of things. Kind of hate snoring away what little time I have left. Graham, park me by the window."

"There you go, *Pops*. I'll get your things out of the car." Without a backward glance, he strode from the room.

"Mr. Jennings, I'll get those linens and be right back."

"Don't you pay someone else to do that?"

"We're short a couple of aides today. My job description doesn't say I *can't* do it! Sit tight."

He chuckled at that.

Adele hurried out the door and jogged toward Graham. From the back, his height and breadth was almost intimidating. The top of his head appeared to nearly graze the low ceiling tiles. His shoulders occupied a lot of hall space.

Why was it she kept *noticing* the man?

"Graham." She neared him.

He stopped and turned, his furrowed brow questioning.

She reached his side and touched his forearm. "It gets better. It does."

"Easy for you to say, Ms. Chandler." He turned on his heel and walked away.

Hurrying down the hallway, Graham tried to shut out the institutional gray-green walls, the faded black-and-white linoleum, the water stain on a corner ceiling tile. The totally overriding bleak, stark *feel* of the place. The vacant stares of wheelchair occupants as he passed them.

The warmth of compassionate fingers touching his forearm.

But of course he couldn't.

Because all of it revolved around Rand Jennings. And the man had always been an integral part of his life. There was no going backward. Adele Chandler, institutional green, the scent of waiting for death...all were permanent fixtures in his foreseeable future.

Graham eyed Adele over the top of his reading glasses. She sat behind her desk, across from him, efficiently shuffling the myriad of papers he was signing.

"Only one more." Her voice was lilting, as if she were always on the verge of expressing something wildly joyful.

"Ms. Chandler."

She didn't correct him by reminding him of her first name. Perhaps she thought as he did, that it was best to keep the distance of formality between them. She met his gaze with a steady one of her own. Her eyes were large ovals that dominated her face. Not quite blue, not quite gray. Like a hazy summer sky. Warm and calm.

"Yes, Dr. Logan?"

He intended to ask another question about hospice, but her tone matched her eyes, and he knew formality was not in the woman's character. Allowing him to vent his pain came with running the nursing home. She wouldn't hold it against him. Still…confession was good for the soul.

He removed his reading glasses. "I'm sorry for being short with you earlier."

"Don't worry about it. I have this annoying tendency to invade people's private space. I think it's because so many of the folks here continuously need it. I forget that healthy adults don't go around hoping somebody, *anybody,* will offer comfort." She gave him a half smile. "I should have read the signals."

"Signals?"

Her eyelids fluttered downward as she straightened papers. "You know. Those manly signals of self-sufficiency."

"Oh, *those.* Evidently I wasn't displaying them very well."

She looked back up as if to say something, gave her head a slight shake, and laughed. "Never mind. All right. We're finished with the paperwork. Any questions?"

He could think of only one. "Will you have dinner with me tonight?"

Eight

Five minutes before Tanner's scheduled arrival, Kate heard the doorbell buzz. Shrugging into her overcoat, she opened the front door. He stood there, bundled in a black jacket, his hair grazing the thick turtleneck rising above the leather, his breath turning into white puffs on the night air.

"Hey, Sir Galahad."

The porch light shone on his puzzled face.

"You could have just honked." She shut the door behind her. "You know how I feel about Sir Galahad, right?"

He followed her down the steps. "Let me guess. Waste of energy?"

"To the max."

"I was just being polite. Fighting noise pollution."

She laughed, hurrying through the cold night air around the big black hood of an SUV. "Man, was I ever wrong! I figured you drove a little red sports car." She opened the passenger side door and climbed up onto the buttery soft leather seat as he entered from the driver's side. "Isn't that the thirty-year-old bachelor's usual mode of transportation?"

"I totaled that when I was twenty-two."

"I see." With exaggerated motions, she tugged the safety belt out as far as it would go and hooked it with a loud click. "Have your driving skills improved since that time?"

"Well, my drinking skills have."

In the relaxed manner she had observed in her brothers, he handled the car as if it were a small toy, steering with one

64

hand, elbow propped against the window. She waited, hoping he would elaborate on his cryptic comment.

"I don't anymore," he said.

"That's great."

"I don't suppose you've ever had to deal with that issue?"

"No. I can't relate."

"Lucky you. Well!" He smiled, his tone flippant. "Enough about me!"

"But I want to hear about your trip."

"Oh, all right. You're such a snoop. But I guess that's your job."

"Tell me who, what, where—"

"There's not that much to tell. Flew out, flew back. Some guy moved his friend here. He was a frail-looking older gentleman."

"In the dead of winter? Poor man, traveling here to the Arctic Circle. I bet it's springtime in Baltimore already. You soaked up some sunshine, didn't you? Your nose has a rosy tint to it."

"Observant little snoop."

"Hey, let's not bring height into this. Observant snoop, okay, but I draw the line at the word 'little.'"

"Okay, okay." He held up a hand in mock surrender. "Exactly how short are you?"

"None of your business."

Like other times, they bantered easily. Teasing, laughing, freely sharing a wide range of thoughts. He never crossed the line into flirting, for which she was grateful. With her plain appearance and career-oriented outlook, she knew she was nothing like the type of woman he pursued. She would have doubted his sincerity if he had behaved that way toward her.

She imagined he had quite a number of ex-girlfriends. Besides being symmetrically proportioned, the guy projected a depth. With a start she realized she'd just described the perfect catch: Adonis with a soul. And she was, at that very moment, by his invitation, sitting next to him.

A highly unusual situation.

~

Tanner watched Kate from a distance at the banquet. As he suspected, she wasn't a needy companion who required his constant attention. Which was why he had offered to escort her there in the first place.

The affair was held in the commons, now furnished with long tables. Girls from the three basketball teams sat together while their families settled in elsewhere. As one of the coaches, he sat at the head table, leaving Kate to her own devices. She was remarkably self-sufficient. Truly one of the guys.

She easily made new acquaintances, slipping into an empty chair beside the Andersons near the back, introducing herself. Who could resist her quirky friendliness? She posed no threat in her too-large coat and one mitten, camera dangling from her shoulder, glasses often sliding down her lightly freckled nose. Her red hair was held in a ponytail by elastic, but still stray ends stuck out. He noted as he had at the Rib House that she was left-handed. It was so *apropos* for a quirky character.

She caught his eye and smiled. He gave her a thumbs-up and turned his attention back to Britte, who was now speaking into the microphone. Anne Sutton, the sophomore coach and Britte's assistant, was off on a Valentine's trip to California with her husband. Rotten timing. Tanner would have to do her presentations as well as his own. Not that he minded the exercise itself of calling names and handing out awards. It was knowing he would let down the ladies. The evening was always an emotional event for every female in the house as they reminisced over the season. Tearful discourses were addressed to the seniors. Tonight would be even more significant with the once-in-a-lifetime third-place trophy from the state tournament. He, on the other hand, would tell one too many jokes and, in general, be a disappointment.

Almost two hours later the crowd had thinned, but Kate wasn't quite finished. Tanner joined her as she photographed a group of varsity award winners. From behind her, he made faces at the girls. They burst into laughter just as she clicked.

She glanced over her shoulder at him, and then she put her eye back to the camera. "Ladies, puh-lease. Try to ignore Coach Adonis."

They roared, breaking rank from the posed lineup, and Kate snapped their picture again.

He leaned over and whispered in her ear, "You'll pay for that one, Kilpatrick."

She laughed and waited for the girls to settle down. "Why don't you go pose with them? Imagine all the future college dorm rooms displaying your photo. You'll be famous!"

He shook his head and backed away. "I think I'll go warm up the car. Maybe, just maybe, I'll wait for you."

Adele twirled the pizza platter around until the last piece lined up with Graham's plate across the table. "This is yours."

"You're sure you've had enough?"

The waistband of her skirt was decidedly more snug than when they had entered the Pizza Parlor. She nodded.

He helped himself to it. "Thanks. It is excellent, isn't it?"

She heard his astonished tone and grinned. "Surprise!"

He laughed. "Well, I never would have expected it in such a small, out-of-the-way place. Did you grow up here in Valley Oaks?"

"No, I've only been here since shortly before Chelsea was born. I immediately developed a craving for this pizza."

He returned her smile. They had spent the evening primarily talking business. Naturally, he was deeply interested in the day-to-day operations of Fox Meadow, how he and his close friend would be affected, what his role was. Now, at last, she sensed him loosening up.

"Adele—"

"Thank you."

"For what?"

"For dropping the 'Ms.'"

He lowered his eyes and fiddled with a fork. "I was resisting this afternoon. Resisting the fact that you and Fox Meadow are now part of my life."

"I know."

He looked at her again. "You must see it often."

"Often enough. Watching a loved one grow old and die is not something any of us would choose to do. Institutionalizing them is a heartbreaking decision."

"Have you had to do it? Oh, probably not. Your parents must be much younger."

She shook head. "They were forty when I was born. My mother passed away about twelve years ago."

"And your father?"

How odd. Like Kate, he was a fairly new acquaintance, a stranger really. Like with Kate last night, she was about to unwrap her past in front of him. At least it was clean now. Long ago she had asked her heavenly Father to forgive her.

But there was a mystique about Graham Logan. Safety radiated from him. Was it his gentleness? His overpowering physical presence? Or the fact that he ate vegetarian pizza with gusto and without snide remark? She didn't know. Whatever it was, she felt secure with him.

"Adele, I'm getting too personal."

"No, it's all right. I was just thinking how we're practically strangers, yet you don't seem like one. You're rather easy to be with."

"*You're* rather easy to be with. I figured this must be a familiar routine for you, that all your clients take you to dinner." There was a definite twinkle in the steel blue eyes that held hers.

"Um, not quite. As a matter of fact, you're the first." She tried to ignore a peculiar tingling feeling now forming at the base of her throat.

"I have a confession to make."

"Oh?" She touched the hollow of her neck. Her beaded choker necklace felt snug, like her waistband, but it wasn't from eating too much pizza. It was from her heart throwing chaotic beats against it.

"Truthfully, it wasn't a simple business invitation. I deliberately took note that you don't wear a wedding band."

She lowered her left hand and studied it. "Uh, no I don't. Because I'm not. Married, that is."

"But that photo on your desk suggests you're...involved?"

"Oh, that's, um, Will. He's a friend. Just a friend. Not like...involved. No, I'm not involved. Nor engaged." Her voice sounded strange to her own ears. Breathy. High-pitched. "So, what you're saying is, you picked me up? At Fox Meadow?"

He laughed. It was a deep, rich sound. "I wouldn't have phrased it quite so crassly."

"But if the shoe fits..."

He still smiled, the crow's feet around his eyes crinkling. "Touché. Are you always this direct?"

Now it was she who broke eye contact and fiddled with a fork.

He went on. "The past six months have been...difficult. I felt like I couldn't take a breath. Until today. You welcomed Rand, and suddenly I could breathe again." As if to demonstrate, he inhaled deeply and let it out. "You were like this great gulp of fresh air."

She was a gulp of fresh air? Then he must be a great gulp of sweet spring water because suddenly her thirst was quenched. And she hadn't even known she was in the desert.

Nine

"Oh, Tanner!" Kate giggled as she climbed into his warm car idling at the curb just outside the high school. "You missed more accolades— Fiddlesticks!" She reopened the door and jumped down.

"You forgot your coat."

"Sorry. I'll be right back." She slammed the door shut and raced up the wide walkway and into the building.

He grinned to himself. She would forget her head. He waited, wondering if she had been as much fun in high school. Of course in high school he wouldn't have noticed her. Girls didn't exist unless they were fashion model material—very tall and preferably blonde—with a bubble for brains. What a jerk he'd been. No doubt still was.

He noticed someone meet her at the door with the jacket. She hustled back out to the car.

"Tanner." Her voice was breathless. "Check me. I've got my camera. Coat." She patted her pockets. "Program, notepad, pen."

"Head?"

"Funny."

He pulled away from the curb. "Are you hungry?"

"Ravenous!"

"Potlucks have that effect. How about a pizza?"

"Sounds great. So anyway, you missed a dozen more accolades from parents, not just the starry-eyed teenagers. They love you."

"You're kind. You seemed to have enjoyed yourself."

"It was such a trip! I didn't think Mayberry existed. My goodness! They opened with a prayer!"

"Is that legal, by the way?"

"Who cares, if nobody's complaining and the students did it themselves? I think the latest ruling said it was all right."

They chatted more about the evening. She was full of questions, nonstop. She even carried her notepad into the crowded, noisy Pizza Parlor where she made a beeline to a table occupied by a couple.

"Adele! Hi. This is Adonis—I mean, Tanner Carlucci."

He glared at her, only half teasing.

"Tanner, be nice. This is Adele Chandler."

"How do you do?" He shook her hand. The woman resembled Chelsea, though her curly hair was shorter. She appeared rather youthful-looking for a junior student's mother. "You must be Chelsea's mom."

"That's right. And this is Graham Logan. Newcomer to Valley Oaks."

Tanner recognized the man from his earlier flight to Maryland. "Hello, again."

"Hi." He smiled hesitantly, and then recognition registered. "You're the pilot."

"Small world."

Graham explained to Adele, "We flew. Much easier on Rand than driving." He turned back to Tanner and Kate. "Adele got him all moved into her home. Well, not her own home."

Kate smiled. "She took me in. I'm sure he'd be welcome there too."

They laughed. Kate declined Adele's invitation to join them, noting they were finished eating and that she was still interviewing Tanner. He followed her down the aisle to a window booth.

"You're interviewing me?"

"I'm always interviewing, Tanner. And besides that, Adele looked a bit off. Flushed and flustered. That's curious, but I didn't want to interfere."

A college-age waitress set water glasses before them. "Need a menu?"

He looked at Kate and intuitively knew her tastes matched his own. "The works? Extra cheese?"

She smiled. "Extra large?"

He turned to the waitress. "That'll do it."

"And coffee," Kate added.

"Make mine root beer."

"Okay. Coming right out." She left.

"I don't know that waitress," Kate said. "Did I mention I eat here all the time? The owner, Mrs. Posateri, lets me work and drink coffee in the middle of the afternoon when they're closed."

"Well, Kate, I'd say you're fitting right in at Valley Oaks."

"I don't know. I'm viewed as a gossip columnist. Everyone is nice to me. They think maybe they'll see their name in print." A frown crossed her face. "I don't mean that. Well, yes I do, but I'm trying to get over it. As Rusty says, it ain't DC. And that's okay."

"Remember it's temporary. For now you just need to relax and let the magic take over."

"You obviously have. You fit right in here, Tanner. Like I said, the parents love you. And you were so at home up front tonight. Why don't you choose one of your hobbies full time and move out here?"

He tipped his water glass back and forth.

"Sorry. You can stop me when I'm being too *much* of a snoop."

He looked at her. "You're not. It's just that..." He glanced out the window before meeting her gaze. Could he tell her? Could he trust her with the vague notion of a dream?

"Hey, Tanner, forget I asked. It's none of my business."

"It's all right." He reached over and swooped up her notepad. "But you can't breathe a word to anyone. Not a soul."

"I smell a story." Her tone was singsong, and then she sobered, solemnly handing him her pen. "But I promise."

"I'm in the process of buying the video store next to the pharmacy."

Her eyes widened. "The one that's shut down?"

"Yeah. The owner's in prison. He tried to kill Cal Huntington, the deputy sherriff."

"I know. I read about that in those old *Times*. Congratulations!"

"Thanks. It's a small place. I can still fly and sub. Another hobby!"

"But it's a start of something. When do you get possession?"

"In a couple of weeks, if I decide to go through with it. And if my dad doesn't back out of the deal. He's giving—make that *loaning*—me part of the money." Loaning. He was done *accepting* money from his old man.

"Is your dad a doctor? I think I know him."

"Yeah, he's a surgeon. How do you know him?"

"He operated on my mom about eight years ago. She had breast cancer."

"Is she…" He hesitated. So much death accompanied his father. Sidney Carlucci had the touch of death. It was unavoidable baggage with his professional life. In his personal life…well, suffice it to say that too reeked of it.

"She's doing great. She liked your dad a lot."

Patients. What did they know?

"Tanner?"

"Hmm?"

"Your eyes are at half-mast. Where'd you go?"

He gave her a cockeyed smile. "You don't want to know."

Graham followed Adele into her house. On the drive home from the restaurant she had invited him to come in for tea, and he had accepted without hesitation. Even if no extenuating circumstances tied their destinies together, if he had simply met her on the street...still he would have said yes. From the first three minutes in her office, the woman had captivated him.

Which was why he should have declined.

Not to mention those extenuating circumstances would most likely work against them, reason enough to not even be making eye contact, let alone—

"Graham." She hung her coat on a hall tree beside the door, twirled a half circle, and headed through an arched doorway. Avoiding eye contact herself?

Waving a hand toward the right, she called over her shoulder, "Go on into the living room and make yourself at home. I'll be right there."

He concluded she was avoiding eye contact. She was quite obviously flustered.

Which was the basis for reason number three. He had no business being in her home.

Shrugging out of his coat, he looked around. It was an old house. The small entryway opened to arched doorways on the left and right, leading to the dining room and living room. Straight ahead was an enclosed staircase.

He hung up his coat and went into the living room, doing as he was told.

Reason number four...

The furnishings were old and worn, but everything appeared tidy and clean. That and a comfortably warm temperature after the frigid winter night created a cozy atmosphere. A scent of spiced apples permeated the air.

The décor was of the homegrown variety. Candles. Pottery. Healthy green plants. Photos of Chelsea and other young people. None of what's-his-name.

Graham sat in an armchair. He heard kitchen clanging noises. There was a fireplace, too clean to have contained burning wood in recent history.

What was going on? She had caught him completely by surprise. The plan had simply been to fulfill the wishes of old Rand: check him into the home and wait for God to finish things.

In whatever way He wants.

Hadn't Graham learned that truth yet? Why did he still insist on reaching for the reins, wanting to do it his way?

Adele entered the room, carrying a wooden tray. "I hope you like peppermint?"

He did. He also liked watching her move. There was a fluidity in her motions that only women confident in their own skin possessed. She was of medium height and build, not tall the way his wife had been.

She poured tea from a ceramic pot and handed him a mug. Brief eye contact, fingertips brushing.

"Thank you. Where were we?"

Adele slipped her stockinged feet out of her clogs and sat on the couch, tucking her legs underneath herself. "My sordid past."

"It gets sordid?"

She smiled. "Graham, we only got to high school graduation from a Connecticut boarding school."

"And your decision to quit college after a semester."

"I was rebelling against my dad. He directed everything. He was a large man, tall, two hundred and fifty pounds. Overbearing. Loud, gruff voice. It wasn't easy to disagree with him face-to-face. I followed his decree that I study business, but one semester of that and no art was all I could handle. He allowed me to go to Italy for the January term. I didn't come home. I had enough money saved to pay my way." Her face was down as if she sought words in the cup of tea.

"And?"

"This is where it gets sordid." She glanced up and then off to the side. "I met a guy. We parted ways in August. I found out I was pregnant. I came home. My father disowned me. Literally lock, stock, and barrel. He ordered the maid to help me pack, and then he escorted me to the door and said, 'I always knew you'd amount to nothing.'" She bit her bottom lip. "He locked the door behind me, and that was the last time I ever saw him."

He waited for her to continue.

"I stayed at a friend's for a while, foolishly thinking he'd change his mind. I gave up and got on a bus headed for San Francisco. A snowstorm stopped us in Valley Oaks. Naomi Sommers befriended me and I stayed." Adele looked at him. "She taught me about Jesus and loved me unconditionally."

"Thank God for those people in our lives, huh?"

"You have one too?"

"I did. My wife."

"When did she die?"

"About five years ago."

A distinct compassion clouded her eyes. "I'm so sorry."

"Well, I'm learning that God uses our sorrows to draw us to Himself." He cleared his throat. He didn't want to go down that road. "What about Chelsea's father?"

"Oh, this is where it gets really sordid. I didn't know how to contact him. He was from Germany. I couldn't spell his last name, let alone pronounce it. I had no clue what city he was from."

It sounded rehearsed, false even, compared to other aspects of her story. Perhaps there was more to add, things she wanted to leave unsaid. So instead he asked, "Did you keep in touch with your mother?"

"I did. But after a while, R.J. forbade her to talk to me. We still did periodically, when she knew she wouldn't get caught." Adele shuddered, set down her mug, and pulled an afghan onto her lap.

"Did you try to contact him after she died?"

"No. I've had enough rejection to last a lifetime, thank you. I figured it was his move. Mother would have left my number where he would find it."

"And what of Christ's command to forgive our enemies?"

"I have. He's off the hook." She wiped a tear from the corner of her eye. "But you know the funny thing? A part of me still hopes he'll call. Isn't that ridiculous?"

"Not ridiculous at all. As Rand would say," he rasped his voice, "it's never too late until you're dead and gone."

She smiled and sniffed. "But for all I know, he is dead and gone."

"I think..." Graham began sliding from the chair. With a start, he realized he was on his way to cross the room, to sit beside her, to pull her into his arms. He crushed that urge in the blink of an eye. "Adele, it seems that you would somehow know if that were true or not. Don't you think?"

"I think..." She touched her necklace. "I think I don't know why I'm telling you these things!"

Ten

Early Saturday morning Kate shuffled into the kitchen and passed Adele sitting at the table. She mumbled, "Morning."

"Morning." Adele's mumble was even less recognizable.

Not one to chat before her first cup of coffee, Kate pushed her glasses up her nose and went about her business preparing a potful. Adele and Chelsea never touched the stuff. A coffeemaker was the only item Kate needed to purchase for her new home, a fact she had unfortunately discovered on a Monday morning. Dear Rusty had saved her on that occasion. The woman knew how to make a mean cup of coffee.

Kate glanced over her shoulder. Something was wrong. Adele always chatted, no matter Kate's reticence, no matter the time or the day. She sat now, her hands clutched around a mug full of herbal tea, staring at nothing in particular.

"Adele, are you all right?"

"Huh?" She shifted her eyes. It took them a moment to focus on Kate.

"What's wrong?"

"Wrong? With what?"

"With you, Adele. You're not chatting."

"I'm not?"

"No."

"It seemed like I was." She made a strange noise, something between a giggle and a cough. "Must have all been in my head!"

Kate pulled the partially filled carafe, interrupting the drip action, and sloshed the coffee into a mug. She clearly needed her caffeine kick before continuing with the conversation.

Mug in hand, she sat down across the table from Adele, who was now humming and smiling into her teacup. Like Kate, she wore a fuzzy robe and slippers, protection against the early winter morning. Frost covered the dark window pane. From outside, light from a streetlamp sparkled through its delicately etched patterns.

Kate remembered how last night she thought Adele appeared somewhat flustered at the Pizza Parlor. She had introduced Graham somebody, a newcomer, a tall, broad-shouldered man in need of a shave. With pewter gray hair.

"Adele, last night at the restaurant, was that guy the toe curler?"

"Toe curler? Oh, that silly phrase of Chelsea's." She shrugged and wound a curly strand of hair around a finger. "I introduced you, right? Graham Logan. His friend just moved into the home."

Kate already knew that.

"We had such an in-depth conversation. He was full of questions about Fox Meadow. Then one thing led to another. It was so easy to open up with him. He exudes *safety*. Do you know what I mean?"

"My dad's like that."

"You're fortunate. Mine was never like that. I know Jesus is, and sometimes I get a real glimpse of that, but to meet someone in person..." Her voice trailed off and her eyes went toward the window. A tiny smile turned up the corners of her mouth.

"Is Will like that?"

"Will?"

You remember, the good friend who just gave you an amethyst ring on Valentine's Day. Kate pressed her lips together.

"Will. He's...not the same. I'm...content with him, comfortable."

"Except for your wardrobe."

"Well, yes. You have a point there. He...he challenges me. In a way."

"Is tonight a date night?"

"No. He has his kids this weekend. And tomorrow night he leaves on a business trip, to Atlanta, I think, for a week or so. Last night Graham and I just talked and talked. Until eleven o'clock!"

Kate hadn't gotten home until midnight. She and Tanner had finished their pizza and then driven to the closed video store. The night was calm. They ventured from the warm car and lingered on the sidewalk, peeking in the windows, brainstorming about what he could do with the place. He balked at making a commitment. She couldn't imagine personally investing thousands of dollars, and offered to pray for him to have wisdom. He brushed aside the comment as if it were simply a nice thing to say. She dropped the subject, realizing that the everyday reality of Jesus was far removed from his life. Which was why she was up early...to pray that would change for Tanner.

Now Kate drank her coffee and studied Adele. She was quiet again, twirling her hair, staring at the frosted window, humming in a distracted way, letting her tea go cold.

Oh boy.

Her friend may not recognize it, but Graham Logan had captured her attention in a way Will Epstein hadn't even approached.

Later that morning, Kate drove through the business area of Valley Oaks. If it weren't for the temperature holding steady at 14 and the wind whipping out of the north at 15 miles per hour with gusts up to 20, she would hoof it to the office. Adele's house was only two blocks from the town square. The *Times* was only another two blocks beyond that. Piece of cake.

Maybe in the spring. No, she'd be long gone by then. Adios, Midwest! *Lord, please? DC by the end of May?*

She rounded the corner and her heart sank. Rusty's car was parked right outside the *Times* office. Kate had hoped to have a quiet, smoke-free environment in which to write her story about last night's awards banquet slash potluck.

She pulled into the space beside Rusty's car and hopped out. Crossing the sidewalk, she inhaled three garlic-scented, deep breaths of air. She held the last one and opened the door.

"Hey, kid. I was just going to give you a call. How'd the banquet go last night?"

"Fine." Kate hung up her coat and went to her desk. "Tanner escorted me in and showed me the ropes. He is a wealth of information."

"Surprising, isn't it, considering how lackadaisical he is." She lit a cigarette, evidently unaware of the one already burning in the ashtray on her desk.

Kate's eyes watered and her throat felt scratchy. She switched on the computer and thought about the balance in her checking account. Was there any way she could swing payments on a laptop?

"Well, Katy-girl, do you think you're ready to cover a boys basketball game? They have a home game tonight. Sophomores start at six."

"Sure." Kate was grateful for the new assignment, though her tone didn't reveal that. "I'd be glad to."

"Townsfolk here are dead serious about their high school athletics."

"I noticed that with the girls last night."

Rusty snorted. "And that was nothing. Wait until you experience how they handle the male aspect of things. I'm heading up to Chicago this afternoon. I've got an old friend coming to the city."

"A newspaper friend?"

She rattled her bronchial laugh. "Is there any other?"

Kate had heard some of Rusty's stories, how she had worked in Springfield and then Chicago, writing city news for years. Some political maneuvering had edged her out. That was five years ago, when she was 57. Not an easy age to start over in another city at a large newspaper. She had come across the Valley Oaks position and jumped at the chance. Not that there had been any competition.

Rusty continued, "Jack and I worked together at the *Trib* in our younger days. He moved on to New York eons ago. We get together every now and then, laugh about our early angsts."

"New York." Kate's voice was wistful.

"You'll laugh someday too about your time in Valley Oaks."

"Mm-hmm." Kate turned to the computer. She'd laugh if she was still breathing in 20 years.

"The pasture for has-beens, but a ripe field for those just cutting their teeth."

Something about Rusty's tone struck an uneasy chord in Kate. She rested her fingers on the keyboard and listened to it. A corner of her heart whispered, *What is it, Lord?*

Rusty Connelly. Crusty. Rough, self-sufficient exterior. Bent on self-destruction. A hurting soul.

It was the type of nudge that Kate recognized. No sense in trying to ignore it. She swiveled around in her chair.

"Rusty?"

She looked up from a paper she was reading, a cigarette dangling from her lips.

"I wish you didn't smoke."

"Blazes, kid, why didn't you say something?" She puffed deeply, and then she crushed the burning tip against the ashtray. "I didn't know it bothered you."

"I can live with the smoke. Well, it's not my first choice of air space, but, Rusty, I really wish you didn't smoke. I mean for your own sake."

"You're not going to read me the list of health hazards, are you? I know all that stuff. The impact has been zilch. Besides, I've been smoking since I was fifteen. Forty-seven years and no problems." She coughed.

"You're worth so much."

"Oh, I doubt that."

"But you are."

Rusty's eyes resembled a basset hound's, mournful and defeated.

"Jesus thinks you are."

"Good grief, you're a Jesus freak. You could have told me that too. I would have cleaned up my language." She tried to smile, but it didn't quite lift all the way. "Somewhat, maybe."

"I don't care about that, either. It doesn't matter. All that matters is that I tell you you're a precious human being and Jesus and I care an awful lot about you."

She blinked. "You sound like He's a person, your good friend."

"He is. Both."

"I suppose you two talk about me."

"At least once every day." Kate smiled.

The older woman turned back to her desk. "Imagine that. Somebody praying for old Crusty Rusty. My mother would turn over in her grave."

"Why is that?"

For a long moment she didn't reply. "Because she never once said a kind word to me."

They were quiet for a time. Kate stared at the computer monitor. Her heart pounded erratically as it had those other times, those few occasions when for the briefest of moments her upper arm tingled...as if the arm of Jesus had brushed against it as He moved beside her.

"Katy-girl?"

She turned to see Rusty walking across the office..

"My friend Jack from New York..." She removed her worn, brown woolen coat from a peg and slipped it on. "He has connections in DC."

Kate's eyebrows rose on their own accord, widening her eyes.

Rusty shrugged, buttoning the coat.

"You said I have to pay my dues."

"That you do, kid. But it never hurts to know somebody who knows somebody." She grinned, lifted a hand in parting, and walked outside.

Eleven

On a record-breaking cold Saturday morning when she could have stayed home relishing in long uninterrupted hours of playing with clay, Adele drove down the county highway. The north wind howled across barren fields on her right, dusting the blacktop with snow, rattling her car, lengthening the trip by seven minutes. At last she pulled into Fox Meadow's parking lot, continuing the dialogue begun at four-thirty that morning.

I have a legitimate reason for being here.

On normal weekends she didn't go in to work, but there were often situations that required her attention.

In her opinion anyway.

All right. So she was a little too hands-on for some people. What did it hurt? She loved Fox Meadow as if it were her own home and loved every facet of caring for the residents. What did it matter that her job description did not specifically prescribe that she give tours, do the necessary paperwork with relatives, welcome newcomers at the door, change linens, or show up on Saturdays? Or tuck in the new guy and have dinner with his close friend?

"Oh my."

She left the car and walked across the lot, holding her hood tight against the icy wind.

There were official reasons for her creative schedule. She had no assistant and only a part-time secretary. The center was short-funded and understaffed, which meant sacrificing those special TLC touches. Adele refused to let that happen.

They were what made Fox Meadow a special place. She jumped in, running herself ragged at times, turning reports in late, not returning phone calls in a timely manner.

Then there was Chelsea's growing independence. Her daughter was smart and artistic. She would easily receive grants and scholarships and in 18 months head off to college. Adele's stomach hurt when she thought about that fact, but she had long ago vowed to never lay a guilt trip on her daughter. Their relationship was not going to resemble the unhealthy one she'd had with her parents.

"Adele!"

She looked up to find herself standing in the middle of the lobby facing Gracie, the weekend supervisor, whose demeanor didn't begin to approach the promise of her name. Another reason for Adele's creative schedule.

As usual, Gracie's hands were planted on her ample hips and her gray-streaked black hair was pulled back severely in a bun. "Except for Mrs. Cantrell's nonstop jabbering, there's no wind blowing in here."

"Huh?"

"You're standing there all bundled up with your hood on."

"Oh. I am!" She chuckled, pushing back the hood and fluffing her hair. "How did Mr. Jennings do last night?"

"Fine, far as I know. Friendly buzzard, isn't he? He made it to the dining room for breakfast."

"Great."

They chatted about business for a few minutes and parted ways. After tossing her coat on a chair in her office, Adele headed out to make the social rounds. Saturday was a good day to touch base with a large group of residents and their visiting relatives. Room 212 seemed as good a place to start as any.

Rand Jennings was sitting in the armchair and looking out the window. Black slacks, a bright yellow cardigan, and a plaid shirt hung loosely over his gaunt form. She was glad not to see him in pajamas. It meant the pain was still tolerable...there was still a reason to get up in the morning.

She knocked on the open door. "Mr. Jennings?"

He turned his head and smiled. "Adele! Good morning. You look especially lovely today. Have a seat."

She dragged a straight-backed chair nearer to him and sat in it. "How are you doing? Did you sleep all right?"

"I slept like a baby." He smiled, his dark eyes nearly squinting closed behind the thick bifocals. "It's a comfortable place you have here."

"Thank you."

"How'd you get to be director?"

"Hey, I came to talk about you."

"No, you didn't. You came to make me feel better. I'll feel better if I don't talk about me. It's getting to be an overdone subject. Now, how did you end up here?"

"Well, I started out as a nurse's aide."

"Baths and bedpans?"

"You got it. And I fell in love with the place! I spent any time I could spare here, learning all I could about nursing. But I found out I wasn't as interested in the medical side of things as in the people themselves. I went to school part-time and eventually got a degree in sociology. In the meantime, I became receptionist, then file clerk, then assistant to the director. I learned about administration, the ins and outs of insurance, and state aid and social work."

"And dying."

She stared at him.

"You must have."

She nodded. It had been the hardest part. Still was.

"Your Fox Meadow is more than likely the last stop for all of us. The only thing that matters is that we're ready. If it weren't for Jesus, I know I wouldn't be ready. I met Him about two years ago. It's been a crash course, making up for lost time and getting to know Him better. How about you? Have you met Him?"

She smiled, thinking about how Graham considered *her* direct. "Almost seventeen years ago, since the moment I saw my newborn baby's face."

He raised his arm slightly, haltingly, as if to reach out to her. The pain would be too sharp. Graham told her the cancer was in his spine. Adele covered his hand with her own.

He smiled. "You're a believer. I hoped you were. My wife was, but I wouldn't listen. Graham never gave up on me, though. Thank the good Lord. Do you go to a church in your town?"

"Valley Oaks Community. Though sometimes I come here. We have a service at nine. Friends and relatives are welcome to attend."

"Which one are you going to tomorrow? So I can tell Graham." His laugh was rough-sounding.

Adele stared at him, unsure how to respond.

"Don't mind me. I'm a meddler. Always have been. Thing is, he's been lonely for a long time." His voice was growing raspier, but still he talked. "Tell me about that baby."

Safer ground. Her turtleneck was beginning to feel tight at the throat. "Um, her name is Chelsea. She'll be seventeen in three months. She looks an awful lot like me. Do you want to lie down?"

"No. But maybe I will. Morning nap time for this baby."

She helped him onto the bed and covered him with a soft afghan that had been folded neatly at its foot. It wasn't Fox Meadow issue. They must have brought it from home. For a couple of men, they seemed to have taken good care of the homey details. She noticed a plant on the chest of drawers and an eight-by-ten framed photo of an ocean sunrise hanging on the wall. A shiny new television with built-in VCR.

"Shall I close the blinds, Mr. Jennings?"

"No, thank you. But you could call me Rand." He smiled.

"You got it, Rand. Sleep tight."

Adele walked down the hall, pulling at the neck of her sweater.

She had known Graham was a believer. She had known he was kind and thoughtful and funny. He had apologized for being rude, paid for her dinner, and made her laugh, all in one day. And he could eat an all-vegetable meal and drink her herbal tea without a hint of complaint. He had great hair, but if it all fell out he would still have that intriguing cleft in his chin.

She had known all of that.

Now she knew he was a devoted friend, evidenced by the good care he took of Rand. By how he hadn't given up on him. By how he rearranged his work and living situations in order to be near him. By the attention to detail in a drab nursing home room.

And now she also knew that he was lonely.

She had no idea any such man walked the face of the earth. Not that she was looking. She wasn't, was she? She hadn't been for 17 years. No reason to start now.

Was there?

Graham entered Rand's room Saturday afternoon and found him sitting up in bed, the afghan tucked around his legs, the television tuned to a basketball game.

"Hi, *Pops.*"

"They don't have cable."

He set down his briefcase and sat on the edge of the bed. No need to remind Rand they knew before the move that Fox Meadow was low-rent district. Hence, no cable. "I'll get some video tapes of your favorite preachers."

"That would be nice." Rand closed his eyes, his pale, skeletal hand clutching the blanket. "Sorry for grumbling."

"When did you take your pill?"

"Thirty minutes late."

Graham's blood did a slow boil. Low rent didn't have to mean shoddy. They had to stay on top of the pain or somebody would have to answer to him.

"*She* came in." A smile tugged at his mouth.

"Hmm."

"She is a lovely young woman, isn't she?"

"She is." But if she couldn't get the morphine distributed on time, her dimpled smile wasn't going to help.

"Her church is Valley Oaks Community. I don't know the time."

"So you think I should go to the same service, do you?"

Rand didn't respond.

Panic clutched at Graham's chest and he leaned forward. Was Rand asleep? He detected his shallow breathing. Graham's own evened out again.

Lord, please don't take him too soon.

Ridiculous prayer. God would accomplish what needed to be accomplished. Time meant nothing to Him.

He eased himself gently from the bed and sat in the armchair. He pulled the *Valley Oaks Times* from his briefcase and opened it in search of a local listing of church services.

He wasn't so sure about Rand's hopes that he and Adele would become close friends as quickly as possible. *Pops* said it would make him happy to be able to leave this world knowing that someone near would offer comfort.

The trouble was, Rand didn't know just how lovely she was. Nor just exactly how available she was, despite that photo of the guy on her desk. Nor had he taken into account exactly how vulnerable Graham was, something Graham himself hadn't even known until last night.

The problem was, he and Adele had blown right on past close friendship status by the time the pizza was gone. By the time they finished the tea, the air between them crackled.

And that simply was not going to work.

Twelve

Kate munched a glazed donut and sipped coffee as she stood at what she considered a discreet distance, but she still overheard every word exchanged between Adele and Graham, Mr. Toe Curler.

After a short wrestling match with her conscience, she concluded it couldn't be all that private of a conversation. It was Sunday morning, between services. Graham had been to the early one; they had just arrived for the second. They stood in the church foyer, a short distance to the left of the exterior doorway, not far from a table loaded with boxes of donuts enticing most passersby to linger. The aroma of coffee permeated the area, which was large and sprawling. It easily accommodated the chatty, milling crowd which probably numbered around 200. Evidently, therefore, the conversation was not all that private.

And besides, she needed to keep an eye open for Tanner's arrival. Near the front windows was the best spot. If she weren't there at the critical moment of his arrival, he might use it as an excuse to back out of his first visit.

And besides that, she truly was a snoop.

"Adele, I was there until *four* this morning." Graham had already relayed this information, but then he didn't appear in tip-top shape today.

The man was big, not like a beefy football player, but rather in an understated sort of way. A sport coat over sweater and corduroys made him presentable, though his height and breadth suggested that the clothes obscured a powerful strength. Which, according to the expression on his face, was scarcely being held in check at the moment. His five o'clock shadow had grown into next-day stubble. His eyes were mere slits, his mouth a grim line.

Adele placed her hand on his forearm in a soothing gesture. It matched her tone, which had remained even throughout the exchange. "I'll go in right now and get to the bottom of this."

"No. I'm on my way there. Stay for church. It's a good sermon." There was a distinct note of calm in his voice now. "Good music too."

Adele smiled.

Kate knew she had stumbled upon another bit of Valley Oaks magic: Adele Chandler's touch.

Graham almost returned the smile. "Isn't this your day off?"

"I'm always on call."

"We'll be fine today. I had planned to spend the day with him anyway. I'll make sure he gets his medication on time. Sorry, Adele, I guess I needed to vent. *Again*. Despite the fact I just came out of church. Guess you walked in at the wrong time."

"No, it was the right time. I'm the one to vent to since I'm the one responsible. I wish you would have called me last night. Please don't hesitate in the future. Okay?" She removed her hand.

"Okay. I appreciate it. I'll probably see you tomorrow?"

"I imagine so. Bye."

"Bye." He nodded at Kate and left.

Adele, still bundled in her winter coat, her back to the crowd, tapped a foot. Emotions flitted across her face, wrinkling her brow, now smoothing it, setting her jaw, now loosening it. At last it all settled into a scrunched frown.

"Kate, may I borrow your cell phone?"

"Sure." She dug it out of her bag, turned the power button on, and handed it over.

Adele punched in a number and muttered, "You know, if he just would have gone home last night and cried like a baby, he'd feel a whole lot better. Hello!" Although her voice remained low, it took on a harsh edge. "This is Adele. Get Gracie for me. Please."

Evidently on hold, Adele looked at Kate. "This will only take a minute. It has to be taken care of right now. I'll pay you for—Gracie!"

Kate watched as the easygoing, artistic woman she was beginning to know switched places with a dragon lady.

"What happened yesterday with Mr. Jennings?" Now Adele's mouth was the grim line. "Mr. Logan was upset and referred to Fox Meadow as a one-horse operation. We're looking like one. Why was the medication administered late *two* times?"

Her foot was tapping again. One hand was propped on a hip.

"Tell her she is skating on thin ice. She will be fired if this happens again. And I want you to get the doctor there today...I don't care what day it is. This is his job. Mr. Jennings probably needs his dosage increased...Yes...All right. Call me at home later. Thanks, Gracie." She handed the phone to Kate. "Thanks."

"Whew. Guess that's why you're the director."

Adele shook her head. "No, that's why I shouldn't get distracted by good-looking friends of the family." She blew out a breath. "Okay. I'd better go sing and try to remember how to be nice." She clanked her teeth together in a forced grin and walked away.

No two ways about it, the woman was in denial.

Kate and Tanner sat on a padded pew along a side aisle in the church sanctuary. Naturally, because he had arrived late, they weren't far from the pulpit.

She glanced at him out of the corner of her eye and smiled inwardly. Hunched over, arms crossed on knees, eyes glued on the pastor, he appeared deep in thought. Kate hoped so. Fun and carefree as Tanner behaved, she sensed that something disturbing lay at the root of his casual meandering through life. Something that only divine intervention could heal.

He had called her early in the morning, inviting her to explore the video store. The real estate agent was scheduled to meet him there at one-thirty. Tanner said he could use a female's opinion on the task before him.

She found it interesting that he noticed she was a female. Their rapport was so in tune, it was as if gender didn't even play a role. They were friends, buds, pals, chums, amigos. In the short time since they'd met, they had "hung" together as though they'd been doing it for years.

Given Chelsea's strong opinion of his looks—since verified by a boatload of girl basketball players and their mothers—Kate knew the guy must have a string of gorgeous women waiting with bated breath for such an invitation. Women who paid close attention to style and lipstick application.

She accepted his offer, with a caveat. It was her turn to introduce him to a Valley Oaks niche that positively overflowed with that special magic.

"Hey," he had said, "*I'm* the expert."

"Do you know about VOCC?"

"What's that?"

"The Community Church."

Silence.

"Yeah, I didn't think so. Meet me there at the front door, ten-twenty. It'll be good for business."

"If I don't show, does that mean you don't show?"

"That's the deal."

"Some friend you're turning out to be. All right. Ten-twenty."

The challenge had worked.

She looked at him again now, noting his rapt attention. Though she had only heard Pastor Peter twice, she sensed he was typically engrossing. Redheaded, Chicago-accented, burly, and streetwise, he captured the essence of Scripture in laymen's terms without masking the unexplicable of the holy.

A guy's guy. Someone Tanner could relate to.

Thank You, Father.

Tanner peered over Kate's shoulder at the bubbling pot of chili she stirred. She had invited him for lunch after church. Because the Chandlers were going to Rockville, she was in charge of the kitchen.

"Mmm," he said, "I smell meat."

She laughed. "You know me. Of course you smell meat. Adele is great. She doesn't mind what I do in her kitchen. Though I think I caught her shuddering last night. I was cooking up a storm of meat dishes. Chelsea will be absolutely *devastated* when she hears Mr. Carlucci ate lunch at her house. She won't want me to wash your spoon."

"Kate, don't tell me that stuff. I'll give up teaching and coaching altogether."

"Oh, Tanner." She ladled the thick chili into bowls. "I hope you're just hungry. You're not much fun to tease at the moment."

She handed him a bowl, and then they sat down at the kitchen table. As usual in the energetic way she did everything, she bowed her head briefly before taking a bite. If he didn't watch closely, he would miss it.

Yes, he was hungry. But...he was also on edge.

"So what did you think of church?"

He swallowed his first mouthful of the best chili he'd ever tasted. "Kate! This is fantastic!"

She grinned. "Thanks."

"Where'd you learn to cook?"

"Cookbooks. When I was twenty-two, my mom got sick. I think I told you she had breast cancer. Anyway, I'm the oldest of four. I'm ten years older than Patrick, twelve years older than Jimmy, and nineteen years older than Sara. They were so young and needed a lot of attention. And since Dad worked, I was in charge at home."

Tanner did the math. "Did she have surgery and go through all the treatments? A year out of her life?"

"Mm-hmm. All told, it was about an eighteen-month detour."

"Is that why you didn't finish college?"

She nodded, no bitterness evident in her demeanor. "It was obviously the thing to do. We could have hired people, but this was my *mom* we're talking about. And my little *siblings*. I didn't want anyone else cooking or cleaning for them, or helping with their homework, or nursing my mom. College just got postponed again."

"Again?"

Watching her talk was more entertaining than flying a plane. He had never seen such an animated person. Those green eyes darted here and there. Her forefinger periodically shoved the glasses up her nose. Numerous strands of her shiny red hair had fallen out of a single braid. She must have spent two minutes on today's hairdo rather than one.

She swallowed a mouthful and nodded. "Again. I didn't go to college right after high school. Well, I went, but only for three days. My dad was transferred to Paris. He works for the government. When he called with the news that they were leaving right after Christmas, I quit. No way was I going to pass up a family junket to Europe!"

Her whole family must be quirky. Considering his own parents and siblings, he couldn't imagine a reason he would go with them to Paris or anywhere for an extended period of time, especially after the age of 18.

"We spent over a year there, then I did a semester at Rockville Junior College. A bout with mononucleosis delayed my start at Iowa. I got in one semester before Mom was diagnosed."

"What happened after she got better?"

"By then, all the scholarships and loans were muddled. And with medical bills, money was tight. I worked full time and went to school part time for a few years. Gradually I've worked less and gone to class more. Only two months now and I graduate. Yay!"

"Your life sounds like a series of delays."

"It has been, though I never doubted that God had it all planned out. I trust His timing is the best for me." She stopped. "All right. Confession. I am doubting His choice of internship locations. I wouldn't have missed those family times or my jobs and school experiences for anything. Good things have come from it all. Things that never would have come about if I'd stuck with my own agenda. So I'm trying to be quiet on the subject of this...location."

"You? Quiet?" He pressed a hand to his chest in mock alarm. "That must be the hardest thing you've ever done."

She wrinkled her nose at him. "You didn't answer my question. What'd you think of church?"

"It was a nice brick building."

"Ha ha." She picked up their empty bowls and refilled them. "Anyway, I'm glad you came."

"It reminded me of my AA meetings."

"Really?" Kate set his bowl in front of him and sat down again. "How's that?"

She hadn't missed a beat. He should have known. Kate Kilpatrick would not use the information against him, nor would she shrink from it.

He smiled. "The guy up front talked about heavy issues. And he talked about a higher power."

"Jesus."

"Yeah. I always figured He had a name. Did I mention this is the best chili I've ever eaten?"

"Want to see where Cal was stabbed?" Tanner asked casually as he inspected the rack of video action titles.

Kate quickly shifted from the comedy section to stand next to him, sidling nearer until her arm brushed against his. "No."

He laughed and glanced down at her. "What kind of a reporter are you?"

"Political."

"No attempted murders, huh?"

"None." She shivered at the thought and looked around the eerily quiet store.

The real estate agent had left them alone, promising to return and lock up in a couple of hours. Kate saw potential in the stale, dusty place. A coat of white paint and some heat would do wonders.

"Tanner, can we turn on the heat?"

"Good idea. We should inspect the furnace. Of course, that's where *it* happened. In the basement."

She poked him in the ribs with her elbow and moved away.

"Ouch!" He laughed.

She went into the back room. "There's a Ping-Pong table in here!" Of course, he probably knew that already. She rummaged around in a closet and found paddles and a ball. If he wasn't going to turn on the heat, they could warm up with a game.

"What do you think, Kate?"

She looked up to see him leaning against the doorjamb. He was brooding. His black leather jacket, black hair, and dark eyes heightened the effect.

He went on. "The inventory is pathetic. The atmosphere is drab. Drugs were sold in this room. And blood has been shed in the basement. Is this a totally dumb idea?"

She heard an uncertain, little boy tone creep into his voice. "Some elbow grease and money put toward new DVDs is all you need. Maybe you could specialize in something, like family videos. You know the choice at Swensen's is really limited. I think Valley Oaks could support this place."

He crossed his arms and looked around, not convinced.

"Ping-Pong can be a fun thing, a healthy diversion. Maybe you could get a big-screen TV and have video nights and sell popcorn. Cater to the young teens who don't fit in with the athletic stuff at the community center and need something to do besides eat pizza."

"Hire a magician? Maybe a motivational speaker?"

She spread her arms wide. "Why not?"

He shook his head. "I'm getting cold feet."

"Tanner, why are you doing it in the first place?"

"I liked the idea of having my own quiet little business." He rubbed his jaw. "No, truthfully, in the first place I'm doing it to please my dad. So he can refer to me as his son, the entrepreneur, instead of the deadbeat."

"What do you want for yourself?"

"An investment that will allow me to retire when I'm thirty-five." He grinned, but quickly became solemn. "It's a big-time commitment, Kate. Major."

"Yeah, it is."

"I talked to Lia next door. She's got an apartment above the pharmacy. She'll rent it to me."

"Really? You'd move to Valley Oaks?"

"Seems the sensible thing to do. If it were you, would you see your God's hand in it?"

She went over to him, grasped his arms, and stood on tiptoe to get in his face. "Tanner, you're overdue for a challenge. I'd say God has just delivered a gift with your name on it."

"How do you do that? Be so sure of something?"

"Years and years of getting to know Him. Hey, are you going to turn on the heat?"

"You think it's cold in here?"

"It's freezing." She went to the Ping-Pong table, picked up the ball, and tossed it to him.

He caught it in midair.

"We'll warm up with a game. Best two out of three. I bet I can beat you."

"What's the bet?" He shrugged out of his coat. "Dinner?"

"Of course." She handed him a paddle. "Is the Rib House open tonight?"

Thirteen

Standing in the produce aisle of Swensen's Market, Adele fingered the broccoli. Grocery shopping, a hit-or-miss affair over the past few weeks, had finally been relegated to the top of her priority list. With threats of staging a strike and shutting down the kitchen, she persuaded Chelsea and Kate to carve time out of their Saturday afternoon to join her.

They had commandeered three carts and set off in three different directions about half an hour ago. Still, Adele hadn't completed inspecting the fresh produce, a misnomer if there ever was one given the fact that it was the dead of winter and the only thing local growers could produce were seed-catalogue orders.

The broccoli was particularly rubbery. Maybe frozen would be the better—

"Hello."

Adele looked up. "Graham! Hi."

The effect of seeing the man was immediate, as it had been each of the five times their paths had crossed at the nursing home that week. Her heartbeat backfired, sputtered, and, after a moment's hesitation, kicked into high gear. She touched at the open collar of her blouse, gently pressing the hollow of her neck where it seemed all the erratic thumping was centralized.

He smiled, nodding at her cart. "So that's what a vegetarian's groceries look like."

"That's it." She observed the contents of the large blue handbasket he carried. It was easier than meeting those intense eyes. "And what is this?"

A stack of frozen TV dinners teetered on the brink of spilling over the edges of the basket. "Uh, that would be a cooking-challenged bachelor with an empty fridge."

"I disagree. That would be indigestion in the making. Come for dinner." *Oh my.* She looked up at him. "I mean, there's no reason for you to eat like that. We're cooking. Chelsea and Kate and I. Just down the street from you. It breaks my heart to think of you sitting alone in your apartment eating that...that stuff."

The more she talked, the more his grin expanded.

"Oh, but maybe you're going to see Rand. Or working on your research?"

His attention flickered over her shoulder. "This must be your daughter."

Adele glanced around to see Chelsea nearly breathing down her neck. The expression on her face indicated she was on the verge of bursting into laughter.

"Chels! Uh, this is Graham Logan. Graham, Chelsea."

He shook her daughter's hand. "Nice to meet you. I'm sure you hear this all the time, but you are the spitting image of your mother."

Chelsea smiled. "Oh, now and then someone comments to that effect. Mom, do you mind if I get the chocolate raspberry ice cream? Tara and I like that the best."

Adele nodded.

"You *do* mind?"

"Um." She shook her head. "No."

Chelsea leaned toward her and whispered, "Toes curling?" In a louder voice, she asked, "So will you come for dinner, Mr. Logan?"

"Thank you. I'd like that very much."

"See you later then." She headed down an aisle.

"What time, Adele?"

"Anytime. I mean, we'll be home in half an hour. Come on over. If you're sure? You don't have other plans?"

"Even if I did, I can't be responsible for breaking your heart now, can I?"

"Silly figure of speech." *Just like toe curling.*

Graham stashed the frozen dinners into his freezer while he talked on the phone to the nurse at Fox Meadow. "Heather, you're a doll."

"No, I'm not, Mr. Logan. Just saving my skin. Can't have you complaining again."

It had become a standing joke between them over the past week. The initially rocky start concerning Rand's medication had been straightened out. Graham recognized his overreaction and Heather admitted her error, but not before Adele's authoritative intervention, which he had heard about from the good-natured nurse. He pictured her now walking to the dining area next to her station, cordless phone at her ear. There were no phones in the room, and so he had called the nurse.

She continued, "And besides, Mr. Jennings is sitting right here. No problem to let him talk. Just don't tie up the line for long. The big boss might be trying to call me."

"Thank you."

"Graham?" It was Rand.

"Hi, Pops. You doing all right?"

"No, but then you know that. Why are you calling?"

"*She* just invited me over for dinner. I found her at the grocery store."

The old man chuckled.

"You okay if I don't get back out there until tomorrow morning?"

"As long as it's Addie Chandler, you know I am fine." There was a catch in his raspy voice. "Graham, thank you."

"This is why I'm here. Sleep well."

Kate slipped into her favorite imaginary role of fly on the wall and observed the busy scene in the kitchen. The thought crossed her mind that flies did not smile, but she couldn't help herself.

Naturally Adele was there, directing vegetable chopping and ignoring Kate's browning of ground beef while Kate ignored Adele's smelly fish baking in the oven. Upbeat Hispanic music blared from Chelsea's CD player on the counter.

Graham Logan was there, casual in jeans and demeanor. Still, something about him—the intense focus of his eyes perhaps—set him apart from the average run-of-the-mill 40-something.

Chelsea and her good friend Tara were there. They both wore overalls, planning on creating pottery in the basement later. Tara was striking with long black braided hair, a brilliant smile, and a cheerful attitude.

Tanner was there, mercilessly teasing the girls as he fried tortillas in a skillet of sizzling oil. Kate almost regretted her insistence that Chelsea and Tara promise not to swoon and giggle within a hundred feet of the guy. At the moment, he deserved some aggravation right back. Well, almost. He was a good sport to join them for dinner. In the past five days he had bought her dinner twice again. When they made plans to see a movie tonight, she invited him over before he could suggest a restaurant. He spent money as though it was a non-issue, but for her it was an issue and she could not, in all good conscience, let him buy again.

He looked over at her now and winked. *Fiddlesticks.* Chelsea would misinterpret that for sure. Earlier she had asked Kate, "Are you two, like, dating?"

Kate had laughed. "He's just a friend! Like you and Tara. We hang out together."

Chelsea had gotten that dreamy, starry-eyed stare. "But we're talking about Mr. Carlucci!"

Kate had shaken her head. Mr. Carlucci might be a dreamboat to the majority of Valley Oaks females, but to her he was fast becoming a good friend. His looks had nothing to do with that. She wondered what she would have done without him. Their ability to connect surpassed what she experienced with either Rusty or Adele.

Tanner wasn't exactly her type anyway. Not that she'd ever met her type. Surely her type would live in a big city and be consumed with news-related pursuits.

She studied Tanner now and tried to conjure up an image of them as a *couple.* It didn't work. He was definitely *not* an average-looking, run-of-the-mill Joe with those long-lashed fathomless brown eyes and thick black hair. On the other hand, she was a plain Jane with a splash of freckles. He was tall, with an athletic build. In comparison she was a runt. Jock and geek. Never the twain shall meet.

To top it off, he was into diddling around with hobbies, and she was single-mindedly pursuing a career in Washington, DC. *And* he didn't know Jesus! She had no idea why they got along so well.

"Kate!" Adele handed her a stack of plates. "The table?"

"Right."

A few hectic minutes later they all gathered in the dining room at the worn, round oak table with its eclectic collection of chairs. Adele's homey ambience centered around hand-me-downs.

Their hostess lit candles while directing them. "Please, sit anywhere. I'll sit here next to the kitchen."

It was like musical chairs when the music abruptly halts. Graham quickly laid one of his big hands on the chair next to Adele's. Tanner took the one next to him as Chelsea tripped over her own feet reaching the one next to *him*. Kate chuckled to herself as she and Tara slid onto the remaining chairs. At least in this game everyone got a seat.

"Graham," Adele said, "would you mind?"

"Not at all."

They joined hands, Tanner a bit slow on the uptake, but he joined in and received Kate's smile with one of his own. They bowed their heads as Graham asked the blessing on the food.

Dishes were passed and jovial comparisons made about fish tacos versus spicy beef ones, the benefits of each loudly debated. Just as Kate sank her teeth into the first yummy bite, the doorbell rang. Chelsea popped up like a jack-in-the-box to answer it.

Graham was entertaining them with a description of a Russian he knew eating his first taco when Chelsea reappeared...with Will Epstein in tow.

"Mom."

Adele's eyes were riveted on Graham as she laughed at his story.

"Mom!"

She looked over, fish taco in midair, and her laughter faded to a gurgle. "Will!"

"Adele?"

"Hi! Would you like a taco?"

"Adele, did you forget? The concert? The one you invited me to?"

Now she popped up like a jack-in-the-box. "Oh my gosh!"

"Dinner reservations are in thirty minutes. If you…" The unfinished thought hung as did Will's outstretched hand, palm up.

At last Adele responded. "Oh! Oh. Yes. Give me three minutes. This is, uh, Kate and, uh, Tara, and—"

Kate interrupted. "Adele, we've met. Go get ready." She flipped her hand as if shooing her away. "Will, have a seat."

As Adele bounded up the staircase, her date continued standing under the archway looking decidedly awkward as they all stared at him.

Kate slid her chair over a bit. "Pull that chair up. Have some chips and salsa."

"I'll just wait out—"

"No!" The word burst forth in her eagerness to leave the awkward moment behind them. "I mean, please, sit. You're reminding me of when I was little and had to wait for my mom to pick me up at Jenny Dubin's. Her mom always made me sit in the living room while they ate dinner, pretending like I wasn't there. I hated that feeling."

Tanner asked, "Then why did you go over there?"

Kate laughed. "I don't know!"

Will carried the chair over to the table, and then he politely shook hands with Tanner and Graham as they introduced themselves. He greeted Tara, whom he knew because she spent almost as much time at the Chandlers as Kate did.

Kate noticed that beneath his stylish, long black wool coat and cashmere red scarf, Will wore a dark suit, white shirt, and silver tie. He smelled nice. It must be a dress-up affair.

"So," she asked, "what's the concert?"

"I believe it's Mozart."

"Mom's favorite. I like Tchaikovsky myself. There's so much more oomph to his works." Chelsea turned to Tanner. "Mr. Carlucci, who's your favorite composer?"

Tanner had just bitten off an entire third of a taco. They all waited politely with bated breath while he chewed. Kate decided things had turned much too polite since poor Will showed up.

At last Tanner swallowed. "Bob Marley."

Disappointment flickered on Chelsea's face. "I meant classical type."

"He's a classic."

Chelsea obviously knew the Jamaican reggae artist had not composed symphonies. Her eyes rolled. Tanner's face remained expressionless. Kate's giggle interfered with eating and came out a cough. She reached for her water glass.

Adele clattered down the steps. "Okay! Let's go!"

In a glance Kate took in her friend's preparations. Or lack thereof. Adele's natural curls required little attention, but she had added a barrette, holding her hair behind an ear. Instead of clogs, she wore sleek fashionable boots. There was the faintest hint of lipstick. Other than that, her outfit remained what she had put on that morning: a deep purple long skirt, white blouse, embroidered vest, hoop earrings, and a few strings of beads.

Kate covertly watched Will and saw what she hoped she wouldn't see...a subtle lifting of a brow. He recovered quickly, though, and rose with a smile.

Still...it had been there. A shadow of disappointment in the way Adele had dressed, as if it were not quite up to his standards. Her friend would have accurately predicted his reaction, and yet she hadn't changed clothes. She'd remained true to herself.

Good for you, Adele. You did it.

Fourteen

As they sped down the dark highway toward Rockville, Adele glanced over at Will. Embarrassment scarcely began to describe her emotional state. Not only had she completely forgotten the concert date for which she had purchased the tickets, she now reeked of hot oil and fried tortillas. The scent rivaled those of leather and masculine cologne.

"Will, I am so, *so* sorry," Adele apologized for the third time, her voice still breathless. "This week has been horrendous."

He reached over and patted her gloved hand, the hand Graham had gently held during the prayer. "Don't worry about it. I should have called you when I got back in town this afternoon. But I was swamped and thought for sure you'd remember, especially since this concert was your idea."

"You'd think so, wouldn't you? I haven't even looked at the calendar since Monday. It's just been one thing after another."

"I hope I didn't interrupt anything."

"Interrupt?"

"You had guests."

"Guests? Oh. No, not really." Her tone sounded as false as it should in telling such a lie. "I mean, it was just sort of a last-minute thing. Tara and Kate are part of the family, of course. Kate had plans with Tanner, so he joined us for dinner. I just happened to see Graham at Swensen's this afternoon. I told you about him, right?"

"No."

"Oh. Well, a friend who's been like a father to him moved into Fox Meadow recently. Graham is alone in town, keeping Mr. Jennings company while doing some research, and there's no other family around. You know me. Bring home any stray hungry dog I come across."

"I hope you didn't call him that to his face."

She joined in his chuckle.

"Tell me about your week, Adele."

Will was gracious and sweet as he steered them onto safer topics as smoothly as he steered the car along the highway's curves. But she knew that the only topic she could think about wasn't safe...and that sooner or later she was going to have to deal with it.

Tanner leaned against his car, watching Kate park Helen nearby in the lot outside the Rockville movie theater. They had driven separately from Valley Oaks because Kate insisted upon it. She wouldn't hear of him making the back and forth trip again in one evening. That would have smacked of Sir Galahad, thereby causing great discomfort to her practical mind.

She approached him, laughing, her breath frosting the air. "Was that awkward or was that awkward?"

"That was awkward."

They hurried into the lobby, still chuckling about Will's surprise appearance and Adele's abrupt departure from the dinner table.

"Hey, Tanner, you didn't mind me inviting Graham along, did you?" Adele's friend had declined.

"No. I was going to ask him myself. I felt sorry for the guy. Of course, I felt sorry for Will too."

"At least he had plans!" They stood in line to buy tickets and Kate smiled up at him. "Isn't it strange how you and I seem to occupy the same wavelength? How we both thought of inviting him?"

It wasn't the first time their thoughts meshed. "It is strange considering you're such a redhead." He liked teasing her about her hair.

"Ha ha." She wrinkled her nose. "For that remark, I should have invited the girls. I'm sure they would have changed their plans."

"Thank you for *not* inviting the girls."

"You're welcome. I think you squelched Chelsea's infatuation with your Bob Marley comment. Her arty side noticed a flaw, Mr. Dreamboat. That was brilliant."

"I really don't know Mozart from a hole in the wall."

She laughed.

He joined in. Kate had an infectious laugh. He suspected the red hair compounded the effect. Silky and smooth as it was, its usual style could only be described as messy. He imagined her mind an overflowing, chaotic place with no room left over for mundane thoughts such as, "hairdresser, style, hair dryer, curling iron."

She pulled money from her coat pocket and shoved it into his hand. "I'm going to get popcorn while you buy the tickets. Want anything?"

He shook his head and watched her scamper off, pocketing her money until he could find a way to give it back. He could afford to treat her, the nonpaid intern. However, that too smacked of Sir Galahad in her mind.

A short while later they entered the theater and found seats. Tanner grinned at her as she dug into a large bag of buttered popcorn on her lap.

She caught his expression. "What?" she asked.

"Nothing." He chuckled.

"You are such a crummy liar."

"I know. I'm trying to figure out where you put the food. Didn't we finish a huge dinner of tacos approximately," he glanced at his watch, "forty-three minutes ago?"

"Mm-hmm." She finished chewing her mouthful and swallowed. "Getting back to Adele and Graham...I think they're in love."

"They just met."

"I know, but it's so obvious. And there is such a thing as love at first sight. That's how my parents got together, thirty-five years ago. What I can't figure out is why Adele and Graham don't admit it."

"Kate Kilpatrick, I never would have imagined you had a romantic bone in your body."

"Of course I do. I agreed to come to this romantic comedy tonight, didn't I?"

He didn't remind her that her yes involved her interest in the screenwriter's work. Nor did he mention that she balked at anything he did or said if it resembled an impractical, Sir Galahad gesture, like driving her tonight in a vehicle that was far more roadworthy than hers. It was almost as if she felt she didn't deserve to be on the receiving end of such things.

Instead he went on to explain why he held the opinion of her. "But romance is such an airy, frivolous thing. Not like you at all."

"Oh?"

"No. You're quirky."

She grinned. "Really? As in offbeat? Unconventional?"

"Yep."

"That's the nicest thing you've ever said to me."

"Well, don't let it go to your head."

"Things don't go to the heads of quirky people."

"I suppose not." He reached over and into the popcorn bag. "May I?"

"I'll go get you some."

Someone bumped into his leg and said, "Excuse me—Tanner! Hi!"

He recognized the woman as he stood to let her and a companion pass. "Hi." *What was her name?* "Sondra."

"How *are* you?" She clutched him in a hug, babbling about how long it had been, introducing her fiancé. At last she spied Kate, who had risen beside him. "You must be Tanner's little sister."

"No." Kate's tone was unsteady, disguising a chuckle.

"Cousin then."

He intervened. "Kate Kilpatrick. *Date.*"

Sondra's eyebrows rose perceptibly and a smirk twisted what he had once considered a lovely mouth. "Oh." It came out as a two-syllable word.

Kate held up her left hand dripping with butter and wiggled it. "But no ring yet!" she whined, elbowing him in the ribs. "He keeps promising though."

Sondra gave an arrogant half laugh before they moved on down the row.

Seething, Tanner sat again as the lights dimmed. *What a snob! And to think I was actually attracted to that.* He should march over there and tell her off. He owed that much to Kate. She didn't deserve that kind of treatment. Man, she had even smiled at Sondra. Not the least bit flustered, she had joined in his charade that they were dating.

He felt Kate's eyes on him and turned. The previews had begun, making conversation difficult. "What?"

She leaned sideways, and he lowered his ear toward her mouth. She said, "You look like you're about to explode. Don't worry about it. Quirks are often mistaken for sisters and cousins."

He laughed so loudly the guy in front of him turned around and frowned.

"Sorry." Tanner called out. He swung his arm across the back of Kate's seat and gave her a friendly hug. She was so easy to be with. She even knew how to defuse his anger. He felt the tenseness go out of his muscles.

She stretched toward him again and said, "You're going to have to do better than that, Galahad. I think she's watching."

"No way. I refuse to hold your hand until you wash off that butter."

Now Kate laughed, prompting another frown.

Same wavelength. Amazing how he could have spent 30 years of his life so blind.

Adele picked at her dinner and only halfheartedly listened to the orchestra play all of her favorite Mozart selections. By the time they got into the car, she was drained of chipper conversation. Evidently so was Will. The ride home was a silent one.

As they neared her house, she noticed there were no extra cars parked in front or in the driveway. Tanner and Kate were gone, as was Tara. Graham Logan was also gone. Not that she had expected him to wait for her. Still, the disappointment pierced somewhere deep inside.

She had to try explaining it to Will.

"Adele." He pulled into the driveway, but left the engine running. The car was warm and comfortable under a starry sky. "I need to say something." He turned in his seat to face her.

"Do you want to come inside?" She settled back against the door.

"No. This won't take long. Listen, something has shifted between us this week."

She nodded. The dear man knew. "I'm sorry."

"No, don't be sorry."

"I didn't mean for—"

"Adele." He pulled her into his arms. "Shh. It's all right. Don't cry."

"I don't know what's happening."

"Yes, you do. You're falling in love."

"But I don't even know him!"

"I guess you know enough. He seemed like a nice enough guy. At least in the three minutes I spent with him."

She sniffled against the fuzzy grain of his coat, half laughing.

"I don't want to interfere. I'll always be there for you, but I probably won't invite you out again. I think that's for the best. All right?"

"I'm sorry."

"You're a beautiful woman, Adele, and I loved having you beside me at functions, having dinner with me now and then, keeping me company. But we both know it was only a friendship for the time being. I'm not ready for another wife. You aren't ready to be a stepmom." He tilted her chin up and kissed her softly. "I will miss you, but there is nothing to be sorry about."

Swallowing her tears, she nodded. "I can't keep the ring."

"Yes, you can." He smiled.

"No, Will. Wait, I'll run up and get it." That had been another source of embarrassment. She had forgotten to wear the amethyst tonight.

"Another time. I need to get home. I'm exhausted." He opened his door and she climbed from hers. At the front door he kissed her cheek. "Thank you for the concert."

"Thank you for dinner."

"Take care, Adele. And if you need anything, call me. Okay?"

She nodded and watched him return to his car. He waited until she unlocked the door and waved to him, and then he drove away. Reluctant to go in, she ran her hand along the inside wall and flipped off the porch light switch. Closing the door, she remained outside in the cold, looking up at the black velvet sky studded with stars.

Will was a good friend, a masculine presence that she clung to not only because he was a man but because he was the only decent, successful man who had accepted her for who she was.

Nearly. Nearly accepted her for who she was.

She let the thought develop. It had been there all along. She had simply chosen to ignore it every time she scrambled for something to wear that would pass his inspection…every time she spoke her mind in a group setting and caught the subtle raising of his brow.

She had been forever trying to please him in exactly the same way she had always tried to please her father. But Will had been so gentle about it, nothing at all like the tyrant who had raised her. Silly how she behaved as though by winning Will's approval she was somehow winning R.J. Chandler's.

Silly how she had let *that* man dictate *this* relationship. Maybe Will would have changed…in time…

Now that really was a silly line of thought. He was gone…and she was ignoring the obvious. Again.

Oh, Lord.

An unknown future lurked, waiting to devour her the moment she stepped toward it. And so it was fear that rooted her to the porch, her companion for a cold night's vigil.

Fifteen

Sunday morning Kate snuggled under the thick down comforter, relishing in the warmth of flannel sheets. It was nearly time to get ready for church, but she chose to luxuriate for a few moments in the coziness of her room and in the knowledge of how she was loved. God had given her so much.

"Even though I'm in Valley Oaks for the duration and not Wash—"

No, she was *not* going to complain.

Sunlight already streamed through the blinds she had twisted open last night when she wanted to see the stars. It was a quaint room, located on the first floor with a view of Adele's backyard. The bed took up most of the space, but it was an old four-poster, and from it she could see out the two windows. A braided rug covered most of the hardwood floor. The vanity and dresser looked like antiques, but knowing her landlady, they weren't. The closet door's handle was a glass knob. Another glass-knobbed door led to her own private bath. The walls were papered in a tiny blue floral print.

The adjoining room was a sitting room, probably a parlor in the old days. Adele designated it as Kate's space. It contained a desk, a couch, and a chair. Kate had added her own small television, CD player, and bookcase. The kitchen was always open for her use.

It was a good home away from home. Adele's character, of course, permeated the situation, welcoming Kate like a beloved relative.

"Which we are, in a way. Right, Lord? Sisters in You."

Chelsea accepted her. Rusty accepted her. The book club women accepted her. She had even been invited to Britte Olafsson's for an open house that afternoon, a postnuptial shower for Britte's brother and his new wife. The place would be crawling with resources for *Times* articles, a perfect networking opportunity.

Spring was a few weeks away, practically around the corner. Warm temperatures were predicted for Wednesday. The snow could melt and not fall again until next winter.

And the cherry on top of the chocolate sundae was Tanner. She couldn't have asked for a better tour guide for this internship phase of her life. The guy was a gem. It was fun being silly with him the previous night at the movies, pretending they were romantically involved. For one brief moment, when he put his arm around her, she was dazzled by what that felt like. She quickly set the impression aside.

"Lord, thank You for the laughter with him. Please smooth things between him and his dad. I get the feeling their relationship is strained. And please bring Him into Your family. He has that homeless look about his soul."

Tanner rubbed his whiskers and poured coffee into a mug. He carried it over to the table and sat in his windowless kitchen, staring at a calendar on the wall.

He wanted to go to church, out in Valley Oaks.

That thought had awakened him, and it wouldn't go away. He let it rumble around in his mind. It was a totally foreign thought that couldn't seem to find its own niche. What was he to do with it?

Last week he had attended church simply on a lark, meeting Kate's challenge. Last night she hadn't brought up the subject and he wasn't about to. Not that he had disliked the service. It was fine. And the pastor had actually given him some new concepts to ponder...like Jesus Christ. God's Son? The way to the Father? A friend who imparts the strength not to drink? Supernatural yet real in the day-to-day of life?

But he couldn't go out there today. He was having breakfast with his dad, the only time available in the busy doctor's schedule. Not that it was a regular appointment. Today's meeting had been planned because the down payment for the video store was due on Thursday. Sidney wanted to hand him the check in person, his dad's feeble attempt to make sure his son knew how much he cared.

Yeah, right.

The phone rang and Tanner leaned over to grab the cordless from its cradle. "Hello?"

"Tanner."

"Hi, Dad." The guy was going to cancel.

"What are you doing tomorrow morning?"

Tanner closed his eyes. "I'll be in Denver. I'm flying a charter out there tonight. Be back late on Tuesday."

"I'm sorry to hear that."

"What? Sorry to hear I'm working?"

"I didn't mean that. Look, something's come up this morning. Marnie needs me here. How about if we postpone breakfast and I'll deposit the check in your account first thing tomorrow?"

"Not a problem."

After a few so-called pleasantries, they said goodbye.

Marnie. Not work, not patients crying for attention, but Marnie, the wife, a woman not much older than Tanner's sister. At least he had married her, unlike the handful preceding her.

Tanner drummed his fingers on the table. It was such a familiar scene, his dad letting him down. He wondered that it still surprised him, still carved fresh wounds. Maybe because for years he had managed to escape it by consistently sinking into oblivion.

Unaware of his movements, Tanner felt cool air and found himself standing in front of the opened refrigerator staring at a carton of orange juice. Automatically he removed it along with a package of bagels. Still he stood, one hand resting on the open door, one hand holding breakfast.

And suddenly he realized what he was doing. He was searching for something that was not stashed in the refrigerator nor in any of the cupboards.

"Okay." He spoke out loud, his voice strange to his ears. "Are You here, Jesus? Is this where You come in? It's been six and a half years and *still...*"

He shoved the items back into the fridge and slammed the door shut. Swiftly he made his way to the bedroom and grabbed a pair of running shoes from the closet.

He would run. He'd do the long route, down to the river and back, 5.2 miles, embrace the arctic blast, the sensation of icicles forming on his lungs.

Then he would go to Valley Oaks Community Church and surprise Kate. It was fun to surprise Kate. Her face would light up like a Christmas tree. He could easily imagine her dancing around like an elf. She was about the size of one, definitely as energetic as one.

Then, if she didn't mind, he would hang out with her, go together to that open house at Britte's. Maybe she had some more of that chili.

The thing about Kate was, she seemed to like him. Just the way he was. No strings attached.

"So, Pops, what do you think?" Graham sat on the edge of the bed, holding Rand's limp hand between his. It seemed swollen. "I'm getting the impression that she is attracted to me."

"What's wrong with that?" His breathing was labored.

Exasperated, Graham placed Rand's hand under the covers and stood. Pacing, he fingercombed his hair. "You don't really mean it. I have no business worming my way into Adele's life!"

"It's not worming."

"Of course it is. I just happened to have become attracted to her in the process!"

"Shh. You'll break Heather's heart." He breathed a soft laugh.

Graham ignored the joking reference to the young nurse. "My sole purpose for being here is to grant your last request. Once you're gone, the strings will be severed. She'll want nothing further to do with me."

"Pure conjecture. Graham, you have my blessing. A relationship between you two is my fondest dream."

In reply, he stuffed his hands in the back pockets of his corduroys. *Stubborn old coot.* "You're a stubborn old coot."

"Thank you. Tell me again about Chelsea. She's as beautiful as her mother?"

He nodded. "Taller. Just as confident and independent. Bit of an adolescent's attitude, naturally."

"And when is her birthday?"

"May twelfth. She'll be seventeen." They already knew that.

"I sure would like to meet her."

"She works here sometimes, during school breaks. The next one is mid-April, Easter week."

"I'd like to see Easter again too. Make up for all the ones I missed."

Graham returned to his side. Rand had had a difficult night. Their hopes to attend the center's church service that morning were waning. "You know those are forgiven and forgotten. I imagine Easter at Home will be somewhat on the magnificent side, don't you?"

He chuckled in his raspy way. "Graham, I have one more last request."

"You're only allowed one."

"Don't fight whatever it is developing between you. She needs someone to take care of her. God told me you're the one."

"Now you're receiving personal messages from God?"

He smiled, his eyes closing. "We're getting chummier every day. He'll be taking me Home soon, you know."

Adele sat in her minivan on the street, a block from the church parking lot, unsure about continuing further.

She had tossed and turned most of the night, finally falling asleep as the stars faded from view. Chelsea had woken her at eight, but she didn't move a muscle except to mumble she would catch up later. Chelsea and Kate should go on ahead to church.

She rested her forehead against the steering wheel. "Lord, what's wrong with me? I feel like an idiotic teenager again with a crush on a good-looking guy. For goodness sake, I'm thirty-six years old! My life was good and balanced and now all I can think about is some man I just met who doesn't even live here! I'm afraid to take another step. I'm afraid to see him. I'm afraid *not* to see him!"

Do not be afraid. Trust in your Father.

It wasn't an audible voice, only a distinct impression reminding her of what she already knew: She wasn't walking alone.

"What am I getting into?"

Like He was going to tell her that one.

Adele wiped her tears and pulled down the visor mirror. She looked the wreck she felt. Maybe she should go home.

That thought felt comforting.

But it was the fearful way out and would only postpone the inevitable.

She opened her compact and did some repair work on her face.

He probably wasn't even around. More than likely he was attending the service at Fox Meadow with Rand. Maybe she would see him tomorrow. Maybe not. Their paths didn't necessarily have to cross at the nursing home. She could probably avoid him for a time. Maybe it would be wise to take that time...

At last she drove into the lot, parked, and walked toward the church, ten minutes after the music would have started. A lone figure stood inside the glass doors, looking out.

Adele stopped in her tracks. There was no mistaking that pewter gray caught in the sunlight, nor the broad outline filling the doorway.

She continued slowly.

When she reached the door, Graham pushed it open for her, and she walked in, scarcely breathing as she brushed past him. There was a tentative expression about his eyes that probably mirrored her own. They stared at one another for a long moment.

Then he extended his hand toward her as a friend would invite another...*come, walk with me.*

Adele reached out and placed her hand in his. He wrapped his fingers ever so gently around it, and they walked together into the sanctuary.

Sixteen

Adele sat in her living room, in the chair beside the window, staring through the parted curtains at the dark street. Her heart was in racing mode, thumping its wild beat into her throat.

She had never felt like this waiting for Will. She had never felt like this waiting for anyone. Eating and sleeping were things of the past. She could not foresee engaging in the everyday rhythms of life again.

Oh, that sounded so silly! Surely the surprise of it all would pass sooner or later.

The day had been one long adrenaline rush from the moment she saw Graham standing in the church doorway. The day had held no interest except in anticipating when she would see him again.

Oh my.

A car pulled into the driveway. It was Graham's white four-door with seats that did not smell of leather.

The lights blinked off and he climbed from the car. Spotting her in the window, he waved and loped in that long-legged way of his along her sidewalk. She went to the door and opened it.

"Hi."

"Hi."

There was an awkward moment as he shrugged out of his coat. She tried to help, and his elbow whacked her arm.

"Oomph."

"Sorry."

Together they hung his coat on the hall tree and laughed. She asked, "Are you hungry?"

"No, not really. How about you?"

"No. But I made some salad."

"Later?"

She nodded, took his elbow, and steered him into the living room. "Shall we sit?"

The room was cozy, with candles lit, the lamps low, Vivaldi playing softly in the background. A teapot and mugs waited on the coffee table.

She sat on the couch. "Tea?"

"Yes, thanks." He sat beside her.

She filled the mugs. "How is Rand today?"

"It was a good day. Thank you." He took the cup from her. "He keeps saying it won't be long before Jesus will be taking him Home. Can you tell when it gets close to the time?"

"In cases like his, sometimes within a week or so before it happens we think, 'it won't be long now.' Not very accurate. You haven't gone through cancer before?"

He shook his head.

"How did your wife die?"

He glanced away. "She was murdered."

"Oh! I'm so sorry." How horrible!

"I'd rather not talk about it. Someday I'll tell you the details." He said it matter of factly, as if they could schedule it into the calendar. Then his eyes met hers. "I don't know why I held your hand today."

She swallowed. Was it all her imagination?

"Obviously I wanted to." He gave her a half smile. "I haven't noticed another woman since the day Sammi was killed. And then I sat down in your office. Suddenly I'm wondering who the guy is in your life."

"He isn't in it anymore."

"Good. Saves me from having to hurt him."

She laughed and he joined in.

He said, "I didn't mean to tell him to get lost last night."

"You didn't!"

"No, I didn't." He hunched his shoulders in an exaggerated way and frowned. "I just kind of circled around him and he got the idea."

She laughed again. "Well, he got the idea all right. Even before I did, I think."

Graham touched her hair, brushing a strand from her temple. "There's so much you don't know about me."

"That works both ways. We just met."

"Adele, your life is an open book. You've created a real home here all by yourself. You have a lovely daughter, a responsible job that you relish, a place in the community, faith in Christ. You're an artist."

"Still, there are things."

"I have more things. I have not always been what I seem."

"Are you a weird psycho that I'm going to read about in the paper someday?"

He smiled. "No. But then I doubt that sort would answer yes to the question."

"I suppose not. Have you committed some horrible, unconfessed crime?"

"No."

"Do you trust in Christ?"

"Yes."

"All right. That covers everything."

"Not quite. When Rand is gone, my project will be finished and more than likely I will be on my way."

"You already know that? That you'll leave? Well, naturally you would. This isn't your home."

"His death is imminent. You and I will have only begun to scratch the surface of becoming acquainted."

She studied the tea in her cup. Why the feeling that she needed to delve no further than the surface? She already *knew*... It was that safety that oozed from him.

"Adele?"

She looked at him.

"It's such a risky business."

She sensed that because his wife's death had hurt him so deeply, he feared loving again. "Graham, there's potential for hurt in any relationship."

He set his cup on the coffee table and rested his arms on his knees, not facing her. "You're right. I'm...I'm willing to take a chance."

She swallowed, letting his words sink in. "Well, given the fact that we don't have much time, I vote we jump right in and get to know each other and not waste any of it by worrying about what might *not* happen."

He turned his head sideways to look at her. "There you go being straightforward again."

"And there you go being moody again."

"I'm not moody."

"You most certainly are. And I won't have it, not tonight."

He sat up, leaned against the back of the couch and took her hand in his. "And what will you have tonight?"

A warmth encompassed her as it had that morning in church, and she sensed again a sensation of pure perfection.

His hand was large, the palms wide, the fingers long, the strength implicit.

She said, "Pottery. Let's go make some."

Graham followed her down the basement steps to her brightly lit studio. The concrete block walls were painted white, as was the floor. It had been a good move to leave behind the candlelit room, soft music, and cozy couch.

Holding hands with her was crazy enough. Wanting to touch that gentle face and kiss the dimpled cheek surpassed crazy. It was out of the question. He reminded himself of his disciplined training. He could hold his emotions in check. He would. He had no business kissing her.

Maybe a hug. She was so...huggable.

"Here." She held out a large man's denim shirt with the sleeves cut out. "This might fit."

"I'm fine."

"You'll get messy, trust me."

He removed his flannel shirt and put the other one on over his T-shirt.

"No tattoos, as far as I can see." She grinned, buttoning another denim shirt over her blouse. "Just getting to know you!"

She kept surprising him like that, sneaking up on his lighter side and urging him to smile in the face of approaching death.

"All right. Sit."

She pushed him toward a strange contraption on the floor, some sort of wheel with a little stool beside it. He inspected it.

"It'll hold you, big guy." She went to a shelf and dug inside what looked like a trash bag. Out came a hunk of clay.

He sat, watching her throw the lump onto a table and begin kneading it as if it were bread dough. She talked the whole time about what she was doing, about different kinds of clay. He liked her chatty way. That lilting voice of hers carried him along, mesmerizing him.

She said, "This is off the subject, but I've been meaning to ask how you met Rand."

"My father worked for him. When I was a little kid, he was the head of maintenance in Rand's office building. The two of them hit it off for some reason. It's not like they were golfing buddies. Dad's the loyal type and Rand appreciated that. Dad even personally washed Rand's windows. Nobody could do them like he did. One day the scaffolding gave way, and he fell three stories. His back was broken; he's been on disability ever since. I was twelve at the time. Through the years, Rand always made sure we had what we needed. He paid for college for me and my two brothers. I'm the oldest, and he particularly took me under his wing. He's been like a second dad to me. Tried to teach me investment banking, but I wasn't interested."

"He said you told him about Jesus."

"That's true. Rand was quite a rough character in his day, but I couldn't give up on him. I owed him too much."

"Did I mention my father's name was Randall too? But I called him R.J. Everyone did. Not Randall or Rand and definitely not Randy."

"Small world."

"Speaking of names, he called me Addie one time."

"I told him I had seen that name on a piece of your pottery in the living room."

"You noticed that?" She sounded pleased. "I sign the name on my artwork, but I haven't been called it since I was a little girl. Hearing it was like déjà vu."

She brought the chunk over, put it on the wheel, leaned near him, and flipped a switch. The wheel began humming.

"You wouldn't have really hurt Will, would you?"

"Well, I would have tried talking to him first."

Smiling, Adele came around behind him. "Here. Dampen your hands in this water."

He reached over to a nearby pail and did as he was told. She seemed to have that effect on him.

"Now put your foot there on that pedal."

The wheel spun like a top.

"Not so much pressure. Put your hands here. We'll make a bowl."

She bent forward beside him and placed her hands on his, guiding them so that one was on the outside and one on the inside of what soon resembled a bowl. As it spun, she pushed on his hands, talking about keeping the pressure equal.

The thing soon grew lopsided. She giggled and he laughed. And then she gave up helping and stepped behind him, watching as he tried gallantly to reshape the bowl. Her giggles grew into uncontrollable laughter, and she buried her face in the back of his neck, hands on his shoulders.

He hoped they'd make pottery again sometime soon.

Seventeen

Cell phone pressed to his ear, Tanner stood at his Denver hotel window and admired a view of the snow-covered Rockies. Sunlight touched only the highest peaks, dazzling white steadily chasing away the deep purple shadows. He couldn't decide which was more spectacular: the view before him now or last night's moonlit view. God certainly knew how to have a good time.

"Hello." Rusty's gravelly voice answered on the other end. "*Valley Oaks Times.*"

"Knew I'd catch you there."

"Tanner? What are you doing up already?"

"The mountains are calling my name. I'm spending the day on the slopes."

"Well la-de-dah." She chuckled. "You must be playing pilot today."

"Flew into Denver last night and have to hang around while my charges attend some business meeting. Is the little elf in yet?"

Rusty barked a laugh. "I knew she reminded me of something! No, not yet."

"Then I'll give the scoop to you."

"I've got one for you. Mind if I go first?"

"Not if it's really good gossip."

"It's not gossip, and I don't want anybody hearing about it." Her tone was dead serious.

"Then why are you telling me?"

"Moral support."

Rusty was asking for moral support? Further proof that God was real. "My lips are sealed."

"Thanks. I've got a shot at a job back in Chicago. The political sands have shifted. Long story short, I'm leaving."

He whistled. He knew she had considered her chances of returning next to nil. "Congratulations, Rusty. That's got to feel good."

"It does. Now for the moral support." She hesitated.

He knew she had no family and was getting up in years. What could the problem be?

"I'm leaving next week. I need the little elf to become editor for the time being."

"That's going to be a problem."

"Tell me about it. She's fully capable, but she only has one foot in the door here as it is."

"Any prospects on hiring someone else?"

"No, and there's no guarantee the owner can find one in two months."

"What can I do?"

"You could marry her."

Tanner hooted. "That's a bit drastic, don't you think? And you don't really believe that would tie her down."

"Nah, probably not. You two seem like friends."

"We are."

"Will you just be on hand when I break it to her? Keep her from slugging me? Or worse yet, crying?"

"Sure."

"Thanks. Oh, here she is now. Kate!" Rusty's voice grew fainter. "Tanner's got a scoop for us. Why don't you take it from him? Tanner." She was back on the line. "Don't be a hotdogger and break a leg now. Okay, here's the elf."

"Elf!?" It was Kate on the phone, the timbre of her voice threatening. "What's that supposed to mean?"

"Uh." He owed Rusty one. At least she hadn't repeated "little," which was probably redundant with the word elf. "You just...just kind of remind me of one. In a good way. You know, energetic, fun-loving..."

"Keep going."

"Cute. Irrepressible. Big pointy feet. Into making toys."

"You're burying yourself, Carlucci. It's a good thing you're in Denver. What's the scoop?"

He looked again at the mountains. A reminder? "I'm going through with it."

Kate whooped. "Yay! Rusty, he's buying the video store!"

He imagined Rusty's expression of disbelief.

"When?" Kate asked.

"I sign the papers Friday. And..." He took a breath. "I'm moving into the apartment."

She laughed loudly. He thought her incredibly easy to delight.

"Want to help me on Wednesday?"

"I'd love to. Why don't you call me that morning? I'll get my schedule figured out."

"Okay. So go ahead and put the sale in this week's edition."

"But it hasn't happened yet, which means it's not news. We'll get it in next week with photos of you inside the store."

"But if it's in black and white, I..." His voice trailed off. Maybe if he didn't voice his fears out loud, they'd go away.

"Tanner, you need to hire people, right? Take out an ad. They can pick up applications on Saturday at the store. We could put in a tentative opening date."

"Put my money where my mouth is." His breathing returned to normal. "Okay. That sounds good. Say late March."

"Maybe a Saturday? That'd be a good grand-opening day. The thirty-first?"

"All right."

"What size do you want?" She gave him a range of sizes and prices.

"You're better at this. Go ahead and choose something."

"Rusty can probably get you a good price. No, never mind. She's giving me a thumbs-down on that thought." She laughed. "We'll take care of it and try not to break your budget."

"All right. Thanks, Kate."

"You're welcome. Have a good time hitting the slopes. And, Tanner?"

"Yeah?"

"People always believe the ads they read in the newspaper. You will go through with this."

Kate, his personal cheerleading elf.

"Katy-girl, you handled that well," Rusty said. "This is a huge step for Tanner. I didn't have a clue anyone was buying the place. He must have mentioned it to you?"

"He swore me to secrecy." She carried her coat to the pegs next to the door. "He's moving into Lia's apartment too."

"Things are changing for our boy. You two are getting to be good friends." There was a hint of pleasure in her voice.

"I guess everyone else my age in town already has a full life. He, on the other hand, is always available."

Rusty smiled. "I imagine he's getting cold feet."

"You've got him figured out. He wanted his decision in black and white, right now. As if that might keep him from backing out of the deal. Why is he like that? He's so down-to-earth friendly and talented. Everybody likes him. He was popular in high school, athletic. You'd think he'd be confident."

"Lack of healthy parental love will cut that right out from under you."

Kate sat back at her desk. "He hasn't said anything about that."

"His dad bailed out of the family when Tanner was thirteen. Hasn't had much to do with them since, except for buying them whatever they want. I think his mom didn't handle things well raising three of them on her own."

That explained a lot, even Beth's remark about him hanging out with the wild crowd in high school. Poor Tanner.

"He'll be all right. He's got good instincts." Rusty leaned back in her creaky desk chair.

Kate noticed she was chewing gum.

"So tell me about the shindig at Britte Olafsson's yesterday." She referred to the postnuptial shower for Britte's brother Brady and his new wife, Gina. "Joel around?"

"Oh, yes. You would have thought he was the host in her house."

Rusty laughed. "The man is smitten."

Kate told her about Brady's outrageous gift to Gina. "He gave her this little bejeweled elephant and everybody in the place knew exactly what he'd done. He'd bought her a *real* one! Do you believe it? The animal currently lives at the St. Louis Zoo. Brady and Gina want to open a petting zoo on the property adjacent to theirs."

"Wouldn't that'd be something. A petting zoo might grow into something more. I imagine there's some controversy brewing over all that. A lot of people wanted a housing development out there."

"Isn't that historical property?"

"The original founder of Valley Oaks lived there. Charles Crowley."

"Seems to me history and a zoo give the place more depth than a housing development. Otherwise, you've just got a bedroom community with people working and playing elsewhere."

"Sounds like an editorial in the making."

"You'd let me do one?"

"Sure. You're ready for anything, kid."

"How about a social column?"

Rusty raised her bushy gray brows. "Something beyond wedding announcements?"

"Oh, yeah. We could write about things like Joel Kingsley taking coats at Britte's door and cutting cake. I thought you said that guy was a Marine. Or Gina receiving an elephant. Or Tanner moving into Lia's apartment. Or Adele and the stranger in town holding hands in church. And you know Joel's going to propose publicly. I mean, the guy was *at home* there."

Rusty chuckled and swiveled her chair around to face the desk. "You are getting into the swing of Valley Oaks."

Swing of Valley Oaks? Given the fact that she'd just devised on her own—all by herself, without any prompting whatsoever from anyone else—a *social column*, she had to say "swing of Valley Oaks" was an understatement. It had to be nothing less than the magic of the place.

"Mr. Jennings." Adele called down the corridor and hurried to catch up to him.

The wheelchair stopped and he peered over his shoulder. "Adele." He smiled broadly.

"Hi. How are you?"

"Better now, after seeing your pretty face."

"Oh, you are too charming. May I push you somewhere?"

"If you call me Rand. I was going to the library."

"I'll take you there, *Rand.*"

"Wheel away, Addie."

"It's funny how you call me that. No one has called me that in years."

"Why is that?"

"My parents used that name. I dropped it when I, uh, left home. Now it's how I sign my artwork." They entered the library. "Where would you like to be?"

"By the newspapers."

She set the chair brakes.

"You seem a bit down, young lady."

"Do I?" Perceptive man. She attempted a perky tone. "Graham came over last night. We made pottery."

"Graham made pottery?" His shoulders shook as he laughed silently.

"His bowl has corners in it."

"Is that why you're down?"

"No." She smiled. "We had a..." *Lovely, fun, fantastic, heart-thumping, unbelievable...* "A good time together. It's my teenage daughter."

"What's Chelsea doing?"

He knew her name? Graham must tell him everything. "She's pulling away. Not communicating."

"Ah, she's just growing up. She'll come around."

It wasn't the first time Adele heard the trace of an eastern accent in some of his words, and she wondered where he had grown up. "I just don't want her wasting time making the mistakes I made."

"What were those?"

"Getting pregnant too soon."

"Then Chelsea's the mistake?"

His response startled her. "No, of course not."

"Have you given her a good life?"

"I do the best I can. She doesn't always have the material things 'everyone else' has."

"Those aren't worth a plug nickel. Just be honest with her. She'll be fine. Of course, I'll be long gone before I see how she turns out." As usual, he was direct and matter of fact.

There was a rap on the door. Nate, a young aide, stepped into the room. "Adele, phone for you. It's the high school. Chelsea didn't show up for school today."

Eighteen

At five o'clock Adele yanked open her front door before Deputy Cal Huntington had a chance to ring the bell. She had seen him park his cruiser on the street.

"They're fine, Adele." He stepped inside.

She put her hands to her face and held back a sob. *Thank You, Jesus.* Before her knees gave way, she went to the staircase, the nearest seat, and sank onto a step.

Cal shut the door and removed his sheriff's hat. "A friend of mine with the State Patrol spotted Tara's car coming from the direction of Chicago."

"Chicago?" The hollowness in her stomach grew. Chelsea had never gone to Chicago alone!

"He followed them to the Rockville exit and just now called to let me know. My guess is they're coming home." Chelsea and Tara hadn't been gone long enough to be reported missing, but Cal had made some phone calls and asked favors.

He rubbed his full beard. "But if you want, I'll head down the highway and find them."

She wiped tears from under her eyes. "It's not Jacob County."

"No problem."

"You don't mind?" Fear still clutched her throat, making her voice sound like a stranger's.

"You okay alone?"

She nodded. "I'll call Tara's mom." *On the off chance she cares.*

"All right. If you don't hear from me, I'm on their tail until they're parked in your drive."

"Thank you."

He nodded and replaced his hat. "Adele, she's a good kid. She's a really good kid from where I sit. Don't be too hard on her." With that he left.

She's a good kid. She is a good kid.

Adele rocked herself and let the tears fall.

She's all right.

Every nightmare she'd ever had bombarded that afternoon. Her greatest terror was always of losing Chelsea, her only child, the love of her life. It made her overprotective. It made her want to cling to the nearly 17-year-old girl and not let her out of her sight.

Not a healthy attitude.

Chelsea was pushing her away. It was a creeping, subtle withdrawing. In recent months their communication had suffered. For the most part, they got along like always, with no major disagreements, but something was fading.

What was it? Rand Jennings' words came to her. "Then Chelsea's the mistake?"

Had she ever breathed a hint of that? Ever inadvertently given credence to that thought by her words or her actions?

Oh, dear Lord, give me wisdom.

She waited. Again. Every breath hurt as they had all afternoon. She had raced home after the school called. After shouting at the school secretary for not knowing sooner. Didn't they keep better track of those things?

Joel had gotten on the line, trying to calm her, promising to talk to all of Chelsea's acquaintances. He had checked in with her twice since then.

She called him now. He thanked her for the news and promised a stiff sentence at school.

Next she called Tara's mom and talked briefly. The woman did not sound like the basket case Adele knew she herself was at the moment.

And then she waited. Again.

Headlights flashed through the front windows. Adele rushed to the door and opened it. Tara's car was in the drive. Chelsea took an eternity getting out.

Adele braced herself against the doorjamb, the cold night air numbing her hands and face.

"Mom." Chelsea approached. "I'm sorry. Please don't yell."

Adele grabbed her daughter by the arm and pulled her into a fierce hug. Yelling was the second item on her agenda.

By eight o'clock the yelling had fizzled. Chelsea was in her room, moping, grounded from phone, computer, and pottery until further notice. Kate had gotten wind of Chelsea's trip and popped in long enough to make sure everything was under control before she went to cover a meeting. Adele's "thank you" had snapped like a crocodile's jaws, sending her boarder quickly on her way.

She paced the living room now, more distraught than she could remember ever feeling. Her prayers were incoherent babbles. She hadn't eaten since lunch, but wasn't hungry. She was exhausted, but not tired. She was totally confused and unsure.

The doorbell rang. She considered not answering. It rang again. She did not want to talk to anyone! Now someone pounded on the door.

She went to it and jerked it open. "Graham."

"Hi. How's it going?"

She shook her head. "I'll get through it." Some way. Some how. Some day.

"May I come in?"

"I'm really not good company tonight."

"I'm not looking for good company."

"What are you, a masochist?" Her laugh was without humor.

"Adele, you don't have to do this alone."

She blinked. "Of course I do. She's my daughter."

"And you're my friend."

"It's my problem."

"But you don't have to deal with it alone."

"Graham, I appreciate the offer, but I really need to be alone right now."

He came inside, shut the door, and shrugged off his coat. "Have you eaten?"

His sudden presence engulfed her home. It felt as if something shifted, tilting her world, throwing it off balance. Throwing her off balance. Blurring her vision. She took a step backward. "Graham, please. I'm all right. Really."

"How about some tea? I bet I could find my way around your kitchen." He hung his coat on the hall tree and turned, his voice a soothing murmur. "After you left the other night, I helped clean it up."

Why didn't he leave? "Look, I don't need any tea! I don't want any company!" It was the tone she had used against Chelsea. The same volume. The same tone. Full of fear. Teetering on the brink of controlled. "I can do this alone! I've always done this alone! For over seventeen years, as a matter of fact! I've been a single mom from day one, perfectly capable—"

"Yes, you are." He held out his arms, nearly closing the gap between them. "But I'm here now and you don't have to do it alone this time."

She felt something begin to crumble inside of her. Courage? Determination? Stamina? *Faith?* That couldn't happen! "Jesus does it with me." The crumbling was gaining momentum. The sound of crashing grew louder. She heard her voice like a distant echo. "I'm not really alone."

"I know. Imagine, though, that He would let me take His place. Physically. That I could hold you for Him."

She shook her head, desperate to shake away that shattering noise whirling in head.

"Let it go, Adele. Just for now."

She sensed him move nearer, his arms held wide. He didn't touch her, but now his shoulders filled her vision, blocking out the world, restoring balance to her home.

And then she knew. All that noise was her fear. Like great waves it crashed against the rocks protecting a harbor. A safe harbor...the one that waited for her now in Graham Logan's embrace.

She laid her face against his soft sweater.

Graham closed his eyes and wrapped his arms around her. She felt smaller than he had imagined she would feel. Perhaps it was only that he was unaccustomed to her display of fragility. Her hair smelled like sweet, freshly crushed lavender. Its springy curls tickled his cheek.

She didn't cry. She had probably cried all day. He would have come sooner had he known, had he been in town.

He felt a shudder go through her. She slipped her arms around him.

It was the first time he had held a woman since...since Samantha. Since that day...

Like Adele, he had gone it alone. Trusting in Christ, yes, but not letting anyone come alongside and see the pain in its full force. Why now? Why with Adele Chandler of all people on the face of the earth? Why now as Rand lay on his death bed, complicating issues? Of course without Rand he never would have come to Valley Oaks in the first place...

They stood in the entryway. He didn't want to break the spell. She needed to come to terms with what she had just done: accepted his comfort. From her outburst he knew she still feared totally trusting any man as she must have once trusted her father, who let her down. Could she trust him in that way, in spite of everything?

He wanted to carry her off, whisk her away from the here and now, away from that *teenager* for whom he was garnering a few choice words. Of course, if she hadn't behaved like a fool, he wouldn't be standing there now holding Adele. Who knew how long before he would have allowed himself?

Adele stirred and lifted her face.

He cradled her cheek in his hand, caressing the ever-present dimple with his thumb. Her eyes were puffy and dark circles surrounded them. As always he found her lips enticing, the upper one a bit fuller than the lower one. He inclined his head.

And then he stopped. "Adele. It's not the right time."

She swallowed and nodded slightly.

"Tea?"

"You'll stay?" Her voice was hoarse.

"As long as you'll let me. Come on." With an arm around her shoulders, he led her through the dining room and into the kitchen.

A short time later they sat at the kitchen table sipping tea, Adele's shoulders wrapped in a blanket. Since arriving he had heard the furnace blasting heat waves throughout the house. Still she was cold. He got up and shut the door leading to the dining room, wondering if she'd mind if he sat around in his T-shirt and shorts. It was hot.

Adele was slowly describing the events of the day. "She refuses to tell me what she was up to. I have no idea what she and Tara did all day. I'm only guessing they went to Chicago from what Cal told me. She says I can trust her. I mean, that's it. That's all she'll say."

"Do you think you can trust her?"

"Before today I would have said completely. Without a doubt." Her gaze wandered toward the windows. "No, before the last few months I would have said that. She has been pulling away. I know she hasn't been opening up, not like before."

"She's never been sixteen going on seventeen before. Perhaps it's merely her age, her need for independence."

Adele's face fell. "I didn't think it would happen. We've always been so close because it's just been the two of us. And I've never discouraged her independence."

"Have you talked with Tara's mother?"

She shook her head. "The woman has…a wild lifestyle. I've lost track of which boyfriend is living with her now. Her daughter doesn't seem to be a priority to her."

"Maybe today was Tara's issue, not Chelsea's."

"I hadn't thought of that."

"Not that you should let her off the hook for skipping school and frightening you half to death, but if she asks for your trust, maybe giving it is a giant step toward letting go."

Tears welled in her eyes. "It's so hard. Harder than I ever imagined."

He reached over and touched her hand.

The kitchen door swung open and Chelsea entered. "Mom—Oh, Graham. Hi."

"Hi yourself. Are you allowed to be down here?"

Her eyes widened.

A tiny giggle escaped from Adele.

Chelsea's eyes grew even larger as she looked back and forth between the two of them.

Graham said, "Would you like some tea?"

"I came for ice water. Mom, it's so hot upstairs. Can I turn down the heat?"

"I'm freezing."

"Do you want some soup?" The child was obviously attempting to rack up good-behavior points.

Graham stood. "I'm sure you both need some. I'll cook." He touched Chelsea's shoulder and steered her to the table. "You two make up."

Now they both stared at him.

He ducked his head inside a cupboard. "Chicken noodle all right?"

In unison they said, "No chicken!"

"That's Kate's stuff!" Chelsea added.

He smiled at them. "I knew that."

"Mom, I am sorry."

Chelsea sat on the edge of Adele's bed where she leaned against pillows propped behind her. Her daughter seemed less exhausted than she did. While watching the late news with Graham, she had fallen asleep against his arm. Now she could hardly wait to sink under the covers. But Chelsea had just walked in. She wouldn't miss a moment with her for the world.

"I know you are, honey. You've already told me a few times. And I'm trying to trust that you knew what you were doing. That you're old enough to not have to tell me details.

But you would, wouldn't you, if someone might get hurt by your silence?"

"Mom, I already told you that too. Yes, I would. Graham seems like a nice guy."

Adele reached out and smoothed Chelsea's hair back. "He is a genuinely nice guy."

"Nicer than Will?"

"Nice in a different way. I think he might be hanging around some. Okay with you?"

"Sure. He's cute too, in an older kind of way. He's bigger and has more hair than Mr. Kingsley, but that's all right. And he fit right in, didn't he? I mean, it was like all of a sudden we had a man in the house, taking care of us and fixing us soup."

Adele didn't respond. She had noticed. With every fiber of her being she had noticed.

Nineteen

"Tanner, you're a man after my own heart." Kate grinned down at him from a standing position on a chair in his apartment kitchen.

"And how's that, Miss Kilpatrick?" He stopped beside her, his arms full of books.

"You travel light. I packed four plates, two bowls, four glasses, two mugs, one frying pan, one pot."

"Still seems like too much. There's only one of me. You really don't have to scrub that cupboard. The manager's not going to check. Trust me, the guy's a slob."

She plunged her hands in a pail of sudsy water and squeezed a sponge. "You never know. And besides, you should leave a place spick-and-span."

"Says who?"

"I do. It's just one of those things."

"One of what things?"

"*Those* things. It's innate."

He laughed and walked around the counter that divided the kitchen from the living room. "Trust me, it's not innate. You're a weirdo with red hair from a different planet."

"The planet of elves."

She smiled to herself as she scrubbed. Not everyone could get away with calling her that. But then, Tanner wasn't everyone.

It was Wednesday evening, and they had spent most of the afternoon in his modest Rockville apartment packing. She had stayed up late the night before to complete some

151

articles. Rusty, who also had an undeniable soft spot for Tanner, told her to take all the time she needed. They both wanted to light a fire under the guy and make certain he didn't dawdle and lose sight of his new commitment.

He truly did travel light. The walls were bare, the furniture—nice, heavy bachelor pieces—was minimal, the closets not overly stuffed with clothes or things.

She called out to him, "Maybe Graham Logan can help you with the big stuff on Friday. He's been hanging around a lot. I don't think the guy does anything except visit his friend and Adele."

"He's a professor on sabbatical. What do you expect?"

"I figured he had to do something. Supposedly he's writing a book. But it's nice for Adele anyway. She seems so content." Kate jumped down from the chair and joined him.

Sitting on the floor, Tanner taped shut a cardboard box. "Cal's giving me a hand. I shouldn't need any more help than his. He could probably move this couch all by himself."

"I'll come do the girl stuff."

He laughed up at her. "I can't believe you said that."

"You know what I mean. Are you about done? I'm hungry."

"Yep. Where do you want to go?"

"I'll surprise you."

A short while later they stood outside next to Helen. Tanner shook his head. "Uh-uh. No way. You drive like you talk. Fast and distracted."

"Chicken."

"I'll drive and not for chauvinistic reasons."

"Then it won't be a surprise." She shoved him toward the passenger door. "Come on. I did all that packing for you. You owe me."

"I don't owe you by putting my life in danger." But he laughed and opened the door.

Kate ran around to her side and climbed in. Soon they were roaring down the street. He grabbed hold of the dashboard with both hands. She pushed his knee out of the way and shifted into third.

"You're taking up too much space," she said.

"These cars are made for elves, not regular people. Why are you shifting into fourth? Kate, this is a twenty-five-mile-an-hour zone!"

"No kidding? Hey, did you notice it smells like spring today? Look at all this melting snow." The streets were wet, dark, and glassy under the streetlights. "I love springtime, don't you? It's probably springtime in DC. I bet the crocuses have bloomed already."

"How often have you been there?"

"Four times. With my dad once when he had to go on business. I was only a kid, but that counts. I went when I was twelve for the national spelling bee. Didn't win, by the way. Then I went with a group from high school, junior year, government class. Mr. Collins went with us. Remember him?"

"Vaguely."

"Then I visited one January between college semesters. It really felt like home, Tanner. Have you ever been there?"

"Family vacation. I was six. Don't remember a whole lot."

They continued chatting, Tanner clinging through the entire 15-minute drive. She followed familiar streets through Rockville to an old neighborhood of mostly two-story middle-class houses, and screeched to a halt in front of one located in the center of the block.

"Kate, what restaurant is this?"

"My mom's kitchen!"

He shook a finger at her. "You could have warned me."

She grinned, reached over, and ruffled his hair. "What? Would you have combed your hair or something? No, you

would have had other plans. Come on in and meet the fam.
They're expecting us."

～

There were times when Tanner questioned his attraction
to Kate. He never liked carousel rides. He didn't like the
world spinning by out of focus...or slowing to a stop and
forcing him to readjust his equilibrium. But that was exactly
what life with Kate felt like.

Especially after a wild ride in Helen and a surprise stop to
meet her family.

To his relief, the "fam" gathered around the dining room
table appeared within the range of normal. They weren't all
redheaded elves.

As one they stood and noisily welcomed them. Kate,
whom they called Katelyn, didn't introduce him. The four
of them already knew who he was and heartily shook his
hand.

Kate's father, Dan, was the only one whose hair and eye
color resembled hers. He was shorter than Tanner, stocky,
friendlier than all outdoors. His wife, Carol, had chestnut
hair and dark eyes, though Kate's button nose and wide
mouth were mirrored in the woman. Danny Junior was
missing, or rather, they said, away at college. Patrick, 18,
and Sara, 11, looked like their mother. Kate was the shortest
of everyone, shorter even than her little sister.

They insisted that he and Katelyn sit and eat. The remains
of dinner still cluttered the table, but Carol disappeared for
a few minutes in the kitchen, returning with two plates piled
high with steaming roast beef, mashed potatoes, gravy, and
broccoli with cheese sauce.

Midway through his meal, Tanner realized he should have felt strange sitting there wolfing down a plateful of the best home-cooked meal he'd eaten in years while four strangers who were not eating tried to get to know him. But he didn't feel strange in the least.

And that was strange. It seemed little Katelyn had a touch of magic right here under her own roof.

About 9:30 she offered to take him home in her mother's car. She was spending the night there rather than driving back to Valley Oaks. While she spoke with her mother in the kitchen, Dan walked him to the front door, where he shook his hand again.

"She says you're just friends." The unblinking green eyes held his attention.

"Yes, sir." *Sir?* When was the last time he'd said "sir"?

"You seem like an honorable young man. I thought I'd ask about your intentions." He waited, his hand still clasped around Tanner's.

"Uh, none. Sir. I mean, we're friends. Rockville classmates who ended up in Valley Oaks for the time being. She's a wonderful person. There's nothing, uh, romantic between us, if that's what you're talking about. Does that answer your question? Sir?"

"Dad!" Kate yelled, striding through the living room and laughing. She wiggled between them, breaking the hand grip, and threw her arms around her father. "Don't ask him that stuff!"

"Good-looking macho man like this? You better believe I'm asking him those questions!" He hugged her back.

She planted a kiss on her dad's cheek and turned. "Ignore him, Tanner."

"Protective papa bear like this? You better believe I'm not ignoring him."

Dan roared. "You can keep him, Katelyn, with my blessing."

Hunched over with his arms crossed on his knees, Graham sat in a straight-backed chair beside Rand's bed. The window blinds were slanted, dulling the bright sunshine because it hurt Rand's eyes. Making a conscious effort to block out the drab room, he studied the dear old man. Rand was struggling after a difficult night, his skin a gray pallor. His hair was beginning to grow back in white tufts here and there. He almost could use a shave. Still in much pain, he dozed only fitfully, his head slightly elevated. His eyes fluttered open now.

Graham said, "Heather says the doctor is on his way."

Rand grunted something unintelligible.

They had talked earlier. The pain was intensifying, the cancer doing what it did best...growing, taking over cell by cell. Gradually, his pain medication would be increased. What Graham still struggled with was why they couldn't know it beforehand, before things were out of control again. He wrung his hands and tried to pray.

"How about some water, Pops?"

"Please."

Graham took a glass from a nearby tray and held it close enough for Rand to sip from the bent straw.

"Tell me about the dinner." His voice was raspier than ever.

"Again?" Graham smiled. "She cooked tofu with vegetables in a peanut sauce. Out of this world."

"I've never had tofu."

"I'll ask Adele to bring you some."

"It sounds nasty."

Graham laughed. "It isn't, not with her gourmet cooking skills."

"Candlelight?"

"Didn't I mention that? Candles. Soft music. Just the two of us."

"Kiss her yet?"

"We're only in phase one. That's not going to happen until phase three."

"I won't be around by then."

"And I may not be either. Miles to go before then."

"Is she like Samantha?"

An image of his wife flashed in his mind. Tall, slender, plain features, short dark hair, hazel eyes, shy except with her classroom children, not prone to chattiness. "She's nothing at all like Sammi. Are you up for hearing more? I learned something last night that could move us into phase two."

Rand smiled. "Her secret dream that only money can buy."

"She wants to build an apartment complex in Valley Oaks exclusively for seniors. Sort of an in-between step from house to nursing home. There's nothing like it for miles in any direction. It could draw on the rural areas. It'd be reasonably priced and have a coffee shop, drugstore, and even a movie theater. She already has the property scouted out south of town. There's some development out in that direction, more land going on the market soon."

Rand's smile widened. "Big dream!"

"She has talked with investors, but she hasn't found any interest. It wouldn't exactly be a big moneymaker."

"But it sure would help a lot of old folks, wouldn't it?"

"That's the idea."

"I like it. Where'd she get such an altruistic heart?"

"My guess is Jesus."

There was a knock on the partially closed door and someone pushed it open. "Knock, knock."

"Chelsea!" Graham exclaimed and stood up. "What are you doing here?"

"No school today. Really. Technically there is no school for anyone today. Mom's put me to work, free of charge. Mind if I come in and meet your friend?"

She was already in.

He glanced at Rand. His eyes were large behind the thick glasses as he stared at the young girl. She neared the bed now. Her long curly hair was pulled back in a low ponytail. She wore a long dark green skirt and baggy purple sweater. Her smile lit up her face. The spitting image of her mother.

"Hi, Mr. Jennings." Like most people when talking to the elderly residents, she raised her voice.

"Addie?" Rand's voice was a rough whisper. Tears welled in his eyes. "Addie?"

She lightly touched his arm. "I'm Adele's daughter. It's so nice to meet you. You know, Graham has been keeping company with my mother. I thought I should check out his good friend. Can't have just anybody courting her, you know."

Chatty, just like her mother.

Rand's tears dripped from the corners of his eyes.

Chelsea picked up the stainless steel pitcher from the tray. "I'll get you some fresh water."

Graham took it from her. "I'll do it. That's all right."

The tears were flowing, puddling on his cheeks and pillow. "Graham," he choked, flailing an arm.

"Mr. Jennings?"

Graham gently grasped Rand's arm with one hand and set the water pitcher back on the tray with the other. "Rand, it's okay. Chelsea, run along now, please. We're having a rough day."

"Can I do something?"

Rand was blubbering now, thrashing about.

"No!" Graham called over his shoulder, louder than he intended. "We'll be fine."

He thought he heard the clicking of the door shutting as he took the small man into his arms. "Shhh. It's okay, Pops. It's okay."

~

Chelsea burst through Adele's open doorway. "Mom!"

"What's wrong?" She walked around her desk.

Chelsea's face was scrunched up, a sure sign she was distraught. "I just met Mr. Jennings and he started crying and he called me Addie!"

She hugged her daughter. "He calls me Addie sometimes. Graham told him about my pottery, and for some reason he picked up on that name. He had an especially bad night."

"You could have warned me."

Adele looked up at the teenager already three inches taller. Her height was one of only two things Adele recognized as being inherited from that young man she had known 18 years ago. The other was a left ear with an upper ridge folded slightly inward.

"Actually, honey, I thought you would help him feel better. You're always so good with the folks."

"Not this guy."

"Well, they all respond differently to their physical pain. Some don't want to see a young chipper face."

"Mom, it seemed different than that somehow. It was like the instant he saw me, he burst into tears. I mean the *instant* he saw me. He was crying before I said *anything*. I tried to ignore it and just jabbered nonsense. He got worse! Oh, Mom, I don't know how you stand this job!"

She hugged her daughter tightly. "Guess this was a little more penance than you bargained for today."

"I felt like I did something wrong."

"I'm sure you didn't, Chels. Was Graham still there?"

"Yes, thank goodness. I kept trying to be polite, and he finally just told me to go. You know what he was doing when I shut the door?"

"Holding Mr. Jennings."

"How'd you know?"

She smiled. "That's just the kind of man he is. If he hadn't come over the other night and hugged me when he did, you and I never would have eaten *and* you would have been on daily volunteer duty here until the day you graduate!"

Chelsea rolled her eyes. "I owe him. Maybe I should bake him some cookies or something. Does he like cookies?"

"Oatmeal with raisins and walnuts are his favorite."

"You know that already? Getting a little personal awfully quick, Mom."

Not as quickly as I'd like.

Twenty

Late Friday afternoon Kate parked Helen in the alley behind the large brick building that housed the pharmacy, video store, and florist. She carefully gathered a bouquet of helium balloons, tucked a potted deffenbachia plant under an arm and a plastic container full of cookies under the other, and got out.

Two pickup trucks sat next to the opened back door of the pharmacy. She guessed one belonged to Cal and the other to Tanner's brother, who wasn't available to help but offered his truck for the occasion. She maneuvered her way around them and walked inside without ringing the bell.

It was a back room with a desk, a kitchenette area, stacked boxes in a corner, and a closed door that probably led into the pharmacy. Voices floated down a staircase on the left. She climbed the steps.

The door at the top led directly into a kitchen where Tanner's table and chairs already sat. Beyond that the space accommodated a living room furnished with his couch, end table, lamp, recliner, and television. The walls appeared freshly painted, the hardwood floor polished.

Tanner emerged from a hallway. "Kate! Hi."

"Hey. This is great!"

He nodded. "I think it'll work. What have you got there?"

She handed him the balloons and plastic container. "Housewarming. The cookies are from my mom. I'll put the plant right here by the window."

161

"Thanks. I can't remember the last time I had balloons. Or homemade cookies."

She heard his wistful tone and wondered if he'd ever had any. "How do you know they're homemade?"

"I met your mom."

"Hi, Kate." Cal joined them.

"Hi, Cal. How'd the move go?"

"Walk in the park. Tanner's got a fourth of what Lia had crammed in here. I think we're finished. Hey, nice piece in today's paper on the village board meeting."

"Thanks."

"Tanner, if we're finished I'm outa here. I'm going to go kiss the pharmacist, and then I'm picking up my little girl at her friend's. I promised her ice cream, but don't tell Lia if you see her."

Tanner shook Cal's hand. "I appreciate all your help."

"No problem. Glad to have you in town. Bye."

"Goodbye."

Cal disappeared through the doorway leading to the staircase.

Kate draped her jacket over a table chair. "He's sweet."

"Sweet doesn't come to mind when I think of an ox." He chuckled as he tied the balloons to another chair. "He did pick up the couch by himself."

"Jesus is like that. Sweet and strong as an ox. He can carry any load. No complaints. He just says give Him some more."

Tanner gave her a quizzical look, his eyebrows almost touching. "I'll have to think about that one."

Thank You, Lord. He's thinking. She leaned over, putting her face between his and the knot he was still tying. "Sooo?" she prompted in a singsong voice. "Tell me?"

His grin said he inferred what she was talking about. "I signed the papers."

She clapped her hands, whooped, danced around in a circle, and then she flung her arms around his neck. "Yay! Congratulations!"

He laughed, hugging her back. "Keep it down. Lia requested I not throw wild parties while the store's open right beneath us."

She punched his arm and whooped quietly.

He tapped her nose once. "Thank you."

"Okay, put me to work." She spotted boxes on the counter. "I bet those are dishes, and I bet the cupboards are clean."

"Have at it. I'm putting the computer together in the spare bedroom. Which has a border of stenciled cat silhouettes on all four walls."

She laughed, ripping the tape off a box. "Where do you want things to go?"

"In the cupboards."

"Any preference? Right, left, up, down?"

"Nope. I'll find them."

"You are so easygoing. I don't know why some pretty young thing hasn't snapped you right up."

"It's a mystery."

"Do you like spaghetti?"

"Love it."

"I'll walk over to Swensen's soon and get some things. Then I'll cook for you." She glanced over her shoulder. "And don't go stuffing money in my jacket again."

"I promise I won't if you're cooking for two."

"Am I invited?"

He grinned. "Since when did you need an invitation?"

She threw a wad of packing paper at him. "Since your bachelor pad suddenly opened up two blocks from my place!"

Adele heard his footsteps echoing in the hall coming toward her office. It was late at Fox Meadow, almost eight o'clock, and things were winding down. Most of the residents were in their rooms.

She felt that funny misbeat in her throat as she anticipated the moment he would stop in front of her open door. That feeling couldn't keep up, could it? Maybe she had a heart condition...which flared up only when Graham Logan was in the vicinity. That was a heart condition, all right.

"Adele." He stood in her doorway.

"Hi. How's he doing?"

"Resting quietly now." He came in and sat in the chair across from her desk.

"I peeked in once. You were both asleep."

"Is Chelsea all right? I hope he didn't frighten her."

"She's fine. It's part of working here. She knows now what she doesn't want to do with the rest of her life."

"That makes two of us. You, on the other hand, are a saint."

"No, just different. Have you eaten?"

"I ate some of Rand's dinner."

She walked around the desk, picked up her coat folded atop it, and reached for his hand. "Come on. How about some leftovers?"

He smiled softly as he stood, his fingers closing around hers. "Sounds perfect."

She flipped off the light switch as they passed it. "I sent Chelsea home awhile ago." They walked down the hall. "There may even be some oatmeal cookies, considering the fact she was grounded from about everything except baking."

"Mmm...oatmeal cookies. With raisins and walnuts I hope?"

"Naturally." She squeezed his hand.

"Why didn't you go home with her?"

"I'm still catching up from that unscheduled day off. And you were still here. I knew I could get a ride."

"What if I hadn't stopped by your office?"

She leaned against his arm. "Not even a chance of that."

"You shouldn't know me so well already."

"Graham, I don't know you at all. I only know..." She closed her mouth, cutting off the words.

He squeezed her hand now as they reached the deserted lobby. He took her coat and held it open for her. "You only know what?"

She slipped her arms into the coat and buttoned it.

He put a finger under her chin and tipped it. "Only know what?"

She searched his eyes for permission to make a fool of herself. Up until that moment he had been distracted, preoccupied. But now...now she sensed all of his energies were directed at her. It was an unnerving sensation that threw her heart rate into double time.

"I only know," she whispered, "that I can't breathe quite right when I'm with you."

"Adele!" Gracie's voice startled her.

Graham dropped his hand, and they turned as one to the weekend supervisor approaching from across the lobby.

A few minutes later, Gracie's questions answered, they hurried through the parking lot. Adele smiled to herself. The moment had passed.

Thank You, Lord. I really did not want our first kiss to be in the lobby of Fox Meadow Care Center!

Graham sat in Adele's living room smelling delectable scents of warm cookies and curry emanating from the kitchen. He held the newspaper and turned its pages, his eyes seeing words, his mind not comprehending a one.

It was a battle of the voices.

He had almost kissed her. He had almost *kissed* her! Exactly what he had vowed—just a few hours earlier—*not* to do.

But you want to. And she wants you to.

It's too soon. The charade isn't finished yet.

She's a strong woman. She will understand.

And then what? Love her like I loved Sammi? So that when she dies I can be a total zombie for a few years?

Who says she's dying?

Daily possibility with everybody. I'm not signing up for it again.

Where's your trust?

Let's just get through Rand first.

"Graham!"

He jumped and snapped the newspaper away from his face. "Chelsea!"

"Sorry, you must have been really engrossed in the sports page." She sat in a chair opposite him. "Dinner's almost ready. Did I do something to disturb Mr. Jennings today?"

You showed up. He wasn't prepared. "Uh, no, no. Don't take it personally. His pain… I can't imagine what he's going through. He just wasn't feeling well enough for company."

"I felt really bad. I thought maybe he didn't like me teasing about you and Mom. Like maybe it reminded him of your wife."

"Uh, no. Actually, he's happy I have a new, um, friend."

She laughed, an echo of her mother's lilt. "Actually, I am too. She would have been mad at me for a *much* longer time if you hadn't shown up."

He folded the newspaper. "Really?"

"She said so and I know so. She can be a tough old broad when she needs to be. And she has needed to be, what with raising me all by herself."

"Do you ever wonder about your father?"

"Oh, yeah. She never says much about him or her family. I know just a little more than zilch. My dad's last name is something in unpronounceable German. His first name is Gregor. Not much to go on, huh?"

"You'd be surprised. With the Internet these days, there are ways. You know he was in Europe eighteen years ago. She could tell you where they were."

"She hasn't gotten to the point of when I was conceived. She keeps saying I'm not old enough yet."

"How about your grandparents?"

"My grandmother is dead. She did volunteer work. My grandfather was involved in arbitrage and made tons of money. R.J. Chandler doesn't sound like someone I'd care to meet. She was an only child, but she could have had aunts and uncles and cousins."

"Your grandfather could have changed by now. Not many people can stay angry forever."

She shrugged. "Then he probably would have found us. We're in the phone book. Let's go eat."

He followed her through the house. They found Adele at the stove.

"Hi, you two. It's almost ready. Chels, why don't you take those things to the dining room?"

She picked up some dishes and disappeared.

Graham went up behind Adele, placed his hands on her shoulders, and whispered in her ear, "She's delightful. You should un-ground her."

She laughed. "In your dreams."

That wasn't exactly what he had in mind for his dreams.

Twenty-One

"You're sure you don't mind?" Adele's eyes sparkled and a smile tugged at her mouth, threatening to reveal those dimples in their entirety.

Graham wondered if there could ever be anything he minded this woman asking him. He seriously doubted it. "I don't mind in the least."

Her smile came then, and he knew he shouldn't be there.

They climbed from his car. It was Saturday afternoon, and they were parked near the video store Tanner Carlucci had recently purchased. As a welcoming gesture, Adele was delivering cookies.

After that they were driving 30 miles to a Swedish historical museum for him to do research. That was also Adele's idea. It had taken him a moment to get the connection. Research?

He shouldn't be there. Between the allure of her dimples, the stress of Rand's decline, the dread of the approaching anniversary of Sammi's death, and the guilt of his deception—compounded now by a trip to a museum—he was walking a tightrope. One misstep and he'd be taking a nose dive into emotional overload. Undisciplined territory. What had happened to his discipline?

"Graham?" She smiled, standing in front of the store. "Coming?"

His discipline? Undermined by pair of dimples.

Inside they were greeted by Kate and Tanner, who both wore jeans and sweatshirts splattered with paint. Two teenage boys stood at the counter, filling out what looked like application forms. A big bearded guy and a little girl with black hair were reading video cases. The girl appeared about eight or nine.

"Cookies!" Kate exclaimed.

"Thanks." Tanner accepted the plastic container and set them on the counter next to a plate of plastic-covered lemon bars.

"Mr. Carlucci," one of the boys said, "you shouldn't tempt us like that."

"Help yourself, guys."

They eagerly dug in.

"If you don't want a job." Tanner laughed at their dumbfounded expressions. "Just kidding."

Adele asked, "Kate, did you bake in the middle of the night?"

"Oh, I didn't make the lemon bars. Lia made those. Graham, have you met Lia's husband, Cal?"

The bearded guy came over, greeted Adele, and shook his hand. "Cal Huntington. That's my daughter, Chloe."

"Graham Logan. Nice to meet you."

"Do you live in Valley Oaks?"

The guy was a cop. It showed in his clear focused eyes and no-nonsense demeanor.

"Temporarily. A close friend of mine moved into Fox Meadow."

Adele added, "He's a history professor on sabbatical. We're going over to the Swedish museum so he can do some research. Tanner, show me where you're painting."

Adele followed Tanner and Kate toward a back room. Graham knew he wasn't dismissed yet.

Cal said, "Have you got an apartment in town?"

"Yeah. There was a furnished one available on a month by month basis. I don't know how long Rand will be around."

A flicker of compassion in the green eyes. "Sorry to hear that. So where do you teach?"

"Northwestern."

"Been there awhile?"

"Awhile. And what do you do?"

"Deputy sheriff."

Bingo. "Now that sounds like an interesting job."

"Oh, lots of digging for facts, just like you. Hey, my father-in-law teaches history at Northwestern. You probably know him."

"It's a huge department."

The other three were reentering the main room.

"He's in American history too. Older guy. Thin. Long hair. You know, how most of you professors look. His name's Lawrence Neuman."

"Oh, yeah. I know who he is." Graham smiled. "Seems like a nice guy. I've seen your mother-in-law in the library." He remembered Adele telling him about her. "How are they as in-laws?" *Let's move it, Adele.*

"They're good ones."

At last Adele said, "We better go. The museum doesn't stay open very late. See you."

Goodbyes were said all around, and then they left the store.

Deputy sheriff. Graham shouldn't have been there.

Tanner closed the door on his young applicants and said to Chloe, "You can borrow any videos or DVDs you want."

Kate smiled to herself. The guy might be short on business savvy, but he was thoughtful. The little girl had been hinting for 20 minutes.

Chloe turned to Cal, her big blue eyes growing larger. "Daddy! Can I?"

"Sure. Go pick one out."

"He said *videos*. Maybe I can have two? I know what Mommy likes."

"All right, two." He grinned as she skipped down the aisle, and then he turned to them. "Kate, what's with the new guy and Adele?"

Even if she hadn't been inclined to answer, she would have. There was something about the man, even out of uniform. "I guess you could say they're dating. They both spend most of their time at the nursing home."

"Is his friend really dying?"

Kate exchanged a look with Tanner. "Well, he lives out there and Adele says he has cancer."

"And she thinks he teaches at Northwestern."

"Doesn't he?"

"You heard him say he knows Lawrence Neuman?"

They nodded.

"My father-in-law is Jack Neuman and he teaches economics. My mother-in-law spends 99 percent of her time in a library office at a computer. People don't see her."

"You think he's a fraud?" Kate asked.

"I think he's a *cop*. Chloe," he called, pulling his wallet from a back pocket, "you ready? Tanner, how much do we owe you?"

"Nothing. I'm not in business yet."

Cal laughed. "Thanks. Hey, don't say anything to Adele, all right? I'll give my father-in-law a call. Maybe there is a Lawrence Neuman who teaches history. If not, there's no law against cops having friends at Fox Meadow. See you later."

After they'd gone, Kate and Tanner stared at each other with wide eyes.

Kate asked, "Where'd he come up with cop?"

"Maybe they have a special radar between them or something that sends out cop signals only other cops can pick up."

She laughed but quickly sobered. "Do you think Adele's in danger? I thought Graham seemed like a really great guy."

"Well, we know he's got a friend out at the home, so I doubt he's an ax murderer looking for a victim. Cal has to be suspicious about strangers in this small town. It's his job. I remember him sniffing around me when I first started coaching. Kate, you're getting that snoop look in your eye."

"I am not."

"You are." He wagged a finger in front of her face. "You think there's a story about Graham Logan."

"You never know! Is it cookie-break time yet?"

Tanner beat her to the counter and grabbed two. "I think there's still coffee in the thermos. Want some?"

"Please." She helped herself to a lemon bar and an oatmeal cookie, and sat on the floor. "I still can't understand why Graham would yank his friend out of Maryland in the dead of Midwest winter when he could have just as easily moved there to be with him. With the Internet, you don't need a Swedish museum located down the road."

"I'm telling you, there's no story." Tanner poured coffee into their mugs and joined her. "May I change the subject?"

She nodded and took a bite of lemon bar.

"I noticed another Jesus thing about Cal today. His beard."

Kate stopped chewing.

"You know, even if all those paintings aren't true depictions, Jesus had to have a beard. I doubt men shaved back then. For certain, itinerant preachers wouldn't have shaved. Walking through desert and sleeping outdoors? No way."

She chewed, nodding.

"But then there's that suspicious streak. Does that fit? Was Jesus suspicious?"

She shook head and swallowed. "He didn't need to be. He knew everything. No secrets from Him."

"Hmm. Then if Graham turns out to be a cop, Cal knew the truth. I'd say Cal's got an inside track on the character of Jesus. A sweet bearded ox of a man who knows everything."

Kate laughed until tears rolled down her cheeks.

Adele sat at the old upright piano in the corner of her living room, leafing through sheet music and surreptitiously studying Graham. His professor's image was in place: He wore a sweater and cords, and his attention was riveted on a local history book. He sat in the overstuffed armchair, his stocking feet propped on the ottoman. The subtle agitation that had plagued him all day seemed gone at last.

That afternoon, after leaving the video store, they had visited the museum. While examining displays of nineteenth-century farm equipment and historical documents, he had excused himself three times. He went outdoors and made cell phone calls, each lasting quite awhile. In way of explanation he said dying was a legal quagmire.

On the return trip home, they detoured into Rockville, picking up Chinese carryout, a favorite of Rand's. The three of them ate dinner in his room at Fox Meadow, visiting until the older man had tired.

Making calls during their time together was atypical of Graham, but other things were even more uncharacteristic. Outwardly he maintained his usual subdued demeanor. Yet he occasionally lost the train of their conversation. His mind seemed distracted, his eyes focusing on something she couldn't see. With Rand he fidgeted. With her...he maintained his distance...in every way.

She quit looking for another piece of music to play and walked over to him now. As she sat on the ottoman near his feet, he looked up, peering over the rims of his half glasses.

He closed the book. "Midwesterners are a strange lot."

"You sound as if you're not one. Weren't you born in Chicago?"

"Buffalo, New York."

"So you're a settler, just like those Swedes." Smiling, she took one of his hands in both of hers and held it on her knees. "Graham. Do you want to talk about it?"

He stared at her a long moment before speaking. "I can tell by the look in your eye you're not about to accept the answer, 'There's nothing to talk about.'"

"If that's your answer, I can live with it. But what I can't live with is pretending nothing has changed. So I asked."

"I think the third thing I first admired about you was your point-blank attitude. Do you want to know the first two things?"

"Graham, you're not answering my question."

"They're part of the answer. The first thing was how very pretty you are. The second was how absolutely delightful you are."

She lowered her eyes.

"Adele, dear, you're blushing." He slid his feet from the ottoman and planted them on the floor.

She felt him shift and lean toward her, but she didn't raise her eyes. Flattery was like a foreign object intruding upon her mindset. It didn't belong there. Compliments concerning an accomplishment for which she was responsible was another thing. Admiration for her looks or the way she spoke had never been a part of her life. Not counting Will's compliments, which were usually when, in his opinion, she wore something especially suitable.

Graham placed a finger under her chin and lifted her face. "I'm sure you hear those things all the time. I didn't mean for it to sound like insincere sweet talk—"

"I've never heard those things, and you sound so sincere, I don't know how to respond."

He removed his hand and smiled. "You don't have to."

"You're right. Now getting back to my question?"

"If I recall, you asked if I want to talk about it. My answer is no, I don't, but yes, I need to. I've been distracted today. I take it you're wondering why?"

She nodded.

"It's Rand's imminent death. It's the fifth anniversary of Sammi's death. It's being more vulnerable than I've ever been in my entire life. It's finding you lodged in my heart while I'm not free to accept you there right now because I'm afraid to trust my feelings. It's keeping a physical space between us, thinking that will dislodge you when the whole time all I want is to kiss you."

She bit her lip.

"Forgive me for not being as direct as you are."

"I'd say your answer was about as direct as you can get."

"There's still much you don't know about me."

She let go of his hand, slipped her arms around his neck, and whispered in his ear, "Graham, I've got the rest of my life to find out."

He held her close. "Let's hope it doesn't take that long."

Twenty-Two

"Tanner, just sit still." Kate held the camera to her eye while he kept repositioning himself in exaggerated poses atop the video store's counter. She lowered it, waiting for him to finish his antics. "No, we don't want *The Thinker.*"

He removed his fist from his forehead, pulled his feet up and sat back on his haunches, scratching under an arm and making wild noises.

"Monkey is no good either."

"This is an orangutan."

"Tanner, you can be so infuriating! Just sit cross-legged. A smile would be nice. You don't want to scare customers away."

They had finished painting walls. Rusty had called and offered to bring over a late dinner, ribs from the Rib House. In the meantime, Kate was taking notes and a photo for next week's article in the *Times* about the store's new ownership.

"All right," he said, stilled himself and smiled.

She put the camera to her eye again, focusing in on his face. The symmetry truly was extraordinary. Square jaw with five o'clock shadow. Perfectly shaped mouth, full lips but not overly so. Strong nose. Beautiful brown-black eyes that weren't squinty, set off with long lashes. Masculine brows. Thick black hair combed back with mousse. Broad shoulders draped in a black sweatshirt, sleeves pushed up.

"Kate."

"Hold on." A smile that must have broken a hundred hearts.

177

"Kilpatrick!"

"Sorry." She lowered the camera and looked him in the eye. "You know you really are handsome."

"You've only just noticed?" He teased. He wasn't a vain man, even if he did use mousse.

"Yeah, I did." She raised the camera again, breaking off the eye contact. "And I rarely, and I mean *rarely*, notice such a thing. Smile, Mr. Entrepreneur."

After she took a few shots, he hopped off the counter. "When was the last time you noticed?"

She replaced the lens cap and put the camera in its case. "David Webb. Sixth grade. He only had eyes for Susie Hall."

He laughed. "Guess that makes me kind of an oddball?"

"No."

"Sure it does." He turned off the lights, and they walked through the back room. "If I'm only one out of two in your twenty-nine years, that makes me odd."

Kate didn't see it that way. She saw it as something...significant. Something she should tell Beth about, but something she didn't want to tell Beth about because her friend tended to read more into things than existed.

She followed Tanner out into the alley and waited while he locked the door. They walked a short distance along the alley to the next door, the one leading to his apartment.

He said, "Of course, odd is a good thing. I mean, look at you. You're odd and you're a good thing."

They went inside and he followed her up the stairs. She said, "I don't think the two necessarily go hand in hand."

"Well, they do with you. What's wrong? You got strangely quiet all of a sudden."

"Nothing." The truth was she felt light-headed all of a sudden.

She pushed open the door at the top of the staircase and flipped on his kitchen light.

"Kate, I'm just teasing when I say you're odd."

"I know, but I am odd. I learned that in high school. There were a handful of people I connected with. A handful out of eight hundred and seventy-four."

"Like I said, it's a good thing. Go sit on the couch. I have a surprise for you. Maybe it'll cheer you up."

"I'm fine."

"Sit down." He disappeared down the hall.

Kate went over to the leather couch and checked her paint-spattered jeans before sitting. Nothing rubbed off.

She sat, remembering for some reason how it had hurt at times growing up out of sync with most of her classmates. It wasn't until halfway through her junior year that she realized the social scene didn't matter, the lack of dates didn't matter. What mattered was that she knew God's love, and she knew that with the brain He had given her, she could probably do whatever she wanted to do.

So why did it hurt now? And what did it have to do with noticing that Tanner was physically attractive? Attraction in that way only interfered with friendships. It confused the dynamics. Not that she had been attracted, but there had been two guys along the way. Perfectly good friends until they started behaving like romantic fools, sending flowers and telling her she was beautiful. She still didn't talk to either one of them.

Kate pushed her glasses up and blew out a loud breath that fanned her bangs. Maybe her body was craving protein. She had consumed way too many cookies that afternoon. Inhaled too many paint fumes.

"Ta-da." Tanner stood before her, holding out a box. Its yellow wrapping paper obviously not put on professionally.

"What is this?"

"A thank-you gift for all your help."

"Tanner," she protested.

"It's not a Galahad thing, though I do want to say you mean a lot to me, Kate Kilpatrick. I am grateful for your friendship." He laid the box on her lap and sat in a chair. "Open it."

"I'm grateful for *your* friendship. I owe you for helping me adjust to Valley Oaks."

"For pete's sake, Kate! Just accept the thing. You're always wanting to make sure you're not in debt, and you go overboard trying to outgive other people."

"I do?"

"Yes, you do. And now you're taking away all my fun in giving you something."

"I'm sorry."

He set his jaw and his eyes narrowed.

All right. "Wow, it's heavy. Nice wrapping job."

His expression remained the same.

Be quiet, Kate. She held her breath and tore off the paper. The box was plain cardboard with the ends taped shut. She pried open one end and reached inside. Her fingers landed on soft leather, and she knew it was a serious gift. Not daring to look at him, she pulled out a black bag that looked like a briefcase. From its weight, it was evident the bag wasn't empty.

"Oh my gosh!" she whispered. She put a hand to her mouth and blinked at him. "It isn't."

He was biting his lower lip, his brows raised. He gave a slight nod.

She unzipped the case and saw the sleek black object that she had only dreamed of holding in her own hands. And then she gasped. "A laptop computer! Tanner!"

As she raised the monitor and gazed at the keyboard, he sat down beside her. "The sales clerk said women seem to prefer this one over some others. But if you don't like it—"

"Oh, Tanner! What's not to like? Look at this." She ran her fingers gently over the keys. "I can't let you—"

"Why not?"

"How can I ever repay—"

He clamped a hand over her mouth. "What did I just tell you?"

Tears came to her eyes and he lowered his hand. "Tanner, thank you. Thank you so much."

He smiled. "You're welcome. Now, that wasn't so hard was it?"

To let someone outside of her immediate family so generously love her? Actually, it had been incredibly hard.

Tanner set the table, watching Kate out of the corner of his eye. She was still on the couch, playing with the laptop, calling out to him as she discovered different features. He knew his enjoyment surpassed hers. She was fun to observe, like a little kid once she had dealt with the discomfort of accepting the gift. Her glasses would slide down, she'd shove them back up, clap, and giggle. As usual, her shiny copper hair was pulled back, stray ends sticking out of a large clip. White paint streaked one side of her head. In the dim light of lamps, her sprinkle of indistinct freckles didn't show. Her soft, creamy skin was like a child's, untarnished by a lifetime of stupid choices.

The gift was totally unexpected, yet something she would use every day. Something she could not afford. Something that would not be in her parents' budget. Something he could give her for the simple reason that he wanted to treat her.

Especially in light of what was coming.

The doorbell rang and he went downstairs to let Rusty in.

"Well!" she greeted him, laughing. "I guess we won't be disturbing the neighbors, considering you don't have any."

"Hi. Come on in." He took two bags from her and reveled in the scent of barbecue sauce. "Thanks for bringing this."

She followed him up the steps. "You're welcome. Do you have free run of the pharmacy?"

"No, the back door that leads into it is always kept locked. Here we are." He shut the staircase door behind her.

"Nice," she huffed, catching her breath. "The lace curtains are you. Hi, Kate."

"Rusty! Look at this." She held out the computer. "Laptop."

"No kidding." She went over to inspect it. "They make me nervous, but I know you've been wanting one."

"Tanner gave it to me."

Rusty glanced at him, back at Kate, and then she settled her gaze on him. "How'd I miss it?"

Tanner exchanged a look with Kate and asked, "Miss what?"

"You two."

"Us two?"

She barked a laugh. "Do I have to spell it out?"

No, she didn't have to, but he knew Kate would bolt if there was even a hint of courtship in the air. And he didn't want her bolting.

"Rusty," he said, "it's a laptop, not flowers or candy or diamonds." *True, she's changed my life, but I'm not going there.*

Kate said, "Rusty, you didn't think—" She hooted. "Us? Not in a million years. He needs some tall model next to him."

"And what's a tall model going to do with a friend he gives laptops to?"

"Okay!" Tanner interrupted. "Let's eat!"

Faced with the imminent consumption of ribs from the Rib House, both Kate and Rusty dropped the subject.

Midway through the meal, Rusty said, "Katy-girl, I've got some good news. You know the DC contact I mentioned?"

She nodded.

"Jack came through. He knows a woman with the *Post* who said—"

"The *Washington Post!?*"

Rusty grinned. "And she said she'd love to show you around and could probably get you into a press conference."

Kate's jaw dropped. "Wow! Rusty! Thank you. I can't believe it. I've never had that kind of a lead."

"And imagine, it came from right here in Valley Oaks. You just never know."

"Tanner, it's another piece of your magic!"

"Looks that way."

"Wow," Kate repeated. "I feel like it's my birthday. Did somebody move it up? Or is it Christmas in March?"

Just hold that thought, hon. Tanner figured Rusty's news about leaving wouldn't be received with the same gratitude.

After dinner, while Kate cleaned up the paper plates and Tanner made coffee, Rusty inspected the apartment. Eventually they settled in the living room with their mugs, and he knew it was coming. He felt uneasy. *God, if You're listening, Your Kate needs some help here.*

Rusty coughed. "Well, I have some good news too." She took a sip of her coffee, and then she looked at Kate. "You know about my friend who made that contact for you. He made one for me too." She paused. "I've got a job in Chicago."

Kate cried, "Rusty, that's great! Congratulations!"

Tanner stayed mute. He already knew.

"Thanks. There's a little fly in the ointment, though. I have to go next week."

"Go?"

"Move. To Chicago."

"How can you do that?"

"Fairly easily. Never did plan on retiring here."

"How can Fred replace you so quickly?" Fred Wilton was the owner/publisher.

"He agrees with me. The new managing editor is right under our noses."

Tanner saw an atypical calmness settle over Kate. The ramifications were sinking in.

Rusty went on. "You're perfectly capable of taking over. You run circles around me. You write better and faster than I do. You're familiar with Valley Oaks, its rhythms, its spirit. Your camera skills—"

"Rusty! I can't do this. You teach me something new every day!"

"No, I don't, Katy-girl. I just reveal something you already know. You're ready. It's like you already know how to swim. This is your shove into the pool. And, hey, you'll get paid for it."

"Shouldn't somebody ask me if I want this?"

"It's basically what you're already doing."

"I'm an intern. I'm out of here in nine weeks!"

"As of this Friday, you're the editor. Nine weeks is plenty of time for Fred to find someone else."

"I don't want to be the managing editor of a small-town newspaper!"

"It's temporary."

Kate sprang to her feet and grabbed her jacket. "Temporary is too long. It's always too long." She rushed through the kitchen and jerked open the door.

As her feet clattered on the steps, Tanner heard her burst into tears. He stood. "I'd better go and make sure she gets home all right. It's only two blocks, but it's late."

Rusty picked up her own coat and followed him down the stairs. "And I need a smoke. I figured she'd balk at first, but she'll be all right once she gets used to the idea. She'll realize it's a good opportunity. It'll look great on her résumé. But what did she mean about temporary being too long?"

"I'm not sure." They hurried outside. "Thanks again for dinner. I'll see you before you go."

"Right. Bye."

Tanner jogged to the corner of the alley. Rounding it, he spotted Kate down the block, running as fast as her short legs would carry her. He followed, keeping his distance, watching until she entered the house.

Hesitating, he stood on the curb across the street. Much as he wanted to go knock on the door, he sensed Kate was the type of girl who preferred to do her crying in private. He would respect that. For now.

Twenty-Three

During the opening hymn at the Sunday morning church service, Graham exchanged a look across the aisle and two pews up with Deputy Cal Huntington. The look indicated they would be talking in the near future.

Adele smiled up at him and nudged her shoulder against his arm, reminding him the hymnal was open for a reason. He joined in the singing.

Last night they had agreed on maintaining the status quo. In his vulnerability, he knew he was growing dependent on her company. In the norm, he would have fought against that. But then, he was losing sight of what the norm was anymore. He never imagined God granting him the ability or desire to love again. That it was happening under the present circumstances completely bewildered him.

Jesus, I don't have a choice. Is that it? I have to trust that You're in this.

Adele tugged on his sleeve, pulling him to sit down. When he settled next to her on the pew, she slid her hand into his. Status quo meant they still held hands while he averted his eyes from her lips. For how long this could go on, he didn't know.

But then I really don't know much.

She was incredibly naïve. He kept looking for cracks in it, for a glimmer of falsehood, of distrust, of evidence that she believed the world owed her one. He couldn't find any of that, increasing his desire to protect her. The discombobu-

186

lating thing of it all was that he knew the source of her danger: It lay in Graham Logan.

He paid the service only partial attention. What might appear as distraction to Adele was simply him praying unceasingly for forgiveness.

After the service, as they greeted others in the crowded foyer, a woman caught Adele by the arm. Adele introduced her as Lia Huntington. A moment later the women were head-to-head and Graham was catching a nod from Cal, who stood near the front door. Two minutes later they were in the parking lot, enjoying a breath of air laced with an early hint of spring.

"Graham." Cal wasn't smiling. "I was hoping you might fill me in. Save me a lot of time from trying to figure out why the dean of Northwestern's history department has never heard of you or Lawrence Neuman. Or how, as of late last night, your name appears on their Website's faculty list. Or where you got the strings to pull that off."

"You work fast, Officer."

His face went rigid.

Of all the schools in Illinois, I pick Northwestern, which just happens to have connections in Valley Oaks? God must be in it. There must be a reason for this conversation. Perhaps for the simple fact that he was growing weary of carrying the secret alone.

"All right." Graham smiled. "I appreciate you not bringing this up in front of Adele. Do you mind uncrossing your arms? Maybe smile a little, like we're anticipating the Bulls game today? It's a long story."

He didn't budge. "Give me the short version."

"My name is Graham Logan. But I'm not from Chicago, nor am I a professor at Northwestern or anywhere. Five years ago my wife was killed, an act of revenge against me."

The face behind the beard softened. Graham knew the information he was about to divulge would go no further until it was time.

Kate heard a commotion in the other room, but she couldn't pinpoint its source. She was lying on the couch in her sitting room, wrapped like a cocoon in a comforter, keeping her head as motionless as possible. Old-fashioned heavy draperies were drawn across two windows, shutting out bright afternoon sunlight.

The pain and nausea had started last night as she ran home from Tanner's place, her head along with every muscle and joint feeling as though she'd been hit by a Mack truck. It wasn't from a truck or the flu. She knew it was her mind and body shutting down, a defense mechanism keeping her from having to deal with the full force of reality.

She slept as if anesthetized, another nifty defense mechanism that didn't leave her in the least bit rested. The dizzying head pain and nausea were there when she awoke along with a bone-deep chill. Awhile ago she had attempted going to the kitchen, dragging the comforter from her bed behind her, but she had made it only as far as the couch.

It didn't matter. She would deal with life later. Her emotional turmoil would dissipate. She would seek God's perspective and try to accept it little by little. For now she simply wanted life to go away.

She heard the swoosh of the wooden door sliding into its pocket between the walls.

"Kate?" It was Adele's voice coming from a great distance.

She didn't respond, a combination of not wanting to and being unable to.

Muffled voices. The door swooshing again, clicking shut. "Hey. Are you in there?"

Tanner? No, not Tanner! He complicated things to no end.

She felt the comforter lift from her face. She opened the one eye not scrunched against the pillow.

Oh, no! Despite the fact her glasses lay in the other room, she saw it. *He's still cute.*

"Hi." He was eye level with her, from a sitting position on the floor beside the couch. "Missed you at church. Yeah, I went. I even went in and sat down after Adele said you were home sick."

She blinked her one eye.

"Flu?"

"It's contagious," she mumbled.

He smiled. "I doubt that."

He knew.

"Kate, I brought over your new toy. I thought you might want to play with it."

Her eye filled. "I'm dizzy," she whispered. "I can't see straight. My stomach hurts so bad."

"I can fix that." He disappeared from her limited view.

The door swooshed open, slamming against the far end of its space. "Oops. Sorry."

She winced.

The tear dribbled from the inner corner of her eye, slid sideways across her nose, and dove onto the pillow. She had experienced such vertigo and nausea only three times in her life. Once when she first learned of her mother's illness. Once when mononucleosis postponed a college term. Once when she lost a chance at a summer job in a Springfield legislator's office.

All unintended turns in the road, twisting the straight way into a labyrinth. God surprising her. God testing her. Refining His gold.

The door swooshed shut, clicked into place.

She heard Tanner moving about, and then she felt his arms grasp the blanket around her legs. He pulled, inching her along the couch.

"Ow!"

"Sorry." He tucked the pillow back under her head and disappeared again. "Adele gave me this. Here's an outlet. Okay." He came back into her line of vision and held out an electric heating pad. "Here."

Something like a whimper sounded in her throat.

"Now, now, Katelyn, don't be a baby. It'll help."

She reached out from under the cover, took the pad from him, and pulled it back underneath with her hand. Doubting its effectiveness, she pressed it against her stomach.

Tanner sat down on the couch beside the pillow, at her head. He placed a hand on her cheek, turning her head until both eyes faced upward. His palm was rested lightly against her cheek, his fingertips stroking her temple.

"It's a good thing you don't get angry too often if this is what happens."

It hurt to talk, but she had to explain. "I'm not mad at Rusty."

"I didn't think you were. I'm sure you're mad at the situation. Understandable."

"I'm upset with God."

"Whoa. What does He have to say about that?"

"He forgives me. He loves me."

He smiled. "He is one quirky God, and you are one quirky redhead. And you're both growing on me. Kind of like mold."

She giggled.

"Mind if I watch the game? I'll keep the volume low."

She closed her eyes and whispered, "No."

At the moment she wouldn't mind anything...except Tanner Carlucci taking his hand from her cheek. She fell fast asleep.

The Bulls still trailed in the third quarter and Kate still slept. She hadn't budged when Adele came in and offered Tanner tea. At halftime, when he went to the kitchen to make coffee, she merely rolled onto her back and snuggled more deeply under the blanket.

He had never seen her without the tortoiseshell glasses sliding down the bridge of her perky little nose. He had never seen her so inert before either. The bundle of energy was revealing a different side altogether.

"Hey."

He looked down and saw her eyes open wider than their previous slits. "Hey, yourself," he said. "I was just thinking how watching the game with you is like watching with the guys. You don't interrupt with unnecessary chatter."

She smiled crookedly. "This is necessary. I've been awake for a while, biting my tongue, but you look like you're going to burst a blood vessel. I only interrupted to say don't hold back on my account."

He turned back to the television, pointing the remote and notching up the volume. "It's only a game."

"Mm-hmm."

He sensed her move from the couch and leave the room. Twenty minutes later in TV basketball time, after seriously, loudly questioning the referee's last call, he lowered the volume and looked up.

Kate was setting a tray on the coffee table. It overflowed with sandwiches, potato chips, sodas, carrots, celery, and cookies. She sat on the floor near it and crossed her legs. "Hungry?"

"Thanks." He joined her, resting his back against the couch and accepting the plate she offered. "This looks great. I take it you're hungry, which means you must be feeling better?"

"I am. Thanks." She moved in a stiff-necked way, though, as if she still hurt. Her glasses were in place, and she wore gray sweats and fuzzy slippers. Her hair was brushed, but not pulled back in its usual manner.

They ate in silence for a few moments.

"Tanner, thank you for sitting with me, but you shouldn't have. You have so many things to do."

"I wanted to. Besides, Sunday is a day of rest. I like *that* idea."

"And which one don't you like?"

He chewed slowly, wondering how to phrase it. "The pastor talked about forgiveness today. He gave real-life examples of people forgiving others who had committed the most heinous crimes against them." Tanner took another bite.

She waited, tearing bits from her sandwich, not eating, watching him.

Something about those green eyes that never condemned pulled it from him. "My dad. Not exactly heinous, but I can't. No way. Never in a million years."

"What did he do?"

"The usual. Left my mother and us three kids for another woman when I was thirteen. Until that day, I didn't have a clue there was a problem. I mean, he wasn't around as much as some of the other dads. He never had time to coach, but he always came to my games. He always took us on vacation." Tanner continued eating.

"What happened after he left?"

"We scarcely heard a word from him, but we never needed anything that money could buy. No sirree." Tanner heard the bitterness in his tone. "He stood by us financially. He was always buying us expensive things and depositing chunks of money in our bank accounts. Still does. Such a hokey way to make up for his absence. Anyway, the fallout was typical. By the time I was sixteen, I only stayed sober during basketball season."

Kate wiped an eye with her napkin. "I'm sorry."

"Obviously I'm still angry. And I don't see a reason to forgive him."

"Does your anger hurt him?"

"I doubt it, but I get this morbid satisfaction from knowing he knows I'm mad. That he can't point to me proudly and refer to our idyllic father-son relationship. He's got a three-year-old son now. Maybe he'll get it with him."

"I can't imagine how that must hurt you." Her voice was on the verge of tears.

He shrugged it off, the innate macho response ripping a hole somewhere deep inside of him.

"My dad was the complete opposite. He's always been so loving and kind, not that he let us get away with anything."

All of those characteristics had been evident after one meeting with Dan Kilpatrick.

"I think because of that, I found it easy to trust in God's love for me. Tanner, He loves you too."

"But you're upset with Him."

"I also get upset with my dad when I don't understand why he does something. Like why when I was little he yelled at me not to cross the street and I watched a truck smash my ball. It's nothing like being abandoned by a father, like you've been."

Time to change the subject. "Why does Rusty's decision bother you so much? I don't think you're afraid of the challenge or the extra work."

"No." She set her jaw, her forehead furrowed.

"Your headache's going to come back if you keep doing that with your face."

"I don't know what God's doing. Is He taking away DC?" She rubbed her forehead. "Why would He do that?"

"Kate, this won't keep you from DC. The job is temporary. You don't have to stay in Valley Oaks."

"Maybe I do. Maybe He's crushing my dream."

"Has He done that before?"

"No. The changes were always obvious choices."

"And they only postponed college, which you're about to graduate from. That was the dream, right?"

"Yes."

"Do you think He's telling you not to cross the street?"

"I don't know!"

"So you're afraid of the unknown future. That doesn't sound very trusting."

She lowered her eyes. "It's not. It's not typical of me."

"Is there something else going on?"

She lifted a shoulder.

"Maybe it's a little of that Magic Kingdom getting under your skin."

She didn't respond.

"Somebody read from the Bible today. I remember it was about not being anxious for tomorrow. Kate, I know life has to be lived one day at a time."

At last she looked up. "Tanner, you sound like a believer."

"I told you. We've been on speaking terms for a long time. Just not on a first-name basis."

"I'm praying you'll meet."

"I know you are." He held her eyes for a long moment, and then he stood. "I'd better go. I've been invading your space long enough."

"Thank you for the laptop. And keeping me company."

"You're welcome."

A minute later he was on the sidewalk, heading under the stars toward his apartment. It wasn't how he wanted to end the evening, but the atmosphere was growing too heavy.

He would have preferred sitting beside her again. Perhaps holding her. Perhaps telling her he was praying that God would keep her in Valley Oaks.

Twenty-Four

Kate sat on a stool in the video store, her laptop computer on the counter, her fingers clicking away at the keyboard. She glanced over at Tanner, who was sorting through the store's collection of video tapes and DVDs in the small glassed-in office.

"Tanner, what was that play at the end of the game when the center caught the pass from the forward and then popped it back out to the guard who scored?" She paused in her typing.

"They did that? Wow, you're good. I missed it."

"You were supposed to be my extra pair of eyes, Mr. Athlete."

"You're doing fine on your own. Thinking you needed help was just a case of first-night jitters."

Continuing with her writing, she muttered to herself, "And tomorrow will be first-day jitters of figuring out what to write. Tomorrow night will be first-night jitters with a county board meeting. Wednesday will be first-day jitters with a deadline."

"What?" He stuck his head through the doorway.

"Nothing. Have I mentioned how slick this machine is?"

He smiled and ducked back into the office.

Still cute.

Half an hour later they had both finished their work.

Kate asked, "Can I sweep for you? Or scrub the front of this counter?"

"No, thanks. After working in here all day, I'm calling it a night. Unlike someone who slept all yesterday, I'm bushed." He sat on the other stool across the counter. "But tell me how the meeting went today."

Though she had seen him at the game earlier and asked for his help on writing the article, they hadn't had a chance yet to talk.

She closed up the computer. "Fred said he'd pay me Rusty's salary, which was more than I expected. He said he's already posted an ad on the Web and in the Rockville paper. The first *Times* ad will go in this week. He said I'm free to leave on the date initially set." She shrugged. "But what's he going to say? He needs me right now."

Tanner reached across and tapped the tip of her nose.

"What?"

"No more negative talk like that. Understood?"

"Fred was so kind. I think he'd take care of the entire paper by himself if I wanted to leave next week. And I saw my first daffodil of the season."

"Much better. Hey, no kidding? About the daffodil?"

"No kidding. The groundhog was wrong. Spring is coming ahead of schedule."

He gave her a thumbs-up. "I'll vote for that."

"I've been thinking about Rusty's farewell."

"I have too, but I didn't know if you were ready to discuss it yet."

"We made up today. She was being so nice it was weird. I told her I wasn't mad at her. After that she was normal."

Tanner laughed. "How about we take her to dinner Wednesday night? There's this place she especially likes in Rockville."

"I think she'd like that. She's not exactly the party type, is she?"

"No. Will you ask her tomorrow? I'm flying to St. Louis for the day and won't be back until late."

"Sure. Speaking of parties, I think you should send out invitations for your grand opening. My family would love to come. You can invite your family."

"My parents never show up at the same place."

"Give them different times. One afternoon, one evening." She reopened the laptop. "I've got a file going on it. I can take care of balloons and cake for you. I also think a bell above the door would be a good idea."

"Here." He reached under the counter, pulled out a key ring and slid it across the counter. "Those are for you."

Her jaw dropped. "Keys for the store?"

"You can come and do whatever you think is necessary whenever you want." He flipped through the keys. "This is for the front door, the back door, and the apartment."

"Apartment?"

"In case you want to leave a pot of chili for me when I'm out of town." He grinned. "Or cookies."

She laughed. "That was a subtle hint."

"It's too late for subtle. Come on. I'll walk you to your car."

Graham stood on Adele's doorstep, anticipating one of his favorite moments of the day.

The door opened and she smiled.

That was it.

She took a step back and he went inside.

"I was driving home and saw your lights on."

"Will you stay?"

He nodded. "If you don't mind."

"Of course I don't."

He wore a sport coat, not one he needed to remove, and so they stood still, looking at each other. Their greetings were growing awkward. Shaking hands reeked of formality. A friendly hug and peck on the cheek far too artificial.

He wanted to hold her.

He took half a step toward her, and in that shy way of hers, she melted into his arms. He set his chin atop her head and held her close. All the angst of the day fled.

"Adele, I take too much from you."

She tilted her head back.

Bad move. Perfect kissing position.

"What do you mean, take?"

He shut his eyes, blocking out the view. "Shall we sit?"

She took his hand and led him to the couch. Not ideal, but better.

"Take," he repeated. "I drop by unannounced at ten o'clock because I know I'll feel better after being with you."

"That's not much taking." She smiled. "How is he tonight?"

"He's well. It's such a roller-coaster ride. One day he seems almost healthy, the next I don't know how he can make it through another day."

She squeezed his hand. "Are you hungry?"

"Only for your company. How was your visit?" An old friend, now living in Rockville, had joined her for dinner.

"Wonderful. It was so great to catch up with Naomi. I told you about her, didn't I?"

"The woman who took you in. This was her house."

"Yes. Chelsea calls her Aunt Naomi. They had a little chat. I don't know that she learned anything, but I'm sure she encouraged my daughter to give me a break."

"Sound advice."

"Naomi also had some advice concerning you."

"Oh?"

"That I should learn more about you before I go off the deep end with my feelings."

"That is sound advice. Are you going off the deep end?"

She turned away and picked up the remote. "Shall we watch the news?"

"Adele."

She clicked on the television.

He took the remote from her and clicked it off. "Please don't go off the deep end until you know me better."

She crossed her arms and frowned at him. "Well, that makes two of you who think feelings can be turned on and off like a spigot. I'm afraid I haven't quite got the hang of it."

"Then maybe we'd better spend less time together."

"That's what she said. More sound advice?"

He nodded.

"Well, you're free to go whenever you want." She tucked her feet beneath her, yanked the remote out of his hand, and turned on the television again.

Go, Logan. Get up and walk out. Don't even look back.

He made it to the front door, his hand on the knob, and then it struck like a blow to his solar plexus. The loss of Sammi, the imminent loss of Rand, and now the loss of Adele. He couldn't breathe.

The coming weeks would change things. She would know more about him than she would ever care to know.

But they had this moment.

He strode back into the living room, grabbed the remote from beside her on the couch, turned off the television, and tossed the control across the room onto a chair, out of reach.

She glared up at him.

He sat sideways facing her, his hand on the back of the couch behind her. "Adele, I will hurt you someday."

Her glare softened. "I know," she whispered. "But all I can think of is that silly old saying. It's better to have loved and lost than never to have loved at all."

"Alfred, Lord Tennyson. It's not a silly old saying."

"But is it true?"

She didn't know. She really didn't know. He knew. Knew it was true. Knew he would gamble again.

He cupped her face between his hands and kissed her with all the emotion that had been building inside him. What had she said? That a spigot could stop it? Not even Hoover Dam.

Early the next day Graham was on a commercial airliner flying east. By 1 P.M. he was at the cemetery. He sat down on grass already thick and green in the southern Virginia sunshine.

"Hi, Sammi."

He laid a bouquet of red roses near the tombstone.

Samantha Abbott Logan.

Today was March 20, five years after the March 20 carved into the stone. The date of his annual visit. The date when his world stopped spinning once again.

"So how are things going in heaven?"

He hadn't figured out why he continued the agonizing ritual. As a tribute to the memory of his wife? As an act of penance? He sensed that despite the passage of years and the lessening of the raw grief, he had not yet felt closure. Unfinished business gnawed in a vague way, nothing he could pinpoint. And so he continued to come.

As always, a tenderness filled him as he recalled how he loved the bubbly young school teacher…how she loved him. And then the guilt would wash over him.

He made the trek alone, in and out of town the same day. He avoided seeing her parents, who lived nearby. They had never cared much for him. Rightly so. He had taken their only child away, taken her north, and then he had *allowed* her to be killed. It was all he could bear to be at her grave site. To see their faces wasn't an option for him.

He first met Sammi in Roanoke. He'd been on assignment...she was teaching...mutual acquaintances had introduced them. When he was transferred, she resigned to go with him. Neither of them had ever regretted the choice.

The end descended upon them swift as an avalanche. Early morning. They were on the lawn, Sammi ready to leave for school. How long had the killer stalked them, waiting for the perfect moment when Graham had a front row seat to his wife's death?

Everyone agreed that it was a professional job. Though it was never proven, he knew the assassin had been hired by a convicted drug dealer behind bars. He had blamed Graham for his wife's accidental death and threatened retaliation. It didn't matter that she had died in a crossfire initiated by the dealer.

Graham wiped away angry tears, hating the feeling of helplessness that still haunted the memory. In his mind he sought the voices of friends, people who had loved Sammi too, telling him there was nothing more to be done, to let it go. Once again, they comforted.

"Sammi, you'll never guess who I finally met. Adele Chandler. Remember that name? She's grown into quite a woman. In a way she reminds me of you. She's full of that deep joy you had. And she's pretty. You'd like her.

"Funny thing is...I kissed her last night. Yeah, I'm head over heels. Imagine that. Not that I want to be, but there it is. I keep telling myself not to sign up for sure heartache again, but it seems I don't have a vote in the matter. I just wanted you to know. Not that you'd care, considering you can't hear me.

"She has a kid. You'd like Chelsea too—"

Graham cringed at his words. *A kid. A kid.* They resounded in his head. *A kid. She has a kid.*

Sammi had wanted children. She had *desperately* wanted children. Graham was adamantly opposed to having children.

It was the single point of contention between them. It was...what they had argued about on the front lawn that morning.

Without advance warning, the memory hit Graham like a tidal wave, engulfing him, taking away his breath.

Sammi had held her own, not backing down as she faced him, her dark eyes glistening with unshed tears. Her hands were propped on her slender hips...hips hidden with the rest of her body beneath that favorite baggy jumper of hers.

He fumed back at her. How many times had they had this discussion? His job was too demanding! It wouldn't be fair to give a child such an uncertain future! What was she thinking? She saw every day in her classroom the devastating effects of parents on children.

And then the bullet struck.

The memory continued to roll over him. Details hammered at him until at last he could no longer fight them, pretending they didn't exist.

Yes, he had ignored the blossoming curves on his wife's body. Yes, he refused to face the truth. Yes, his inflexible line of reasoning was the cruelest response he could have given her.

And now here he was, falling in love with a woman who had a child. He knew full well that loving Adele would mean caring for Chelsea. He knew that loving Adele would mean facing the possibility of her wanting a baby. *And those two caveats did not disturb him in the least!*

"Sammi, I'm sorry. I am so sorry."

Graham cried unreservedly now as he finally acknowledged the truth he had buried with her, the truth that still had the power to rip him apart five years later.

Two people had died in his arms that day. His wife…and his unborn child.

Twenty-Five

Seven o'clock. Saturday night. March twenty-fourth. The *Valley Oaks Times* office.

Her birthday. Her *thirtieth* birthday.

With a dramatic sigh, Kate shut down the computer.

Is melancholy a sin, Lord?

What a week! She and Rusty had finished the paper's weekly edition together and filled the vending machines Thursday night. After sharing a pizza at the Parlor, they had said their goodbyes.

The woman had grabbed her in a tight embrace right out there on the sidewalk. An unfamiliar hint of softness laced her familiar foghorn of a voice when she said something highly irregular. "Keep praying for me, Katy-girl?"

"Of course I will, Rusty."

She had patted her shoulders. "Oh, call me Crusty. All my closest friends do." With a smile and a wave, she was gone.

And Kate felt a sadness.

Friday had been a whirlwind. By 7 A.M. she was cruising in Helen across the countryside, distributing the *Times* to outlying gas stations and a truck stop. Back in Valley Oaks, she hit the grocery store, pharmacy, and gas station. In the office she gratefully worked with the receptionist on next week's schedule. As if that would hold. Alice, a young homemaker with way too many things on her plate, worked more or less when she could. Nine out of ten callers were greeted by the answering machine rather than Alice.

The afternoon hours were consumed with phone interviews and writing articles. The evening ended with yet
another boys basketball game. Kate felt a twinge of guilt for
her silent "amen" when a Viking player missed the last
chance at a three-point shot, thereby losing the game and
abruptly terminating their season. No more games. No more
out-of-town late-night tournaments. Whew! *Finis.*

She had fallen exhausted into bed last night, thinking that
perhaps her limitless supply of energy had, at the age of 29
years and 364 days, a limit. It was a new thought, and it
made her sad.

Saturday dawned with her cell phone ringing beside the
bed, her parents calling to wish her a happy birthday. The
usual family celebration was scheduled for Sunday.

They had invited Tanner. They liked him. Kate hadn't
informed him that it was her birthday. It was just a Kilpatrick Sunday gathering. She didn't want him feeling obli-
gated and buying another gift, for goodness' sake, after the
laptop.

And besides, the thought of turning 30 had interfered with
her rational thought processes. Jesus had started His public
ministry at that age. Here she was, still not finished with
school, still not settled in a high-profile political journalist's
career the way she had promised Him.

And *that* made her sad.

Kate flipped on the office night-light and turned off the
other lights.

Tanner.

They planned to have dinner together, but with both of
them inundated with extra work, they scheduled it for no
earlier than seven. She told him if he didn't show up by then,
she would head to the video store and drag him from his
mess.

Tanner.

The melancholy felt like molten lead flowing over her shoulders now, weighing her down.

Tanner. Her feelings were getting tangled up in a perfectly good friendship.

And that made her really sad.

Tanner stood outside his darkened video store in the chilly night air, stuffed his hands into his jacket pockets, and admired his adopted town. The corner streetlamp cast a soft glow on the sidewalk and the square across the street. He chuckled. Who would have imagined he would wind up out in a rural village with a business? With a spunky, redheaded geek for a best friend?

Life was indeed growing stranger by the minute. For the first time ever, he considered each day something other than an endurance test. Was it the anticipation of a fresh start? The challenge of running the store? The relief of placing physical distance between himself and the childhood memories that haunted Rockville? The pleasure of a community already welcoming him? The unconditional acceptance of the redhead?

Speaking of which, where was she? He turned around and studied the video store. Nothing but darkness filled the large plate-glass window. He paced along the sidewalk. At last he heard old Helen chugging, drawing closer. He watched her approach, zipping along Fourth Avenue. Across from the store, she whipped around at breakneck speed into a parking space.

Kate rolled down the window and called out, "Hop in. She's warm."

He cringed. Riding with Kate was a surefire way of agitating nerves he didn't even know he had.

He opened her door. "Come on. Ride with me."

"Your leather seats are freezing."

"I'll get you a blanket."

"You're chicken." She turned off the engine and climbed out.

"So? At least I'm man enough to admit it."

She laughed. "That's true."

He pulled on her arm as she veered toward his car. "Come inside a minute. Let me show you what I did today."

"All right, but let's make it quick. I'm hungry!"

"I knew that."

He pushed open the door and a bell jingled above.

"You put up the bell! Nice."

"Thanks." He fumbled for the light switch, complaining loudly, "I don't know why anyone would put this switch here—"

"Surprise!" loud voices sang out as the lights flickered on. "Surprise!"

Kate screamed and, although expecting the moment, Tanner jumped. The timing had been perfect.

Kate screamed again as her parents and friends surrounded her, everyone shouting again, "Happy birthday!"

Tanner almost felt sorry for her. She looked terrified. After screaming again she burst into tears. As her mother hugged her, he exchanged a puzzled look with her dad, who only shrugged and mouthed, "Women."

It was Kate's birthday. He had invited Britte and Lia, who passed the word to Joel; Cal; Chloe; Anne, Alec, and their kids; Gina and Brady; the pastor and his family; and a few folks he didn't know. Kate's family had brought along her friend Beth and her family. Adele, Graham, and Chelsea completed the crowd filling his two rooms.

He had made space by moving aside shelves and opening up the Ping-Pong table for the caterers to use. The Posateris, owners of the Pizza Parlor, had cooked all of Kate's favorite dishes and now served them. Adele had ordered the cake from Swensen's Market; it looked like a newspaper with the headline "New Editor Turns 30." Chelsea and Chloe had hung crepe paper everywhere and provided a CD player that now blared Kate's favorite oldies radio station. People had brought lawn chairs for seats.

The party was well under way before Kate smiled at him. She slipped through the crowd, approaching him, hands on hips and frowning. "Tanner Carlucci, you are in trouble. Big trouble."

"Happy birthday!" He laughed and caught her up in a bear hug, twirling until she squealed to be set down. "So, were you surprised?"

She shook her head, smiling. "I have no idea how you did this. I never even told you when my birthday was."

"Rusty did. It was on your application form."

"And she's the only one missing."

"But she left a gift. Did you see your pile of gifts, by the way?"

She appeared thoroughly embarrassed.

He leaned over and whispered in her ear, "I told them not to bring gifts."

"I hardly know most of these people," she whispered back.

"Just a little bit of that Magic Kingdom shining through." He kissed her cheek. "Go eat, birthday girl."

Magic Kingdom indeed.

When Kate was a little girl and all of her grandparents, aunts, uncles, and cousins would come to her birthday party, the crowd equaled tonight's in number. However, it had never approached the outrageous gesture of acceptance displayed by the Valley Oaks group. Nor could she remember such laughter.

And to think that Tanner planned it all.

She closed the door on Beth and her family, the last to go, and joined him in the back room where he was tying up trash bags.

"Tanner, thank you so much!"

He grinned like a little boy. "You're so welcome. It was great. Do you think they'll all come back next week for the open house?"

"More free food? And prizes to boot? Of course they will!" She sat on a lawn chair, making a mental note to remind him that tomorrow they could buy the chairs she had spotted in a Rockville ad. "How long have you been planning this?"

"Since Rusty told me she was leaving. Just under two weeks." He sat down beside her. "She had been reviewing your application and noticed the date was close to your big 3-0 day. Did you have a good time?"

"I had such a good time! Did you see my folks and Beth mingling with everyone? I love that they got to see Valley Oaks up close. And all the yummy food! And didn't everyone seem to laugh a lot?"

"And without booze. I guess it can be done." He seemed genuinely bewildered.

"Is that an eye-opener for you?"

A little smile lifted the corners of his mouth. "Thank you for having a birthday party to show me."

"Anytime." On the rare occasions when he let her in like that, she realized she didn't have a clue how harsh the world could be.

"By the way, when were you going to let me know this was your birthday?"

She shrugged.

"And tomorrow? I take it the family gathering is for you?"

She shrugged again. "No big deal."

"Kate! I'd feel kind of ridiculous being the only one there who didn't know."

"Maybe I would have told you at dinner tonight. I would have let you buy."

"Do you have birthday issues?"

"Well," she hedged. "It's just not something you go around announcing. It's like asking for a gift. Or saying I'm special so you better treat me like it. I wanted to crawl off in a corner when I saw those gifts tonight."

"But they were just-for-fun gifts."

"True, but I didn't know that while they were all wrapped up. Besides the fact I've only been here for two months."

"I can't believe you're going shy on me."

"I'm not."

"Yes, you are."

She turned away. "Am not."

He laughed. "Speaking of gifts, Miss Birthday Girl." He went to a closet and pulled out a red gift bag.

Her stomach somersaulted. "You gave me a laptop."

"That wasn't for your birthday. That was a thank-you gift." He set the bag on her lap.

"You gave me a party."

"Doesn't count."

"You spend money like it grows on trees."

"Habit I picked up from my dad."

She swallowed. "Why didn't you put this out with the others?"

"Mine's private. It's not a just-for-fun. Will you open it?"

"Tanner, why do you do this?" As the words flew from her tongue, she yearned to snatch them from the air, to take them back. In unguarded moments tonight she had noticed him watching her. When he sensed her eyes on him, the mask quickly adjusted itself into place. She knew why he did this. She didn't need to hear it out loud. "You don't—"

"The simple answer," he interrupted, "is because I want to. And that's because—at the risk of sounding totally sappy here—my life hasn't been the same since you walked into it." He settled back into the chair and crossed his legs, ankle to knee. He folded his hands and twiddled his thumbs. The nonchalant demeanor was firmly back in place. "Besides, I get a kick out of making you smile."

"And you think *I'm* quirky." Her tone was flippant. Her heart, on the other hand, was flip-flopping to a ragtime beat.

She pulled tissue paper from the red bag. Underneath that lay a pair of red mittens. "Aww, Tanner. You think I need these?"

"You don't? Look." He reached over as she put them on and touched the palm of one. "They've got leather pads. Better for driving."

"Thanks." She clapped her hands together. "Wow, two hands covered."

"There's more."

She knew that. She'd spied the thick white envelope in the bag. With a quiet sigh she slowly removed the mittens and pulled out the other gift. Her name was scrawled on the front.

The return address belonged to a travel agency.

She met his eyes. He only waggled his brows.

There didn't seem to be any choice but to open it. Airline tickets fell onto her lap. Pages of a printed itinerary followed.

Kate struggled to focus on the fine print.

Washington, DC.

"Tanner..." she whispered.

"Rusty helped. She worked on the schedule with that contact she set up for you. You go in two weeks, on a Thursday. Fred said he'd print the paper without you. I'll fill the vending machines and do the subscription mailings. It's only for a long weekend. You're not smiling."

"I will," she blubbered through her tears. "In a minute."

It took more like ten minutes, but the shock began to wear off and giggles eventually chased off the weeping. She leaped from the chair and whirled around the Ping-Pong table, coming to a stop in front of Tanner.

"I can't accept this!"

"Sure you can."

"How can I ever *ever* thank you?"

"Use it. Go and find your place out there in the big world. That's all the thanks I want." He smiled.

"How about a hug?"

"That'd be nice too."

She pulled him to his feet and wrapped her arms around him. It was like trying to squeeze a solid oak tree. But it felt awfully comfortable...especially when his arms came around her.

Twenty-Six

Adele locked her front door and walked to the driveway where Graham was leaning inside the opened back end of her minivan. It was a beautiful sunny morning, a Tuesday, a rare, self-proclaimed holiday from the nursing home. Sunshine and a gentle breeze out of the south teased that spring was around the corner. A false hope, but nonetheless it fostered spring fever, encouraging that the daily routine be pitched out the nearest window.

Which was the same effect Graham Logan was having on her. She couldn't help but wonder if that too was a false hope. He said he would hurt her. She understood that the threat of his old life and Rand's death hung over them, that things would soon turn complicated. Still, weren't complications innate to relationships? Then again...what did she know of such relationships? Her teenage affair had been pure rebellion. Her friendship with Will and the two or three other men she had dated occasionally didn't begin to compare with what was happening now.

Well, she didn't know. But God did. She had given it to Him, tossed her routine out the window, and cherished each moment she could spend with Graham.

She walked up behind him now and looked around his arm. An array of single layered, cardboard boxes covered the folded-down backseat, the center seats, and floor.

"Thanks, Graham."

He smiled. "You're welcome. I don't think they'll slide."

214

The boxes held her pottery. Each vase, bowl, and casserole dish was individually wrapped and bound for Manning's Art Gallery to be sold on consignment.

"Do you mind driving?" She handed him the keys as he ducked out from under the car door.

The bright noon sunshine glinted off his sunglasses and cast highlights in his pewter gray hair. He smiled that slow smile of his.

"Dear lady, you could ask for anything and I wouldn't mind obliging you." He leaned toward her.

She met his kiss, his lips fresh and cool with the outdoors. Scents mingled...spring air with masculine shaving cream.

"How did you know what I was going to ask?" She reached and fingered that curl behind his ear.

"Lucky guess." He chuckled. "Anything else?"

Stay. Don't leave Valley Oaks. She shook her head. "No."

His eyes were hidden behind the dark glasses, but she felt them, mere inches away, studying her face. How much could he read in her expression? She glanced aside and dropped her hand from his hair.

He kissed her cheek softly. "Well." His voice rumbled indistinctly, and he cleared his throat. "Shall we go?"

A short time later as they sped down the highway toward Rockville, Graham asked, "So how is it with Chelsea?"

"About the same. She's so distant. I want to ground her again until she stops behaving like an adolescent. Somehow I don't think that would work. I feel like we've lost something between us."

"You have. Her childhood."

He was right. Saddened, Adele gazed out the side window. And then there was that unresolved issue. Naomi had suggested she take care of it soon. It involved old secrets she had never shared with anyone but her friend. Maybe it was time.

"Graham." She hesitated, wondering why it was she trusted this man above her friends. Women friends from church, those who had walked beside her for years, some since Chelsea's birth.

"Adele, what's wrong?"

She looked at him. "How do you know there's something wrong?"

"You seem tense."

"I was just thinking you seem...safe. Like Smokey the Bear, Santa Claus, and Big Bird rolled into one."

He laughed. "Is that good?"

"Very good. Do you mind if I unload something on you?"

"Of course not."

"About my sordid past...there's more. Chelsea's father is American. His name is Greg Findley. He was from San Francisco." She paused.

"Not from Germany with an unpronounceable last name?"

"No. I lied."

"Does he know about Chelsea?"

"He knows. The thing was...when I found out I was pregnant, he asked if I needed money for an abortion. I said I wouldn't get one. He said in that case, he was splitting. He wanted nothing to do with a baby. We were in a youth hostel in Rome. Half an hour after I told him, he was gone." She wiped a tear from her cheek.

"You didn't see him again?"

"I waited there for two weeks, and then I went home. When Chelsea was three months old, I tracked down his parents' phone number. His mother gave me a number for him in Los Angeles. I called him. He denied ever having met me."

He let that sink in. "And Chelsea knows nothing of this?"

"I couldn't tell her she had a daddy who wanted nothing to do with her except to pay for an abortion. All she knew of my father, her grandfather, was more or less the same scenario. I didn't want her thinking she was doomed to always being abandoned by men." She picked at dried clay around a fingernail. "And I couldn't tell her that it was the farthest thing imaginable from being a romantic European affair. I couldn't tell her the truth: We were two aimless, spoiled rich Americans, stoned most of the time we spent together." She squeezed her hands into fists. "But I have to tell her."

"Yes, she should know. Adele, it was so many years ago. You've been taking the blame long enough by saying he never knew about her. He knew and that's his burden, not yours."

"She'll resent me."

"Probably, but she'll resent you more the longer you wait."

"I know. It's so unfair to dump this on her though."

"You've given her seventeen years of being cherished, of not having to deal with the painful truth. Now she's old enough to handle it. You know, it's not going to take away those seventeen years. That's what will carry her through."

"Will you fix us soup again?"

He reached for her hand and brought it to his lips. "You can count on it."

Graham leaned against the kitchen wall, out of the way. Watching three women prepare dinner was far more entertaining than television. Well, perhaps not any three women, but Adele, Kate, and Chelsea captivated him.

Adele, of course, captivated him just by being. The way she moved, her lilting voice, the little-girl dimples, the womanly mouth he had been kissing on a daily basis now for over a week...her warm attention to Rand and all the Fox Meadow residents...her dreams...

Kate was stir-frying chicken and talking nonstop about a meeting she had covered last night. Her total lack of self-awareness made her the most refreshing person he had ever met.

Chelsea seemed to have caught something of Kate's spirit and behaved more normally than she had since before her mysterious truancy. Still, there were moments when she withdrew, her face a blank, her mind obviously elsewhere. Graham hoped she would clue her mother in on the problem soon.

"And then..." Kate bit off the end of a carrot, "I asked the village board president why he thought Brady's land was unsuitable for a wildlife refuge. Given the fact it's full of wildlife as it is. The man sputtered." She held up her right hand. "No lie. He absolutely sputtered. I'm going to write an editorial."

Chelsea laughed. "About him sputtering?"

Kate grinned. "No. About the positives of having a refuge, even one that includes an elephant."

"That would be so cool to have an elephant down the road. I have a friend who would love to work at Brookfield Zoo in Chicago. Obviously he can't do that for a few more years. I bet Gina could train people, couldn't she?"

Kate pointed the carrot. "Excellent idea. I'll run it by her and maybe include it in the piece. Think of the possibilities! A petting zoo would be fun."

Graham asked, "What about zoning matters?"

"The property is out far enough. It's not prime farmland. I don't see a problem." She pointed the carrot again. "But that's a good point. I'll have to find out."

Adele pulled a casserole from the oven. "I'm ready. How about you, Kate?"

"Two minutes."

Chelsea asked, "Is Mr. Carlucci coming?"

For the briefest of moments, Kate grew still. Graham hid a smile behind his hand. Mention of the young man threw her into self-awareness.

"No." She recovered quickly. "He's flying a charter back from Maryland." She turned to Graham. "*Again* Maryland. That guy is all over the country like it's no big deal. I bet your friend misses being near DC. I know *I* would."

He caught Adele's puzzled look. Another twist he'd have to explain, very likely sooner than later. He had led her to believe Rand came from Chicago. Only God could have arranged for his path to cross that of the charter pilot's in Valley Oaks. Professors and pilots... Was he out of practice or what?

Adele untied her apron. "Maryland?"

"Maryland?" Chelsea echoed. "Kate, a charter plane crashed in Ohio late this afternoon, near Columbus. I just heard it on the news. It was coming from Maryland."

The women stared at one another, shock on their faces.

Graham said, "What kind of plane was it?"

"They didn't say. They won't release any details yet."

Kate ran from the room.

They all followed.

She was in her sitting room, cell phone to her ear, squealing in a high-pitched voice, "Tanner! Call me the very minute you walk in!"

"Kate." Adele pulled her into a hug. "We need to pray." She held her close, whispering quiet words into the younger woman's ear.

Graham closed his own eyes and prayed silently for Tanner's safety...for the people on the plane...for the families affected...

"Thank you, Adele." Kate grabbed her coat from the couch. "I've got to go."

"Where?"

"I don't know. The airport, I guess."

Graham said, "It's a charter. They won't know anything at the ticket counters. He works for a company that owns the plane. They're not at the airport. Do you know the name?"

She shook her head, her eyes wide behind the glasses.

"Let's study the yellow pages."

She shook her head more violently, pulling on the coat. "You look. I'm going. I'll find somebody."

"What's your cell phone number?"

Her face looked blank.

He eased it from her hand and searched through the menu until the number was displayed. Committing it to memory, he handed the phone back to her. "I'll make some calls. I know somebody who knows somebody with the National Transportation Safety Board. They'll be investigating. I doubt I can get any names, but maybe we can learn what kind of plane, where it was headed."

She nodded.

"Kate." Adele grabbed her again. "Honey, be careful."

Chelsea hugged her next. "He'll be okay."

They walked her to the door and watched her walk down the sidewalk and get into her VW. A few false starts later, she was chugging down the street.

Chelsea headed back toward the kitchen.

"Adele." She was staring at him. "This is where I say trust me. Though you've no apparent reason to do so."

"You didn't write her number down."

He pointed to his head and gave her a little smile. "It's here."

"You know somebody who knows somebody on a national level with information like that." Though her tone made it a statement, her facial expression questioned.

"From the old days."

"The ones you always avoid talking about."

He nodded slightly.

"Why would Rand miss being near Washington, DC?"

"Adele. It's complicated." He left it at that. He had to leave it at that.

"Are these the things that will hurt me?"

He winced. "Unintentionally."

She crossed her arms, staring at him.

"I'll go."

Her face crumpled. "But then who will tell me everything's all right?"

He enfolded her into his arms and, when she didn't resist, breathed a prayer of thanks.

She mumbled, "Why is it I keep listening to my heart instead of my brain?"

"Hey!" Chelsea was in the dining room doorway. "Dinner's ready. Let's move it, lovebirds."

Adele laughed against his shoulder. "I guess that answers my question." She wiped her eyes and looked up at him.

He smiled. "Lovebirds never listen to their brains."

Kate fished the ringing cell phone from the deep pocket of her jacket as she strode through the airport. It displayed a number she didn't recognize. "Hello?"

"Kate, it's Graham. Are you all right?"

"No! They won't tell me anything! They can't even figure out when he's due in. The entire airport staff is clueless!"

"Take a deep breath."

His calm voice broke through, and she stopped yelling. She had been tearing around the airport, cornering every employee she came across. The only worthwhile piece of information she learned was that the control tower security was tighter than Fort Knox.

"Listen, Kate. I found out the plane that went down is a Beechcraft Bonanza. Tanner told me he generally flies their larger one for longer trips. He would have been flying a Cessna Citation. It's what we flew on."

"But that doesn't mean—"

"It happened outside of Columbus. That might have been their destination."

"Here comes an official-looking woman. I think it's the manager I'm waiting for. Maybe *she* knows what a press ID is. I'll talk to you later."

"Kate!"

"What?"

"My friend's calling me back as soon as he has more information. I'll let you know."

"Thanks." She pushed the off button and stuck her right hand toward an approaching woman wearing a black suit. "Hi, I'm Kate Kilpatrick with the *Valley Oaks Times*."

"Haley Weckel." She shook Kate's hand. "How do you do. Security tells me you're giving them fits." Her dark eyes lit up in silent laughter as if she doubted it.

"I have been."

The woman's eyebrows rose.

"A small plane went down outside of Columbus, Ohio. A Beechcraft Bonanza, chartered, coming from Maryland. Was it headed here?"

"I can't answer that question."

"Do you know the answer?"

"No comment." The woman was digging in her heels.

"The people have a right to know."

"I agree. Certain people. Family, for instance, and they don't need to hear about it from the news media."

Kate's bravado faltered. "What if I'm family? Or very nearly so?"

"How near is nearly so?"

Good question. She was under the impression he didn't have much to do with his family. She knew for a fact that he spent more time with her, as if she were family or, at the least, a close friend. "We're close." Her throat was tight, choking the words. "Tanner Carlucci. He's piloting a chartered plane from Baltimore, Maryland. I don't know what time he was due in tonight." She covered her mouth with a hand before a sob escaped.

Haley Weckel's demeanor softened. "Let me see what I can find out. Wait right here."

As she walked away down the brightly lit open area, Kate sank onto a chair near one of the front doors.

"Oh, Lord. Please keep him safe."

Her pleading hadn't ceased since Chelsea relayed the news. Nor had the biting of fingernails. She removed her thumb from her mouth. Maybe she should wear the mittens. Two mittens. She still had two of them.

Kate dug again into the pockets and pulled them out. At the sight of the red fuzzy things with leather padded palms, she started crying. She removed her glasses and pressed the mittens to her eyes.

Fiddlesticks. She was a nervous wreck. No two ways about it. What was wrong? She reminded herself of Beth when her husband was out of town on business. Or her mother when her dad was grouchy about work. Or her little sister already idolizing boys.

Kate Kilpatrick was never a nervous wreck. She was excitable, true, emotional...even hyper at times...but never high-strung over the safety of a guy. That was in God's hands. She was doing all she could by praying. For goodness' sake! It was only an unconfirmed news report that *might* concern a new friend she hardly knew in a town she was *leaving* in a few weeks!

She chewed on the end of a mitten and sniffed.

Tanner was a friend.

All right. Admit it. He was a *guy*. A good-looking guy who bought her *extravagant* gifts and made her laugh and was incredibly easy to hang out with.

Too good-looking to be interested in her *that* way. So? She was leaving in a few weeks.

Whose faith was wobbly at best. *Oh, Jesus, please don't let him die until he knows You.*

It seemed to take hours before Haley Weckel stood before her again. Kate flew to her feet, grabbing her glasses as they sailed from her lap. She stuck them back on.

"He's landing in two minutes."

Kate whooped and threw her arms around the stranger. "Thank you!"

She laughed. "He must be one special guy. Do you know where private aircraft park?"

Kate shook her head, and Haley quickly gave her directions, walking her to the exit. Before the automatic door had swooshed completely open, Kate was through it, racing across to the parking lot. It would take at least five minutes to drive out of the lot and pay the attendant. From there she had to drive down one highway parallel to the runway, down another highway around the end of it, and turn onto another road that would take her to a flight school building she didn't know existed and into its parking lot.

"Oh, Lord, please start Helen on the first try!"

She climbed in, turned the key, and the engine popped off. One prayer answered.

No...two prayers answered.

"Thank You for keeping him safe!"

She turned into a parking lot in front of a low building closed up for the night. A discreet sign posted alongside the walk indicated she was in the right place. She parked and climbed out. From here she needed to walk. There were rows and rows of hangars behind it. Haley told her it was best not to go driving around. She wouldn't miss the small jet taxiing or her friend's car.

As she jogged along the driveway, she noted everything was deserted. Lights were dim with long passages of dark space between them. She heard distant voices and walked toward them. As she rounded the corner of one row of hangars, she saw Tanner and a group of people.

She stopped. It felt as if her bones had liquified.

There he was, laughing and talking with the others. The plane was already parked inside the oversized garage. He appeared to be inspecting it as he moved around it.

They were all behaving so normally. Didn't they know they had almost crashed? Of course not, because they hadn't. That was her interpretation.

What was she doing here anyway? She slunk back around the corner, into deeper shadows.

The lights went out, the big doors were rolled shut. Goodbyes were called out. Tanner climbed into his SUV as the others got into a second car. Both drove away, not passing near Kate.

She waited a few moments, and then she found her way back to Helen. By then the other cars were gone.

As she got in, the cell phone rang. She dug it out from underneath a mitten.

"Hello?"

"Kate, he's on his way."

She smiled. "Thanks, Graham. He just landed."

"He just landed!" Graham's voice was muffled. Loud cheers reached her ears.

"Your source is a little slow," she teased.

"Sorry about that."

"No problem. Hey, will you tell Adele I'm staying in town tonight at my folks?"

"Sure. Bye."

Kate ended the call and turned off the phone's power. She was done for the evening. She felt sapped of all energy and wanted nothing but to climb into her old bed.

Tonight's events made no sense, and that made her very, very tired.

Twenty-Seven

Kate didn't turn down her mother's offer of bacon, pancakes, and eggs. By 6:30 A.M. her appetite had returned, and she remembered she hadn't eaten dinner the night before.

Her dad left for work, taking a bacon-and-egg sandwich with him. Her brother and sister passed through the kitchen, stopping long enough to down a pancake before heading out the door to school. Kate finished her last bite as her mother joined her with two mugs of coffee.

"Thanks, Mom. Wow. I'm thirty years old and you're still doing this."

She smiled. "Waiting on all of you is my favorite thing." She took a sip. "How's Tanner?"

Kate's swig of coffee tangoed with a gulp for air, sending her into a coughing fit.

Her mother handed her a napkin. "Is that what the problem is?"

"What—" she coughed, "problem?"

"Katelyn, you drop in unannounced to spend the night, which is not unusual. Going right to bed without talking is unusual. Do you want to talk now?"

"You're still doing that too."

"What?"

"Seeing beneath the surface. Yes, it is Tanner. I think I'm developing a *crush* on him. Mom, thirty-year-old women do not have crushes. This is so ridiculous."

"How do you know thirty-year-old women don't have crushes?"

227

"Because it's time to work and get on with your life or else *wham!*" She brought her hands together in one loud clap. "Love at first sight. Meet the right guy, and you know he's the one because he's everything you've ever wanted."

"I didn't know you had a checklist."

"I don't. Not consciously, but I know he'll be involved with journalism and probably older because guys my age are inane. Tanner's just a friend."

"But?"

"But last night a charter plane coming from Baltimore crashed. I thought it was his and I went bananas. I was a basket case. Look at my nails." She held out her hands. "There's nothing left to chew."

"But it wasn't Tanner?"

"No." Should she tell her the rest? She needed to confide in someone. Maybe that was why she came home. "I saw him at the airport. He didn't see me, and I didn't go over to him. I was so thankful to see him, but I couldn't talk to him."

"Why not?"

"There were other people around and I...I knew I'd just start bawling."

"Oh, honey."

She was crying now. "What's wrong with me?"

"Well, I don't think it's a crush."

She pulled off her glasses and wiped her eyes with the napkin. "No?"

"No. My guess is..." Now Carol's eyes filled with tears. "It's way beyond crush. I think you're in love."

"Oh, Mom! I can't be! Not with Tanner Carlucci!"

"Why not? He seems like such a nice young man. And now he has his own business—"

"Mom! Do you remember what he looks like? The girls in Valley Oaks and their *mothers* refer to him as Adonis. He's built like a Greek god. Or maybe Roman, in his case."

"He is handsome, but so what?"

"Mom, this is me, Kate, not our beautiful Sara. This guy could have any girl who walks by. Actress, model, Miss America."

"Katelyn." She smiled and touched her daughter's hand. "You're the one who received a laptop and plane tickets from him."

"But we just met!"

Carol laughed and smartly clapped her hands together once. "Wham!"

Using the hair pick on her wet curls, Adele studied her reflection in the bathroom mirror. The image staring back at her begged for sleep. Crows' feet were pronounced, the skin drying from lack of attention before bed. Again. The eyelids drooped above puffy bags. Proof of another short night.

Toe curling was serious business.

She opened the medicine cabinet, pulled out her facial lotion, and went to work.

I'm behaving like a fool. From last night's conversation, I know he's carrying around secrets.

So he knew high-level people in government. So what? So...maybe he used to work for the government. There were years and years worth of unknown information between them. It took time to really get to know another person. That was the purpose of a lifetime together.

But he wouldn't even talk about it. And he wouldn't explain what Rand had to do with Tanner flying to Balti-more.

"Father, please help me figure this out. Am I just a totally naïve idiot? Should I stop seeing him? Why doesn't he stop seeing me if he has to keep secrets?"

Because...he's falling in love with me.

"Mom!" Chelsea rapped on the door. "Tara needs the bathroom!"

"Coming." She put away her lotion and opened the door. She and Tara squeezed past each other. The girl quickly slammed the door shut. "Morning, Tara," Adele said to herself and went to her room to dress. Tara had stopped by to pick up Chelsea for school.

Enough introspection. She was already behind schedule having slept late, a highly unusual occurrence...until recently, at any rate.

She paused in her doorway. She could hear Tara being sick. The poor girl. A flu was going around the school. It sounded as if she'd better go home for the day.

A few minutes later, as she was zipping her skirt, Chelsea came in and dove onto the bed.

"Chels, I can take you to school— Are *you* feeling all right?" She went over and placed the back of a hand on her daughter's pale forehead.

"I'm not sick."

"Are you sure? You and Tara usually share colds and—"

"We're not sharing *this*."

Red warning flags waved before Adele's eyes. She sat on the bed and breathed a silent prayer. Chelsea had been touchy lately, more standoffish than usual. Would she accept a mother's prying?

"Honey." She smoothed the long tendrils of hair down her back. "What's wrong with Tara?"

"Isn't it obvious? She's barfing."

Adele pressed her lips together and waited for her huffy response mode to fade. "That could mean a number of things…but something you can't catch? Something not contagious. Like…food poisoning."

No response.

"Or bulimia."

Chelsea buried her face in the chenille bedspread.

Tara walked in then, her face a white sheet against disarrayed black hair.

Adele met her eyes. Tara had been a part of their lives since the girls started school and became fast friends the second day of kindergarten. She was like another daughter.

"Honey, what's wrong?" She held out an arm and drew Tara down beside her.

"Nothing." Her lower lip trembled.

Adele hugged her. "This is me. You know I'm not taking that for an answer."

Chelsea sat up, wiping her eyes, though the tears kept falling. "Tara, we've got to tell her. It's not going to go away."

Her friend burst out crying and nodded.

"Mom, she's pregnant."

Now all three of them hugged as one, the girls wailing, Adele fighting back her own tears.

When Adele could find her voice, she went to her bedside phone and called the high school and then Fox Meadow. The three of them would not be arriving anywhere on time.

Adele straightened her skirt and cleared her throat, forcing the weeping from her voice. "Well, girls, I've been there and done that. First of all, Tara, let's get some crackers in you. They'll settle your stomach. After that you can tell me about your mysterious trip to Chicago."

A corner of Kate's mind registered the bell jangling, which meant the door of the *Times* had opened and shut. Another corner bemoaned the fact that Alice the receptionist had sick kids keeping her at home. Every other fiber of her being was glued to the computer screen and the editorial she was writing.

She could imagine no downside to a wildlife refuge a few miles west of town. Deer and other animals already lived there anyway. Adding a parking lot on vacant land, widening some of the existing trails, installing a small petting-zoo area, and placing signs to the site of an early settler's house hardly seemed a detraction to Valley Oaks. There might be a little extra traffic on the weekends...which would mean oodles of business to local establishments. How cool was that?

She erased the last sentence and saved her document.

She leaned back away from the computer monitor and jumped. Tanner stood at the counter, resting his arms on it and watching her.

"Sorry, Kate!" He grinned. "Didn't mean to startle you, but from the intense look on your face, I thought I shouldn't interrupt."

"Thanks. I needed to finish my scathing editorial about the zoning problem for Brady and Gina's place."

"Good for you. Do you think Fred will run it?"

She shrugged. "We'll see. This is my first attempt at such a thing. Rusty's material was a lot tamer."

"Seriously?"

She eyed him as she walked to the counter and wondered if he was serious. Even lounging against the counter he was much taller than she was. As usual, he appeared fresh from a magazine ad for cologne...a sports car...leather jackets...blue jeans... Or merely as decoration for a female modeling the latest slinky fashion. What on earth did she see in him?

"Yeah, seriously."

"Oops. Did I hit a nerve?"

"You don't think I'm capable of scathing, do you?"

"No, I'm sure you are. I only meant you look so much nicer than Rusty." He wrinkled his nose and sniffed in an exaggerated way. "You smell so much nicer too."

His antics made her laugh. As usual.

"I called you back." He referred to the frenzied message she'd left for him when she'd first heard about the crash.

"I know." She'd listened to his voice mail message on her phone.

"It was late last night. You must have been asleep already."

"Probably. I spent the night in Rockville."

"You sounded like you wanted something?"

"Oh, um, no. I can't remember anything in particular." No way was she getting into her overdone reaction concerning his well-being. "Maybe it was about the village board meeting."

"I was hoping it wasn't something we'd forgotten to do for Saturday's grand opening. Speaking of which, my dad's wife responded to the invitation." He never referred to her as his stepmom. "They're all coming."

"Really?" She knew it was a milestone. "Great!"

"Yes. I was so overcome with goodwill at the news that I extended another invitation to her." His heavy dark brows knit themselves together. "Marnie's kids have been begging me to take them flying since the day I met them. I told her I'd take them on Sunday. I already reserved the plane. Kate, come with us. I need your moral support."

"Flying?" She felt her own brows shoot upward. "In a small plane?"

"There are seats for four."

Her brows wouldn't come down. *"Four?"*

"Katelyn Kilpatrick, are you afraid of flying?"

"Only the crashing part." Her voice squeaked.

"Birthday and flying issues. You get more interesting by the day. Now I'm insisting you come. It's the only way to dispel the fear. How will you make it to DC?"

"Big jets with the pilot out of sight are not a problem."

"But I'm the pilot!" He grinned. "Believe me, it's no different than riding in the car with me. I'm an okay driver, don't you think?"

"Yeah."

"You don't sound convinced."

"There was a charter plane crash last night."

"I heard about that. They got caught in a storm. If it's not clear weather Sunday, we won't go." He reached over and kneaded her forehead. "Stop worrying."

"Maybe I'll pray for rain and snow and sleet and lightning."

"That'd be okay too. Then I wouldn't have to be nice to the rug rats."

"You don't mean that, do you?"

"I might. You'd better come. Else I might try scaring them." He drew large airy circles with a finger and grinned wickedly. "A few loop-de-loops should cure them of ever asking again."

"Tanner."

"You'd better come to protect them. Or me from myself."

She chewed on what was left of a thumbnail.

"Kate, I'm only joking." He gently pulled her hand down and rubbed it between his. "I'm sorry. You really are afraid. I forget how terrifying it is for some people. But isn't this where Jesus comes in? He gives you courage to face your fears, right?"

She nodded reluctantly.

"Then I'm going to challenge you. If He's real, you'll prove it to me by getting on that plane."

"That's not fair!"

"Why not? Put your walk where your talk is, girl, and I will get down on my knees."

"Tanner, don't look to me to save your soul."

He laid her hand on the counter beneath his. "Where else am I going to look?" His tone was resolute. "I need to see His reality firsthand."

"You're asking Him for a sign. He doesn't always do that."

"But He can if He wants to."

Of course. "That's too heavy a responsibility."

"For you or for Him? All you have to do is climb into that plane and entrust your life to me, knowing the whole time it's not really in my hands."

He had her there. She was only thinking of herself. "Nothing's too heavy for Him."

"That's what I'm hoping." He bent toward her and said in a low, urgent voice, "You've been walking with Him for a long time. I just want to see how that works."

"You're that desperate for moral support on Sunday?"

"Yep. About as desperate as you are terrified."

She took a deep breath, not sure what either of them was getting into. He was practically asking to see the face of God. Talk about heavy. She needed to pray. But first she needed to lighten up. The feel of his hand on hers threatened to scramble her thought processes. How did they usually settle challenges? Dinner.

She asked, "Throw in dinner?"

He tapped the tip of her nose and smiled. "Right after I get up off my knees."

Graham inched the chair he was sitting in as close as possible to the wheelchair and put his nose a few centimeters from Rand's. He spoke through clenched teeth. The conversation was far too private to chance it being overheard.

"I respect your strong sense of God's timing, sir, but phase two starts today. You will not leave me with this woman until you have answered all of her questions. And she is beginning to ask them."

Behind the thick bifocals, the elderly man's eyes wavered for the briefest of seconds. Long enough for Graham to understand the hesitation. Why hadn't he seen it before? The courageous old coot *did* know fear.

"Rand, she has a right to know even if she's not ready. Even if she tosses you out on your ear."

He nodded. "When?"

"By this weekend. There are a few loose ends to tie up."

He nodded again. "I'm tired."

Graham reached down and released the wheelchair's brakes. "No you're not. You're going to go flirt with the ladies in the lobby. Do you want to know why?"

Rand did his best imitation of a glare.

"Because Adele Chandler is the most genuinely kind person I have ever met. She will not toss you out." *Me, on the other hand, she very likely will.*

Twenty-Eight

Tracking down Greg Findley wasn't all that difficult. Adele could have done it herself had she been so inclined. But Graham knew she thought it a hopeless battle. Foisting the reality of a daughter onto a disinterested father threatened the emotional stability she had built around her little family of two. There was no reason to go there.

Graham saw every reason to go there. Chelsea would want to know about Findley, had a right to know about him. Adele, whether she admitted it or not, needed closure on the subject. And Graham himself? He needed the closure as well. What if the woman he loved met the father of her child and old sparks ignited? He had seen far stranger things than that occur.

Some brief late-night Internet surfing garnered the information he needed. A few Wednesday morning phone calls completed the process. Greg Findley lived in Denver, Colorado, where he was a branch manager for a software company founded by his father, Greg Sr. Sitting in the small kitchen of his furnished apartment, Graham reviewed his notes, reached again for his cell, and punched in the number to that branch office.

"Mr. Findley, please."

"May I ask who's calling?"

"It's a personal matter. He won't recognize my name."

"Just a moment, please."

A moment later another female voice answered. "This is Mr. Findley's personal assistant. How may I help you?"

"I need to talk with Mr. Findley."

"He's unavailable. If you care to leave your name and number—"

"Tell him," Graham interrupted in a patient but firm tone, "it's about Adele Chandler. He'll want to know."

She hesitated. "Just a moment, please."

True to her word, he waited only a moment, but it was her voice, not Findley's.

"Sir, I'm sorry. Mr. Findley doesn't know an Adele Chandler."

"I see. Would you relay just one more message? Tell him the DNA testing won't take long. All we'll need is a stray hair, which we will easily find in his silver Porsche when it's towed in to the garage this afternoon for some unscheduled repair work."

"Hold on."

It took less than a moment.

A male voice barked, "Who is this?"

"A friend of Ms. Chandler's. You do remember her, don't you? Pretty nineteen-year-old, naturally curly hair. Surely you recall the youth hostel in Rome, which you hastily fled eighteen years ago this summer?"

"What if I don't?"

Graham knew he had made the correct choice by calling on the phone rather than going in person. Had Greg Findley been standing in the same room, he would have throttled him. "I think the question is, what if you do?"

"You just threatened to harm my car."

"No, I just got you on the line. Look, Findley, money is not an issue. Ms. Chandler is not after seventeen years of back child support. She's independently wealthy."

He laughed. "So she did get her old man's money after all?"

"As you did your father's. Half a mil a year declared income for running a branch office that scarcely nets that much isn't bad at all." He paused, letting the breadth of his knowledge sink in. "Findley, you have a charming daughter who turns seventeen in May. She's not looking for a new family. Your wife, Vicky, does not have to be her stepmother. Your children, Alyssa and Greggy, do not have to be her half-siblings in anything beyond fact. She's simply curious about her biological father."

Except for his audibly labored breathing, Findley was silent.

"I take it your wife doesn't know. She doesn't have to. My question is, are you willing to talk to your daughter Chelsea Chandler on the phone?"

"I'll think about it."

"Don't take too long. Why don't you give me the number of your direct line? It would be much more discreet, don't you think?" He let the implication hang. Going through secretaries or family members would complicate matters.

After another moment of heavy breathing, he gave it to him.

"Thank you. One word of caution. When she calls, please don't deny who you are." *Or we'll be talking again, you sleazy lowlife bum.*

"I get the message. Who are you, anyway?"

"As I said, just a friend. I appreciate your cooperation. Have a good day." Graham disconnected.

Tanner jogged the two blocks between the video store and Cherry Street. It was dark, but spring was definitely in the air, a week ahead of its scheduled appearance. He wore warm-up pants and jacket, glad to leave behind winter's layers.

There was Helen parked on the street ahead. Kate must be home. He trotted up to the front door and rang the bell.

A moment later Chelsea opened the door. Beckoning him inside, she grinned and yelled over her shoulder, "It's Mr. Carlucci!"

"Hi."

Adele and Graham walked in from the living room and smiled broadly at him.

"Hi." Now they were all grinning at him. He resisted the urge to turn around and see if something was going on behind him. "What?"

Adele said, "It's just so good to see you after last night. You scared us half to death."

"Mom! Not exactly a good choice of words."

Tanner was lost. "What'd I do?"

Graham said, "You didn't do anything. We just heard the report about the charter plane crash."

Adele added, "And Kate went berserk."

Graham touched her shoulder. "Only hyper. I'd say berserk kicked in when she was at the airport calling every employee there clueless."

The three of them laughed.

Tanner still didn't get it. "Back up. Kate was at the air-port?"

Adele asked, "Didn't you see her?"

He shook his head.

"She insisted on rushing out the door the moment she heard the news. She didn't even eat!"

They laughed again.

Kate didn't eat? Because of a plane crash? He was still lost. "Is she home?"

Adele nodded. "Go on in." Still laughing, the three of them went back into the living room.

Why hadn't Kate told him she'd been at the airport? Berserk? Why would she be that upset?

He knocked on her sliding door located at the other side of the dining room. He could hear the television.

"Come in!"

He slid the door open.

She was sitting on the couch, her nose in the laptop.

"Hey."

Her head jerked up.

"Sorry. That makes twice today I've startled you."

"No problem." She used a forefinger to push the glasses up along her nose.

"I thought you were coming over tonight?"

"Was I?"

"We talked about it this morning. About rearranging the shelves. You had ideas."

"I talk too much sometimes, don't I?"

"No. I'm always ready to listen to your ideas."

"You'll do fine. It's your store." She looked down at the monitor and bit a fingernail.

He had never seen Kate bite her nails. She was quirky, not hyper or prone to going berserk. "Adele said you went to the airport last night."

Her eyelids fluttered. "I thought I could find out some information about the crash. If it were a local plane, think of the scoop."

"You would have written about my fiery death?"

"And gotten it in this week's edition too." She tried to smile, but the attempt failed.

"You're one tough reporter."

"I probably belong in DC."

"Maybe." Maybe she did if she couldn't own up to last night's episode, which included a frantic phone message on his machine. It was like the birthday and flying situations, other issues she didn't want to address. What was her problem now? He changed the subject. "I hired Mick and Betsy."

"Good choices. Tanner, I really need to work. Deadline's today. Tonight. Before 8 A.M. tomorrow."

"First solo week, huh?"

"Yeah, and I'm a little behind."

"Okay. Catch you later." He backed out and slid the door shut.

Newspaper deadline. Maybe that was her problem.

He doubted it.

Graham knelt before the fireplace and crumpled newspapers. The other night he had checked the chimney and flue and declared them fire worthy. With a small load of wood in his trunk and a discount-store poker, he went to work. Adele was dubious, but she liked the thought of a cozy fire and trusted he knew what he was doing. He had inwardly cringed at her words.

Now he inwardly cringed as he did whenever Tanner Carlucci was near. Nice enough guy, but he knew too much for Graham's comfort. If the pilot were to mention he had flown Graham and Rand from Baltimore to Rockville, Adele might be inclined not to let him off the hook again.

He was growing weary of the misrepresentations, of taking advantage of Adele's trusting nature. How in the world had she developed such an attitude?

He straightened and surveyed his handiwork. It just might work. He pulled the old screen across the front of the fire.

Adele clapped from her seat on the couch beside Chelsea. They both were reading.

He said, "Success! No smoke. I'd better wash my hands."

In the dining room he passed Tanner, who was on his way out. The guy appeared a little miffed. He nodded curtly and mumbled, "See you."

"Bye."

He hadn't yet figured out that relationship. Kate had been visibly upset last night. Why didn't she tell Tanner she had been at the airport? It was a curious household tonight. Kate hadn't come out of her room. Chelsea had been downright clingy with her mother, not her usual aloof, breezy self. Adele had been uncharacteristically somber.

A few minutes later he returned to the living room and paused in the doorway. Mother and daughter were hugging, Adele murmuring something.

She spotted him and gave Chelsea a final squeeze. "Okay?"

The girl nodded and stood. "Well." She smiled first at him and then at Adele. "I have some serious homework to do. I'll leave you two lovebirds to enjoy this romantic fire."

"Chels—"

"'Night, Mom." She leaned over and kissed her mother's blushing cheek. "'Night, Graham."

"'Night."

As she left the room, he took her place on the couch near the fireplace. "Sorry. I didn't mean to interrupt anything."

"You didn't."

"You're blushing." As always, the woman's loveliness intrigued him.

"I wish she would stop the teasing."

"Except for that remark, she seemed very sweet to you tonight. Did something happen?"

"You're awfully observant of details for a man."

He shrugged.

She peered over her shoulder toward the doorway. "You are so strange at times. A puzzle." She looked back at him. Her face went slack, as if some inner resolve fell away.

His breath caught. Did she suspect something? He wasn't ready to explain.

"It's Tara," she whispered. "She's pregnant." Adele put a hand to her mouth and gazed at the fire.

Relief flashed through him, and then he comprehended what she had said. Tara was like another daughter to her. He slid to her side and wrapped his arms around her as the first tear glistened on her cheek.

"Oh, Graham! I've been holding it in all day." She sobbed softly. "I didn't want to cry in front of Chelsea."

He held her close. Unbidden comparisons flashed in his mind. Sammi hadn't been as open with her emotions. He recalled holding her when she cried over her father's death. There was the time she had broken her arm. Other than that...

Or was it him? Had he just not been as receptive to her emotional needs? Work consumed him in those days. Now he knew better. What had Sammi done with her tears? What had Adele done with hers?

"Graham, I'm sorry." She straightened and brushed them away. Curling her legs beneath herself, she huddled sideways against the back of the couch and faced him.

He touched her hair. "Don't be."

"I don't know why I open up to you. You're like this guardian angel God sent to watch over me. Do you affect all women this way?"

All women? He hadn't even affected his wife that way. "No. Jupiter must be aligned with Mars or something."

She smiled softly. "Remember that day the girls skipped school? You were right. It was about Tara. They'd gone to Chicago. Tara wanted an abortion. Chelsea talked her out of it, but not until they were inside the clinic."

Her voice barely above a whisper, she went on to tell him about that morning, about the girls' confession and Adele's counsel.

"I'm afraid she won't get much help from her mother or from the boy. Chelsea's committed to going with her to the doctor appointments. I imagine if she doesn't opt for adoption, you're looking at an honorary aunt and grandma." She sighed. "Thanks for listening."

"You're welcome." He reached over and traced the outline of her cheek with his fingertip. Her day was about to grow more complicated, but the timing was unavoidable. "Speaking of teenage pregnancies, I found Greg Findley."

She stared at him, motionless.

"Am I stepping on toes?"

"Not yet."

He glanced over her shoulder toward the doorway and lowered his voice even further. "I called him."

She jerked herself to an upright position. "You *what?*"

"We talked. He's willing to chat with..." He lifted his chin, indicating Chelsea upstairs. "He works for his dad's company in Denver. Has a wife and two kids, ages seven and nine."

"Graham!" She hissed his name through clenched teeth. "I can't believe you did that!"

"Why not?"

"It's not your concern!"

"Of course it is."

She leaned close to him, her voice a hoarse whisper. "What do you mean of course it is?"

"Adele, I don't mean to interfere. It's just information that you can totally ignore. But look, she has to know. I simply saved you the time and effort of searching on the Internet."

"Once she knew the name, the Internet wouldn't have been any time or effort for her. My concern is his response! I don't want him hurting her!"

"He said he's willing to talk with her. He admitted knowing you and about her." In a manner of speaking he had admitted it anyway.

"How did you get that from him? Seventeen years ago I got *nothing.*"

"People change. Even cads grow up."

She flopped back against the couch and looked at the fire, quiet now.

He waited, giving her time to sort through the wreckage of old emotions colliding with new ones. His own were on edge.

At last she said, "I hadn't even considered the possibility that *he* could change. And I even prayed for him, in the early days, when I first became a Christian."

"Well, he's older now and has a family. That tends to change a guy. And I told him…" He paused. "I told him you weren't after money."

She turned to him. "So that's why he's willing."

Graham shrugged. "Could be a major factor."

"The creep. He hasn't changed." Her voice was agitated again. "I don't want my daughter anywhere near the sound of his voice! I wish you hadn't done this."

"I was only trying to help."

"Well, I think you went beyond guardian angel duty. That man will not disrupt our life. Did you tell him where we live?"

"No, nothing like that. I only said I was your friend."

Her eyes narrowed.

On second thought, perhaps he wasn't her friend. "I think I'll go now. You have a lot to sort through."

She nodded curtly and rose. He followed her to the door and retrieved his coat.

"Graham, this really isn't any of your concern, in spite of..." She bit her lip. "In spite of whatever these feelings are between us."

"My mistake. I apologize for intruding." *I just have this idiotic tendency to go after the bad guy.*

She shut the door behind him. No goodbye, no hug, no nothing.

The woman's independence would not crumble easily.

Twenty-Nine

Late Friday afternoon, Kate turned on the sidewalk and backed into the video store, yanking the strings of a dozen helium-filled balloons. They bopped her in the face and wouldn't fit through the door. Laughing, she called out, "Help!"

She felt the door give way as Tanner came alongside and helped her guide the balloons indoors.

"You didn't bring these in Helen. There's no way."

She laughed again. "Absolutely no way. I borrowed my mom's car, and there are more out in it. Hi, Mick," she said to the boy closing the door. She spotted the other new employee behind the counter. "Hi, Betsy!"

The teens greeted her. She had met them last week when they came in to fill out applications. Tomorrow was the big grand opening, Tanner's first day of business. Tonight they were putting the finishing touches on the place.

Taking the balloons from her, Tanner asked, "What are we going to do with these?"

"Tie them down. Let them float around. Whatever."

"Okay." He sounded dubious. "Let's go with whatever. Whatever you decide."

"Let's take these to the back room."

He followed her. "They'll make things look festive, I guess."

"I've got this too." Kate dug into her jacket pockets and pulled out three rolls of rainbow colored crepe paper. "Ta-da."

"Well, you're certainly perkier than you were the other night. I suppose you'll be a regular Miss Grump on deadline days."

On the pretense of removing her coat, she turned her back to him. In his innocuous observation he threatened to undo all of her preparations for the weekend. She had buried her feelings and her mother's words in work. With the weekly edition put to bed, the weekend loomed with all of its Tanner-related plans. How could she nonchalantly be with him when all these emotions fizzed so near the surface?

Early that morning she tackled it in prayer, followed by a pep talk to psyche herself up. She was giving no credence to the idea she was falling in love with him. Impossible. In the first place, she was leaving town. Even more important than that, though, was the fact that he was totally out of her league. His wealthy background and his gorgeous good looks—all right, yes, she admitted he was gorgeous—set him apart. He *did* resemble Adonis, a contemporary American version. Their paths could cross, but they could never ever walk the same one. It would be like the prince marrying the scullery maid, with no queen mum to train her in proper royal etiquette. No adoring public to cheer her on.

With all that settled in her mind, she felt geared up to help him with the grand opening. By sheer willpower she would simply ignore his magnetism and that ridiculous meltdown sensation which started the other morning when she looked up from the computer at the office and saw him watching her.

She laid her coat on a chair and faced him. "I apologize for Wednesday night. I was an awful grouch."

"Downright rude."

"I'm sorry!"

"Apology accepted." He grinned. "Thanks for coming."

"I wouldn't miss it. You promised pizza." She wrinkled her nose at him.

"That's kind of an easy route to your heart, Kilpatrick."

"I know." She avoided his eyes and went to work on untangling the balloon streamers he held.

"I'm surprised you don't have suitors lined up around the block."

"Mm-hmm. And what would I do with a line of suitors?"

"Besides eat well?"

She laughed. "Tanner, you're all thumbs here. Can I borrow Betsy? Decorating is kind of a girl thing."

"What exactly is it you have against Sir Galahad? I know you said his efforts are a waste of energy." He yanked on the ribbons, which only tightened them around his fingers. "What's a waste of energy is fiddling with these balloons."

"But they'll add so much to the event that it's worth expending the extra energy."

"I believe that's Galahad's intention." His eyes met hers. "Some women are worth the extra energy because they add so much to the event of his life."

She looked at the snarled mess in his hands, blotting out the brown-velvet warmth gazing at her. "I'll get the scissors. And Betsy."

"Kate, you're worth it."

Why didn't he drop it? "I suppose I will be to the right man, if there is such a one. Maybe God has plans for me staying single."

"And maybe He doesn't. Maybe He has one particular Sir Galahad waiting in the wings until you get over your *issues.*"

Her laugh was derisive. "Why are we on this subject?"

"Because you don't want to be on it. You have Galahad issues too, don't you?"

"I don't."

"Do too."

"Don't." Her voice rose.

"Do!" His was louder.

"Don't!" she yelled.

He burst out laughing, grabbed her hands, and deftly wound streamers around them, joining their hands together in a tangled web.

Tanner Carlucci was flirting with her.

Shivers chased that meltdown sensation until she felt giddy.

"Betsy!" she shouted. "Bring scissors!"

But take your time. I doubt I'll get another chance like this again.

~

Late Friday evening Adele huddled on the couch under an afghan, staring at the cold fireplace. There weren't any romantic flames burning tonight. There weren't even any ashes left. She had cleaned those out as if that would erase the memory.

She waited for Chelsea. In typical teenage fashion, the girl would sleep half tomorrow away. Now that Adele had made her decision, she couldn't afford to lose a Saturday waiting while anxiety chomped slowly through the hours. It had been doing that for two days now.

The Graham-induced anxiety threatened to undo her. It was his fault. If he hadn't pushed the matter of Chelsea's father, she could have let it go. Again. Still. Oh, why had she ever told him in the first place? The notion that he represented safety was a silly pipe dream. She hadn't been looking, had she? Why had she succumbed to his masculinity so easily?

Lord, I'm sorry for replacing You with him!

The two days since his bombshell had been like running through a maze trying to lose the anxiety-driven thoughts. *He had no right. I do not have to tell Chelsea now. She's still too young.* Adele worked as usual. Though she worried how to avoid Graham, it hadn't been a problem. He didn't call or come by her office. She didn't go to Rand's room. Last night she worked in her basement studio until the wee hours of the morning. Tonight she had tried to do so again, but her nerves were frazzled. The matter obviously wasn't going away.

She called Naomi, who spoke soothingly and pointed out that Graham had indeed done her a service by forcing the issue. It was time to let Chelsea know the entire truth. After all, hadn't *she* just shared the truth with Adele about Tara?

Headlights flashed through the living room curtains and continued along the driveway. Chelsea was parking the minivan in the garage. Given her recent confession, she had been allowed out tonight, with the car. Adele glanced at the clock on the mantel. Ten fifty-five. Good girl.

She would come in the back door. Adele waited. She felt as though she'd been waiting for 17 years.

"Hi, Mom!" Chelsea bounded into the room and plopped on the couch. "I'm early!"

"I noticed."

"Thanks for letting me go out tonight." Her eyes were bright, her smile wide.

Maybe Adele would wait.

"We all got together at Jackie's and Tara told them. She'll go through with the pregnancy now. No way would she want them all to know she'd had an abortion. And, Mom, they were all so supportive."

"That's good. You have a loyal group of friends, honey."

Chelsea babbled on for a while and then was about to head upstairs.

"Chels, can we talk a minute?"

"Sure." She settled back into the couch. "What's up?"

Adele took a deep breath. "Well, I'm not sure where to begin. Honey, I haven't been completely honest with you." She paused again.

"Mom, you're scaring me. Can't you talk faster?"

"I know your dad's name. He's an American."

Chelsea stared at her. "What's his name?"

"Greg Findley. I've been waiting until you were older before I told you everything."

"Why?"

"Because I didn't want you to know how foolish I was. It was hardly a romantic fling. I met him in Europe. We were both spoiled brats with access to unlimited funds. We were out to have a good time." She covered her mouth with a hand and whispered, "I'm so ashamed." On second thought, she needn't go into the entire truth. Ugly details didn't need to be relived.

"Mom, you were just a kid."

She clasped Chelsea's hands. "Who should have known better. Anyway, I told him I was pregnant. He told me to get an abortion."

Her daughter winced.

"I have always been so grateful for refusing. You are the joy of my life." She leaned over and kissed her cheek. "He picked up his backpack and walked out. I never heard from him again. I tracked him down once, when you were about three months old. He said he didn't know me."

"Oh, Mom! How awful!"

"Well, we didn't need that influence in our life, did we?" *Do we need it now?*

"No way. How did you do it? I mean, first your dad rejects you, then him."

"You know how. Aunt Naomi and Jesus. But..." Should she? "Graham...Graham tracked down Greg."

"Graham?"

"Yeah. He seems to have a way with the Internet. And with words, I guess. He actually talked to him."

Chelsea's jaw dropped.

"Your dad lives in Denver. He has a wife and two kids. I think they're seven and nine. He said he's willing to talk to you if you want to talk to him. You don't have to decide right away. You need some time to decipher all this."

"Not really."

Now Adele felt her own jaw drop.

"I mean, what's been your biggest regret ever, Mom? Not ever talking to your dad. Right?"

She nodded. She'd never kept that a secret.

"I don't think I want to live with that for the rest of my life."

"Honey, I don't want you to get your hopes up. He might still be a creep who'll just say hello, have a nice life, and don't look to me for anything."

"I have to find that out for myself."

"Even if it hurts?"

"You keep telling me life hurts."

She smiled. "You could stop quoting me, child."

"You could let me grow up."

She let go of Chelsea's hands and wrapped her in a hug. Her daughter snuggled into her arms like a two-year-old. "Well, I let you take a baby step tonight by telling you this."

"How about letting me take another one?"

"So soon? What is it?"

"You could give me his phone number."

Adele felt herself go still. "Graham has it."

"So will you get it?"

Adele rubbed Chelsea's back and nestled her face against her curls. "Sure."

It was midnight when Tanner locked the door on the last customer and leaned against it.

Kate watched him. The grand opening celebration had been a success, a day full of wall-to-wall customers and well-wishers. He should be ecstatically happy over the town's enthusiastic support, but he appeared to be brooding. She knew why, and she didn't want it to be the first thing out of his mouth.

She applauded her hands and let out a piercing whistle. "Way to go! That had to have been the grandest grand opening Valley Oaks has ever seen. Front page article for sure."

He smiled. "Above the fold?"

"Most definitely. With your photo. Your photo will sell lots of papers. All those moms and daughters. You want to count the money?"

"I'm too bushed. How's that for an entrepreneurial answer?" He laughed in a mocking way. "The bankers would cringe."

"Well, it can wait." She had already cleared the Ping-Pong table of food and tableware trash. "Shall I take down the crepe paper?"

"No. I'll let one of the kids do that on a slow day. I suppose we could have one."

"Maybe now and then. Well, I'm bushed too. I guess it's time to call it—"

"He didn't come."

"I know. Something probably came up."

"Something always comes up. Something is going to come up tomorrow to cancel a certain outing that involves a plane."

She went to him. "Tanner, don't do this to yourself."

"What am I doing to myself? I think my dad took care of things quite nicely without my help. At least my mom had a good excuse. She's in Arizona."

She grabbed his hands, pulled him behind the counter, and shoved him into a chair. "It's an old emotional tape you're playing." She boosted herself atop the counter. "Let him go. Forgive him for all the times he's wronged you and for all the times he's going to again."

"One good reason?"

"You're letting him ruin this perfectly perfect day. It's your new start, Tanner. Don't let him interfere. And besides, you're not so cute when you're feeling sorry for yourself." *Whoops.*

He smiled at her. "It's hard to let go of thirty years."

"I can't imagine. But if you let him off the hook, you're really pulling out the hook that keeps cutting into your heart. I dare you to keep the date tomorrow. It'll be a tangible thing you can do to pull that hook out. How he treats you does not have to dictate what you do or how you feel."

"I've tried."

"Well, try again and stop whining." She scooted off the counter. "Oh. You could pray about it too. There's no way on God's green earth that by your own power you can forgive a person who's hurt you like he has."

He rubbed his jaw.

"I think we both just dared each other to go tomorrow. What do you say?"

"I don't know, Kate. This is a new one, daring to do the same thing. Who will pay for dinner?"

She laughed. "Let me at that cash register."

Thirty

Adele spent most of Saturday with Chelsea. The girl was full of questions about Greg Findley. She didn't seem to mind that the answers were 18 years old.

It was a painful journey for Adele, but she knew it was no longer avoidable. She hauled the ladder from the basement to the second floor hallway and climbed up it and through the attic opening. The shoe box was in the bottom of a larger box which was tucked beneath a stack of baby clothes. Neither box had been opened since she packed them when Chelsea was a toddler.

They sat together at the dining room table. Pushing aside mementos, Adele searched for what Chelsea would want to see first: the photo album. It was small and plain, the photo edges somewhat yellowed. Flipping the pages quickly, she went as if by reflex straight to the picture. It was the best one of Greg, alone, standing near a canal in Venice.

"Mom, he's cute!"

"Well, of course." She studied the tall, laughing blond, more southern California surfer than San Franciscan. Yes, he had been a cute 21-year-old, though now she recognized the softness about his chin, a clue to his lack of character. At least she hadn't had to confront it every day. "But you know, Chels, I've always been grateful you resembled me."

"Except for my ear." She touched her left one where the ridge folded over slightly. "Look, you can see it on him."

"Mm-hmm. And he was tall, like you. His eyes were bluer than ours."

"How did you meet?"

Chelsea listened with rapt attention as Adele relayed an edited version of the story.

When it ended in Rome, Chelsea hugged her. "Thanks, Mom. This means so much to me, just to know. I should thank Graham too, don't you think?"

"Yes, I think so."

And I owe him thanks as well as an apology.

Even as a teen, Graham Logan's chin would have been firm.

Late Saturday night, Graham sat in his drab furnished apartment, staring at four empty walls. Temporary surroundings never disturbed him all that much. To put up with uncomfortable chairs, a lumpy mattress, and a kitchen with few conveniences was not a hardship. He could tolerate almost anything for three months. On the other hand, being disconnected from Adele for three days was sheer torture.

He had purposely avoided her at the nursing home, determined to give her the space she needed. Should he call and risk further alienating her? Not only was time running out, he feared his chances of winning her over faded with each passing hour. Now that he knew what it was like to kiss her, he longed to commit to a relationship with her. Surely that longing was nothing short of a gift from God.

The whole problem with this assignment was letting his personal feelings get involved. Of course, he knew they were involved going into it. Rand had suspected as much, and it had fueled his determination which, in the end, was what had brought them to Valley Oaks.

Adele was as determined and as stubborn as Rand. She may not make the first move. She may not accept any first move he could make. What was the way to her heart? He assumed it had been Chelsea. That backfired. Roses? A ton of clay delivered to her door? Blueprints for a senior housing complex?

His cell phone rang. The caller ID displayed Adele's number. He breathed a prayer of thanks.

"Hello?"

"Graham?" It was the younger version of the lilting voice.

"Hi, Chelsea."

"You recognized my voice! I just called to thank you for finding my dad."

Whew. She had told her. "You're welcome."

"Maybe...maybe you could give me his phone number?"

"Of course."

"Later. Mom wants to say hi now. Thank you."

"My pleasure."

There were muffled voices, and then hers, clear, the lilting subdued. "Graham? Hi. How are you?"

"Better since the phone rang." Too strong. "How about yourself?"

"I'm okay. I...I want to apologize. You can say 'I told you so' if you want."

"I don't want to."

"Well, you were right. Again. She needed to know. Thank you for forcing me into telling her."

"I apologize for not asking you first. I overstepped the bounds by taking things into my own hands."

"My guardian angel."

"All right. I also apologize for that self-appointment."

"Accepted." There was a smile in her voice.

"Did the conversation go all right?"

"Yes. We didn't even need soup!"

"Pity. I would have come."

"I know. Graham, I think I'm getting too used to you being here."

"Is that a bad thing?"

"I don't know yet."

He closed his eyes. "May I see you tomorrow? I thought a drive up the river would be nice. Dinner."

"I hate leaving Chelsea. You know how clingy she was the other night? I'm behaving like that. Something feels so tentative about life right now."

Could she sense his unease, the impending dialogue? Still… "Adele, you've been overly anxious about this situation. Perhaps a few hours away is exactly what you need. I don't think you give yourself much time off, do you?"

She didn't reply.

"Please, give yourself a break. And me."

"Give you a break?"

"I've missed you. Don't hang up."

She didn't hang up, but neither did she answer.

"Sorry, Adele. I'll go do my grumbling in private. Why don't I call you in the morning? You can sleep on it."

"I haven't slept in three nights. I'd better not sleep on any more unfinished business. I'll see you," she whispered, "tomorrow."

Kate suspected she had a problem with bravado. She didn't mean to portray it by accepting challenges willy-nilly. The fact of the matter was her faith had instilled in her the ability to readily accept anything thrown her way. She trusted God would cover for her. It added quite a bit of zing to her life by always saying yes. Nothing to worry about.

Except single-engine four-seater planes.

Bravado had nothing to do with it this time. Zing had nothing to do with it. Clever Tanner had turned what would have been an automatic "no" into a faith issue, leaving her no choice but to face her biggest fear.

God will cover for me. Mantralike, the phrase replayed in her mind as she waited not far from the runway. The bright early afternoon sunshine didn't penetrate the khaki trench coat, her favorite spring outerwear, a hand-me-down from her father that usually enveloped her in comfort. Not today. From her innermost depths fear rendered her numb. She stood stiff as a board next to Tanner and met his dad's family while pointedly keeping her back to that *thing*.

One glance had convinced her that *thing* was made of popsicle sticks and rubber bands and model glue. It could not have reached her height of 5´2˝. And he referred to it as an *airplane*.

Tanner excused himself now to complete his preflight tasks.

"Kate." It was Dr. Carlucci. He was a mature version of Tanner, his hair still thick and black, though shorter and not moussed. "Have you ever flown in one of these before?"

She shook her head violently.

"You'll love it."

Mm-hmm.

"Just like riding in a car, but you can see the entire countryside. What a gorgeous day for flying." He turned to the children, repeating something about seat belts.

Jenna, age eight, and Jake, ten, danced around, clearly thrilled at the prospect before them. Marnie, a tall slender woman with long, smooth blonde hair and a young face like Adele's, ran after little Sidney Jr., their three-year-old.

Kate hadn't slept well. She probably resembled a zombie. Horrifying visions of flying had filled her dreams...scenes of mountains suddenly appearing, of green hills rushing at her, of spiraling downward—

"Kate!"

"Huh?"

Tanner was in her face. "Ready?"

She shook her head.

He glanced at the others, smiling. "She's a little nervous."

His dad said, "I'll strap the kids in."

Tanner took her face in his hands and whispered, "Show me, Kate. Show me it's not all talk. He's with you, isn't He?"

She blinked until his face came into focus. "Jesus." Her lips felt shot with novacaine.

"You'll come fly with me?"

Yea, though I walk through the valley of the shadow of death...

"Okay."

He led her to the *thing* and helped her climb into it. The kids were grinning from their seats.

"Up front, Kate."

She found her voice. "Maybe Jake wants it. He can—"

"Front seat is yours. It's a weight thing."

She sat. And then she squeezed her eyes shut and gritted her teeth. *Thy rod and thy staff—* She balled her hands into tight fists pressed together on her lap.

She sensed Tanner pulling the safety belt around her, lifting her arms out of the way, clicking it into place.

"Here we go, kids!"

The engine started, drowning out everything but the crash of her heartbeat in her ears.

The sensation of careening came over her. She imagined them hurtling down the runway. Would they never lift off? How could they lift off?

Please, Lord, can You please just make it quick? I don't mind coming Home, I really don't.

A hand touched her shoulder. She peeked at him.

He sat on her left, nearer to her than when they were in his car. He was grinning, his cheeks cupped by a headset. He pointed forward.

Behind his head she saw blue sky.

They were off the ground?

He took hold of her chin and gently nudged her face frontwards.

Her heart leapt and a whimper escaped her throat.

And then a brand-new world burst into existence, imprinting itself on her vision. The resplendence of creation flooded her, spilling over onto her tongue. Her delighted laughter was a hymn of praise to the One whose hand had made it all.

~

Adele slipped her arm through Graham's, relishing in his closeness. They sat side by side atop a picnic table, their feet perched on the bench seat. The deserted park was located on a bluff overlooking the river. Sunlight danced on the distant silver gray water. Surrounding brown hills were covered with bare-limbed trees that seemed out of place. Though it was only the first of April, with the record-breaking 70-degree weather it seemed they should be loaded with spring green foliage.

He placed his hand over hers.

Her heart still occasionally did its funny little foxtrot number in her throat. Like now, when his physical presence overwhelmed her... Or when she thought of how quickly they had grown close... Or when she thought of what she didn't yet know about him...

She had never been in love before. Was that what it was? Or had she just signed up for heartache? How was she supposed to know?

He kissed the top of her head. "A penny for your thoughts."

"I'm thinking how on earth can a woman reach my age and be so naïve?"

"About what?"

"Come on, Graham. Don't pretend like I'm not."

"All right. You are so naïve it's frightening. I'm surprised some scuzzy creep hasn't waltzed right into your life and stolen you blind."

"I don't have that much to steal."

"It's figurative. I meant your emotional well-being."

"Oh." She stared out at the river. "Don't you think I could smell a scuzzy creep?"

"No, I don't. What amazes me is your ability to trust after the way your family treated you."

"Ancient history. God has been taking care of me since Chelsea was born. Without a husband or a scuzzy creep around, I had to learn to depend directly on Him."

"What happens when you cry like you did the other night?"

When she didn't reply, he gently pressed her hand and waited. She met the piercing blue gaze. "Why do you ask that?"

"I was wondering. It particularly concerned me for some reason."

"I imagine Jesus holding me." She blinked.

"And that works?"

"It did...until that day Chelsea skipped school. I couldn't quite get a handle on my emotions." It was the first time Graham held her. And then she got a handle on them.

He smiled briefly as if he too remembered. "I cannot imagine dealing with kids."

"Did you ever want them?"

"No." A brusque tone underscored the lightning-quick response. He cleared his throat. "How about you? Did you ever want another?"

"Sure. Giving birth, holding that newborn, watching her grow year after year. There is no word to describe it. The benefits obliterate the struggles. But..." She shrugged. "Not by myself again."

"Maybe if you had others, letting Chelsea go wouldn't be as tough."

"Oh, it probably wouldn't make a difference. For the first time I'm getting a glimpse of what I put my mother through. I've been so determined that Chels and I would have a different relationship, I didn't think I'd notice this part. We do have a different relationship, but I'm sitting here concerned she's going to grow up today while I'm not at home. I have this irrational fear she'll run away and get pregnant like I did. Which was why I was so crazy the day she skipped school."

"Then, dear, you definitely need something else to think about. Don't go away. I'll be right back." He sprang from the picnic table and loped off toward the parking lot.

Adele noted what she had seen before. He moved with the agility of an athlete. There was a subtle physical strength about him that greatly enhanced the sense of safety she always felt emanating from him. She had no doubt that if she were threatened by someone with a weapon, Graham would know just what to do.

Just like he knew what to do when they were worried about Tanner.

Just like he knew what to do about Greg Findley.

Adele hesitated as she connected the pieces of the Graham Logan puzzle. Another naïve reaction? Or self-preservation? If she saw him clearly, would he resemble the man she loved?

Of course he would. A leopard couldn't change his spots. Graham would still be kind and gentle, attuned to her. And the best-looking guy she had ever seen.

Still, the missing pieces begged for attention.

Rand Jennings was more than likely from Baltimore, her *hometown*, not Chicago.

Graham never talked about his work, but he talked of a wide variety of other personal experiences. He had obviously lived in more places than Chicago.

He had sources high in government.

He was overly alert, though he downplayed his physical and mental prowess. The details he noticed, the way his eyes took in the surroundings, his instant memorization of Kate's number, his intimate knowledge of Rockville...

"Adele." He was standing in front of her, smiling. "You're not looking at the river. Lost in thought again?"

"Mm-hmm. But not about Chelsea."

He cocked his head to one side, studying her. "Do I want to know about what?"

"Oh, just you. What are you holding behind your back?"

"What about me?" he teased.

"You don't want to know!"

"Was it good stuff?"

"Well," she drawled out the syllable, "some of it was."

"Not most of it?"

"No."

He heaved an exaggerated sigh. "I'll have to try harder."

"Yes, you will."

"I have something here that might help."

She caught a glimpse over his shoulder of a long rolled sheet of paper. "What is it?"

"Let me preface it by saying I found an investor for you."
Stunned at this statement, she felt her smile fade.

He swung a leg over the bench seat and straddled it, watching her intently. "Your dream has merit, Adele. I knew someone who would agree." He unrolled the large tube of papers. "He's a seasoned businessman, wealthy, not accustomed to waiting. These are—"

She gasped, struck with the realization that she was looking at blueprints.

"Plans for your complex. If they're not what you have in mind—"

"Graham!" she whispered, quickly deciphering floor plans of an apartment building. "How...? What...? This is incomprehensible!"

"I'm sorry. Let me explain—"

"Not the diagrams! Oh my goodness! There's the coffee shop! And an enclosed walkway connecting it to the theater!"

"Here, underneath." He rearranged the papers. "This shows the individual units."

"Oh my!"

"And here." More shuffling. "That acreage south of town. See the entrance is here, and another here."

She gasped again.

"Did you picture it this way? It can be changed."

"Oh, Graham!" She put a hand to her mouth. "Who...?"

"Anonymous."

She needed to stop gasping. Lowering her hand, she took a deep breath and tried to think rationally. "You said *an* investor. One *person?*"

He nodded. "As I said, he's seasoned, he's familiar with such investments. And, he's wealthy."

"How...how does something like this work?"

"Simple contract. Your attorney is drawing up the papers now. We have an appointment with her on Tuesday. She'll come out to Fox Meadow so you won't have to—"

"You know who my attorney is?"

"I figured someone at the nursing home would know. I asked Gracie."

A faint warning bell dinged in the back of her mind. He knew more about her than the name of her lawyer. She ignored the thought. "Good heavens! I feel like I just won the lottery. It's unbelievable. Is it unbelievable? I mean, is it too good to be true?"

"No. It's a straight business transaction."

"I'm not familiar with business transactions."

"Do you trust your attorney?"

"Yes." Laura was a friend of Naomi's. Adele had known her for years.

"She'll explain everything to you. I don't have to be present. I won't interfere with your meeting. Bottom line, you make all the decisions. If the investment falls flat, it's not your fault. You don't have to repay a dime."

"How can Mr. Anonymous sign a contract with me?"

Graham blinked as if surprised at her question. "I have power of attorney. I can sign his name to legal documents."

"You can sign his checks?"

He smiled. "Naturally. You'll have to receive one, won't you?"

Rand Jennings. "Will he identify himself someday?"

"He may."

Why? Why would a complete stranger on his deathbed put up—"How much are we talking?" Goodness, the man had already paid for these plans before her.

"Four point two million."

Her eyes grew wide. *Incomprehensible!*

"That includes the land. There's more if it's needed, but we anticipate residents prebuying units, which will offset expenses. See here." He pulled out one of the bottom sheets. "The first ten could be ready for occupancy by fall. People could move into them while the rest are under construction."

"Can you tell me..." Concern tightened her throat. "Can you tell me *why?*"

"Dear Adele." He rolled up the blueprints, set them aside, and hopped back onto the tabletop beside her. "Think of it as a gift, like grace from your heavenly Father. Did you understand that in the beginning?"

She shook her head. "It was incomprehensible. Like this."

"Will you just think about it?"

It began to sink in then, the whole wildly outrageous joy of her dream taking shape. She smiled. That stretched to a grin. She giggled. "Oh, Graham!" She slid her arms around his neck and laughed loudly. "What's to think about?"

Thirty-One

"Was that the coolest thing you've ever seen or what?" Kate grasped the hands of Jenna and Jake and whirled the three of them around the airplane in a silly dance, each trying to out-"yahoo!" the others.

Off to one side, Tanner laughed, relishing in a deep sense of satisfaction. The kids were delighted with the plane ride. Though he recognized that, as usual, his first reason for doing something was to please his dad, he also got a kick out of putting those smiles on the little Marnie faces.

And Kate had come. She had risen to the occasion as he suspected she would, embracing the moment with all of her energy. She would give Jesus the credit, of course, but she had been willing in the first place to step out into unknown territory. He admired her for that. Even if the landing terrified her.

"Oh, Tanner!" she cried now. They danced over to him, and, letting go of hands, she and Jenna grabbed his.

He joined their circle and hopped around, wondering at the picture. Wouldn't his dad think them ridiculous? Thirty-year-olds prancing like preschoolers? His dad was probably still shaking his head over Kate, assuming she was his latest girlfriend. Her shiny copper hair would be described as *red* in a derogatory tone; her clogs, baggy pants, and billowing coat as urchinlike.

Tanner let go of hands, grabbed Kate around the waist, and twirled her. She was none of those things his father, so consumed with appearances, might think.

She squealed till he set her down. "Thank you!" She kissed him on the cheek.

He slipped his arms around her back and held her a moment longer than their brief friendly hugs usually lasted, his face against her neck. She smelled clean...fresh...of soap...of innocence.

She pulled back. "Hey! It's time for ice cream, big brother! You promised!"

He wanted to kiss her. Instead he tweaked her nose and went off to finish his postflight duties. It took twice as long as it should have. His mind kept wandering, imagining what it would be like to kiss those shapely lips. In so intimate a touch, would her energy feel like an electric shock?

Eventually he joined the others at his car. They were taking the kids home, right after a stop at the mall for ice cream. He hadn't spent much time with Jake and Jenna. They were likable kids and well behaved.

Although dinnertime wasn't far off, Kate ordered a cone. No surprise. They found a table in the open food court and sat, while the kids carried their cones over to the stage where a magician was performing.

He couldn't help but smile at the sight of Kate's vanilla ice cream mustache.

She caught his eyes on her. "What?"

"Is this the same woman who wrote that scathing editorial?"

She laughed. "I think so. Oh, Tanner!"

He had lost count how many times she had said that since they landed. "You don't have to thank me again."

"But I do! That was the most magnificent thing. All the fields and trees and sky and the river and creeks. Can we do it again when things are in bloom?"

He didn't remind her that by then she would be gone. "Anytime."

"Is it horribly expensive?"

"No. I get a significant discount, and we don't have to pay a pilot."

"But 'expensive' is a relative term."

"True. Don't worry about it."

"What you did today was magnificent too."

"What'd I do?"

"You forgave your dad."

He frowned. "How's that?"

"He didn't show up yesterday, inflicting even more emotional damage on you."

He flinched. "Do you ever consider mincing your words?"

She lowered the cone. "I'm sorry."

"I'm only kidding."

She didn't look convinced.

"Partly."

"Anyway, in spite of that, you did something for him that cost you a lot of time and energy. You had to swallow your pride to do what you did today."

He shrugged. "I love flying."

"That's beside the point. Don't shrug it off, Tanner. What you did was an act of forgiveness." Her green eyes filled. "It was a really big deal."

He glanced away before his own eyes resembled hers. "Not as big a deal as what you did."

"Oh, Tanner!" There it was again, that ecstatic, bubbling tone.

He looked at the face lit up like a Christmas tree. "Don't thank me again. All I did was invite you. You came, you got on board, you opened your eyes."

"None of it possible without your encouragement. God is so amazing. You knew He wouldn't let me down, but I didn't want to take Him at His word. Not when it came to flying in small planes!"

"Kate, what you did spoke volumes to me about God. More than anything I've heard in church so far."

She lowered the ice cream cone again. The white mustache was still there.

He picked up the napkin lying on the table in front of her and dabbed away the ice cream. If faith were contagious like a cold, he would have kissed away the creamy line right there in front of everyone. Maybe with her it was contagious. Maybe that electrical shock of energy would be infused with the spirituality she wore so eloquently.

"Tanner." She pushed aside his hand. "If that spoke volumes, then you'll keep up your end of the bargain?"

"I don't know. It would appear that I simply cannot take you out in public. However, if you promise not to spill, I'll take you to Antonio's."

"Dinner is not what I meant."

He knew what she meant and dropped his joking tone. "A deal is a deal. But let's do dinner first. For some reason I don't want to get down on my knees in the middle of the mall."

Her eyes bore into his as if she wanted to read his mind.

"I promise, Kate. I promise I will."

Kate fidgeted in Tanner's car. And it wasn't only because she couldn't stop thinking about Tanner's hands on her waist, effortlessly lifting her off the ground and twirling her around. Or about her impulsive kiss on his scratchy, solid cheek. Or about his face pressed against her neck. Or about his hand patting a napkin at her mouth.

Dusk was falling, and they sat in a driveway in an old established neighborhood of Rockville. Large lawns and hedges separated homes. She had seen the hidden backyards from River Parkway below. They melded into the edges of bluffs, no doubt providing spectacular views of the river.

The house before them was a white, three-story colonial. Enormous oak trees rose around it like an elegant canopy even in their early spring barrenness.

Tanner turned to her. "So this is where I grew up. Would you like to see the inside? No one's home. Mom's still in Arizona."

"Uh, no thanks. Some other time."

They had just completed a tour of Sidney and Marnie's house, a newer sprawling brick affair with an indoor swimming pool. The plan to simply drop the kids at the door was foiled by Marnie's friendly invitation to a cup of tea. It would have felt rude to turn her down.

Kate thought her imagination was pretty good, but the two homes owned by Tanner's father went far beyond anything she had anticipated. They solidified her notion that Tanner's background would be impossible to relate to hers.

He spoke again. "He makes an obscene amount of money."

Obviously. "Hey, do you mind if we stop at my parents' house before dinner?"

"Not at all. I'd love to." He sounded relieved and quickly shifted into reverse.

They rode in companionable silence to yet another section of town. Kate felt quieted after the wild exuberance of the afternoon flight. It wasn't only the fact that she had actually flown in the small plane that fueled her sense of silent awe. It was most of all that Tanner had chosen an act of forgiveness toward his dad...that he saw God's faithfulness in her climbing into the plane...that he promised to get down on his knees. *Hallelujah.*

He interrupted her thoughts. "I made reservations for seven."

"Great. That gives me plenty of time."

"For what?"

"Changing clothes."

He glanced over at her. "Why would you do that?"

Because her mother would have a fit if she knew she wore baggy khaki slacks and an oversized sweater to Antonio's. "Antonio's is…" She shrugged. "Upscale."

"Since when would anything affect what you wear?"

"Since I saw the two houses that belong to your family."

"I'm wearing blue jeans."

And a soft black sweater over a white collared shirt, a combination that emphasized his dark good looks. "Tanner, you look presentable in anything."

"So do you."

She bit her lip, wishing he hadn't said that. "I don't need to hear empty flattery. I'm sure you know that by now."

"It wasn't and I do know that. You have a rare, colorful, individualistic look about you. It doesn't matter what you wear."

"You're pretty good at dishing out compliments."

"Kate, give me a break. Why won't you accept what I say at face value? Is it because my dad has money?"

She squirmed, uncomfortable as much with her tone as with his probing. "Partly."

"Partly. What's the other part?"

"Well, good grief, Carlucci, women refer to you as Adonis."

He burst out laughing. "What do my looks and my dad's money—two things I can hardly take any credit for—what do they have to do with you not accepting what I say? What? They're proof I'm shallow and insincere and a prig?"

Put that way... "No. I just don't want to embarrass you at Antonio's. Even Beth makes me change clothes sometimes before she'll go out with me."

He laughed again. "Trust me. You don't have to on my account."

"But if you don't mind waiting, I think I'll change. My brother says I clean up pretty good."

He smiled at her. "I'm sure you do, Kate Kilpatrick. I'm sure you do."

Tanner watched Kate walk down the staircase, well aware of her dad standing nearby. He made an effort not to gawk as her legs came into view.

Kate had legs. Slender calves in black hose, small feet in black flats.

She had a feminine shape, evident now in a knee-length black knit dress.

She had normal hair... No, not normal. It was a rich, beautiful, unusual color and hung in soft waves just above her shoulders.

Eyeshadow enhanced her pretty eyes and a glossy hint of color emphasized those lips—

"Tanner! We're running late!" She jumped down the last two steps. "Sara insisted on trying to curl my hair. Ready?"

Good. She hadn't lost her energetic quirkiness. He nodded.

Her mother trailed behind her, carrying a plastic grocery bag. "Katelyn, wear my black coat. Dan, get it out of the closet."

"Mom," she protested.

"You'll ruin the effect wearing your dad's old raincoat."

Dan held a long wool coat open for his daughter. "Thanks, Dad. Let me have my clothes." She took the bag from her mom and they exchanged a hug. "Bye. Bye, Dad. Tanner, will you bring along my favorite raincoat there?" She pointed to the coat draped over a chair. "Thanks."

Tanner waved his goodbyes to her parents and followed Kate out to his car...still speechless.

The inner beauty of Kate Kilpatrick had just leaped into a different realm, fanning the flame that already burned steadily within him. It didn't need any fanning. What was she trying to do? Break his heart?

He reached around her before she had a chance to open the car door herself.

"Tanner, we don't have time for Galahad!"

He took the plastic bag from her and put a hand under her elbow as she stepped up onto the running board. "On the contrary, Guinevere, we have all the time in the world."

She sat down, complaining, "But I've never eaten at Antonio's! What if they give our table away?"

"They won't." He shut her door, opened the back one, and laid her bag and coat on the seat.

"How do you know they won't?"

He shut that door, went around to his, and climbed in. "Because my dad owns it." He started the engine.

"Really?"

"Mm-hmm. I hear the food is excellent."

"Haven't you been there?"

"Not since I made a total fool of myself by overturning a table and yelling at the wait staff. Lifetime ago." He flipped on the heater.

"Tanner." Her tone was thoughtful, almost awestruck. "This sounds like another act of forgiveness."

He hadn't thought of it that way, but then he didn't have the ability to see things from her upside down, inside out perspective.

"Actually." He turned to her, his arms crossed on the steering wheel. "I haven't met anyone I wanted to take there. I kept waiting for a quirky redhead to walk into my life. You know, someone I could show off."

"It's a good thing I dressed up for the occasion."

"But I made the reservations before you did. Dressed up or not, you are something to show off."

"Tanner."

He heard the reservation in her tone and knew he tread on thin ice. If he went with the Galahad speech, she would most likely fling herself from the car and hightail it back into the house. *Adios, bud.*

"Anyway, Kilpatrick, your brother was right. You clean up real good."

She could handle that. With a grin she settled back against the seat. "Thanks."

He turned on the lights and shifted into drive. Maybe some other time he would tell her exactly how intoxicatingly beautiful she really was.

Late that night Tanner stood at the window in his darkened bedroom. The blinds were open, allowing in dim light cast from a streetlamp. He gazed across the street on the town square at the trees, walkways, and band shell. A handful of teenagers hung out, lounging against their cars. Cal or one of the other deputies would be by soon. They'd chat and eventually leave. He'd watched it happen on a nightly basis since moving in above the pharmacy.

Life was peaceful in Valley Oaks, almost as peaceful as it was at ten thousand feet. He felt a relief when leaving Rockville and a pleasant anticipation to check the store, make sure the kids had locked up properly, and climb the stairs to his quiet apartment.

There had been a competing pleasant anticipation, that of kissing Kate goodnight. He knew it wouldn't happen, but the anticipation had been there to savor.

She insisted he not walk her to the door, but he did anyway. It was true, what she had said. She could at times talk too much; he gave himself permission to ignore some of her wishes...the ones that sounded like orders. She thanked him profusely for the day, and then she was in the house. Not even her semi-customary hug. And dinner had been quite good, their conversation thoroughly captivating.

Wouldn't you know it? He had finally got the hang of falling for a woman, and the one he chose wasn't the least bit interested in anything beyond friendship.

He thought of their earlier conversation at the mall. Why had he promised "on his knees"? Twice?

A memory tucked deep into the folds of his subconscious wiggled its way to the surface. Grammy Stanton. His mother's grandmother. She had taught him to pray on his knees. Always on his knees. When he was nine, she had died. He prayed on his knees that she would come alive again. He had never gone down on his knees since.

Kate would ask. Kate would hound him.

He lifted his eyes to the stars. *Well, God, I've always known You're there. Just look at that sky.* Between his great-grandmother and his flying, he never doubted His existence.

But what Kate did today...put her fear in Your hands and then ended up loving it...You're more than just existing out there in the big cosmos. My only gripe is You'll probably insist I forgive my dad. Forgive and forget.

Today's attempt hadn't been all that difficult. Of course Kate the cheerleader had drawn his eyes to the children's fun, away from the man who...

Kate would ask.

He went to his bedside and slowly got down on his knees.

"Okay," he whispered, "I'm here. Jesus. I guess I'm talking to You."

He paused, not exactly sure what was expected of him. Maybe he should just keep talking. He had certainly done a lot more foolish things than talk to the air. But he knew...he *knew* it wasn't just air.

"I saw You today. Alive and well in Kate. I've never seen anyone so afraid of anything, and she's about the least fearful person I've ever met. She never could have gotten on that plane and then reacted the way she did unless her faith is in something, someone who is real. I guess what I'm asking is...though I have no right to ask for anything..."

He didn't. He was filth. So why was he there pretending otherwise?

Because Kate would ask.

Because the pastor said in the morning sermon that Jesus hung out with prostitutes, thieves, and drunks in order to invite them into His kingdom. He was only waiting for them to RSVP.

"Okay, I'm RSVP-ing. I want to be part of Your family. I want what Kate has. I need You at some inner core of my being. Please come in. Please make me clean and whole?"

By now Tanner's face was buried in the bed covers, his arms stretched out in surrender. The instant the tears came he knew they were why he had put off this meeting. He hated crying. It brought back those wasted years when he cried often. It brought back that last time he had been on his knees, crying for the old woman who had shown him such love.

A warmth came over him, the sort of warmth that satiated... Hot chocolate after a cold day of sledding... Grammy's arms around him, the hint of lavender in her cheek... His parents laughing together at his first-grade acting debut... A three-point buzzer shot at the end of a quarter...

The warmth comforted, and Tanner realized he was smiling. The tears still fell, but he was *smiling*. A lifetime of sorrows and regrets mingled with unspeakable joy, and he knew that he was loved.

Thirty-Two

Monday evening Kate parked in the nearly empty high school lot and climbed out of the car. Streetlamps were just beginning to flicker on in the twilight. The snow had completely melted away. The parking lot was bone dry, though the ground remained soggy. It gave off a rich, damp, green scent, evidence that beneath the earth unseen new life was being diligently nourished. Already crocuses had popped through, blooming all over the place. She loved the spring.

Yesterday had been a day full of shivers. The fear of flying had blotted them out for a while, but once she opened her eyes and saw that glorious view, they returned with magnified intensity. Magnified because the flying experience itself was enough to thrill. Added to the day-long close proximity of Tanner, she had been surprised she could breathe.

"Kate!"

She recognized his voice now and his distinct easy gait as he approached through the dusky parking lot. He had left a message on her voice mail sometime that morning when she had been unavailable, just to say he was subbing and that he would see her at the school board meeting.

He neared her now, grinning broadly. "Hi."

"Hi, Tanner."

"I figured you'd come early to get the best seat in the house."

"You'd think they could reserve seats for the press so I wouldn't have to do this."

"Yes, you would think so, wouldn't you?" he teased.

"If I were staying in Valley Oaks, I would do some serious training about press protocol. We are the link to public opinion. Groups like school boards need us, and we need a little special treatment."

"You're only half joking." He shook a finger at her.

"What makes you say that?"

"It's in your voice. Rough day?"

She blew out a noisy breath. "I didn't have a chance to remind myself today that this is the best experience I could ever ask for. I do not know how Rusty did it."

"She would be proud of you." He leaned beside her against the car. "Nice night."

"Did you walk?"

"Of course. It's great being able to hike everywhere in town."

"I keep saying I'm going to, but I'm always in a hurry."

He chuckled. "No kidding. You're always trying to be in two places at once."

They stood together in the comfortable quiet of old friends for a few moments. The night's first stars twinkled to life. By now others were arriving. Car doors slammed, people hurried to the building. Time to go.

"I'd better get in there."

He cleared his throat. "Aren't you going to ask me?"

"Ask you what?"

"You know."

She studied him from the corner of her eye. Ask him what? If he could feel the shivers running through her? Maybe Helen was picking them up and vibrating behind him.

He let out a dramatic sigh. "Oh, well. Guess it wasn't important. See you inside." He walked away.

What wasn't important? Was she going to ask him something important? About what? What had they talked about yesterday? What hadn't they talked about? They always talked and talked... A feeling of dread hit her. She was letting him down. What had he expected her to—

"Tanner!" she yelled, running after him. "Tanner!"

He turned around and waited for her to catch up.

She stood before him, breathless at the thought. "Did you?"

He gave her his cocky grin, the one he reserved for teasing. "Did I what?"

"Did you get down on your knees?" Awe pressed her voice down to a whisper.

"Did I say I would?"

Yes. He had said he would. And yes, he kept his word. She nodded. "And?" Still a whisper.

"And I told Jesus I know He's real. I see Him in you. I told Him I wanted Him in me too."

Kate covered her mouth with her hands. Tears sprang to her eyes and spilled over onto her face.

"I don't know if I got the terminology right—"

She went to him and slid her arms around him. They held each other tightly. *Thank You, Father.*

Tanner Carlucci wasn't the only one who kept his word.

The board meeting was grueling. In anticipation of a large crowd, it was held in the high school gym. A good choice. The folding seats on the floor were filled. The bleachers remained shut. Another good choice. Kate suspected the clanking boards would have made noisy seats for the large number of students who had gathered.

She sat near the front, on a side aisle, scribbling furiously on her notepad. It was after ten-thirty, and they were still discussing Joel Kingsley, the principal. The floor was open to the public. At the moment, things were very close to getting out of control.

The lines were clearly drawn. Kingsley supporters far outnumbered his opponents among the parents and students in attendance. Still, those against were as vociferous as the bigger crowd.

Tanner leaned against her arm and whispered, "We may be here all night."

She wished he wouldn't do that...touch her arm and put his mouth near her ear. It seriously disrupted her train of thought.

At last the president called an end to the discussion and asked for a motion to table the decision to renew the principal's contract until a special meeting next week. There was an immediate motion, a second, a vote in favor. Kate's eyes were on Bruce Waverly, the superintendent. She thought she detected an expression of "that's absurd," the same one she was trying to suppress.

A recess was called. The majority of the people trailed out through the exits. Kate spotted Joel and Britte, her first choice for a quick interview.

Tanner touched her elbow. "You okay by yourself?"

"Why wouldn't I be?"

"The natives are restless, and I see another scathing editorial mushrooming in your head. I'm going home. Stay out of trouble."

She rotated her shoulders, trying to relax. "Okay. See you."

"Bye." He turned away.

"Tanner!"

"What?"

She smiled. "Thanks for telling me."

"Thanks for asking." He returned her smile.

"Do you mind if I share your news?"

His smile faded. "Who would want to know?"

"Adele. Your friends at church."

Those dark lashes hid his eyes.

"The idea takes some getting used to. Forget I asked."

"Well, wait a minute." He put his hands on his hips and glanced around the gym, evidently pondering the thought. His shoulders rose as he inhaled. "I guess if everyone knows I'm friends with a quirky redhead, my reputation is already shot. It doesn't matter if they know I talk to Jesus now too." He let out his breath.

"You are so into appearances, Carlucci."

He grinned. "Why don't you put an announcement in the *Times?*"

She laughed as he walked away.

Kate then made a beeline for Joel and Britte exiting through a side door. She caught up with them in the hallway and fell into step alongside.

"Hi. Mind if I ask a few questions?"

Britte's face was flushed, her mouth a taut line, her deep-set eyes flicking daggers. Joel's demeanor was his usual one of disciplined control. Even on bended knee the guy had defined military.

Britte said, "I'm livid."

Joel added, "Off the record. Let's go find a quiet corner. How about my office?"

That suited Kate. Two minutes later they were behind closed doors.

"Joel!" Britte exploded.

He pulled her into his arms and smiled at Kate. "Off the record."

"But the headline would be so great: Principal Hugs Livid Woman Behind Closed Doors on School Property."

He chuckled. "Thanks for joining us. We've sworn off closed doors for the duration. A third party changes the rules. Do you mind if I kiss my livid woman?"

"On the record?" She shrugged the camera from her shoulder.

Britte pushed herself away from a laughing Joel. "Will you two stop?"

He pushed aside some papers and sat on the desktop. "A little comic relief was in order after that ridiculous show in there. 'Ridiculous show' is off the record, by the way."

"What else is your reaction to the board's nondecision? On the record."

"Everyone had their say. It's a wise decision to sleep on it. A few more days isn't going to matter."

Britte paced the small area. "Except if we have to find new jobs, we should be getting started. Yesterday."

"Off the record," Joel said.

"On the record."

"Off."

"On."

Joel turned to Kate. "Britte is a Valley Oaks native. The town knows what she's like. If she doesn't speak her mind, people will think something's seriously wrong with her."

"Britte," Kate said, "is it true you'll quit if Joel's not rehired?"

"My letter of resignation is already written."

Joel held up a finger. "Off the record."

"On."

"Britte, you can't blackmail the board."

"I'm not irreplaceable!"

Kate didn't want to go there. "Joel, what does the board president have against you?"

The couple exchanged a glance. Kate twisted the crick out of her neck. Britte was tall. Joel was tall. Tanner was tall. She had to start hanging out with shorter people.

Joel said, "Why do you ask that?"

"Just a shot in the dark." The board president could have kept better control, he could have wrapped things up by now.

Britte stopped her pacing and placed a hand on Joel's shoulder. She turned to Kate. "Last fall Harrison's son was stopped in Rockville for speeding. He and his buddies had open beer in his car. Mandatory suspension. His football season ended that night. He was starting quarterback, a junior. They were well on their way to making it to the play-offs, some say state tournament. Several people contacted Joel, suggesting the whole incident be pushed under the rug." Her brows went up.

There was no reason for her to say another word. Joel Kingsley would not bow to that kind of pressure. The kid's dad and others would resent him to no end. Kate asked, "How is the boy doing now?"

Joel smiled. "Mick's doing great. I made him spend some of his suspension in here right beside me. Now he's like my shadow. The kid would probably do anything for me. And he's making good grades."

"Mick? The one Tanner hired at the video store?"

"Yeah. Mick's pretty proud of that job. He landed it without his dad pulling strings, which is a first."

"He's a great kid from what I've seen." Kate tried not to grin. She had her editorial piece. Mick Harrison with his fall from grace worshiped the ground Joel walk on. Who better to extol the man's virtues and personalize his impact on the community?

She lifted her pen from the pad. "So, gang, what do we have here that's *on* the record?"

Britte said, "The math teacher is livid."

Joel slung an arm around her shoulders. "But she's in love with the principal. Who thinks the decision to wait is a smart one. Who's not worried because it's all in God's hands."

"Speaking of God's hands." Now Kate let the grin expand. She knew they were believers. She knew Tanner had worked with Britte for a couple of years. "Tanner is a Christian."

Britte's eyes widened. "Tanner? Our cool Coach Carlucci with the duck feathers who pretends everything rolls off his back? Woo-hoo!"

"Amen," Joel added softly.

Kate said, "Kind of puts things in perspective, doesn't it?"

Britte nodded. "Yes it does. Tonight is pretty silly in comparison."

As they headed out the door, Joel smoothed the back of Britte's jacket with sweeping motions. "Speaking of feathers, yours are a bit ruffled, my dear."

Thirty-Three

Reality crisscrossed with never-never land. For three days Adele was convinced her feet did not touch the ground. Each step she took felt as if it landed on a cushion that gently bounded her upward.

She spent hours pouring over the architect's designs. Fox Meadow staff members teased Adele about her ever-present grin. She had even stopped worrying over Chelsea.

She had shown the plans to Chelsea and Kate, told Naomi about them over the phone. All three began dreaming with her, pointing out possibilities, making suggestions for changes. Kate took notes, already composing a future article for the *Times*. It would be major news for the area. Senior citizens would be given a lovely option for downsizing.

Now, on Wednesday afternoon, she stood outside Rand Jennings's room wearing a purple dress he had complimented twice. She twisted her hands together. It had to be him. The anonymous millionaire blessing her with the possibility of seeing her dream come true. He was on his deathbed. She wasn't about to let him slip away without a thank-you.

Her attorney had explained all the legalities to her that morning. Reality interlocked with never-never land, making them one. It really was true, everything Graham had said and then some.

She went inside the room. Rand was statuelike still, his head to one side. He sat in his wheelchair by the window. The television blared a game show. Although she couldn't see his eyes behind the thick lenses, she assumed he was dozing.

He appeared to have lost weight since arriving. His already gaunt figure had shrunk even more, causing his nice clothes to hang haphazardly. He still dressed every morning and made gallant efforts to eat, indications that his attitude remained upbeat in spite of the increasing pain. A downy covering of white hair had sprouted, replacing his earlier baldness.

"Heather?" He thought she was the nurse.

"No, Mr. Jennings." She went to him. "It's me. Adele."

"Adele." He smiled. "Sit down."

"I don't want to interrupt your nap."

"Plenty of time for napping. Will you turn down that noise?"

She found the remote on a table, lowered the television's volume, and sat on the edge of the bed next to him. "How are you?"

"Fair to middling. How about yourself?"

"Well." *Oh, Lord, please don't let me cry.* "I've never been better!"

"Good for you."

"I didn't do anything. But I think I know who did."

"That Graham. You like him, do you? I knew he'd fall for you. I couldn't wait for you two to meet."

Typical. He was confusing the timing of the recent past. "No. I mean, well, yes. I do like him. A lot."

"He's a good boy. He's lonely. But I think he loves you. Just too stubborn too admit it."

She placed a hand lightly on his. "I was talking about you."

"Yes, I'm stubborn too."

"About the money. The investment."

"Money? Do you need some, honey? Talk to Graham. I've got plenty to spare. A loan would be no problem."

The elderly man wasn't that confused. "You're trying to get me off track, aren't you?"

"What track would that be, Addie?"

The old name he sometimes used threw a wrench into her thinking. It took her a moment to refocus. "Rand, I think you're my anonymous investor for the senior housing complex."

He grunted.

"I want to thank you."

"Graham should be here soon."

"Thank you."

"What's for dinner tonight?"

"Rand, I won't sign the contract unless you accept my thanks."

At last he looked at her. "Why would you do that?"

Tears stung her eyes. "Because it's just too magnanimous of a gesture. It's like I can't get my mind wrapped around it. I need to express something concrete. I have to try to tell you how grateful I am."

"You could have told Graham."

"It wouldn't be the same. It is you, isn't it?"

He nodded slightly.

"Thank you," she whispered and leaned over to kiss his withered face. "You've changed my life."

Again the little nod.

Her tears fell and her voice was unsteady, but she had to ask. "Why did you do it?"

His mouth remained clamped shut.

She waited, wiping her face with a tissue, knowing he wouldn't answer. "That's all right. I don't need to know. You are an amazing man."

"No, I'm not. Just a rich old coot."

Smiling, she stood and smoothed her dress. "Well, I'll go now. I have some papers to sign. Can I get you anything?"

"Will you turn the volume back up?"

"Sure." She did so and walked to the door.

"I love you, Addie."

She paused, her hand on the doorjamb, not sure that she heard correctly. She turned.

Rand's head was tilted again to one side as if he were fast asleep.

Evidently she'd asked the rich old coot enough questions for one day.

Thirty-Four

Washington, DC.

The rising sun glinted off Abraham Lincoln's steadfast face.

And Kate was *there*.

She had to tell somebody. She dug the cell phone out of her bag and dialed Tanner's apartment number. Since he had dropped her at the Rockville airport yesterday, she hadn't had a chance to call. Not that he expected to hear from her. He knew she had packed her agenda. Every hour was filled with a landmark, the theater, or an event arranged by Diane, her connection through Rusty's friend. But she had to tell somebody!

"H'lo," he answered on the fifth ring.

"Tanner! Good morning!"

"Kate?" She heard him yawn.

"Oh, Tanner! Thank you for sending me here."

He chuckled. "You already told me that. Once or twice."

"Yeah, but not from the Lincoln Memorial. This city is so incredible. And today! Diane is leaving a pass for me at the White House! There's a press conference scheduled this after- noon! On the lawn with the president! And I get to go!"

Tanner laughed. "You're talking in exclamation points. You're not excited, are you?"

"Oh! This is a dream come true! And without you and Rusty—" Her throat caught.

"You're welcome, Kate. It's our pleasure. You know treating you is my new most fun thing to do."

Fiddlesticks. Listening to his heartfelt comments while standing under Abe's inscrutable stare would have her blubbering in no time. "Hey, Carlucci! Why are you still at home? Shouldn't you be out taking care of my newspaper?"

"It's all done. Mick helped me deliver last night. He couldn't wait to get 'his' editorial into readers' hands as soon as possible."

When she had interviewed the teen, he gladly shared his version of Joel Kingsley's influence on his life. He credited the principal for setting him on the straight and narrow. It wasn't a scathing editorial. It was a simple portrait of the man in action. His actions would speak louder than any words she could add.

"Thanks, Tanner. No problems then with Fred?" The publisher had been kind enough to work with her Wednesday night on layout and articles, something they normally did on Thursday mornings. Her flight to DC left on Thursday morning.

"No problems. The papers were ready to go when I picked them up at five."

"Thanks, Tanner."

"Stop with the thanks and get going. Your city is waiting."

She smiled. "Abe says hi."

"Hi back, and be sure to greet the president for me. I'll see you Sunday night."

"I told you my dad can pick me up. I'll just stay in Rockville."

"No need to. I'll call him. Okay?"

He was doing way too much for her. She sighed to herself. "Okay. Bye."

"Thanks for calling. Bye."

"Thanks!" she yelled.

His laughter reached her ears before he hung up.

Late Sunday night Tanner entered the all-but-deserted airport and went to the nearest screen announcing flight arrivals. He groaned. Kate wouldn't be in until eleven-thirty, an hour later than scheduled. He should have called before driving all the way in to the Rockville airport.

Hold on! He smiled and headed back out to the parking lot. There was a plethora of reading material in his car.

As a history buff and eternal college student, he enjoyed reading, but never so much as in the past week. On Tuesday, when he'd gone in to substitute at the high school, Joel greeted him with a copy of the Bible. Later that afternoon he stopped in the pharmacy and discovered Brady Olafsson's books, fictionalized accounts of people meeting Jesus face-to-face two thousand years ago. He bought all four novels. On Wednesday evening the pastor had stopped in the video store, chatted, rented a video, and given him two books on the subject of walking with Christ.

After that Tanner stopped being surprised at the deluge of information coming his way. He just read.

And he learned. It was as if a new section of his brain had opened up. He wandered through it like a kid in a toy shop, investigating shelf after shelf of fresh thoughts, untested ideas, and unfamiliar emotions.

What were formerly vague sentiments became earnest prayers. His desire that Kate remain in Valley Oaks changed. What if that weren't the best for her? He prayed that she would find her ideal niche wherever that was. Loving her meant putting her needs before his own.

Loving her?

He kept stumbling over that little tidbit lurking on those shelves too. He wasn't sure what to do with it.

Sixty minutes later he closed his book and went as far as security allowed. He joined a small crowd waiting for the plane's arrival.

Kate's red hair made her easy to spot through the glass barrier. He waved but her eyes were downcast. As when he had dropped her off, he noted her ability for traveling lightly. She pulled a piece of luggage on wheels and wore a knapsack on her back. Those two items were her only baggage. Even her trench coat and laptop were packed. She wore a belted peasant-style yellow blouse over matching skirt. It was a good color for her hair and green eyes.

"Kate!"

She looked up.

He swam upstream through the other arriving passengers and met her. Something in her demeanor checked his impulse to gather her into his arms. "Hi."

"Hi." She didn't slow her pace, continuing on past him.

He fell into step beside her and reached for her rolling suitcase.

"I've got it."

"Oh, come on. Let Galahad do something."

"You came to pick me up. That's enough."

He bit back a smart remark about her nasty attitude. Which wasn't like him. And she wasn't like herself. Well, he didn't need to dance to that tune. He stepped in front of her, forcing her to halt. "Kilpatrick, you got a burr under your saddle?"

She glanced up at him briefly. "I'm exhausted."

"I've never seen you exhausted, and there have been plenty of times when you should have been."

"So this is a new side. The DC reporter side. I haven't slept—"

"Reporter? You got a job?"

She pursed her mouth and fluttered her eyelids in a look of disgust. "Things don't happen that fast. Now can we go home?"

"Sure, but I'm taking the luggage." He firmly grasped the suitcase handle and pried off her fingers. "Do you want to stop and get something to eat?"

"No. Thanks."

Kate turn down food? Definite burr under the saddle. As they neared the door he said, "You need your coat. Spring left while you were gone."

"I'm fine."

Her outfit appeared to be made of cotton or linen. Too thin for the night air. He waited until they reached the door, and then he stopped her again, pulled the knapsack from her back and set it on the floor. He shrugged out of his jacket and held it open for her.

"Tanner," she protested.

"Just be quiet. You're too tired to think sensibly." She slid her arms into the coat. He lifted out the loose hair that caught inside of it. "Valley Oaks needs their editor strong and healthy so she can write her next editorial. They're waiting with bated breath."

She turned, pushing up her glasses. "Really?"

"Really."

"What are they saying?"

He grinned. "You're the talk of the town. That piece about Mick says it all. The consensus is, why would anyone vote against rehiring Joel Kingsley?"

At last a genuine smile erased the tension on her face. "Really?"

"Really. I'd say you did it. You made a difference. Congratulations." That called for a hug.

Ignoring the standoffish vibes emanating from her, he put his arms around her and crushed his coat. Her small shoulders were in there somewhere. He hoped the old Kate Kilpatrick was somewhere in there too.

Thirty-Five

Kate walked into the church sanctuary 45 minutes early for the Good Friday evening service. Except for the choir director and three soloists practicing up front, the building was deserted. On the platform was a large wooden cross draped in a black cloth. She gazed at the dimly lit empty pews, deciding at last upon the center section, a center row, the center spot of the pew.

With a quiet mirthless chortle, she sat down and acknowledged the message: She needed to get *centered*.

One of the choir members lifted a hand in her direction. She waved back. People would assume she was there because she was a newspaper reporter. Funny, the things she got away with. Press members could go early, stay late, move around, take photos, talk to behind-the-scenes people as well as the hotshot stars. No one questioned their audacity to do so. At least, no one had to her face, and she had been doing that sort of thing since she was 12 years old.

She had even bluffed her way into getting invited to a Washington, DC, presidential press conference. The dream of a lifetime. Fireworks should have lit up the sky. Evidently someone forgot to light them… And that had only been the first indication that dreams of a lifetime weren't all they were cracked up to be.

She fast forwarded to the work week in Valley Oaks. Since the printing of her editorial, the town had rallied behind Joel Kingsley, inundating board members with phone calls and letters. Flyers appeared everywhere around town, many

300

quoting Mick's story verbatim. The closed session of Wednesday's meeting lasted all of ten minutes. Five minutes after that the formal vote was taken before a packed gym. It was unanimous in favor of rehiring the principal. The president and his cronies would have looked like supreme fools if they'd voted against him.

Small potatoes…but deeply satisfying. She smiled wryly. Three obscene phone calls were made to the office yesterday. The hate mail began arriving today. Those things didn't compare to the flowers from Joel and Britte, the homemade apple pie from Britte's mother, the high fives in the grocery store.

The whirlwind of the past week served nicely to muddy the waters of her life. Which suited her.

Then why was she sitting in the quiet hoping with every fiber of her being that no one would talk to her?

She crossed her arms and crossed her legs.

She needed to get centered. She knew how to do that. In the forced quiet she would focus on Jesus, on His death, on what He had done for her.

It was the only way she could forget that other…thing. The thing that revealed itself like the unexpected flash of a shooting star as she ate lunch in a busy downtown DC deli while reading the *Post*. The thing that clung like some computer virus to every thought she'd had since then, affecting the very essence of each one. The thing that made standing ten yards from the President of the United States the equivalent of eating a peanut butter and jelly sandwich.

She swung her legs, recrossing them, and twisted the crick from her neck.

If she couldn't escape the thing in this holy setting, it wasn't going away.

Sunday night he had loaned her his leather jacket and driven away before she realized she still wore it. It was so big she could swim in it. Instead, she slept in it. How sappy was that? Insipid, mushy sentimentality.

Fiddlesticks. She was in love with Tanner Carlucci.

Tanner entered the sanctuary with some trepidation. He was getting accustomed to Sunday mornings, but he didn't know what to expect on a Friday night. He didn't even know churches held Good Friday services.

Right off he knew something was different. The pews were packed, but no one was talking. There was no music. The lights were dim. A large cross was up front, a spotlight focused on it, a black cloth draped over its crossbeam, a wreath of thorny vines hung over its top. The somber ambience impacted him, causing a feeling of heaviness in his chest.

He couldn't spot Kate. Maybe she hadn't arrived yet. Not that she had specifically said she would sit with him. They had talked briefly. She mentioned she was coming.

He walked up the left side aisle and slipped into the first pew offering space.

She hadn't been herself at the airport. Things hadn't improved through the week. All of their conversations had been brief. They had all been initiated by him. He had stopped in the office Monday to retrieve his coat. She hastily put on her own, saying she was on her way out to an appointment. He had left voice mail messages that she didn't return. It had taken him until Thursday to catch on that she was avoiding him.

Quirky turn of events.

He turned his attention to the Bible on his lap. At least there was one thing in his life that made sense.

The service had no official conclusion. After an hour of Scripture readings and low-key music, all of which dealt solely with the crucifixion, a collective hush fell over the sanctuary. A note in the program indicated worshipers could leave whenever they chose.

Tanner remained seated, scarcely registering people pushing past his knees or filing down the aisle. His mind's eye saw only the end of the story. Jesus was dead. His body lay in the tomb.

His friends must have felt as hopeless as Tanner did now. The Man had loved the unlovable and healed their diseases, and in turn they tortured Him to death.

Tanner thought he might cry again. That would make twice in two weeks. Nobody told him he'd signed up for a truckload of tenderness. Like the tidbit about Kate, he wasn't sure what to do with sentimental feelings either.

Pinching the bridge of his nose, he surreptitiously wiped the inside corners of his eyes and looked around. The place was empty. He sniffed and leaned back in the pew. Maybe he should turn out the lights?

He found his lone coat hanging in the lobby and headed out into the night. Although the day had been more wintry than springlike, he had walked to church. Because most of his destinations were within a six-block radius these days, he saw no reason to drive anywhere.

Not wanting to disrupt his thoughts, he abandoned the idea of stopping in the store. Mick and Betsy could handle it. He crossed Main Street intending to go down the alley to his apartment entrance when a pounding noise drew his attention elsewhere. It seemed to be coming from the direction of the square. Probably just kids fooling around. He pictured the proximity of his store's large plate-glass window. Maybe he should check things out.

He rounded the corner onto Fourth Avenue and saw Kate's light blue Volkswagen sitting at the curb halfway down the block. She was swinging her fists against its hood.

He ran to her. "Kate!" She straightened as he huffed to a stop on the sidewalk. "What are you doing to poor old Helen?"

"She died on me!"

"Let me take a look." He unlatched the back end. *Dumbest place for an engine.* "Do you have a flashlight?"

"No. Hey, don't worry about it."

He peered inside, trying not to block the feeble light from a nearby streetlamp. "Did she start up all right?"

"She usually *doesn't.* I'll just call the garage in the morning."

"Why don't you wait in the store where it's warm? I'll get a flashlight."

"No!"

"Suit yourself. Wait out in the cold. I'll be right back—"

"Tanner, how many ways do I have to say it? I don't want you doing anything with my car!"

"It's not a Galahad thing. I'd do it for anybody—"

"Why do you always talk about Galahad?"

"I don't. You do. You're the one who has *issues.*" He straightened and stepped away from Helen.

"I don't have issues." Her hands were perched on her hips.

"Whatever." Man, she was exasperating. "I know a little bit about engines."

"I don't have Galahad issues!"

Now his hands flew to his hips and he leaned forward. "You do so. You cringe every time I do something for you. I'm not putting down your womanhood. I don't think you're a damsel in distress."

"Well, you come across like you do, Mr. Macho Cool."

"What's that supposed to mean?"

She barked a laugh. "Just what it sounds like. You've always been able to pay for getting your own way. Money means nothing to you, so you can just dabble in this or that career. Or pastime. Or relationship. Give extravagant gifts to whomever currently tweaks your fancy."

Her accusation hung for a long moment in the still night air. "Kate," he said quietly, "you're the snob if you can't accept a gift that has no strings attached. You treat people like projects, like news stories. You hold them at arm's length and pretend it's God's plan for you to keep moving on to the next town, the next school, the next job."

"And now you're lecturing me about God! Oh, fiddlesticks!" She turned on her heel and strode down the sidewalk.

It was cold. She had almost four blocks to walk in her clogs, wearing only her dad's trench coat for warmth. He should offer to give her a lift.

Not in this lifetime. He slammed shut the engine lid.

So much for that truckload of tenderness.

Thirty-Six

After a night of fitful sleep, Kate kicked off the tangled covers and stared at the ceiling, its normal bright white grayish in the predawn hour.

Well, there was nothing to be done with Tanner's words of last night except to forget them. *Treat people like projects? I don't think so!* What did he know about her anyway? He'd known her for two whole months! There was no way he could even relate to her life, let alone pass judgment on it. *Pretend it was God's plan?* What could *he* know about God less than weeks—*less than weeks!*—after committing his life to Christ?

She sprang from the bed, rushed into the bathroom, and twisted on the shower faucet. No time to dillydally pondering ridiculous notions. She had a newspaper to write.

In love with Tanner Carlucci? What a laugh! It must have been her great disappointment in DC blurring her grasp of reality. So the city hadn't been what she expected. So what? Had a challenge ever slowed her down in the past? *I don't think so!*

Less than an hour later, after a short, vigorous hike, she was at her desk at the *Times* office, engrossed in writing an article about the planting season. She lost track of time until her cell phone rang. Assuming it was the garage calling her back with news of Helen, she absentmindedly answered it.

"Kate?"

"Hmm."

"This is Graham."

"Graham?"

"Logan. Adele's friend."

"Sorry. I was a million miles away."

"Is this a bad time?"

For what? Curious now, she recalled noting that the guy hadn't been around the house for a while. Cal's suspicions about the stranger came to mind. "What's up?"

"I have a favor to ask. You're the only friend I really know of Adele's."

Her antennae hummed upward.

"She may need a ride home from Fox Meadow later today. Would you be available to pick her up?"

"Uh, yes. My car's in the shop, but they offered me a loaner. What time would it be?"

"That's the problem. I'm hoping you can be flexible. If things go badly, it could be two o'clock. If things go not so badly, it could be later, perhaps much later."

She leaned back, away from the computer keyboard. "You're saying things are going to go badly, it's just a matter of degree?"

"Yes."

"May I ask why Adele isn't calling me?"

A hesitation. "She doesn't know yet."

"Doesn't know what yet?"

Another hesitation. "She's going to receive some difficult information. She may blame me for it. She may not want me to drive her home, and Chelsea isn't available."

Kate knew Chelsea planned to visit a friend today at a college located an hour's drive away. Adele, friends with the girl's family from church, granted Chelsea permission to take the van and spend the night.

"Kate, I know it's a lot to ask. I can give you a call if and when she needs you."

"Is your real name Graham Logan?"

That hesitation. The guy was an expert at weighing his words. "Yes, it is."

"But you're not a professor at Northwestern?"

"No comment."

"Is there a story in this?"

"Can't you just do this as Adele's friend?" He lost his moderate tone. "Not as a reporter?"

Tanner's words echoed in her mind. *You treat people like projects, like news stories.*

"Look, Kate, I love Adele. No ifs, ands, or buts. Her best interests are at stake here. I'm simply trying to cover all the bases, and I need your help."

"All right. Give me a call if and when you need me."

Work on the *Times* abandoned, Kate soon lost herself in cyberspace. At last she discovered something.

The article was in a Newark, New Jersey, newspaper dated five years ago last month.

> Samantha Logan, 35, was pronounced dead at the scene outside her townhouse, the apparent victim of a single gunshot wound to the head. Though her husband, FBI agent Graham Logan, was in the vicinity at the time of the shooting, he was unharmed by the unseen sniper, who is still at large...

FBI agent, not professor.

New Jersey, not Chicago.

Rand Jennings from Maryland. Baltimore?

Adele Chandler from Baltimore.

What were the connections?

Tanner's voice again, hands on hips, his beautiful deep brown eyes narrowed at her...

The question was not what were the connections. Rather, she should ask, how hurt was her friend going to be by the information? What could Kate do to help?

She grabbed her cell phone and coat and headed out the door. She'd better hoof it over to the garage and pick up that car they had offered to loan her.

As they walked across Fox Meadow's parking lot, Adele let go of Graham's arm. It was Saturday, and she was at the nursing home on pleasure, not to work. Still, in her own mind she was always on duty. It didn't seem quite proper for the director to waltz about the property on the arm of a good-looking guy whose friend was a resident.

Graham smiled down at her. "Remember when you told me it would get easier, my coming here?"

She nodded.

"It has. And not just because you're here. It's Rand's home, the one he chose. It's not a particularly happy place, but it's real life, isn't it?"

"It is. And there is a joy here, when someone smiles back and you know your hearts have connected."

"Afraid I'm not there yet. Not at saint status like you are."

"But don't forget. You are a guardian angel."

He laughed.

It was good to be able to tease about that remark. Their friendship had eased into a daily crossing of paths at Fox Meadow. Every other night or so they shared dinner. When Adele didn't cook, he treated her at a restaurant. Sometimes Chelsea accompanied them.

Adele kept a distance between them, tried to keep her heart from totally succumbing. Rand was holding up remarkably well, but his death was inevitable. Graham's life would snag him right out of Valley Oaks. She couldn't imagine either one of them pulling up roots. It didn't help any that the vague future was one of those subjects he avoided. It was as if he was waiting to get through his friend's death before committing to anything.

But that he cared for her was evident. For now it would have to be enough.

They entered Rand's room. He sat in his favorite spot, near the window.

"Hello, young'uns."

"Hi, Rand." She greeted him with a kiss. As Graham's "other dad," he was a notch above most residents. Since learning that he was her benefactor, he had risen even above that. She settled into the armchair beside his wheelchair. "How are they treating you today?"

"Heather wants to elope with me," he said, chuckling.

She joined in his laughter. "What did you promise her?"

"Rubies and diamonds."

"You know her well."

"I think well enough for an elopement."

She looked at Graham. His head was buried in the armoire. He appeared to be searching for something.

"Addie."

The childhood nickname didn't startle her anymore. "What?"

"You know I won't be around much longer." His voice was more breathless than usual.

"I know. But we will meet again."

He nodded. "I have something for you."

"Rand, for goodness' sake, you've already given me the moon."

"This is just a little something extra." He looked up at Graham, who stood at the bed, opening a briefcase on it.

He fished out a paper and looked back at him. They held each other's gaze for a long moment.

Graham turned to her. "Adele, this could be...upsetting for you."

His tone was one she'd never heard before. It was devoid of emotion.

"Rand and I both want to apologize beforehand. Please remember we care very much about you. It may not appear so at first, but we have only your best in mind."

She felt herself tense. Her stomach lurched and then sank with the feel of a deadweight. Something wasn't right.

Graham handed her a piece of paper that looked like a legal document and sat on the edge of the bed, just behind and to the side of Rand's chair. They both faced her. "This is the deed to your property. Rand's making it an outright gift, not an investment. It's yours, to do with whatever you choose."

She held the paper, shifting her gaze back and forth between them. What were they up to? At last Graham's words sank in and she exclaimed, "You already bought it?"

Rand gave that half nod of his.

"*Why?*"

"I...wanted..." Rand paused for breaths between his words. "Wanted you...to have a head start...No payments."

She studied him closely. His pallor was gray. He shouldn't be sitting up. In spite of his efforts to promote a different image, he wasn't having a good day. Rather than fuss at him, she looked down at the paper.

And then the room began to spin.

R.J. Chandler...conveys and warrants to Adele Christine Chandler...the following-described real estate...

R.J. Chandler!

The familiar half nod. The hint of a Baltimore accent. That catch in his laugh. The way he called her Addie.

"No," she whispered.

Graham said, "Yes."

She shook her head vehemently. "No way!"

"Addie." Rand's soft voice was barely audible. "I am sor—"

"No!"

Graham knelt in front of her. "Adele."

She pushed away his hands. "He's not my father! My father is tall. He weighs two hundred and fifty pounds. He has black hair. He doesn't wear glasses." Their faces receded, drowned in the tears flooding her eyes. "He didn't even know how to smile at me, let alone—" Her throat closed, choking off the words. She waved a hand to fill in the blanks. So many blanks.

"Adele, he loves you."

"No!" As if watching herself from afar, she saw herself gasping for breath and losing control, sobbing, nearing hysteria. But she couldn't move, couldn't run from it.

"Shh. It'll be okay."

She cried unabashedly now. It was too much to comprehend.

Graham knelt helplessly before her, watching her cry it out, praying she would get past the shock, past the denial. From behind him, Randall Jefferson Chandler's hand trembled on his shoulder. Graham knew tears were streaming down the old man's face. He couldn't turn around and watch. If Adele refused to forgive her father— He didn't want to consider the repercussions on all three of them.

He had stepped out into the hall and called Kate, asking her to come and wait in the lobby. Things were going badly. Well, what had he expected? Exactly what he was looking at. Not that it made it any easier. But what had been their choice? There hadn't been another.

It was a little late to second-guess. Besides, they had considered and reconsidered ad nauseam ever since the cancer had first been diagnosed. What was done was done.

He handed her a box of tissues. Her face was beet red. Great sobs racked her body, and he longed to hold her.

Tears filled his own eyes. He wanted to die and be spared the knowledge that he had caused this.

Several minutes passed before her crying slowed. Her breathing was ragged. "Why didn't you come sooner?" Her voice was a raw whisper, her tone accusatory. "Ten years ago? Five years ago? *Any*time before *now?*"

Graham heard the implication. *Now* meaning before he was on his deathbed.

Rand said, "I wasn't ready."

"Why didn't you tell me *sooner?*"

Rand nudged Graham's shoulder. The old man didn't have the breath for the long answer, and so Graham began, "We couldn't just walk in and announce it. With all the baggage between you two, we thought there was a good chance you'd turn us away."

"You could have called or written! Given me a warning!" She addressed her words to her father. She hadn't yet taken her eyes from him.

Graham went on, "There wasn't time. At first he was too ill from the chemotherapy and the radiation. When the treatments were no longer beneficial, we had to move quickly. He thought his best chance of winning your forgiveness was for you to get to know him as you would a complete stranger. As if you'd never known him before."

Fresh tears streamed down her face. "You are a complete stranger! You don't resemble R.J. Chandler in the least!"

Rand said simply, "Thank God."

Graham waited while she cried silently. "Adele, he also wanted time to get to know you and Chelsea. To find out what he could do for you. To try to make up for the lost years."

"And so you bought me something." She wiped her tears and took a deep breath. "Money always did cover a multitude of sins. The thing is…" She stood clumsily, stepping around Graham. "It would have been more acceptable from a *stranger*."

He stood and intervened before she said anything else she would later regret. "Adele, you need some time to sort through all this. Why don't you go home?"

She nodded and looked down at Rand. "It's too much. I don't know you. I—"

Graham touched her elbow, intent on ushering her out before Rand started sobbing. "Kate will pick you up."

"*Kate?*"

They walked to the door. "I asked her if she'd be available. I figured there was a chance I wouldn't be driving you home."

Adele stared at him. "I don't know you either, do I?"

Before he could open the door, she had it yanked back and was rushing down the hallway.

Kate leaned against the nondescript sedan parked in the circular drive at Fox Meadow's main entrance. She studied the low brick building and its pretty yard. Yellow tulips and daffodils waved gaily. The place looked like Adele's home.

She saw her coming now, through the glass doors. At least she thought it was Adele.

The woman was out the automatic door before it was completely open. Her face was contorted, her eyes red and swollen. Something dreadful must have happened.

"Adele?"

"Will you take me home?"

"Of course. Get in." She walked around to the driver's side.

Her friend remained silent until they had driven out to the highway and were going 55 miles per hour. Her breath more or less shuddered through her. "Kate, I'm sorry. I've just been through… I have no idea how to describe it. I don't have a clue who Graham Logan is. And Rand Jennings…" Another shudder. "Rand Jennings is really R.J. Chandler. My father."

Kate stared at her until the car began to drift toward the shoulder.

Adele was rambling. "He came from *Baltimore,* not Chicago! How did they do it? All that paperwork? Names, dates, doctors, hospitals. They must have forged it all! How would they know how to do that? How did they get away with it?"

"Whoa! Back up. Graham's friend is your *father?*"

"He says he is. He doesn't resemble the man I knew eighteen years ago in any way, shape, or form. My father is a huge, overbearing prig. That man in there is small and charming and one of the kindest men I have ever met. And he loves Jesus."

The two images didn't compute in Kate's mind. She couldn't imagine how Adele was reconciling them in hers.

"Adele, he loves Jesus."

She turned a dazed face toward her.

"Which means Jesus obviously, totally changed him from the man you once knew. Wow. That's truly awesome. Isn't

God awesome? Beyond anything we can think or imagine! To see such an outright, black-and-white—" One glance at Adele cut off her ecstatic stream. "Don't you think?"

"I don't know what to think! I'm angry he didn't come sooner. Why didn't he change eighteen years ago? Why didn't he tell me even last month? *Now* what am I supposed to do?"

"Forgive him?"

"I did. A long time ago." And then she began to cry.

Saturday afternoon Tanner sat in his little glassed-in office behind the store's checkout counter. Betsy was in the front room, glued to the video playing on a television suspended from the ceiling. There were a few people browsing through video titles, a few young teens playing Ping-Pong in the back room. Things were running smoothly as he reorganized his desktop.

For the third time since calling his dad three hours ago.

Kate would be proud of him for making that call. He imagined her elfin demeanor, her voice cheering him on. "Oh, Tanner! It's an act of forgiveness!"

He wanted Kate to be proud of him. He wanted to have a clean slate before her because in spite of his accusations to her last night, she was nearly perfect. In many ways, but most of all in the fact that she could lay her head down at night with no regrets. He knew that beyond a shadow of a doubt.

But it wasn't only her voice he sensed. There was a new inner voice within him. When he was quiet long enough, he could feel it, like an air current lifting him along, steering him a direction he hadn't considered. It was the source of that voice that he wanted to please even more than Kate.

And so he had called his father, because he knew somewhere in the core of his being it was the right thing to do.

Forty-five minutes later when the man himself walked through the door, Tanner battled the usual instant reaction. Like a wave of solar heat, shame rolled over him, creating a burning sensation about his ears.

His dad wore pressed black slacks, a crisp white shirt under a gray tweed sport coat, and a proud expression. Brows raised, he remained just inside the door, eyeing the place with sweeping glances. *Here, Kate, is the original Mr. Macho Cool.*

Tanner couldn't shake the old feeling, but he stood and went out to greet him. Passing Betsy, he asked her to turn down the video.

"Dad. Hi."

"Hi, Tanner." He shook his hand. "You are out in the boondocks, aren't you?"

"It's a world unto itself. Bet you didn't have any trouble finding the store, though." He smiled.

"No chance of getting lost in this town." He chuckled.

"Well," he spread his arms, "this is your investment. How about the grand tour? Over here," he stepped to the front door, "we have a handy-dandy return slot. Videos can be returned twenty-four, seven." He led his dad up and down the three short aisles, pointing at the racks, mimicking a tour guide's tone of voice. "Videos are organized by category. Here's drama, comedy—"

"Dr. Carlucci!" A short, round-cheeked elderly woman greeted them. "You probably don't remember me. Edna Harmon."

His father shook her hand. "Of course I remember you. We took care of that nasty tumor in your abdomen. How are you?"

The woman beamed. "Never better. It's been four years."

"That's wonderful."

"This young man must be your son. He looks like a younger version of you."

"Yes. This is Tanner. He owns the store."

She shook Tanner's hand. "Well, you have a lovely place here. I never liked coming in when that other owner was around. He was a rather unpleasant man. Your selection is much better too."

"Thank you, Mrs. Harmon."

"Call me Edna. Have a good day. Bye now."

Tanner walked her to the door and opened it. "Come back again."

"Oh, I will."

He rejoined his father, who was introducing himself to Betsy. The man knew how to be gracious. They stepped into the office.

In the past, the compliment on the tip of Tanner's tongue would have stayed there. But the exchange with Edna Harmon had mellowed his dad, making him seem approachable. "Dad, you're amazing. Remembering Edna after all these years."

Sidney, hands stuffed in his pockets, jingled change, and did a 360 turn. "Oh, it comes with the territory. Patients are my bread and butter. Like your customers."

"Supplying videos is hardly on the same level as performing life-saving surgery."

Sidney smiled and glanced at his watch.

"Would you like to see my apartment? It's just next door."

"Why not?"

A few minutes later they had finished the store tour, gone out the back door, into the pharmacy's back door, and upstairs to his place.

Tanner showed him around. Back in the kitchen he asked, "Would you like some coffee?"

"Uh, no thanks. I need to get home. So, you're comfortable here?"

"I am. It suits me. The community is friendly."

"Does that redhead live here?"

"Kate? *Here?* No. She lives in town, but only temporarily. She's moving to Washington next month."

"That's too bad. I liked her. The kids haven't stopped talking about her. Seems like she'd be fun."

Tanner kept a straight face, hiding his surprise. Who would have thought? "She is." *And I miss her.*

Sidney cleared his throat. "How about...uh...the other..."

"I'm not drinking."

Relief showed clearly on his father's face. "I'm glad to hear that."

Another window of opportunity? The average number of Sidney's approachable moments in one setting hovered between zero and point five. Tanner knew he had to jump at the chance.

"Dad, I've been thinking. I want to apologize for all the problems I caused you through the years."

Sidney blinked, rumbled a nervous chuckle, jingled the change in his pocket. "I didn't know kids apologized for being kids."

"Being a kid isn't an excuse. And..." He inhaled deeply. "I forgive you for leaving us."

The jingling grew silent. He glanced at his feet and then looked out the window. "I made some mistakes of my own."

Men being men? Tanner refused to let him off the hook. But a few seconds later, the man removed the hook himself.

"There is some good though, eh? Marnie. Little Sidney. Well, I'd better get home. We have some benefit to attend tonight."

"Sure. I'll walk you down."

After a few minutes of generic chitchat, the man drove off in his late-model Lexus.

Tanner stood on the sidewalk, fingers wedged in the back pockets of his jeans. He gazed at the square across the street, smelled the greening grass, and the damp spring earth, noticed the bright bed of blooming tulips and daffodils.

After a time his heart slowed. The burning sensation about his ears cooled. A smile began somewhere in his unconscious, emerging gradually until it pulled at the corners of his mouth and dislodged his resistance.

Kate would be proud. Yes...she would.

Thank You, Jesus.

Thirty-Seven

Each footstep required effort. Graham made his way across the parking lot at Fox Meadow.

On the horizon, across a neighboring barren field, the eastern sky glowed. It would be a magnificent sunrise. He should stop, take time...

He listened to his own advice and halted. A sliver of pulsating yellow radiated on the earth's edge.

Why hadn't she called? Why hadn't she come? He and Rand thought they had prepared themselves. How naïve, to think they could prepare for the incomprehensible. How naïve to not believe Adele could actually walk out.

It would kill Rand. Could he recover? Hang on, give her more time?

They had misjudged the timing. Graham had misjudged Rand's decision-making ability. The old coot had been more fearful than anything, postponing the inevitable. He should have insisted on pushing up the timetable. But when had Rand Chandler ever been fearful?

The sunlight blinded him now, and he headed into the nursing home. The corridors were empty. In Rand's hall, he caught sight of the nurse and night orderly in someone else's room. No one was at the desk. He stepped quietly into Rand's room.

It was like another sunrise.

Adele slept, with an afghan about her shoulders, curled up like a kitten in the big chair. She had shoved it against the bed. Rand also slept, his hand atop the covers...Adele's atop his.

Graham smiled and backed out of the room.

~

"Who's there?"

Adele opened her eyes to see R.J. blindly studying her without his glasses. It was the second time she had awakened that morning. The first time had been at home, long before dawn. That time, the instant her eyes opened, she knew the decision had come sometime during her sleep. It never would have come about in the hours of wakefulness when self-righteousness stood guard.

Kate had fortuitously left her a note and car keys, urging her to take the car. She dressed and drove to the nursing home in record time.

She leaned in closely now. "It's me."

"Addie?" His eyes looked different without his thick glasses. They were smaller, more like the ones she remembered.

She shook off the hint of revulsion. "Can I get you something?"

"My glasses." He moaned slightly. "In that drawer."

Twisting in the chair, she opened the nearby nightstand drawer. "Do you want some water? Coffee?"

His breathing was labored. "Will you put them on?"

She slid the glasses onto his face. "There. Is that better?" He smiled.

Her stomach lurched. The unfamiliar smile was at odds with the familiar memories. Ambivalence rendered her speechless.

"You came, honey."

The endearment washed over her. She soaked in it, the dry pockets of her heart drinking it up.

"I was afraid you wouldn't."

She touched his hand again.

"I'm sorry."

"I know you are. I..." She had to let the past go, once and for all, now, in reality, up close. Not in her head, not separated by miles and years from the one who had hurt her as a child. She had to say the words aloud. They came out in a whisper. "I forgive you, R.J."

Tears seeped from the corners of his eyes.

With one hand she dabbed a tissue on his face, with the other she held a hankie to her nose. "No more crying. I did enough yesterday."

"Will you call me Pops?"

She laughed. That wasn't a term she had ever considered. *Daddy* had evolved directly to *R.J.* by the time she was nine. *Dad* had been too intimate, *Father* too deferential. The name her mother called him fit best. "You want me to call you Pops?"

He chuckled his raspy laugh. "It's true. I always wanted to be called that."

"Okay. Pops it is. Hey, Pops, it's Easter. I thought we could go to the service together. Are you up for that?" She felt an ache, an imaginable longing that he was up for it.

"Yes. Honey, I love you."

Evidently she hadn't cried enough yesterday.

A short while later Adele went to the home's kitchen to make herself a cup of tea. R.J.—make that *Pops*—wanted the orderly to help him dress.

She greeted the cooks only briefly. They were busy preparing breakfast. She was busy processing emotions. She sat in a vacant dining room, sipping her tea.

Graham walked in, cup in his hand.

Graham Logan. She'd forgotten about him.

He stopped at her table, smiling hesitantly. "You came."

She tilted her head.

"We wouldn't have blamed you if you hadn't. But I'm so grateful that you did. Thank you."

"Thank you for bringing him."

"I'm sorry for the deceptions."

"I'm sorry for falling for them." She squeezed the warm teacup between her hands. "I guess that's the way it is when you're naïve. You fall for any nice guy, for any story…" Her voice trailed off.

"Do you want to talk?"

Talk to him? Not now. Maybe not ever. All she could think of was the numbered days ahead, of living through them with her new father, of introducing Chelsea. She hadn't even thought of Graham for hours. He was a stranger who didn't fit. "No. I don't have any space for you. I don't know where to put you in the scheme of things right now."

"I understand. You have a lot to deal with. Perhaps later." He turned to leave, and then he came back. "Adele, there were only three deceptions. I've called your father Rand for years. It's what his close business associates called him. Obviously, we lied about his last name. I'm not a professor. I'm not from Chicago or Buffalo. Everything…" He paused, his blue eyes never wavering. "*Everything* else was true."

She held back her teenage retort. *Whatever.*

Thirty-Eight

Kate slipped out a side door after the Easter morning service, bypassing the pastor's main-door handshake, perfunctorily greeting others, intent on finding the right spot.

She hadn't enjoyed the service one iota. What should have been a glorious celebration only deepened the conviction that she was one lousy representative of the risen Christ. She owed apologies all over the place, but Friday night's atrocious display of rudeness hung over her like a thundercloud. If she didn't take care of it soon, surely lightning would strike.

She strode across Main, leaped over the curb onto the sidewalk outside the hardware store, and turned. Minutes ticked by as she watched cars stream out of the church parking lot. He must be one of the last ones out. He certainly seemed to be getting the hang of going to church.

Finally, she saw him coming. He looked nice in a pale green polo shirt and tan slacks. With a start she realized the sun was shining and the temperature was warm. When had spring sprung?

The problem with the particular apology before her was it involved Tanner Carlucci.

The guy she loved. The guy who sent shivers up and down her spine by *looking* at her.

Such things tended to mangle emotions and eliminate words from her vocabulary.

He crossed the street, smiling at her. "Hi."

"Hi." She waited for him to reach the sidewalk. "I wanted to apologize. I'm sorry for what I said Friday night."

"Not a problem. I'm sorry for what I said—"

"No, don't be. Everything you said was true."

He cocked his head to one side. "Everything?"

Avoiding his eyes, she shrugged out of the trench coat and twisted it around an arm. "Everything. I can't accept gifts. I treat people like news stories. I keep them at arm's length and hide behind God's so-called plans. And I have...*Galahad* issues." She took a breath.

"I exaggerated. I shouldn't have—"

"Don't interrupt. And you're not Mr. Macho Cool."

"Aww, shucks. I wanted to be."

She tucked a strand of hair behind her ear. "Well, you're not. Not in a derogatory sense anyway."

"Is there a good sense to being him then?"

"Tanner! Just accept my apology, okay? Please?"

"Apology accepted."

"Thank you."

"You're welcome. What are you doing today?"

"Uh, going home to soak my head and try to figure out how to be nice to people."

He laughed. "Don't overreact, hon."

The nonchalant endearment zinged through her. Lightning had struck after all.

He must not have noticed. "Wasn't church amazing? And afterwards three people invited me over for Easter dinner. *Three.* Do you believe it?"

She gave him a quick smile. "That's great. I'll see you—"

"But I turned them all down because I had other plans. I made lasagna, and I hoped you would help me eat it."

She swallowed and turned her head, watching the sparse traffic. "Uh..."

"Come on. It's my grandmother's authentic recipe. You'll love it. And it's baking even as we speak."

With her whole heart she wanted to spend the day with Tanner. That was the problem—*with her whole heart*. Could she fake it for a couple of hours? She caught a glimpse of those dark-lashed eyes, the velvet brown-black, and hesitated. But then...given the fact that she was a pro at holding people at arm's length, faking it with him for a few hours should be no problem.

He went on, "You know the best way to figure out how to be nice to people is to just do it. Say yes."

"Okay, yes."

"Thank you. You get a point for being nice. But that was an easy one. I knew you couldn't turn down food."

Today she could have. Today she wasn't in the least bit hungry. Not a good sign.

By the time they reached his apartment, Tanner knew something was seriously wrong with Kate. He had chalked up last week's strange behavior to her hectic trip to Washington followed by six days of newspaper work packed into three. That had all culminated in their argument Friday night. But they had just made up. Normally, Kate would have bounced back by now.

They climbed the steps, her feet dragging ahead of him.

"Hey, how's Helen?"

"Still dead."

"Did they give you a loaner?"

"Mm-hmm."

All of her answers were like that, nearly monosyllabic.

In the kitchen she glanced around, her eyes growing wide at the table already set for two, but she didn't comment. Kate always commented.

He said, "Go sit down. I have to put garlic bread in the oven and finish a Caesar salad."

"I'll help." She sounded as pathetic as she looked. Pallid all the way around.

Placing his hands on her shoulders, he steered her to the adjoining living room area, gently pressed her down into the recliner, dropped the Rockville Sunday paper in her lap, and pulled back on the handle. The footrest popped up, jerking her back. "Stay put."

She looked like a little urchin sitting there in the big chair. Resisting the ever-increasing urge to take her in his arms, he strode back into the kitchen and yanked the lettuce out of the refrigerator. He slapped it onto the cutting board and began chopping it while berating himself.

Physically moving her had shades of macho cool. Setting the table—with *candles* in the middle of the day—and rescuing her from an afternoon of soaking her head smacked of Sir Galahad. Kissing away her frown would definitely send her over the edge. He'd better strike a balance fairly quick before he scared her away once and for all.

Should he pray? What had he read in one of those new books? That he could pray about anything. Well, this qualified. *Lord, You know how I feel about her. Give me a chance with her? She's the best thing that's ever happened to me. By the way, remember I said she could live wherever? I take it back. I want her here. I really want her here. This past week without us connecting has been... Man, if I hadn't had You to talk to—*

"Tanner? The buzzer's going."

"Whoops. Thanks." A few minutes later he had water glasses filled and food on the table. "It's ready, Katelyn." He pulled out a chair and waited.

She pushed on the handle to release the footrest. It didn't budge.

"It sticks. I'll get it."

"I'll just climb—"

By then he was across the room and leaning over her to push the lever.

She was half out of the chair when the footrest clunked down. The rocking motion of the chair threw her against him. "Oomph."

He caught her in his arms. "Sorry. Galahad the klutz to the rescue."

A look of terror crossed her face, and she pushed herself away from him, shoving her glasses back up her nose. "The lasagna smells great."

He followed her to the table, deciding against holding the dining chair for her. He'd better quit. She was holding him at least *two* arm length's away.

"I didn't know you could cook."

"I'm full of surprises." He sat across from her. "Guess who came for a tour of the store yesterday?" He cut a generous portion of steaming lasagna from the casserole dish between them and slid it onto her plate.

"Who?"

He grinned. "My dad."

"Really? Did you invite him?"

"I did." He set down the spatula. "We should pray."

"Yeah." She folded her hands. "It's your house."

"Okay." He thrust his hands across the table.

She stared at them.

"We held hands at Adele's. And at your parents' house."

"But that doesn't mean we *have* to."

"But it's my house and I *want* to."

She frowned but slowly unfolded her hands and placed them in his.

"You know this is my first time, right?"

She nodded and bowed her head.

"Dear Jesus. Thank You for this food and for this day and for Kate. Help her to feel better. Amen."

She jerked her hands away. "I feel fine."

"You don't appear fine."

"Well, I am."

"Fine."

"Fine!" She picked up her fork.

Tanner watched her for a long moment as he took a bite of salad. She didn't move, but simply stared at her plate. Another minute ticked by while he tasted the lasagna and drank his water. It was a record for Kate Kilpatrick silence.

He wiped his hands on a napkin. "Kate, hon, you're not fine."

Her fork clattered against the plate. "I am."

He went to her, placed his hands on the arms of her chair, and leaned down until he was at her eye level. "Look at me and say that."

She tried to scoot the chair back, but he held it firmly in place.

"Why won't you look at me? You haven't looked at me all day."

"Let me go."

"You're doing it again. Holding me at arm's length. Or further. Try the length of a football field." He palmed one side of her face and gently tilted it. "Kate, don't you know by now that I don't ever want to be that far from you?"

At last she raised her eyes to meet his. It was the unfamiliar crease between them that gave him hope. "What?"

She really didn't know! "Oh, Kate. Kate! I adore the ground you walk on, to say nothing of you. And if that's too Galahad for you, deal with it."

"But I'm not your type!"

He smiled. "Says who? You're everything I could ever hope for in a woman. Why are you so afraid?"

"I'm going to DC."

"And what does that have to do with the price of eggs?"

She shrugged.

He lowered his face, brushed his lips across hers, and murmured, "I haven't been able to take my eyes off of you since we met. I don't know why it took me so long to figure it out, but I love you, Katelyn Kilpatrick."

The crease between those beautiful translucent green eyes melted away, and she stared at him.

At last he saw what he longed to see...the real Kate cared for him.

He slid the glasses from her face and set them on the table. "I know you can't see without these, but they're in my way."

"That's okay." Her voice was breathless. "If I see you, I'll think it's all a dream. That I have to wake up."

He pulled her to her feet and folded her into his arms. "It's no dream."

"You know this is my first time, right?"

"To be kissed?"

She shook her head. "Loving someone."

He grinned. "You're too precious. Was my first prayer all right?"

"You don't rate prayers."

"Ditto. I'll never..." He lowered his head. "Ever..." His lips nearly touched hers. "Rate you."

He kissed her then.

She kissed him back.

And the lasagna grew quite cold.

Tanner Carlucci loves me.

Kate had felt positively frothy since early that afternoon, and it wasn't going away.

Beside her on his couch, he smiled. "What?"

"What what?"

"You just giggled."

"I did?"

"Mm-hmm." He squeezed her hand.

The day had pretty much gone like that since she'd made eye contact with him. Especially lip contact.

"You giggled again."

"Hmm."

They had finally gotten around to eating his scrumptious lasagna. After cleaning up the kitchen, they'd taken a walk and browsed his store's video selection. The entire time they'd talked nonstop like two giddy teenagers.

Her early fears of ruining a good friendship proved ridiculous. Openly loving him only enhanced what they already shared. As usual, they talked about everything. His dad, Adele, church, books, and nonsense. There were only two subjects that hadn't come up. But it was Sunday, and she had just discovered a joy she never thought possible. She didn't want to talk about DC or the fact that, no matter what he said, she truly was not his type.

"Kate." He pointed the remote at the television and stopped the video he'd just started. "I have a confession to make."

She met his eyes and was reminded why she had avoided them. First there was the shiver up and down her spine. Then there was the inability to look away, so strong was the desire to search in wonder for what could lie in those gorgeous dark depths.

"Kate."

"Huh?"

"You're zoning out on me again."

"Sorry."

He laughed. "It's okay. I love watching your face. Did you know it actually lights up?"

"It does not." She leaned against his arm so she wouldn't have to look at his eyes.

"Does. Anyway, about my confession. I was telling God that wherever was best for you to live, that was all right by me. But...now I'm praying you won't leave Valley Oaks. I just thought you should know."

"Okay."

"That's all you've got to say?"

"Yes."

"What do you think God does when two people pray for the opposite thing?"

"Well, He says yes to one and no to the other."

"I suppose so. Do your prayers count more than mine?"

She smiled up at him. "No, silly."

He touched her nose. "When are you going to tell me about your DC trip?"

She moved as he pulled his arm up and placed it around her shoulders. Snuggling against him, she felt an unparalleled contentment. The real world could wait. "Not tonight. Okay?"

"Okay. And you're not upset about my prayer?"

"Tanner, at the moment you could tell me my writing is the stinkiest drivel you've ever read and I wouldn't be upset."

His laughter rang out, filling her with a greater joy than she had ever known.

Thirty-Nine

Adele went home Sunday evening, numb with exhaustion and yet overflowing with affection. A new affection for her father. Of all people.

Chelsea greeted her at the kitchen door, excited about her weekend away, grateful to her mother, eager to share her fascination about college life, her hopes to apply to that school next year. Adele listened, asked questions, and saved her news.

Later upstairs, she went into her daughter's room, sat down on the bed, and patted the covers. "We need to talk, honey."

Eyeing her strangely, Chelsea sat down and drew her legs up Indian style.

That wouldn't work. The tears were starting again. Adele reached over and pulled her daughter close.

"Chels, you know Rand Jennings?"

"Graham's friend? Oh, Mom, did he die?"

"No." She sniffed. "He's...he's your grandfather."

"What!" She sat back, her eyes wide.

"He's R.J. Chandler."

"You're kidding! No, you're not."

Adele shook her head and told her the story.

When it was finished, Chelsea said, "Wow! Is that why he called me Addie?"

"You resemble me at your age. You must have shocked him. But he wants to see you now."

"Oh my gosh. My grandfather! What do I call him?"

"I imagine he'll have an idea. Instead of working all day tomorrow, I'd like you to spend some time with him, okay? I want you to get to know him. He's so completely the opposite of the man I knew. Of what I've always told you he was like."

"Wow."

"Exactly. Wow. What a day. I thought I knew what forgiveness meant. I didn't have a clue." Perhaps in the norm she could have eased into a relationship. They didn't have time for easing in now.

"And Graham's his friend?"

"I guess…I guess everything he told us is true. His dad worked for my dad. R.J. paid his way through college."

"But you didn't know anything about him when you were growing up? That your dad was paying for someone else to go to school? How old were you?"

"I guess I would have been about twelve or thirteen when he first went to college. And no, I didn't know anything about my dad's acquaintances or what he did with his money. As I've told you, I spent most of my life away at boarding school."

"Wow," she said again. "A new dad and a new grandfather all in one week. Nobody's going to believe it."

Believing was one thing. Accepting it was quite another.

"Chelsea." R.J. smiled.

Adele watched her daughter smile shyly, lean over, and gently hug the unknown man who sat in his wheelchair.

"You look just like your mother. She had long curls like that. Was too skinny."

"I've seen pictures. But this ear here," she touched it, "that's my dad's. What should I call you?"

"Grandpops."

Chelsea giggled and sat in the chair next to his. "Okay. Grandpops. What was she like when she was little?"

Like he would know. Adele said, "I'll let you two get acquainted. I have some work to do."

They barely acknowledged her departure. A few minutes later, having bypassed her office, Adele sat outdoors on a garden bench facing a newly plowed field, her back to the building. Some of the early perennials were blooming, others were poking through the dirt, but most of the beds were empty.

Resentment bubbled.

Oh, Lord.

Chelsea and R.J. had a clean slate before them. No baggage between them. Nothing to get over. Nothing to forgive.

I hate feeling like this. Please take it away, Lord. Just take it away.

"Adele!"

She turned to see Naomi Sommers walking briskly toward her, elegant in her navy blue business suit, high heels clicking on the sidewalk. Naomi was the dearest of friends, the woman who had taken her in 17 years ago. Fifty-ish, she was every inch a professional with neatly coiffed short brown hair and a kind but direct manner. She worked with a temporary staffing agency.

Adele stood and accepted her hug. "What are you doing here?"

"You'd better sit down." She settled beside Adele on the bench. "Graham Logan came by the office first thing this morning."

"He told you."

"Yes. What a shock. You know my heart goes out to you, sweetie. So I've come to interfere."

Adele smiled. "You always know exactly what I need."

"I just like to be bossy. I called Pastor Eaton. Is that all right?"

"Oh, Naomi, of course it is. I didn't know where to start."

"Praying friends are the best place. And then the church. They'll send food. I'm sending you a temp. I have a perfect one in mind. She can follow you around and take over details you won't have the time or inclination to do. Personality wise, she may even fall in love with the old folks too."

Adele protested. "Naomi, we can't—"

"I know. It's not in your budget. Don't worry about that. It's covered."

"Graham."

Naomi missed a beat, and Adele knew she had guessed correctly. Her friend placed an arm around her shoulders. "Speaking of Graham. Everything I said before? Forget it. You've found yourself quite a man."

"I don't even know what he does for a living."

"He was an FBI agent before his wife was killed. After that he did some private eye work until your dad hired him."

Adele drew back and studied her friend's face. "How'd you learn all that?"

"Are you kidding? He was ready to burst if he didn't confess soon to someone, and since his first choice refuses to speak to him, he went to her good friend."

"*FBI?* That explains a few things. Like his mysterious contacts. Like how he managed to forge all the documents to get R.J. checked into this place. Naomi, I can't talk to him yet. I can't take in anymore emotion. I can't even take in anymore information!"

She hugged her. "Don't worry. He's not going anywhere."

Forty

"Tanner! She's dead. Just totally dead!" Kate found it impossible to keep the whine out of her voice as she wailed into the cell phone.

"I'm sorry, hon."

"Maybe I should get a second opinion?"

"Look, I know she was a good friend, but she was getting awfully old. I don't think another opinion will change things. Just remember all the good years you had together."

"I have to go now. They want me to take my things out of her. And they want their car back."

"I'll be right there."

"You don't have to come. I can walk home. I just wanted to tell you."

"I'll see you in two minutes. Bye."

She turned off her cell phone and gazed across the parking lot of the car repair shop. Helen looked so forlorn sitting off to one side, her faded blue washed out in the late afternoon sun.

She was only a car.

No...she was Kate's past...and she was Kate's future. Named after the political journalist Helen Thomas, the old Volkswagen represented Kate's dream. As if on cue, the dream and the car had died together.

No, that was being melodramatic. Just because one visit to DC had been a bust didn't mean the dream was gone. It just meant it was more challenging.

A black SUV turned the corner.

Doubly challenging. Why would she move away from that guy?

She sighed and walked over to her car.

Tanner joined her as she dug through the trunk. "Hi." He pulled her into his arms.

"Oh, fiddlesticks. Now I'm going to cry."

"Go ahead."

"She's just a car." Kate buried her face in his chest.

Two hours later they sat at a small candlelit table in Antonio's, Tanner's solution to Kate's grieving.

She knew she was hooked, but she pointed a finger at him and said sternly, "You think you're pretty good at this Galahad business, don't you?"

He smiled and winked at her. "Don't you?"

Kate felt a distinct sense of warmth creeping up her neck. Good grief! Now he had her blushing!

"I must say, Katelyn, you are dealing rather well with the issue. I comforted you over Helen. I helped you pick out a car to lease, which I strongly suggested you do. And now I've brought you to Antonio's."

"Hey, I drove myself here in my own car."

"I got the reservation."

"But I'm not a damsel in distress."

"No, definitely not. You were simply temporarily without transportation and hungry. As your friend, I came along to keep you company."

She burst out laughing. "It's still an issue with me, isn't it?"

"We've only been at it for a little over twenty-four hours now."

"It's not fair though. You've spent years as a practicing Sir Galahad. That places me at a disadvantage."

"How's that?"

The waitress interrupted as she set salads before them. Before leaving she smiled at Tanner. Typical.

Kate speared a forkful of lettuce. "Oh, Tanner. I don't know how to respond. I don't mind your help. I appreciate it, but I don't want to lose sight of my independence."

He touched her wrist. "Let's pray."

And then he said things like that. The frothy, shivery sensation hadn't yet subsided.

"Dear Jesus. Thanks for this food and Kate's car that wasn't too overpriced. Please help her to understand it's not a game with me. Amen." He patted her wrist and let go. "Why would you lose sight of your independence?"

"By getting accustomed to you doing things for me."

"But there are thousands of things that only you can do for yourself."

"Name one."

He swallowed a bite of salad. "Write."

"You took pictures at today's track meet. I'm sure you could write the story too."

"Okay. Put on makeup."

"I don't wear any."

"Ah, you had some on the last time we came here."

"You noticed?"

He grinned. "That wasn't all I noticed."

The guy unnerved her. "Moving right along. Try naming another."

"Only you can decide about DC."

She studied the napkin on her lap.

"Only you can love me. Only you can let me love you."

"All right." She glanced up at him. "I get it. Therein lies my independence."

"Yes. The Galahad stuff isn't important. If I'm in the way, just say so."

"Oh, you've been in the way for a long time, Carlucci."

"Really?"

She took a bite of salad, delaying her answer, then deciding she may as well air things now as later. "You've been filling all the nooks and crannies inside of me, interfering with...everything."

He smiled. "I know the feeling. I keep tripping over you."

"Sounds like we're in each other's way."

"But that's a good thing."

"Is it? What happens when...?" She bit her lip.

"When what, Kate?"

"When you...find someone else. Someone who fits you."

He reached over and covered her hand with his. "Kate, no one could fit me better than you. Believe me, I've never felt this way about anyone."

"Oh, Tanner, I believe you, but... Remember your old friend at the theater, that woman who thought I was your sister?"

"Yeah."

"Don't you see that with others? At the car lot today. The waitress here tonight. The way they look at us. People from church invite you over. I've never been invited over except to Britte's, and that was because they wanted press coverage. Tanner, I'm fine with who I am, that I'm short and have red hair and don't get a lot of admiring attention. That I'm not a soul mate to Adonis. You, on the other hand, *are* Adonis with the most gorgeous eyes and lashes I've ever seen. If you hang out with me, you're going to be spending all of your time explaining why."

A slight frown furrowed his brow.

The waitress returned. Kate moved aside her salad, which she hadn't finished yet because she'd been talking so much.

The wafting steam smelled delicious as the girl set a plate of seafood linguini before her.

"Miss, I'd like you to meet the woman I love." Tanner was addressing the waitress who now fastened her attention on Kate.

"Her name's Katelyn. Isn't that pretty?" He turned to Kate now and continued speaking softly. "She reminds me of a Christmas elf, petite, witty, energetic, bubbling with joy. And then there's her color. Her hair's really a copper, like a shiny new penny, but it's close enough to red. And her eyes are green. Can you see them? They're this wonderful translucent color. Sometimes I think I can see all the way into her soul, which is incredibly beautiful. Of course, on the outside she's intoxicatingly beautiful. That creamy skin. I couldn't believe how soft it was the first time I touched it. And her lips. Mmm." He kissed his fingertips in the manner of a chef. "*Magnifico*. She's got great, and I mean great, legs and—well, you get my drift. But you know what the best thing is? She makes me feel like Sir Galahad, a knight on a white horse who's bigger than life. You know, like I'm something special. What more could a guy ask for? Excuse me."

He stood up, walked around the waitress to Kate's side, cupped her face in his hands, and kissed her soundly. "I love you." And then he sat back down.

Kate stared at him, speechless.

"Sir," the waitress said, "will there be anything else?"

Still looking at Kate, he replied, "No, I don't think so. Thanks."

Kate could only blink at him.

Tanner smiled and shrugged. "I don't have a problem with explaining why."

Forty-One

Graham sat in the surprisingly well-stocked library at Fox Meadow. It had become one of his corners at the home where he could hole up with reading material or chat with residents and visitors. At the moment he gazed out the window at the rainy Saturday afternoon, reliving the past two weeks.

Since Adele's pronouncement that she had no space for him, he had remained in the background, allowing her a wide berth. Though their paths inevitably crossed in the halls or the garden, she scarcely acknowledged his existence. It didn't matter. For now he was content to watch from afar and allow her to work through a lifetime of hurt in her own way.

While she was understandably subdued and not her usual attentive self to the other residents, she poured herself into caring for Rand, or, as she called him, R.J. She spent an inordinate amount of time with him. Her office hours fluctuated between early morning, late night, and her father's nap times. Her closest friends came to meet him. Naomi…women from her book club…the pastor…Kate, who took family photos.

Graham avoided going into the room when Adele was there. Chelsea's visits were another matter. Like him, Rand quickly grew fond of his granddaughter. She was delighted when Graham brought in the photo albums made by Adele's mother. The two of them spent hours delving into Adele's childhood through pictures. Sadly, Rand was growing vaguer about the details.

Now, from the corner of his eye he saw a blue skirt swish by. "Adele!" he called out.

She appeared in the doorway. Her face was haggard. It was obvious she was pushing herself too hard.

"Can we talk?"

Hesitantly she entered and glanced about the vacant room.

"Have a seat." He indicated the armchair near his.

"I need to get to the office. He's sleeping." But she sat, clearly tired. Her powder blue cardigan accentuated the blue in her eyes.

He leaned forward, propping his elbows on his knees. "I just wanted to thank you for going through this with me."

She looked at him, silent.

"If you need a break, I'm here."

"I don't want to miss any time with him." Her voice was a strained whisper.

"I know." He let the unsaid fill the air. Rand was surprisingly resilient, but his feet were swelling. He ate little. They didn't have weeks left.

She stood, walked to the door, and paused. "Graham." She turned. "I hadn't thought...I hadn't thought about you spending these last days with him. I'm...I'm sorry. I've been selfish, keeping him to myself while you sit in here."

"You have every right to keep him to yourself. He's your father. Don't worry about it."

Her lips parted, as if she had something to say. Instead, she nodded and left.

It was the longest conversation they'd had since she'd learned Rand's identity. Suddenly he realized how very much he missed her.

Kate and Tanner sat on the couch in Adele's living room. A blazing fire chased away the chill of a rainy spring evening. The remains of take-out pasta from the Pizza Parlor littered the coffee table.

Her arm brushed against his arm, and she wondered when his physical presence would stop affecting her. Shivers and froth...

He smiled down at her.

Coherent thought disintegrated on the spot.

He tapped the tip of her nose. "Good dinner."

"It was great. Thank you."

"You're welcome. Too bad the kitchen doesn't look like we had take-out."

The kitchen was a disaster area. They had prepared home-made soup and salad for Adele and Chelsea, a surprise for whenever they showed up. Their hours at the nursing home had grown long.

Kate gazed at the fire. "I don't know how Adele cooks like that all the time."

"Ditto. Veggies and herbs and spices all over the place."

"And no recipe. I hope she likes it."

"It tasted fine." He put an arm around her shoulders and kissed the top of her head. "We'll clean up later. They won't be home soon, will they?"

"Probably not, but I'll do it. You don't have to help."

"But I want to. I think I feel a little like Adele. She wants to spend every possible moment with her dad. I want to spend every possible moment with you."

"I'm going to DC," she murmured her favorite phrase. She sensed it was a defense mechanism to keep her newfound emotions manageable.

"Katelyn." He always used his serious tone when he called her by that name. "I called your father today."

"Really? Why?"

"I wanted to tell him my intentions. Remember he asked that the first time I met him? Well, my intentions have obviously changed since then."

She peered up at him. Watching that handsome face was not going to get her through a serious conversation. She turned back to the fire. "I imagine he appreciated that."

"He did. He likes me, you know."

She knew. Both her parents did. Not to mention her sister was gaga over him and her brothers always monopolized him, dragging him outside to play basketball. Not that he didn't go willingly.

"Aren't you going to ask me what my intentions are?"

"No."

"Chicken."

"Mm-hmm. I'm going to DC."

"Sometimes you sound as if you're trying to convince yourself of that."

The truth of his statement settled about her shoulders like a mantle of concrete.

He put his other arm around her and held her close. "Hon, tell me what happened out there."

"It won't make a difference. I'm going."

Abruptly, Tanner stood and left the room.

Honestly, the guy pouted just like a little boy.

Kate bit her lip. That wasn't true.

She found him in the kitchen fixing coffee. "Tanner, I'm doing it again, aren't I?"

Keeping his back to her, he replied, "Yep, holding me at arm's length, just where you want me."

"I'm sorry."

He switched on the coffeemaker and turned. "Are you?"

"I don't want to do it."

"What are you so afraid of?"

"What you said, the other night at Antonio's?"

He nodded.

"I never even considered *imagining* that anyone would ever feel that way about me. While most girls were daydreaming about some future Galahad, I was reading a newspaper."

"So what you're saying is either you still aren't interested or you don't trust me?"

"Tanner, you're beyond the wildest dreams of all of those girls. And you're hanging out with *me*. Maybe I just have to get used to the idea."

He smiled, folded his arms, and leaned back against the counter. "That's nothing compared to what I have to get used to."

She raised her brows, not sure if she wanted to hear it.

"I have to get used to being concerned that I'm going to blow it. That somehow I'll remind this angel of a girl she's not my first and that I'm an alcoholic."

Tears sprang to her eyes. He still struggled with his worthiness. She went to him and wrapped her arms around his neck. "Oh, Tanner, those things won't ever stop me from loving you."

He placed his hands around her waist and nudged her away until her face was before his. "I don't deserve you."

"No, you don't. I'm pretty special. Not that I know anyone else who would have me."

He grinned and rested his forehead against hers. "What happened in DC?"

She took a deep breath and exhaled.

He kissed her cheek and straightened, still holding her.

"I hated it."

"You what?"

"I was totally bored out of my mind."

"But you were so excited the morning you called."

"I was, but talking to you was the highlight of my weekend. After that, everything just went downhill. At the press conference I asked the president a question—"

"No way! You asked the *president* a question?"

"Yeah. Something about that farm bill before Congress. No big deal."

He laughed. "Kate! That's an enormously big deal!"

She shrugged a shoulder and studied his button-down collar. "It didn't feel like one. I met people from the *Washington Post*. Diane said there was a good chance I could get some entry-level job later this summer. And from what she saw of me on the White House lawn, I'd be moving up fairly quickly."

"That's wonderful!"

"But all I could think about was my editorial on Mick, wondering if people were reading it, if it would make an impact. And..." She laid her head on his chest. "You. All I could think about was you."

He embraced her in a bear hug and the silence stretched between them.

"Still," she said, "I have to go."

"It's been your lifelong dream."

She lifted her head. "You understand?"

"Of course I do." He kissed her gently. "It's what makes you Kate Kilpatrick. Dreams and challenges. No reason to change your mind at this point. It was probably just a bad weekend."

"But where does that leave us?"

"Long distance. Aren't you going to ask me what I told your dad?"

"Okay. What'd you tell my dad?"

"My intentions are to let you go...for a month. If you're not back by then, I'll be looking for a new career in DC."

She smiled. "Hobby."

"Hobby. Career. Whatever."

His kisses sealed the promise of his words. Time and distance were not going to prevent Tanner Carlucci from loving her.

Forty-Two

A week had gone by since Adele talked with Graham in the library. Life had settled into a routine of more or less living at Fox Meadow. She considered packing a bag and finding a bed for her own use. While her father grew more frail by the day, his conversation seldom weakened. He seemed as determined as she was to catch up on the years.

Long ago a friend of her mother's had communicated with Adele. Now she learned more details of her mother's life since Adele had left home. Of how her faith had deepened after hearing of her daughter's. Of her hidden box of Chelsea's photos. Of how the stroke had taken her quickly.

Adele's initial reconnection with R.J. had been easy compared to the following days. At every turn he asked her forgiveness, and yet she couldn't look him in the face without a distressful memory reminding her he didn't deserve it. Each encounter was a fresh struggle.

Out of necessity she had pushed Graham and even Chelsea from the forefront of her thoughts. They were distractions that interfered with the difficult process of responding rightly to her dad. She didn't have a choice but to go it alone. Prying her fingers from their white-knuckled clutch on a lifelong grudge consumed her.

Now, on a late Saturday night, watching R.J. breathe, she became aware of a joyful peace. It was as if it literally enfolded her, speaking new thoughts into her heart. Until a few weeks ago, he hadn't shown her love in 36 years. But in a sense, he had pushed her into the loving arms of her heavenly Father, who had granted her these last sweet moments, a goodbye that could never make up for lost time. Nor could any amount of clutching ever bring it back. That was life. Choosing to let it go was forgiveness.

She flexed her fingers. *Thank You, Lord.*

Suddenly she was tired of going it alone.

"Gracie! Gracie!" Adele called through the front office window, a distinct note of unease raising her voice above its normal tone.

The weekend supervisor appeared from an inner office. "What's wrong?"

"Have you seen Mr. Logan?" She'd searched all the usual nooks for him: library, kitchen, lobby.

Gracie reached the window. "No, I—" She smiled, her attention diverted beyond Adele's shoulder.

She turned and relief flooded her.

He stood a few feet behind her. "Rand?" he asked, his tone anxious.

She shook her head, absorbing the familiar lines of his handsome face. He'd been gone so long, sent away by her. Was he angry? Resentful? Had coldness replaced the warmth? No, she saw none of that. She held out her hand.

Without a word he stepped over and took hold of it.

They walked in silence through deserted halls, entered the library, and settled in opposite corners of one of the couches. Facing him, she tucked her legs beneath herself. "Forgive me?"

"For what, Adele?"

"For pushing you away."

He smiled. "Nothing to forgive. You needed the time."

She leaned over and kissed the corner of his mouth. "Now. Tell me who Graham Logan is."

"Straightforward, as usual." Graham would have liked to return the kiss, but Adele was back in her corner of the couch, and he wasn't yet sure of the ground rules.

"I had a good teacher growing up. You knew that, though, didn't you?"

"Yes, I knew that. I also knew you were a precocious child, quite advanced for your age. I remember I was about ten when I first heard that word, precocious. You would have been four. I heard all about your ice skating lessons, your horseback riding, your dance class."

The soft light cast her face in shadow, but it didn't hide the confusion. She didn't understand.

"Adele, you've been in my life since the day you were born. I think I've had a crush on you since you were about three. You were so cute with a headful of bouncy curls."

"How can that be? I never met you before in my life!"

"My dad really did work for your dad. They really did have a close relationship. Until he got hurt, I spent most Saturday mornings working with Dad at the office. My job was to clean your dad's bookshelves. Often your dad was around, and he would tell me about you."

"He talked about me?"

"Yes. I remember the day after you were born. He gave my dad a cigar and me one made of bubble gum. We'd never seen him so excited. And do you know what was on those bookshelves I cleaned?"

"I can't remember being in his office but a few times. Mom and I never felt welcome there."

"Well, the shelves were covered with photos of you. One held only your school pictures, all lined up in order by grades."

"What happened after your dad got hurt?"

"Rand hired me just to clean his office. It remained exclusively my job until the day I graduated from college. He stayed current with me. If our paths didn't cross when I went in to work, we'd meet for breakfast. He kept on me about grades, sports, friends."

"Graham, it's like you're not talking about the same man I knew."

"I'm sorry. He seemed unable to communicate with women. His father wasn't much of a role model. You didn't know your grandparents, did you?"

"No. They died before I was born. All I knew was that R.J. grew up poor."

Graham only nodded, choosing not to go into the grim details. "Even after I left Baltimore, we kept in touch. I remember how unreasonably he reacted to your desire to study *art*."

"You thought that?"

"Yes. I told him what I thought too. I rooted for you when you didn't come home from Europe as scheduled."

"You're kidding."

"No. I always thought of you as this poor little princess locked in an ivory tower. The only time he'd get angry with me was when I defended you. He was never quite the same after he kicked you out. There was this heaviness about him."

"Why didn't he come after me?"

"Too stubborn. Too proud. I was working in Washington when I went home for a visit. I caught him stuffing all those photos of you in the trash. They've been in my parents' attic since that day." He smiled. "The crush saga continued."

"Why didn't *you* come after me?"

"Then?"

She caught the implication. He had come now.

"Then I had a life. I'd just met Sammi. I'd already graduated from the University of Maryland and was with the FBI.
My path was set."

"Tell me about her."

"She was a teacher. Little kids, first, second grade. She was
such a *good* person. I didn't know what she saw in me. But
we married and then I fell in love with her Jesus. End of
story."

"It's not, Graham."

No, it wasn't, but...

Adele twisted around on the couch until she was in front
of him, her face inches away, her arms around his neck.

He slipped his arms around her. "The past is over. Let it
be."

"Tell me everything," she whispered. "Don't run from it
anymore. Please. It's still between us."

He shut his eyes, blocking out the woman he was afraid to
let see inside of him.

She kissed his cheek. "Why did she die?"

It came out, haltingly at first. Adele caressed his face,
drawing the words from him, most words never whispered
aloud to anyone. The killing...the aftermath...the horror of
the argument...of losing Sammi and the baby he hadn't
allowed her to tell him about.

At last the vivid images receded, the anger and regrets dis-
sipated. Adele's tearful face came into view.

She sniffed. "Did you quit the FBI then?"

He nodded. "I couldn't work, couldn't focus on anything.
Your dad came to the funeral. Sometime later he called. He
had a job, tailor-made just for me. Security, confidante,

chauffeur, companion, finder of lost daughters. I did everything but clean his office."

She smiled. "You left out creator of elaborate schemes."

"No, I can't take all the credit for that. Rand always thought I should be a professor. With an Illinois university, naturally."

"Oh, you needn't to have gone to all that trouble. Our waiting list is full of people from *Maryland*."

He chuckled, and then he grew silent gazing at Adele. "You're so beautiful, inside and out. Any more questions?"

She shook her head.

"Good. Because once I start kissing you, I don't want to be interrupted."

"Is that so?"

"No more questions." He kissed her dimple and whispered, "I love you, Adele."

"Is this that old crush of yours resurfacing?"

He gave her a stern look.

She smiled. "And I love you, Graham Logan. By the way, is that your real name?"

When she met his kiss, he knew that for now, all her questions were answered.

Forty-Three

Kate intended to do her fly-on-the-wall routine and simply take the photos. Somehow a man eating birthday cake with his seventeen-year-old granddaughter for the first time made that stance impossible.

"Kate, I'll take some." Eagle-eye Tanner must have noticed her blinking back tears and not clicking. "You're never in the pictures."

She let him take the camera from her hands. At least he knew how to use it.

It was as festive an affair as possible under the circumstances. Balloons and flowers filled the small room. Adele and Graham stood together. Chelsea sat beside Rand on the edge of the bed. His bare feet, which appeared abnormally large, were flat on the tile floor. Unlike the other times when Kate had stopped by, he wore a robe rather than daytime clothing. He gallantly ate two bites of the cake and three of ice cream. It took him 40 minutes. Afterwards, they helped him lie back down.

Four weeks had passed since Adele first learned her father's identity. Kate had watched her transition from angry to tense to gentle. Along the way she and Graham had reconnected and were now seldom out of each other's company as far as Kate could tell. Chelsea had blossomed into a young woman, taking over chores at home and daily visiting her grandfather.

Kate watched the four of them now. Despite the passage of years and Graham's strange role, they were a family.

"Tanner," she said, "let's do a family photo."

He waited while she posed the four of them, Rand in the center, the others leaning, surrounding him.

"Okay, one, two, three, say cheese!"

They cooperated and Tanner snapped a few shots. Kate knew they would be precious.

Rand said something, his raspy voice more difficult to understand.

"What, Grandpops?" Chelsea asked.

"Open. Mine." He smiled.

The man possessed one incredibly strong constitution. From what Kate understood, his pain should be unbearable without drugs keeping him asleep most of the time.

Chelsea sat on the edge of the bed and accepted a business size envelope from Graham.

Standing off to the side of their little circle, Kate backed against Tanner, wanting the comfort his physical presence offered. He wrapped his arms around her shoulders and settled his chin lightly on top of her head. She brought her hands up to clasp his arms, imagining he must be comparing his own distant father to the scene before them.

Chelsea pulled a piece of paper from the envelope and gasped. "Mom! It's a deposit slip for my bank account." Her eyes widened. "For five hundred thousand dollars! *Five hundred—*Grandpops!"

"Multiply that...by a hundredfold. That would be the number of times...I regretted...not knowing you."

The girl buried her face in his shoulder. Adele, on his other side, kissed his face and murmured something.

Kate figured they should slip away, but Graham cleared his throat.

"You old coot, you're always stealing the show."

Tanner laughed. Chelsea and Adele sat up smiling and wiped their eyes.

Graham said, "Chels, I have something for you too." He walked around the bed to Adele's side and took her hand. "It involves your mother. And," he turned to Rand, "with your permission, sir?"

The old man smiled and gave a half nod.

Graham returned the smile. "Dearest Adele, will you be my wife?"

Chelsea squealed and Adele started crying. As Graham leaned over and kissed her tears, Chelsea shouted, "Mom! You're supposed to answer!"

Adele smiled at her new fiancé. "She thinks I don't know anything." She pulled Graham nearer and whispered in his ear.

He whispered something back and then straightened. "She said yes."

Rand beamed and Chelsea clapped.

Tanner whooped quietly for only Kate to hear.

"Now, Chelsea." Graham walked around the bed again and took her hand. "I love your mother very much. And I love you because you are an extension of her. I promise to do my best at being a dad. Will you be my daughter?"

His words silenced her.

"You're supposed to answer."

Now Chelsea started crying.

Graham hugged her. "I hope that means yes. Kids these days don't know a thing. Nobody move." He went to his sport coat draped over the back of a chair and dug into its pockets. Out came two small, foil-wrapped gifts. Grinning, he handed the gold one to Adele, the silver to Chelsea.

The women, still speechless, unwrapped...lifted tops off boxes...pulled out smaller, velvet boxes, pushed back lids. Rings sparkled. The mouths of mother and daughter formed round O's.

Even from across the room, Kate could see Adele's ring was of diamonds, a large central one with chips along the band.

"Oh, Graham. It's beautiful." She slipped it on. "It fits!"

"I called Will. He seemed to know your size."

They laughed, but Kate wondered if he teased. The guy knew how to get information.

"Mom, look at mine. Is this an emerald? My birthstone!" She tried it on the ring finger of her right hand. "It fits too! Graham. Thank you!"

Tanner raised his chin from Kate's head. "One more picture, everyone? With ring fingers held high?"

The family laughingly agreed.

Kate leaned against the wall as Tanner the photographer went to work. A deep sense of belonging bubbled inside of her.

Washington, DC, couldn't hold a candle to the magic of Valley Oaks.

⌒

Adele sat beside her father on the edge of the bed, facing him. Graham and Chelsea had left to take the cake and ice cream to the kitchen.

"R.J. *Pops.* Don't go to sleep yet." She touched his shoulder.

He opened his eyes and smiled.

"I didn't thank you."

He waited, an expectant look on his face.

Adele gave up trying to swallow away the tears. She whispered, "Thank you for bringing Graham into my life."

"It's where...I always wanted him."

She kissed her father's face. "I love you."

"I love you too, Addie."

In the predawn hour of a glorious Sunday in May, Randall Jefferson Chandler passed quietly away, surrounded by his loving family.

Forty-Four

Kate's hands literally itched to pick up her cell phone and call Tanner. Instead, she scratched first one palm and then the other. After weeks of blossoming love, it was second nature to turn to him whenever she needed to talk. Like now.

The newspaper publisher's best—make that *only*— prospect for a new editor sat at Kate's desk, working on the computer. His name was Murray. He was sixty-ish, tall, slender, a retired Rockville dentist who wanted to be a writer.

Kate chewed her thumbnail, reading a lead paragraph. He'd spent 15 minutes agonizing over the writing of it.

At last she said, "This isn't bad."

"If you weren't staring over my shoulder, it could be better." He smiled at her, softening the complaint.

"You're going to have people staring over your shoulder all the time. Like after it's in print and all of your readers are next door or just down the street. You see them at the store, at the post office. You will move to town, won't you?"

"Well, my wife's opposed to the idea. She's still working at an office in Rockville, so we'll probably stay put for a while."

"These are long hours out here."

"That shouldn't be a problem."

The bell over the door jangled. Kate turned to see Joel enter.

"Hi."

"Hi, Kate." He eyed the stranger at the desk.

"This is Murray. He's thinking of taking over as editor here. Murray, this is Joel Kingsley, high school principal."

Murray loped over to the counter and shook his hand.

Joel said, "Nice to meet you. Kate, I'd like to buy a page."

"You mean a full-page ad?"

"I guess. Though it's not exactly an ad."

Kate sensed a story. She smiled. "What are you up to now?"

The cool, calm, ex-military man returned her smile. "It's just between us, okay? Until the paper comes out."

"Sure."

"I'm proposing."

"Marriage?" Kate clapped her hands. "In a full-page ad?"

"Gotta keep it public, you know."

"You are bonkers."

He crossed his arms. "I don't recall ever being referred to as bonkers."

She laughed at his sudden military demeanor. "Not to your face. Sorry, but I've seen you on one knee in the commons and hugging a teacher in your office. You're bonkers. What makes you think she'll respond favorably?"

"That's personal."

"Okay. What do you have in mind?" She grabbed a piece of paper and laid it on the counter between them.

"The usual."

She cocked her head.

"Miss O, will you marry me?"

"Signed Joel. Or Mr. Kingsley?"

"Mr. Kingsley. Big print."

"How about inserting the photo from the other time? We could enlarge it." She sketched on the paper. "Put it here. Maybe some floral border here. Don't you want to put something about love in it?"

"Well…"

"Joel, if you're going public, you're going public. If you're not going to be there when she reads it to say it in private, it better be in here."

"Excuse me."

They turned to look at Murray.

"What are you two talking about?"

Kate answered, "Joel is asking Britte the math teacher to marry him. Since he's a public servant, he wants to do everything possible in public."

"So he's taking out an *ad?*"

"Sure. Only it's not really an ad. Now, Joel, we could do this." She wrote on the paper. "Dear Britte. You are the light of my life. I would be honored to have you as my wife. Hey, that rhymes."

Joel's chin jutted out. "Kate. I want it simple. Miss O, will you marry me? Mr. Kingsley. Bold print. No flowers. No pictures. No extra words. I'll tell her the rest in private."

"Okaaay." She pulled out a fresh piece of paper. "Short and sweet it is."

Murray leaned across the counter. "You're both joking, aren't you?"

Joel narrowed his eyes at him.

Kate said, "Murray, this is just the way things are done in Valley Oaks."

⁓

Chelsea opened the front door for Tanner, talking into the cordless phone while smiling at him. She pointed toward Kate's rooms and promptly headed upstairs.

"Knock, knock," he called out and went into Kate's sitting room.

She entered from her bedroom. "Hi. You're early."

He gathered her in his arms and held her a long moment, nuzzling against her neck. It was her last night in Valley Oaks. "All packed?"

In reply, she kissed him. "Tell me what happened at school. I haven't heard."

He laughed. "Nobody said a word to Britte. There were about six of us in the teachers' lounge when she came in. She saw the paper lying there and sat down to read it." He laughed again. "She turned all red and snapped the paper shut. Like none of us had seen it, right? Of course I had to say something. I asked if there was anything interesting in the *Times*. Man, if looks could kill. She marched out the door and muttered something about him paying big time for this one."

Kate chuckled. "The guy is merciless."

"Trust me, she can match him in that department. So..." Their arms were still around each other. "I came early to give you your gift. Tomorrow's the big day."

He and her family were accompanying her to Iowa City in the morning for her graduation ceremony.

"Yeah. It's hard to believe I finally did it. But you weren't supposed to get me anything, Carlucci. After the laptop and the trip—"

"Sorry, I haven't kicked that habit yet. Can't pass up an excuse to buy a gift for my girl. It's outside."

"Outside?"

"Close your eyes. Tighter. Hold my hand." He pulled her through the house and opened the front door. "Now you can look. Ta-da!"

When the volume of her squeal surpassed Chelsea's the night she received the ring from Graham, Tanner was quite pleased with himself. Her face did its Christmas-tree–light number, green eyes wide.

"Tanner!" She flew out the door, and then raced back to give him a quick hug. "You can't do this!" She ran to the curb.

A spanking new sunburst yellow Volkswagen convertible sat there, its top down, revealing a creamy interior.

He joined her beside it. "What do you think?"

"Oh, Tanner, it's beautiful. It's so bright and shiny!" She danced around it, oohing and ahhing. "I cannot accept this! Can I drive it?"

"Of course." He handed her the keys. "But not with me in it."

"You chicken." She got into the driver's seat and turned on the engine. "Oh, she even *sounds* beautiful. What do we name her? If I keep her, that is. You can't give me something this extravagant!"

"Who says?"

"Conventional society."

"Like I care."

"I'll look like a kept woman."

He winked. "I'd like to keep you a kept woman."

She ignored him and shifted into first. "Come on, Tanner. Come with me. I'll tell you a secret if you do."

He eyed her skeptically.

"It's true. I was going to wait until tomorrow, but now—oh, I can't believe you did this! Hop in. We'll just go out to the baseball fields."

How much harm could she get into in that short distance? He climbed in. She roared away from the curb and he questioned his decision, hurriedly snapping on the seat belt. He held his breath for five minutes while she laughed, waving to every driver and pedestrian they passed. She slowed as they neared the ball diamonds, all occupied with teams and fans. The lot and side street were full of cars. Shouts could be heard even from a distance.

"This is too crowded. Let's just go down the road a bit."

Before he could protest, off they went. A few minutes later she stopped along the side of a little used country lane bordered by newly planted cornfields. She cut the engine.

"Kate, from here on out, I'm driving. I can't handle Mr. Toad's Wild Ride outside of Disneyland."

"I'm not that bad. We made it, didn't we? Not even one close call." She wrapped her arms around his neck. "Thank you so much."

He returned the hug. "You are so welcome. Happy graduation."

She kissed him and sat back, gazing at him, her feelings undisguised. It never ceased to astound him that she truly cared for him. What was he going to do without her nearby?

Carefully, he undid the hair clip, freeing her hair, and smoothing it back from her face. "Well, what's the big secret, Kilpatrick?"

"You know I can't think straight when you do that."

"And you know I can't think straight when you look at me like that."

She wrinkled her nose and laughed. "We are disgustingly sappy."

"So." Reluctantly he stopped caressing her hair. "Go ahead."

"I fired Murray today."

"You fired Murray," he repeated in disbelief. "The temporary editor fired the newly hired permanent, for-real managing editor."

"Yep."

"You can do that?"

"Of course I can. The man just did not get it. No way was he ever going to get it."

"Get what?"

"The magic, Tanner. The Valley Oaks magic."

"But that's not your problem."

"Of course it is. How could I let someone like *that* take over? I'd feel guilty for the rest of my life! Not to mention I'd be without a job."

He waited, hoping he wasn't reading too much into her words.

She smiled. "Why would I go to DC when my life is here?"

"But what of your dream? Of recording history? Of influencing people?"

"My goodness, that's been happening on a weekly basis right under my nose since I wrote my first article for the *Times*. But that's only icing on the cake. You're the real reason. You're the essence of Valley Oaks magic for me."

He brushed away a tear pooling in the corner of her eye. "Kate, I love you so much I would let you go if it's best for you."

"I know. That's why I'm staying."

"Are you absolutely sure?"

"I am *so* sure, Tanner. Watching Adele with her father, I realized how quickly time passes. I don't want to waste any of it. My life has been a long winding road. God kept throwing in one curve after another. He sure went to an awful lot of trouble to get me here. I think I should stay put."

"It ain't DC, kid."

"No, it ain't." She grinned. "But it's home."

Sally John is the author of several novels, including the popular The Other Way Home and In a Heartbeat series. She has recently coauthored a book with Gary Smalley, A *Time to Mend*, in Nelson's Safe Harbor series. A two-time finalist for The Christy Award and a former teacher, Sally lives in Southern California with her husband, Tim.